NEVER SAY NEVER

The homes grew larger as Luke drove closer to Cherry's neighborhood. The woman represented everything he'd sworn to never go near again.

He winced.

What an idiot. He'd agreed to have dinner at the curvy stranger's house faster than a Ferrari went from zero to sixty. How had he been so weak?

Cherry sighed and shook her head, her short blond hair fluttering in the breeze, whispering through the car. Her spicy scent enveloped him, wrapping its fingers around his lack of self-control.

Right, he reminded himself. That was how.

<u>BOOK YOUR PLACE ON OUR WEBSITE</u>
<u>AND MAKE THE</u>
<u>READING CONNECTION!</u>

We've created a customized website just for our very special readers, where you can get the inside scoop on everything that's going on with Zebra, Pinnacle and Kensington books.

When you come online, you'll have the exciting opportunity to:

- View covers of upcoming books
- Read sample chapters
- Learn about our future publishing schedule (listed by publication month *and author*)
- Find out when your favorite authors will be visiting a city near you
- Search for and order backlist books from our online catalog
- Check out author bios and background information
- Send e-mail to your favorite authors
- Meet the Kensington staff online
- Join us in weekly chats with authors, readers and other guests
- Get writing guidelines
- AND MUCH MORE!

Visit our website at
http://www.kensingtonbooks.com

Kathleen Long

Cherry On Top

ZEBRA BOOKS
Kensington Publishing Corp.
www.kensingtonbooks.com

ZEBRA BOOKS are published by

Kensington Publishing Corp.
850 Third Avenue
New York, NY 10022

All Kensington titles, imprints, and distributed lines are available at special quantity discounts for bulk purchases for sales
promotion, premiums, fund-raising, educational, or institutional
use.

Special book excerpts or customized printings can also be created to fit specific needs. For details, write or phone the
office of the Kensington Special Sales Manager: Attn. Special
Sales Department. Kensington Publishing Corp., 850 Third
Avenue, New York, NY 10022. Phone: 1-800-221-2647.

Zebra and the Z logo Reg. U.S. Pat. & TM Off.

ISBN 0-8217-7849-8

First printing: November 2005
10 9 8 7 6 5 4 3 2 1

Printed in the United States of America

One of the most amazing perks about my new career has been the friendships I've made. For all of you out there who have made my journey lighter, brighter, full of laughter and support, thank you. You know who you are. This one's for you.

PROLOGUE

"I think we won." Cherry Harte glanced at the lottery ticket in her lap and patted down the flounce of her wedding gown to gain a clear view of the television screen.

"That"—her sister, Liz, raised her bottle of Budweiser and tipped the brim of her chartreuse bridesmaid hat—"I'd drink to."

"I'm serious." Cherry's voice dropped to a whisper. "The numbers match."

Liz set her beer on an end table and leaned forward. "How many? Maybe we won a few thousand or something."

"All of them." Cherry's heart beat a steady rhythm against her ribs. She had to be dreaming. *Right?*

"What about the power thingy? You know, the extra number."

Cherry's mouth turned to cotton, her hand trembling as she gripped the small ticket. "It's a match."

"Hot damn." Liz hoisted the beer bottle to her lips and took a long pull. "That'll teach Bart Matthews to leave us at the altar."

Cherry frowned, shifting her focus from the winning ticket to her sister. *Us?* Last time she'd checked, she'd been alone at the front of the church. All alone.

"I mean us . . . the family," Liz stammered, looking uncharacteristically nervous. "Collectively."

Cherry tuned out her sister, narrowing her attention to the set of numbers quaking before her eyes. She unhooked the veil still anchored in her hair and dropped the netting to the floor, suddenly quite sure of one thing. From now on, the rules were going to change.

No more worrying about what town her father was working or what trouble her mother had gotten into. No more being left behind . . . on the bottom . . . forgotten.

"I mean, he left us all." Liz continued her babbling, slugging back a gulp between sentences. "I can't believe he'd pick his campaign over you. So what if Mom missed her hearing—"

Cherry shut out the words. Shut out the sound. She focused on one thing, and one thing only.

Her luck had changed.

Maybe being named after a slot-machine symbol had finally paid off.

First up on the agenda? Leaving New Jersey and the Harte legacy far, far behind. She'd buy a new house. A new car. New clothes. Hell, with her half of the winnings, she'd be able to buy herself a new life.

A new life.

Cherry hugged herself and rocked back against the worn, nubby weave of the sofa. A sudden, numbing assurance spread from limb to limb, muscle to muscle.

From this moment on, she was headed nowhere but to the top.

CHAPTER 1

Four months later

Luke Chance had had his fill of holier-than-thou, high-heeled, well-bred women. So when his grandfather towed in a Jaguar for repair and announced the female driver needed to speak to Luke *immediately*, it came as no surprise. Such was life in Mystic Beach, Florida. More millionaires than any other city in America. Or some claptrap like that.

He frowned. Millionaires. Most of them only lived here during the winter, hightailing it north come summer. They all had one thing in common, though. They wanted what they wanted *now*, as if their money gave them a right to bark out orders to the little people.

"She can come talk to me here," he answered his grandfather. "I'm working."

"I think you might want to come out. This one's got a light in her eyes."

Luke tightened a bolt and grimaced. "They've all

got lights in their eyes, Gramps. We're in Florida. It's called the sun."

The sound of the old man's laughter warmed Luke's belly, and he smiled. His grandfather never failed to see the positive in anyone—even his grandson.

"I'm telling you." Gramps's voice was nothing more than a hoarse whisper. "This one's something else."

"I'll bet," Luke grumbled. Weren't they all?

"Heads up, boy. Here she comes."

Luke heard the sharp rat-a-tat of heels crossing the concrete shop floor.

"He's right here, Ms. Harte." Luke rolled his eyes at the dripping sweetness in his grandfather's voice. "Are you sure I can't get you anything?"

"Oh, no," a soft, feminine voice answered. "I'm absolutely fine. Well, I mean, except for my car."

"Cherry Harte," Gramps said. "Meet my grandson, Luke Chance."

"Pleasure," Luke growled.

"Likewise," she answered. "I don't suppose you could come out for a moment so we could talk?"

"No, ma'am. I'm in the middle of a big job, and I promised this car to the owner before five."

Luke glanced toward the woman's tapered ankles. Multicolored, sparkle-covered sandals barely encased her slender feet. She squatted next to the battered old Cadillac, her position affording him a view of a soft floral skirt as it draped her slim, inviting knees.

He swallowed, then refocused on the belly of the car above him.

"I'm in a bit of a pinch," she said. "I have an

important meeting, and I really need to get my car fixed."

"What seems to be the problem?"

"Somehow, I thought that's where you might come in."

Great. Killer legs and a mouth to match.

Luke lowered his wrench long enough to slide a stick of gum from the opened pack in his pocket. He counted to ten as the sweet juice filled his mouth. He'd learned the trick in the anger management workshop he'd failed so miserably after the sudden end of his journalism career.

"Mr. Chance?"

The woman was patient, too.

"I can look at it as soon as I'm done here. That's the best I can do."

"How long will that be?"

"Two hours."

Her sigh was audible and sexy. *Damn* sexy. He chewed faster.

"I can pay you double. Or triple."

That did it. Luke gave the wrench a sharp crank. The core of reserve deep inside him snapped. Anger management or not, he was hot, he was tired, and he was sick of his customers' demands.

"Ma'am, some people care about a job well done more than they care about money. I'm one of them. You may be used to buying whatever you want, but it won't fly in my shop. I know your type. Understood?"

"What *type?*"

Was it his imagination or had her voice gone up three octaves?

"Type? You're kidding, right?" He chuckled and

a splotch of lubricant landed on his cheek. "Tourist. Big house. Lots of money."

"I'm not a tourist. I live here."

"How long?"

"A few months."

"Ah." Luke stole a glimpse at her sparkle-covered toes, then scowled at the belly of the car. "*New* money." *The worst.* "What did your husband do? Make a few million in the market?"

"No." Her voice had grown clipped.

"But you have money? You did offer to pay triple, and those sparkly things on your feet must have cost a small fortune."

"I really don't see where my footwear is any of your business, Mr. Chance. All I want is for you to fix my—"

"Let me guess. If it wasn't the market, it must have been the Internet." Luke knew he was way out of line, but he couldn't help himself. This was the most fun he'd had all day. Hell. All month. "Dot-com company?"

"You're a little off." Her voice dropped to a whisper. "Not that I plan on telling you my personal business."

He pushed the dolly out from beneath the Cadillac to gaze up at the woman. Short blond hair fluttered around her oval face. Her sheer dress billowed beneath the force of the overhead fan. His stomach twisted.

"I like to know my customers. Am I right? Did he earn it in the market? Or Internet?"

"Who?" Her pale green eyes narrowed.

"Your husband."

"I don't have a husband." She raised her chin.

"Do you have a problem with that, or is it just my bank balance that concerns you?"

"No problem." *No problem at all.* "I still can't fix your car any faster."

She glanced around the service bay, placed one hand on her hip, and leveled a nerve-wracking glare at him. Gramps was right. There was a light in this one's eyes.

"I'm sure you've got a spare Jag or something at home you could drive for the day."

She shook her head. "Are you this charming to all of your customers?"

He met her frown with a silent grin.

"All I have is this one," she continued.

He shot her a disbelieving look. "When it starts."

She squinted. "I don't suppose you have a loaner I could borrow for a few hours."

"Not unless you want to drive my truck."

"What kind of truck?" She wrinkled her upturned nose.

Luke sat up and wiped the lubricant from his face with a rag that had seen more than its share of spills. "Are you going to get picky? Or do you really have to get to your meeting?"

Her brows furrowed, her full lips pressing into a tight little line. Luke's heart raced, and he mentally scolded himself. He knew better than to let one of the local lovelies turn his head. He'd been down that road before and it had been bumpier than hell.

"Okay." The woman tipped her head to one side, her smile forced, as if meeting a dare. "I'll borrow your truck. Thank you."

"Great." Luke flopped back onto the dolly and pushed himself under the Caddy. "I'll have your Jag fixed later tonight. Tell Gramps you're borrowing Christine."

"Christine?"

"My truck."

"Like the car in the Stephen King novel?"

"Only meaner." He bit back his laughter as the sound of her retreating heels paused, then clicked away.

Fifteen minutes later, Cherry pulled her perspiration-soaked dress from her chest and stuck her head out the open window. How could anyone in Florida drive a truck with no air-conditioning? She'd be a sopping-wet mess by the time she got to her interview.

She'd jumped through every hoop the local Women's League had thrown at her during her time here in southwest Florida. She'd run raffles, organized luncheons, served soup at the local shelter. She'd volunteered like a madwoman, all with one goal in mind.

Lifetime membership in the Women's League. Her ticket to belonging—really belonging—in the local community.

Back home she'd always been one step removed. A misfit of sorts. Thanks to her parents' antics, she'd had to work two jobs to make sure she and her younger sister, Liz, kept a roof over their heads and food on the table.

The lottery had changed all that. She and Liz had possessed the only winning ticket to the multi-million, multistate jackpot. They'd kissed their old life good-bye, and Cherry had gotten to work creating their new one. Membership in the

Women's League would finalize her carefully planned transformation.

She had only to survive the final interview and prove her genealogy worthy of membership. It was nothing that couldn't be accomplished with a few well-chosen statements about her heritage.

She'd simply explain that Monty Harte, her missing-in-action father, had made a career in security at a variety of Western casinos. No sense mentioning he'd made a career out of outsmarting security . . . well . . . usually outsmarting.

Cherry wondered for a passing moment what dear old Dad's latest scam was. Card counting? Poker?

The amazing thing was he hadn't turned up looking for a handout from her or Liz. He hadn't made time for either Harte daughter in years, but Cherry secretly thought their lottery win would have brought him out of the woodwork.

Then there was the issue of her mother. What tale could she weave about Fran Harte? The woman was currently serving time for embezzling funds from a pizza parlor, for crying out loud. She'd been assigned kitchen duty on the inside since word of her culinary skills had spread right along with her reputation as a thief.

Cherry frowned and rubbed her chin.

Executive head chef at Café le New Jersey?

Laughter spilled from her lips and she smiled. Her breeding was so pathetic, it was funny. As long as Monique Goodall, the Women's League president, wasn't up to date on the names of New Jersey restaurants or correctional facilities, enhancing

Monty and Fran Harte's identities would be a piece of cake.

The tattoo just below Cherry's belly button itched. Oh no. *Not now.*

She caught herself just before she sank her ruby-red nail into the spot.

The last time the tattoo itched, she'd hit the lottery. Now then, that particular life change had been a good one—a very good one—but the itching usually signified major upheaval.

Cherry shrugged. Maybe this time the itch simply meant the Women's League was the place for her to make her mark on Mystic Beach society.

She nodded. That must be it.

The engine pinged and knocked as she pressed the accelerator. The borrowed truck abruptly stalled, and the miniature grass-skirted woman on the dash looked about to snap off at the ankles.

"Men," Cherry growled at the figurine.

She was able to restart the truck long enough for it to limp to the shoulder. Scanning the gauges for any sign of trouble, she quickly zeroed in on the cause of her woes. The fuel gauge read empty.

She let out a frustrated breath, plucked the computer-generated map from the bench seat, and climbed down out of the truck's cab. She'd get to this meeting come hell or high water. She glanced again at the map and counted. Seven blocks.

How hard could it be to walk seven blocks?

Five minutes later, rivulets of sweat ran between Cherry's breasts and down her back. She hobbled between one intact heel and the one hanging by a thread. She glanced at her favorite Weitzman sandals and groaned. So much for casual elegance.

And so much for dazzling Monique Goodall from behind the wheel of her new Jaguar. The thing was, she hadn't had a lick of trouble with the car until today.

The tattoo itched again. Mind over matter. She refused to give in and scratch. Surely scratching didn't fit the new, improved Cherry Harte image.

Her car had been the first thing she'd bought with her half of the lottery winnings. Her sister, Liz, had dashed right for the BMW dealership, but not Cherry. She'd read somewhere that Jaguars were considered the most beautiful automobiles on the planet. For Cherry, there was no other choice for her new life in the tropical paradise of southwestern Florida.

Well, she had no doubt Mr. Mechanic-with-an-attitude would get to the bottom of the problem. Lord knew his cocky arrogance alone should be enough to ignite the car's engine . . . along with a few other things Cherry could think of.

Warmth simmered in her belly, spreading upward toward her chest. She fanned her face as she hobbled down the sidewalk. Had the summer heat kicked in early, or what?

Luke Chance. There was something to be said for a man who could give as good as he got, and she wouldn't mind seeing what he had to give.

She blinked. Where in Hades had that thought come from? The tropical heat must be playing with her self-control. She had to admit she'd gotten spoiled using her newly found wealth to get her way, but Mr. Chance hadn't bought the routine for a second.

Nope. He'd piled her into his yellow nightmare

of a non-air-conditioned truck and sent her on her merry little way with no gasoline. Sure, it had been nice of him to loan her his vehicle, but somehow she pictured him back at the station having a laugh at her expense.

After all, the guy hadn't tried to hide the fact her money was a turnoff. Oh well. It took all types to make the world go around—at least, that's what her mother had always said—usually in the moments following an arrest.

Cherry blinked her focus back to Luke Chance, his grease-stained hands and the rumble of his less-than-sociable voice. She swallowed down the lump that materialized at the memory of the way the man's tanned skin crinkled around his eyes when he grinned.

She stopped in her tracks, forcibly shaking the image out of her head.

She was too close to achieving her dream of a totally new identity to let some quick-witted mechanic throw her off track. No way. There had definitely been chemistry, though. At least, she thought that's what it was. She'd never actually had much experience in the sexual chemistry department.

Hell. Bart Matthews had agreed to marry her simply to round out his campaign for New Jersey State Senate. Theirs had been more of a mutual neither-one-of-us-have-gotten-a-better-offer-so-why-don't-we-get-married arrangement than it had been love.

And look how splendidly that had turned out.

No, Cherry had a plan, and she intended on working it—right to its successful conclusion.

* * *

Eugene Chance watched as his grandson pulled a bottle of Pepsi from the shop's ancient refrigerator. A smile tugged at the corner of Luke's mouth, and Eugene's matchmaking radar kicked to life.

Was the young man thinking about Cherry Harte? How could he not be? She was some knockout and a spitfire to boot. Not many women would have met Luke's dare and headed out in Christine. The girl had gumption, plain and simple.

Luke disappeared into the stockroom but reappeared a split second later, his brow furrowed. "You gassed up Christine today, right?"

"Nope." Eugene shook his head. "Thought you did it yesterday."

Dread tickled its way up his neck. The girl might have gumption, but she certainly hadn't been dressed for walking.

Luke snatched his car keys from the pegboard. "I'll be right back," he hollered as he dashed for the parking lot.

Eugene rubbed his chin as his grandson peeled out of the parking lot, waiting until the tiny sports car disappeared down the street before he headed back to the shop's office.

He'd seen the spark in Luke's eyes, and he wasn't about to ignore it. His grandson refused to admit he wasn't getting any younger. Heck, neither one of them was.

If it was the last thing he did, Eugene planned to see his grandson settle down before the grim reaper called. After all, he could kick off any minute, and he had no intention of leaving Luke alone in the world. The boy had had enough of that as a child.

He flipped through the customer files until he

found the folder he wanted. Pettigrew. Anxiety bubbled in his gut, but he ignored it. Sometimes a man had to do what a man had to do.

Right now, he needed information. From what he understood, Cassandra Pettigrew knew her way around a DSL. Word at the senior center was the retired librarian could do a reverse lookup quicker than you could yell *Bingo*.

The widow Pettigrew had made it abundantly clear she wouldn't mind more than an oil change from Eugene. After all, he was no fool. He'd seen the way she eyed him when she'd been in for her last tune-up. He might be getting up there in years, but he still knew the signs.

He sucked in a breath and held it, trying to fortify himself as he dialed the number. Never let it be said Eugene Chance wasn't willing to sacrifice for his grandson.

The feisty woman answered on the second ring. "Eugene?"

"Tarnation. How do you do that?"

"Trade secret."

The soft edge to her voice distracted him for a moment. Not only was she smart as a whip, but Cassandra had recently been voted most eligible widow in Mystic Beach.

Eugene shook himself, refocusing on why he'd called. "Cassie, I think we've got a live one." He smoothed a hand over his white hair, checking his reflection in the office mirror while he waited for her response.

"Do you want me to run a background check?" The woman's velvet voice purred across the phone line, stirring a traitorous longing deep inside him. *Dang*. How did she do *that*?

He turned sideways, sucking in his gut. "You're just the woman I need." He caught the potential double meaning of his words and quickly clarified his statement. "For finding facts."

A moment of silence stretched across the line. Then she spoke. "Come on over. I'll get my connection warmed up."

As Eugene set the receiver back into its cradle, he realized getting Cassie Pettigrew's connection warmed up was exactly what he was afraid of.

Luke couldn't help but smile at the mental picture of Miss Perfect tooling down Tamiami Trail in Christine. The woman would never make it crosstown with the gas he'd left in the truck after his last fishing trip.

Guilt teased at his gut. Annoying as she was, she didn't deserve to be stranded in the midday tropical heat.

Several minutes later, he spotted the truck at the intersection of Tamiami and River Oak, but there was no sign of Cherry Harte. Damn. She wouldn't be stupid enough to walk in the flimsy excuse for shoes she'd worn, would she?

He had his answer three blocks later.

She sauntered down the sidewalk, filmy dress stuck to her generous curves, hobbling on what appeared to be at least one broken heel. She held her head high, as if refusing to acknowledge the way her body bobbed with each uneven step.

A chuckle caught in his throat. The sight gave a

whole new meaning to the term *well-heeled*. He slipped a piece of gum into his mouth, braced himself for another encounter with the woman, and eased his restored Karmann Ghia convertible to the curb. "Car trouble?"

She spun toward him, her pale eyes wide with surprise. At the moment of recognition, her gaze narrowed, invisible daggers trained directly on him.

"Very funny. Thanks to your . . . your . . ."

"Careful." He held up a finger. "I don't take kindly to strangers who badmouth my truck."

"Your truck"—she frowned—"left me high and dry."

"Lady, you don't look very dry from here."

Splotches of hot color fired in her cheeks and his gut caught again. He popped another stick of gum into his mouth as she neared the car.

"You ought to hand out towels with that monster." She frowned. "Or at least spa coupons. Matter of fact, a bubble bath sounds about right just now."

The guilt playing with his insides was replaced instantly by an image of the woman naked, surrounded by bath bubbles. He blinked it away. Uh-uh. *Not* going to go there.

He patted the passenger seat. "Come on. I'll take you to your meeting. Then I can wait around or come back to run you home. It's the least I can do."

"I can get home on my own." She hobbled toward the convertible. "A lift to my meeting would be great, though." She plopped onto the passenger seat, tossed her sandals into the floor well, and shoved a hand through her damp hair. "I loved those sandals." She cut her eyes at Luke and frowned. "*Loved* them."

"Not very practical," he mumbled.

Cherry squinted at him, as if measuring his remark. "Why are men always so worried about everything being practical?"

Luke shrugged. "Because we're not women?"

She rolled her eyes, then turned to stare out the window. Luke leaned toward the driver's door, hoping to put some space between himself and the intoxicating, spicy scent of whatever perfume she wore.

After a few uncomfortable moments of quiet, she turned to face him again, a teasing smile playing at the corner of her lips. "So, do you get a lot of positive feedback on that loaner-truck service you offer?"

He grinned but quickly caught himself, forcing his features into a serious expression. Ms. Harte could be the poster model for the type of woman he'd vowed to stay away from—beautiful and rich. He stole a quick glimpse at her curious expression, forced to silently admit there seemed to be a whole lot of life beneath the pretty package.

"I forgot she was out of gas." He shifted his gaze back to the traffic ahead, ignoring the warning bells chiming inside his brain.

"Hmm." The woman refocused her attention out the front window. "Let's hope your other services provide a higher level of satisfaction."

Of that, he had no doubt, but Luke had zero intention of testing the theory. He slipped another stick of gum from his pocket and added it to the wad he already worked between his teeth.

He thought about the truck and its lack of air-conditioning and gasoline. "Listen, I made an honest mistake about the truck, but they don't make them like her anymore. Solid and decent."

He shifted his gum from one cheek to the other, and when Cherry made no attempt to counter with a snappy comeback, he kept talking. It was better, after all, than trying to deny her nearness was slowly driving him insane. "Some people recognize a classic when they see it and appreciate exactly what they're getting. Most times, it's the flashy packages that cause nothing but trouble."

Cherry wrinkled her nose, her chest now flushed to match her cheeks. "You're talking about cars, right?"

Luke grinned. "Right."

Just then, a breeze kicked through the open top of the convertible and Cherry clasped a hand to either side of her head. "Could you put the top up? I can't afford to look any worse than I already do."

If she had any idea of how sexy the particular combination of windblown, annoyed, and overheated looked on her, she'd ask to have the potion bottled.

"It's a shame to be so worried about your hair you can't enjoy a beautiful day." He arched a brow in her direction, resulting in the immediate narrowing of her eyes. "Seems to me you've got some serious packaging issues."

She frowned and crossed her arms beneath her chest, the move doing nothing to help him ignore the fullness of her breasts beneath her sheer, damp dress.

"My packaging issues and I are on our way to a very important interview. There!" She pointed as they zipped past a large pink structure. "That's where I need to be."

"I'll circle back." Disappointment seeped through

him as he recognized the building. "The Women's League?"

Cherry brightened. "You know it?"

The familiar ache tugged at Luke as he nodded. He knew it. If she was a member there, she'd soon become a carbon copy of the one woman in his past he'd worked very hard to forget.

He mentally chastised himself, knowing he'd been a fool to enjoy their banter. The smartest thing he could do now would be to drop off the Harte woman and never look back.

Try as he might, he couldn't ignore the disappointment that had settled in his gut as he headed back toward the shop a few moments later.

Damn.

Luke added yet another stick of gum to the lump in his mouth.

What the hell. He'd be better off choking to death on a ball of gum than giving in to the temptation of Cherry Harte.

CHAPTER 2

A short while later, Cherry did her best to sit still, pinned by the watchful eye of Monique Goodall, the group's president. The woman was a study in elegance, her raven hair falling sharply into a chin-length bob. Flawless make-up subtly accentuated her patrician features.

She couldn't be more than five years older than Cherry, yet she oozed refinement. As Monique's steely gaze took inventory of her appearance, Cherry fancied she dazzled the woman with her fashion sense but had a sneaking suspicion that wasn't the precise thought reflected in the president's pinched expression.

Cherry glanced down at her broken sandals and winced. Of course, her appearance wasn't helping matters. She fidgeted waiting for Monique to speak, then caught herself, focusing on sitting still.

Monique's focus shifted from Cherry to the file spread across the impressive desk, and Cherry allowed herself a nervous swallow.

If only she'd listened to her affirmation CD one

more time. Of course, the Jaguar refusing to start hadn't helped at all in that regard. Her CD sat trapped in the dashboard player now inside Luke Chance's garage. That was all right. She was perfectly capable of pumping herself up silently while Monique reviewed her paperwork.

All I need is within me now. All I need is within me now. Every day, in every way, I'm getting better and better.

Monique sighed and circled something on Cherry's application. Cherry's heart sank.

I'm getting better and better. Better and better. Better and better.

"Pardon me?"

Monique's clipped tone startled Cherry from her apparently not-so-silent chant. "Nothing. I apologize."

One of Monique's perfectly plucked brows lifted. "Are you nervous, Ms. Harte?"

Cherry blinked, wondering what answer the woman would prefer to hear.

"Because if you are, it's perfectly understandable," Monique continued. "Membership in the Mystic Beach Women's League is reserved for the crème de la crème of our region." She narrowed her piercing gaze, seeming to measure Cherry's appearance once more. "I'd like to make some recommendations for image improvement if you're to be a member. May I?"

Cherry nodded, then mentally corrected herself. "Yes." She spoke loudly and confidently. "I'd be most appreciative of your expertise."

Why not? The woman represented everything Cherry had ever dreamed of becoming. The new and improved Cherry Harte planned to be nothing like the old. No matter what it took.

Ten minutes later, she felt as though she'd been drawn and quartered.

Monique Goodall had played constructive criticism from the tips of Cherry's open-toed sandals to the top of her naturally blond head. Apparently, she needed to learn to wear longer skirts, close-toed shoes, higher necklines, and darker hair.

Even worse, Monique had dictated every word into a small digital recorder. Cherry hadn't seen anyone dictate that quickly since the surgeon who'd taken care of her ankle after she fell off her clogs the winter before last. Even more disconcerting, Monique had left the recorder on to capture the conclusion of the interview.

Cherry delivered her practiced lines about Monty and Fran Harte and their illustrious—if fictitious—careers.

"Very well." Monique nodded. "I think you'll bring a freshness to the Women's League. Consider yourself a provisional member, pending final approval."

Cherry's chest swelled, excitement spiking through her veins.

"There is one other project I'd like to discuss with you."

Cherry straightened. "Yes?"

"*Mystic Living* magazine is doing a profile on the Women's League and its membership. Would you be interested in being profiled as our newest member? I trust your home is suitable for photographing?"

Cherry held on to the arms of her chair to keep

herself from catapulting across Monique's desk. A magazine profile? Unbelievable. She nodded, unable to force her voice past her excitement and nerves.

"How about artwork?" Monique asked. "A nice, original piece is always smart for a backdrop." She nodded. "You'll learn these things as you go."

Cherry thought quickly. Original artwork? She hadn't gotten that far in the grand plan.

Monique didn't wait for her verbal response. "Let me give you the number for my man. He's a genius, did the mural behind my back. His name is Yogi. Simply brilliant. He specializes in entry-way artwork."

As if the name weren't bad enough, the artwork was even worse. Cherry stared at the mural hanging behind Monique's desk. She squinted at the hallucinogenic representation of Monique floating superhero-style above the Mystic Beach skyline. She shuddered, hoping the artist had been having a bad day. A very bad day.

"Is he popular?" She squeezed out the question.

"Tremendously." Monique waved one hand in the air. "His waiting list is months long, but I can get you bumped to the front of the line. Would you like that?"

Cherry swallowed. Good Lord, if she had to see that in her foyer every day, she'd die of fright long before she made full membership in the Women's League.

"I'd love it." Her voice cracked as she forced the words past her better judgment. If a nightmare of a mural would enhance her image, so be it. "Thank you."

Monique flipped open a personal organizer. "I'll have him at your house tomorrow for a consult. He owes me a favor. Ten o'clock?"

"Perfect."

"You know." Monique dragged out the words, then pursed her lips. "I have a feeling you're going to love it here at the Women's League."

Cherry brightened. For that, she could tolerate a mad artist at work in her foyer.

"Of course," Monique tipped her head from one side to the other, "all this would be contingent upon your support of the Horticultural Center project."

"Not a problem." Cherry slipped her checkbook from her purse. "I'll write you a check right now."

Monique shook her head. "Your word is fine with me, Cherry. Interesting name, by the way. Where did you say it originates?"

My daddy's favorite slot-machine symbol. Probably not an answer fit for the pages of *Mystic Living.*

"Cherries Jubilee," she offered instead. "My mother's signature dish at her restaurant."

"Lovely," Monique cooed. "Absolutely lovely."

Cherry made a move to gather her things. "Thanks for your time. I'll see you tonight at the Development Commission offices."

"Quite right. Why don't you plan to stand onstage with me while I make the presentation."

Cherry's stomach flipped. "I'd be honored."

Monique waved her tiny recorder in the air. "Would you care for a copy of our interview?"

Only if she could destroy it. "No." Cherry shook her head. "Should I?"

"Some candidates have a hard time keeping their

stories straight." Monique rocked back in her chair and laughed.

Cherry forced a weak smile.

"I'm joking, of course," Monique continued.

Cherry kept her phony smile pasted in place as she slipped the strap of her purse over her shoulder and headed for the parking lot.

If Monique only knew how right she was about keeping her story straight. But then, Cherry knew this new life inside and out, and why not? She'd dreamt about it since the day her father had finally left for good, and she'd come too far to let anything go wrong now.

"You're freaking rich." Cherry's sister, Liz, flipped through a rack of dresses at Dillard's. They'd headed straight there after Liz had picked Cherry up outside the Women's League.

"That's why they want you as a member," Liz continued. "You can bankroll all of their little projects. For crying out loud, you could probably buy and sell those Women's League people a hundred times over."

"It's not about the money." Cherry fingered a warm white sheath with a matching hem-length jacket. "It's about respect. They like the new me. The me that people look at and say, 'There goes a woman of refinement and good breeding.'"

Liz frowned and rolled her eyes. "You are so bizarre. I'd rather be on an island somewhere drinking a piña colada and rolling around with the cabana boy. But you, you're worried about some plant center and impressing a bunch of stuffy broads with money in their bank vaults and ice in their veins."

"Horticultural Center," Cherry mumbled.

"What?"

Cherry yanked the suit off the rack and turned toward her sister. "It's the Horticultural Center." She straightened. "The project will elevate Mystic Beach to a level comparable with other high-end communities along the Gulf Coast. It's vital for the tourism and relocation business, and I'm proud to be part of the effort."

"And what's in the Horticultural Center, Miss Smarty Pants?" Liz arched an eyebrow. "Hmm?"

"Plants." Cherry shot a look at her sister. "*Important* plants."

"I rest my case." Liz threw her arms into the air and shrugged. "I don't see why membership in this group matters so much to you. You never used to care what people thought."

Cherry spun, leveling a disbelieving glare at her sister. "I always cared what people thought. Aren't you glad to be away from home? Aren't you happy that when people look at us now, they don't whisper behind our backs about our missing-in-action dad or our kleptomaniac mother? Aren't you?"

Liz's features hardened. "I think you're having an identity crisis."

Cherry eyed her sister's wig, today's version a spunky throwback to Raquel Welch's heyday. "*I'm* having an identity crisis? You emulate a different person every day. I hardly think you're one to be talking to me about identity."

Liz rolled her eyes and waggled a finger. "That's where you're wrong. My wigs are my identity. I can afford to be eccentric now, so eccentric it is." She shrugged. "I like it."

"Fine." Cherry turned to flip through a second rack of clothing, still clutching the white suit in one hand. "You be the eccentric one, I'll be the cultured one. It takes all types to make the world go around."

"Now you sound like Mommy."

Cherry shuddered. Had she really just uttered that phrase out loud? She'd have to do double duty with her affirmation CDs later on.

"Just answer me one thing." Liz narrowed her eyes. "Why the plant ladies? Why not something like what I do? Do you think if you go high-end, Bart will reconsider?"

Bart Matthews. Cherry tripped over an invisible snag in the carpet. Four months ago she'd been dismayed by his missing presence at their wedding, but once she held that lottery ticket in her hand, she knew she possessed the ticket to a new life. "Water under the bridge."

Liz flipped through a rack of short leather skirts. "Don't you miss him? I mean, you were friends your whole life. We all agree the marriage thing was a mistake, but don't you miss him?"

"He's part of my history." She pinned Liz with a glare. "Our history. Let's leave him there."

"Whatever." Her sister blew out a frustrated breath. "Maybe we should start a family foundation and forget the plants."

Cherry laughed. What was Liz . . . nuts? "No one would take us seriously. We have to prove ourselves in the community first."

Cherry shook her head. She couldn't fault Liz for dreaming big. Heck, her parents had done nothing but dream big. Look how well that had turned out. They'd been filled with entrepreneurial spirit. Of course, Liz's idea of giving away money instead of stealing it *was* a novel concept, but Cherry planned to stick with the tried and true.

"We don't need to prove ourselves. We're rich." Sincere determination fired in Liz's eyes. If Cherry didn't know better, she'd swear her sister was serious.

"Puhlease." Cherry made a face as she walked toward the dressing room. "Come on. Monique says I need to make more sophisticated clothing choices. Help me decide if this suit conveys the right image for tonight."

Luke frowned as he corrected the wiring on Cherry Harte's Jaguar. Someone had definitely screwed with the car, but who? Did the lovely Ms. Harte have enemies? She said she'd only been in town for four months. Maybe she'd left a checkered past behind. A jealous lover. An enemy out for revenge.

He sighed.

There went his reporter's brain again. Always working overtime. It had been two years since he returned to Mystic Beach from Miami, but the old habit of digging for a story never went away.

He shot a glance at the shop's clock. Less than an hour to get showered and dressed for the Development Commission meeting. Better get going. The repair would have to wait until the morning. He'd call her later to give her the update and ask if she'd let anyone else work on the car.

He plucked his apartment keys from the pegboard and looked toward the side parking lot. Gramps had left a note about a call from the widow Pettigrew, but he should have been back by now. A hearty chuckle burst from Luke's lips.

If he knew Cassandra Pettigrew, she'd invited his grandfather in for tea and sandwiches. The woman was determined to get the poor man down the aisle, even if she had to drag him kicking and screaming.

Halfway to the door, Luke remembered the meeting materials. He retraced his steps to pull a large portfolio from the narrow space between his desk and the soda machine. The Youth Center's development officer had entrusted him with tonight's presentation. This would be his first significant role since becoming a board member, and he planned to nail it.

He swallowed down his nerves as he tucked the case beneath his arm. He could do this. After all, he knew how important a place to gather and belong was to a bunch of kids who had been in the system too long. He'd been there after his parents had died. Until Gramps had returned to Mystic Beach to raise him, Luke had been alone. Now he had a chance to make a difference, and he didn't plan to let a case of the jitters get the best of him.

He drove past Christine on his way down Tamiami. He hadn't thought to toss a can of gasoline into the back of his car. The short time he'd spent with Cherry had left him distracted. Her and the damn light in her eyes, the spark in her voice, and those curves. From her waist, to her hips, to her knees. Damn.

Luke pinched the bridge of his nose. He had no intention of letting the woman get under his skin. Not that she'd tried. Not that he'd mind if she did.

He shook his head. *Forget it.*

The funny thing was, he'd avoided cherries all of his life—ever since he'd broken out into a record-setting case of hives after his first hot fudge sundae. There was a lesson there. Steer clear of cherries, even the ones in sparkly sandals and flimsy dresses.

He needed to leave Cherry Harte alone and focus on maintaining the status quo—just him, Gramps, their shop, and his work with the kids.

Cherry climbed out of her sister's convertible and pulled her suit jacket from the backseat. She slipped the long swing coat over her snug sheath, smoothing the lines of the crepe. She wiggled her toes in her new, conservative ivory pumps, low cut to set off her ankles, generous heels to add height.

"What do you think?" she asked Liz.

"You're gorgeous." Liz winked, her platinum blond wig swinging in the breeze. "Knock 'em dead."

Cherry couldn't help but smile at the beauty mark winking back from the space just to the left of Liz's lips. "New addition?"

Liz beamed. "Like it?"

"Love it. Have fun at your party tonight."

"You sure you won't need a ride home?"

Cherry shook her head, pulling her briefcase from the well behind the passenger seat. "I'll call a cab. You go have a good time."

She watched her sister's bright red BMW speed out of the lot and smiled. Liz might be a bit off as far as her wig fetish was concerned, but she had a heart of gold. Most locals with her looks and money would be headed out on the town tonight, but not Liz. For all of her big talk about rolling on the beach with a cabana boy, she spent most nights singing songs and making balloon animals over at the local Ronald McDonald House. Tonight would be no different.

Cherry often wondered where Liz got her good heart. Heaven knew, Monty and Fran hadn't been around enough to instill the values Liz seemed to have by the truckload.

As for her own night, Cherry's palms suddenly grew clammy. Monique had invited her to be part of the Women's League presentation, and she wasn't about to blow it. She drew in a deep breath, then exhaled slowly to calm her nerves. Cherry turned toward the massive marble steps leading to the county offices, and that's when she saw him.

Luke Chance.

What on earth was he doing here?

She froze momentarily, completely unnerved at the sight of him, her pulse kicking into overdrive. What was the matter with her? It wasn't as if she'd never seen a well-dressed man before.

Oh, who was she kidding?

Good Lord, the man cleaned up well. His charcoal gray business suit looked as though it had been tailor-made. The jacket hung unbuttoned, draping handsomely from his broad shoulders to his trim hips. The long, lean line of his trousers left no doubt about his fit physique. A classic burgundy tie and crisp white dress shirt completed the ensemble.

Cherry's mouth went dry. The vision before her deserved to be on the cover of some male fashion magazine. One thing was for sure. This Luke Chance was a far cry from the grouchy mechanic who'd rolled out from beneath his repair job earlier that day.

She steeled herself, heading straight for him.

Luke couldn't believe his eyes. What the hell was *she* doing here?

"Good evening, Mr. Chance."

His stomach clenched at the swish of the long jacket above Cherry's knees as she crossed the parking lot. Knees, for crying out loud. He willed his body to have no response.

"Ms. Harte."

"I'm surprised to run into you." Her eyes shimmered in the early evening sun, her expression a cross between confusion and amusement. "Delivering a car to someone? Another one of your services?"

He hoisted the portfolio and smiled. "Delivering a presentation."

"Oh." Her stare widened. "Not for the Framingham Estate, I hope."

"Exactly." He nodded, then squinted at her. "What do you mean, not for the Framingham Estate?" He tipped his head toward the building behind him. "You going in here too?"

She frowned, letting out a small sigh. "I'm working with the local Women's League to convince the commission to make the estate a horticultural center."

He took a step backward. "Really?" Frustration

began to simmer in his gut. "That's just what we need around here. More plants."

"It's not just plants." Cherry's voice grew pinched. "The center is an opportunity for Mystic Beach to elevate itself to the level of our surrounding communities and—"

Luke held up a hand. "Save it for the commissioners, Ms. Harte." He turned, starting up the steps. "I've got my own reason for being here."

Her heels clicked loudly on the steps behind him. "And that would be?"

"My group is proposing a new youth recreational facility. An after-school and weekend program for kids who have no place else to go." He turned abruptly to face her. She stopped in her tracks. "I grew up without parents and I know how difficult that is. If I can make life a bit easier for even one other kid, I intend to do so."

"Oh." Cherry's features softened.

Luke bent toward her, lowering his voice. "And I don't intend on losing to a bunch of hoity-toity plant lovers who have nothing better to spend their money on."

Cherry stepped backward, her heel slipping off the edge of the step.

Luke grabbed for her arm, pulling her close to prevent a fall—much closer than he'd intended. Her lips parted with surprise, her vibrant stare locking with his. Heat simmered low and heavy in his groin. Damn.

"You okay?" He eased away from her, hoping his body's reaction had been a fluke.

Cherry nodded, not saying a word and never taking her eyes from his. If he didn't know better, he'd think the momentary embrace had affected her as much as it had him.

Luke jerked a thumb toward the entrance. "Guess we'd better head inside."

She pressed her lips together, causing dimples to appear at the corners of her mouth. As she moved past him, the hem of her jacket brushed against his leg, the soft contact sending his nerve endings reeling.

Her spicy scent teased his nostrils. Shampoo? Perfume? He didn't know. He just knew he wouldn't mind burying his face in that scent all night.

At the top of the steps, she stopped, turning back to face him. She blinked once, as if trying to shake herself from a trance. A tinge of pink fired in her cheeks. "It was nice to see you again, Mr. Chance."

His own cheeks warmed. "Call me Luke."

"Luke." She spoke the word slowly, as if testing out the feel of his name on her tongue. His stomach gave another unwanted twist. "Good luck with your presentation. It sounds like a wonderful program."

"Good luck with yours, Ms. Harte."

"Cherry."

He watched her turn and push through the building's revolving door, head held high. He popped a piece of gum into his mouth, making a mental note to get rid of it before it was time for him to speak.

Of all the luck. He and Cherry Harte were competing for the same property.

Just perfect—and damned distracting.

CHAPTER 3

Cherry was in agony. Her tattoo itched like it had never itched before. The most unnerving thing was that it had kicked into action the moment Luke had pulled her into his arms.

She wiggled in her seat, not about to claw at her stomach under the watchful eye of Monique Goodall.

Once Luke and his group took the stage, Cherry forgot all about squirming. She sat mesmerized by Luke's presentation. He and the Youth Center's development director took turns walking the commissioners and others in attendance through the logic and value of earmarking the Framingham Estate for use by children to whom life had been unfair.

She watched him casually brush a wayward lock of black hair from his forehead as he gestured to a large chart. Warmth puddled deep inside her as he smiled at one of the commissioners who asked a question. Her eyes teared up as he told the story of his own childhood and how he'd bounced from home to home prior to his grandfather's move to Mystic Beach.

Amazing. You just never knew what caliber of man was going to roll out from under an old Cadillac. Not that it mattered. She had no plans to do anything more than file away their brief encounter in her memory bank.

A shiver rippled through her at the remembered feel of being pulled against his firm chest. He'd caught her in a way that left absolutely no doubt about the man's testosterone levels.

Cherry glanced around the crowded meeting room. Was it warm in here, or what? Somebody needed to crank the air-conditioning.

She banished all thoughts of Luke's masculinity to the recesses of her brain and glanced down at the printed agenda in her lap. The Woman's League presentation was next. Cherry opened her purse and slipped a mint from a tiny tin. Sliding the morsel between her lips, she shook her head, awestruck, as Luke wrapped up his group's presentation and thanked the commissioners for their time.

"There's been a change of plans." Monique Goodall's curt voice jarred Cherry's attention away from the meeting.

"About what?"

Monique hoisted her tiny recorder to her lips and uttered something. She spoke so softly Cherry couldn't make out her words, but she had the distinct impression she was the subject of the verbal notation.

Monique clicked off the recorder and leaned

close. "I can't have you up onstage with a hemline that short. You'll have to watch from here."

Cherry's heart sank to her toes as she tugged at her skirt. "But it's classic."

"Flashy." Monique shook her head dismissively. "The county commissioners will see you as nothing more than a pretty little lottery winner, when what they need to see is a polished presentation from someone of stature in the community." She patted her chest. "Like me." The smile she tossed in Cherry's direction reeked of condescension. "Don't worry. Your day will come."

Cherry frowned but could find no words to counter Monique's sentiments.

Monique waved to the other women in the group, then refocused on Cherry. "Wish me luck."

"Good luck," Cherry muttered as Monique headed for the stage.

What if Liz had been right? What if Cherry had been invited into the inner circle simply because of her money? She sucked in a deep breath. If that was true, she had nobody to blame but herself. After all, hadn't that been what she wanted all along? To create a new persona with her wealth?

Cherry glanced at the way Luke's dress shirt draped across his broad shoulders as he slipped back into a row of seats. He'd shrugged out of his jacket moments after his group had cleared the stage.

Maybe Liz had been right about everything.

Maybe Cherry *should* be on a beach somewhere sipping umbrella-laden drinks between rolls in the sand with the car repair . . . er . . . cabana boy.

Monique took the podium and introduced herself.

Cherry turned, scanning the faces of the Women's League members not onstage. They all politely clapped, elegant smiles plastered across each face. Every strand of hair on their heads fell into place. Every rope of pearls sat perfectly at the throat of each conservative, neutrally colored suit.

Dread teased at the base of her skull. They all looked alike. Little society clones, clapping for their leader.

Cherry swallowed. This was what she wanted, wasn't it? A new life? A respectable life? A life without worries?

She nodded, letting herself relax as she settled back to listen to Monique's presentation. Each time the memory of Liz's voice whispered at the back of her brain, she tuned it out.

Her plan had worked just as she'd hoped. She was on her way to becoming all she'd ever dreamed of becoming.

She glanced again at the Women's Leaguers.

She was on her way to becoming one of *them*.

Suddenly, she didn't feel very well. Cherry slipped out of her seat, pushed open the room's heavy wooden doors, and sank onto a long bench in the deserted hall.

Disappointment seeped through her as she fingered the hem of the suit's dress.

She obviously was incapable of selecting a simple outfit. What had Luke called it? Packaging issues?

How would she ever pull off a profile with *Mystic Living*? Or a commissioned art mural with the infamous Yogi? Sooner or later, someone was bound to realize every inch of her life had been carefully created. Fabricated using her wealth.

All I need is within me now. All I need is within me now.

She needed that CD from her car, but for now, the simple mantra was enough to help re-center her thoughts.

She wasn't about to let doubts stop her. The Women's League might not think she had the skirt length to be part of the presentation, but she had the money to be a crucial piece of their project. If she had to buy her way in, she would.

She was a woman on a mission, and nothing was going to knock her off track.

Cherry paused in front of the closed meeting room doors to glance down at her suit. Perfect. Polished and refined.

That's when Luke came barreling through, stopping a fraction of an inch from sending her careening onto her perfectly refined rear end.

Luke's phone had begun to vibrate just as the Development Commission had begun the question-and-answer period. Now, at least five full minutes later, he snatched the device from his belt loop, frowning at the display. He didn't recognize the number, but it was local. Maybe Gramps had run into a problem out on the road.

He slipped out of the meeting and headed toward the hallway in search of privacy. He pushed against one of the exit doors just as Monique Goodall interrupted another speaker on behalf of the Women's League. Leave it to her to find an excuse to grab the limelight. Hers would be one remark he'd enjoy missing.

He paused for a beat. What had happened to

Cherry? Grimacing as he caught the mental slip, he shook his head. He needed to chase the woman out of his thoughts once and for all. He had no business worrying about her or her knees.

As he shoved open the door, the approaching figure registered just before he crashed into her. *Cherry.*

Luke reached for both of her arms, hoping to steady her. "Sorry."

"We've got to stop meeting like this." Cherry shook her head and stepped away from his grip.

"I wasn't paying attention."

Her green eyes sparkled and a smile spread across her face. "Well, I hope you're more attentive with your customers' cars than you are with your customers."

At that moment, he realized he hadn't asked her about the wiring on her car. Maybe she could wait for him while he returned his call.

"Speaking of that." He held up a finger as he flipped open his phone. "I need to ask you a question, but I've got to check on something first."

Confusion washed across her face as she glanced at the meeting room door, then back at Luke, but she stood her ground and nodded. He watched with more than mild interest as she slipped out of her jacket, then twisted sideways and back, apparently scrutinizing her dress.

Between the short cut of the skirt and the height of her heels, one thing was clear. The woman had some killer curves.

He turned slightly away from her, but not before she caught his attention by pointing to the hem of her dress. "Would you say this is too short? Or professional?"

Heat warmed his face, and he tugged at his necktie as he shrugged. "Packaging issues." He pressed the Send button on his phone, yet continued his visual assessment of Cherry's outfit.

Her now-exposed dress hugged every inch, leaving little to his imagination. The woman had meat on her bones—in all the right places. But what really captured his attention, now that she'd pointed it out, was the hem of her dress where it stopped well above her knees.

Too short? Hardly.

Luke pinched the bridge of his nose and looked away. Since when had he developed a knee fetish? He needed to regain his commitment to avoidance of all things female and all things wealthy, especially the wealthy—but tempting—female standing in front of him.

Nothing good could come of admiring Cherry Harte or the way her dress hugged her waist, her rump, her—

"Mystic Beach Memorial," the voice on the receiving end of the phone call chirped.

Luke's heart lodged in his throat, sending all thoughts of Cherry and her knees scattering from his mind.

Cherry watched as Luke's features fell slack. He ended the call and brushed past her.

"Gotta go. Something's happened to my grandfather." He turned, rushing toward the doors to the parking lot.

"What happened?" Cherry called after him. "What about the rest of the meeting?" Darn it. The man walked so quickly, she'd never keep up. "Wait. Do you need help?"

She bent to pull off her pumps just as Luke spoke.

"He's in Mystic Memorial's ER. Had some kind of an episode out on a job."

Cherry froze, scrutinizing Luke's expression. The color had drained from his cheeks.

"I've got to get over there." His voice had grown hollow, monotone.

Her heart ached for the fear she saw etched across his face. Before she could talk herself out of it, she moved quickly, closing the gap between them and gripping his arm. "I'm going with you."

"The meeting," Luke murmured.

She hesitated for a moment. Her disappearance wouldn't make Monique happy, but she'd get over it. Hell, she'd probably be delighted to leave herself another note on her little recorder about Cherry's shortcomings.

Cherry felt she owed something to Luke and his grandfather. After all, the older man had gone out of his way to be kind to her earlier.

"I'll deal with them later." She jerked her head toward the exit door. "Let's go."

Her rational inner voice screamed at her to stop. What was she doing? She didn't even know this man. Worse, this man had stirred up an attraction she had every intention of fighting.

Her irrational inner voice didn't give a damn— compelling her instead to throw her plan out the window and help Luke however she could. After all, this *was* an emergency.

Cherry and Luke raced through the lobby and

out the doors to his car. "Give me your keys." She held out an upturned palm.

Luke squinted at her as if he weren't quite sure she was real.

"Keys." She touched his arm lightly. "You shouldn't drive."

He wordlessly dropped his key chain into her palm, then climbed into the passenger side.

Cherry threw her pumps into the backseat and dropped into the driver's seat. The car protested noisily as she shifted into first and pulled away from the curb. She stole a glance at his rugged profile. He'd squeezed his eyes shut, and one hand white-knuckled the edge of the door.

"He'll be fine." She patted his arm when she paused for a stop sign. His startled gaze met hers, sending her heart slamming against her ribs.

Something long dead inside sparked to life, much to her dismay. Maybe her emotions had been tricked by the excitement of the moment. *Yes. That must be it.*

There was no way the tangle of desire and concern tumbling through her was real. Right? After all, she'd left no room for romance in her new life.

Her tattoo itched. Just once, as if it disagreed with her train of thought.

She savored one last look at Luke, then refocused on the road, jamming the car into gear.

Nope. No room for romance. Even if Luke Chance was just about the most intriguing man she'd laid eyes on in . . . well . . . forever.

CHAPTER 4

Gramps looked mad as a bull. Wires led to a monitor quietly beeping his vital signs to the nurses' station down the hall. "It was that damn poodle," he grumbled.

Luke patted his grandfather's shoulder and shook his head. "You scared the hell out of me. I thought you'd had a heart attack."

"Angina." Gramps winced. "Could have killed me. I keep telling you I could go any minute."

"Now, come on," Luke admonished. "Doc says you're going to be fine. They'll keep you overnight to make sure it's nothing more, and I'll take you home tomorrow."

Relief eased through Luke, but he had to admit his grandfather's episode scared the hell out of him. In the time it had taken to reach the ER, he'd been a little boy again—orphaned and alone. Gramps wasn't getting any younger. Damn.

"Darn that Cassandra Pettigrew." His grandfather's voice broke through Luke's inner turmoil.

"Darn her, that derned dog, and the broom they

both rode in on." Gramps looked up, his eyes more full of life than Luke had seen them in a long time. "They snookered me into tea. *Tea.* And finger sandwiches. It's a wonder I didn't keel over right then."

"Better watch it, old man." Luke tucked away all thoughts of his grandfather's mortality and gave the older man's shoulder another pat. "You've got a little light in *your* eyes."

"Balderdash."

The vitality in his grandfather's voice sent relief rushing through Luke. "Doc said it was too much excitement." Luke waggled his eyebrows. "Maybe the widow is more woman than you can handle."

"Hmph." Gramps crossed his arms over his chest, his white eyebrows meeting in a bushy peak. "Is she here?"

"Who? Cherry?" Luke realized his mistake as soon as the name slipped from his mouth.

"Cherry?" A crease formed between the old man's brows. "Cherry Harte?"

Luke nodded. "She drove me." He glanced down at his polished loafers, fervently hoping to avoid a line of questioning.

Gramps brightened instantly. "Was she picking up her car?"

Luke shook his head, meeting his grandfather's curious look. "Haven't finished it."

Gramps narrowed his gaze. "You going to explain? I could kick off any minute here, son."

Luke pinched the bridge of his nose. If he had a dollar for every time his grandfather had uttered that phrase, he could have funded the Youth Center himself.

"She was at the presentation for the Framingham Estate."

Gramps answered only with a puzzled frown.

"Her women's group wants it for their plants," Luke continued.

"Well, what do you know?" Gramps grinned. "Got a light in her eyes, that one."

Luke paused for a beat. She sure did.

"Why is a rich woman like her doing something nice like driving you to the hospital?" Gramps screwed up his features. "Thought people with money were no good? Thought they changed. Only worried about themselves. Only—"

"Maybe she thought I'd give her a break on her car repair." Luke interrupted before Gramps could continue. He measured his grandfather's expression, flashing back on the original question. "Who were *you* talking about?"

"The widow." Gramps rearranged the blanket covering his lap. "I thought she might be concerned about me."

"As a matter of fact," Luke stood and jerked a thumb toward the door, "she's in the waiting area. I'm sure they'd let her see you for a bit."

"Guess that would be okay." Color blossomed in the older man's cheeks. "She doesn't have that gosh-derned dog with her, does she?"

"No." Luke stifled a laugh as he pushed open the door to the hall. "I think she left her at home. Something about giving you her full attention."

"Is that so?"

Luke glanced back in time to see Gramps smooth the white waves that capped his head. Very interesting. *Very interesting, indeed.*

As Luke rounded the corner, his focus fell to where Cherry sat waiting. As if on cue, her eyes met his.

His stomach clenched. *Damn.* There really was a light in the woman's eyes. She smiled, and Luke's pulse quickened.

Perhaps Cassandra Pettigrew would keep Gramps's mind off any matchmaking he had planned. It would be all Luke could do to resist the blond bombshell without any additional urging from his grandfather.

He had no intention of taking this encounter any further than driving the woman home. After all, he was far too old for a case of Cherry-induced hives.

Eugene pulled himself up straight against the pillows. Cassie Pettigrew peeked her permed, silver head around the edge of door. "Can I come in?"

He cleared his throat. "Sure thing. Thanks for checking on me."

She settled into the chair alongside his hospital bed, the skin around her blue eyes lined with concern. "Sorry about your indigestion."

Tarnation. If that wasn't embarrassing as all get-out. "I believe the proper medical term is *angina.*" He frowned. "You know, this could be the beginning of the big one."

She gave a quick nod, a flash of amusement in her eyes. "Pish posh."

Ignoring her remark, he shifted toward her. "What did you do with the info once the ambulance came?"

Cassie reached into her oversized tote bag and

pulled out a large envelope. She set it on his lap, smiling. "Everything's there. Are you going to tell Luke she's a lottery winner?"

Eugene shook his head. "Lottery money's even worse. He got burned over new money, remember? We need to keep this between us. Let's not give him any excuse to hide from Cherry Harte."

"She's a lovely girl." Cassie patted Eugene's knee and he tensed.

"Don't get my blood going, woman." He patted his chest. "My heart."

Cassie looked to the ceiling. "Lord, give me strength." When she refocused on Eugene, the intensity of her scrutiny set his teeth on edge.

"What?"

"You Chance men are a bunch of cowards."

That did it. "Cassandra Pettigrew, don't you start that lecture again. After all, you just about killed me today. I'd expect you to be more sympathetic."

She settled in her chair, pursing her lips. "You have any intention at all of telling that boy who he really is?"

"He knows exactly who he is."

Her silver brows lifted. "Does he?"

Eugene straightened. "He knows exactly what he needs to know. For now."

"I think it's a bit silly—"

He shot the widow a glare, and she fell silent. "I know what I'm doing."

Her gaze widened. "I hope so. I think he'd take the news just fine as long as it came from you."

"The time has to be right."

A smug smile pulled at the corners of her mouth.

"Let's just hope you live long enough to see it, you old fool."

Luke's eyes softened as he approached Cherry and sank into the chair next to her. Her insides caught ever so slightly, clearly communicating her body's response to the man's nearness. There was no denying the attraction. Based on the expression on his face, the feeling was mutual. "How is he?"

"Ornery and stubborn." Luke's smile kicked her belly into a second twist. "He'll be fine. Doctor thinks it was a bad case of heartburn or angina."

"Finger sandwiches and tea." Cherry smiled at Luke's raised brows. "Cassandra told me. Said she made cucumber sandwiches without trimming off the skins."

Luke grimaced. "No wonder the man's in the hospital."

Cherry rearranged the folded jacket in her lap, stalling for time to gather her wits. She tipped her head toward Luke and smiled, doing her best to resist reaching for him—touching him.

His features fell slack and his eyes darkened. "I'm sorry for today. First the truck running out of gas, and now taking up so much of your time."

Cherry shook her head. "It's okay." She quickly lifted and dropped one shoulder. "Apparently my skirt was too short for me to properly represent the group, anyway."

Luke's eyes narrowed. "How long have you been a member?"

"Provisional member," she corrected. "Since this afternoon."

One dark brow arched. "Did Monique Goodall tell you about your skirt?"

Cherry nodded. "You know her?"

A shadow rippled across Luke's face. "We've met." His gaze dropped to his loafers for several moments. Slowly, he retrained his attention on Cherry.

She resisted her desire to melt beneath the rich brown heat emanating from his eyes.

"I'll run you home." His voice had grown thick, as if he had to force the words through his throat. "I've taken up enough of your time."

"What about your grandfather?"

"He's in good hands with Cassandra. I'll say good night then get you out of here."

Luke stood, offering his hand. Cherry slipped her fingers into his calloused grip, a shiver tracing its way down her spine.

"You cold?" he asked.

Cherry shook her head, glancing down at her rumpled dress and bare feet. "Just a mess." She smiled. "Packaging issues."

His features grew serious. "Not from where I'm standing."

His words sent awareness humming through her veins. "I'll wait for you outside."

Luke nodded, releasing her hand to head back toward his grandfather's room.

Cherry took a steadying breath as she watched his departing back, unable to shake the feeling she was treading on dangerous ground. He might be a harmless flirtation, but she was fairly certain that what she felt came closer to distraction.

Her tattoo itched and this time she gave in to the

urge to scratch, stilling her hand as Luke glanced over his shoulder, flashing a wide smile.

She held her breath as he disappeared around the corner, then raked her fingernail over her tattoo, scratching with abandon.

Oh, what a tempting distraction the man was.

Luke drove in silence toward the address Cherry had given him. The early-summer sun sat low in the sky, and the air held a chill unusual for June. "Should I put up the top?"

Cherry shook her head.

"What about your hair?" he teased.

"My hair's off duty." She propped her elbow against the open window. "I was thinking." She spoke slowly, as if choosing her words carefully. "You must be starving. Why don't I make us a quick dinner?"

Luke hesitated, sensing the attraction in her tone. He could drop her off now, drive away, and only have to deliver her car tomorrow. Then Cherry Harte and her fiery eyes would be out of his life for good. He'd be safe.

He glanced at her, her expression a cross between nervousness and hopeful anticipation.

If he said no now, the worst that could happen would be he'd wonder "what if" for days—or months. "I really need to get back to Gramps."

"Sure." Cherry's disappointment rang palpable in her voice. "Another time."

Damn. Guilt gnawed at Luke's gut. The woman had gone out of her way for Gramps. "Can you cook?"

Soft laughter slipped between Cherry's beautiful lips. "Like you can't believe."

"Then how can I refuse?" He gave himself a mental slap for his lack of willpower. In his own defense, it had been a long time since he'd been with a woman as intriguing as Cherry, and he was hungry. What harm could come from sharing a quick meal?

A few minutes later, Luke rethought his decision.

The homes grew larger as he drove closer to Cherry's neighborhood. The woman represented everything he'd sworn to never go near again.

He winced.

What an idiot. He'd agreed to have dinner at the curvy stranger's house faster than a Ferrari went from zero to sixty. How had he been so weak?

Cherry sighed and shook her head, her short blond hair fluttering in the breeze whispering through the car. Her spicy scent enveloped him, wrapping its fingers around his lack of self-control.

Right, he reminded himself. That was how.

At some point during the evening, he'd decided he might have been wrong about her type. It had probably been when she'd yanked off her shoes and driven him to the hospital. Gramps had a definite point about that.

Luke couldn't remember the last time a stranger had done something so selfless on his behalf.

Somehow, though, her exterior package seemed like it didn't quite fit. Every now and then, the polish slipped and glimpses of the real Cherry peeked from beneath the surface. His reporter's nose itched for the full story. "Why the Women's League? And the plants?"

"Horticultural Center," Cherry corrected.

He grinned. "Right. Horticultural Center. Why?"

"Because I want to be taken seriously." Her voice had grown soft, sedate. "The Women's League has been around forever and they're well respected. Membership is a smart way to establish myself in the community."

Luke thought about Monique and the other Women's League members he'd met over the years. He stole a glance at Cherry's delicate features. They'd eat her alive. Or worse. They'd turn her into one of them. He tamped down the old anger.

"I still don't get it."

Cherry hesitated visibly. "It's important to me. Haven't you ever set a goal?"

A vision of the proposed Youth Center flashed through Luke's mind. The kids. His work. "Yeah." He nodded. "I have."

"Well." Cherry straightened in the passenger seat. "My goal is to make a good life for myself here in Mystic Beach. Let's just say I have my reasons."

He'd have to be a fool not to pick up the defensive tone in her voice. "Forget I asked."

An awkward silence beat between them. Cherry finally let out an exasperated breath and spoke. "I'm going to help the Women's League secure the Framingham Estate. Then, they'll welcome me with open arms. That's all that matters."

Dread flip-flopped in Luke's belly. He'd gotten so caught up in Cherry, the person, he'd forgotten she was a competitor for the estate—and a competitor who obviously valued her own society status over the welfare of kids in need. "If you ever get tired of the plants, remember there's a group of kids who could use a new recreational facility."

"Oh." Cherry slumped in her seat. "We're on opposite sides here, aren't we?"

Disappointment washed across her features, but Luke braced himself, refusing to be drawn into the emotion reflected in her face. He'd be a fool to get involved with the woman.

He reached up to slip a pack of gum from behind the visor. "Gum?"

She shook her head. "You chew that stuff like it's your lifeblood, don't you?"

She had no idea. He nodded, then popped a stick into his mouth, the sweet rush of sugar sending instant relaxation through every inch of his body.

Their approach to a gated community captured Cherry's attention and she pointed. "There's my entrance."

Luke pulled in, braking to a stop as Cherry waved to a spectacled security guard. "Evening, Bob."

"Evening, Ms. Harte." The man nodded as he pressed a button, raising the black and white striped arm of the gate.

"Nice neighborhood." Luke's jaw tensed, a tight knot coiling at the base of his skull. *What* was he doing? He cut his eyes at each villa as he drove past. Cherry Harte wasn't just out of his league, she was out of his stratosphere.

He glanced at her profile. She must be having second thoughts as well, especially as a competitor for the Development Commission's favor. They'd both been swept up by the day. Nothing more.

She turned to meet his gaze, smiling. His stomach tightened in defiance of his thoughts.

"It's this next drive." Her words cut through his inner turmoil.

Luke downshifted, steering the car onto a stone driveway. Sensor floodlights blinked to life, bathing an exquisitely landscaped walk and a two-story Victorian villa in white light.

"Very nice." *Damn.* Out of the stratosphere had been an understatement. The woman was out of his universe.

Cherry gave a quick shrug. "It's home."

Luke cut the ignition and hesitated. She unfolded herself from the car, waiting for him to follow. Should he call their dinner off now, or give it—and her—a chance?

Cherry gestured toward a walkway that disappeared around the side of the house. "Come see the view."

It wasn't the view out back he was worried about. Not in the least. What worried him was the way the view in front of him—that of Cherry Harte—had tied his stomach up in knots. If he were a smart man, he'd leave now while he could still make a clean escape.

Luke slowly opened the driver's door and stretched. His muscles ached, a wave of fatigue washing through him. The episode with Gramps had caught up—that and he had rapidly developed a case of cold feet.

As he followed Cherry to the back of the house, a second set of floodlights blinked on, illuminating a wrought-iron table, chair, and glider. Large ceramic pots of flowers filled the corners of the patio with various shades of pink, white, and purple.

She reached for his hand, and the contact ignited a fire deep in the pit of his stomach. Her eyes widened, as if their shared touch had startled her, and she dropped her hand, instead gesturing to a stone-edged path.

"Why don't I show you the beach?"

He nodded. "Lead the way."

He followed her toward the water, all the while marveling at how soft her fingers had felt when they'd grazed his own. How soft—and how hot.

The late-day sun reflected brightly off the mirrored surface of the Gulf. The amber semicircle slipped beyond the horizon, tossing a brilliant ribbon of pink across the water to where they stood. A pair of sandpipers skittered along the water's edge, just steps away.

A tangy, spicy fragrance teased the air, and Luke couldn't help but wonder if the scent came from the potted flowers or from Cherry herself.

He stared at her profile, filled with the urge to forget about her net worth and pull her into his arms. He suddenly could think of nothing but tasting her lips, her neck, her knees.

As if reading his mind, Cherry turned, touching her fingertips lightly to his chest. "What do you think?"

He looked into her pale eyes, searching for the now-familiar flash of life. And there it was—vitality, spunk, spark. Gramps had been right. The light hadn't been the sun at all. It had been Cherry.

"Breathtaking."

She slipped her hands to his shoulder, pulling

herself to her tiptoes. Luke gripped her elbows and tensed. He couldn't do this. He *shouldn't* do this. But, oh, how he wanted to do this.

She closed her eyes and pressed her lips to his cheek. The soft, sweet contact surprised him, but was gone in an instant, nothing more than the brush of a butterfly's wings.

Cherry lowered herself from her tiptoes, her lovely face mere inches from Luke's. Without thinking, he angled his mouth over hers, drinking in the sweetness of her kiss. He cupped her face in his palms, ruffling his fingers through her short, feathery hair.

He might be low on willpower, but right now his willpower could go to hell.

Cherry's lips parted and their tongues tangled, tasted, explored. He skimmed his palms down over the soft curve of her shoulders, down her slender arms and around her waist. He gathered her close, pulling her lush body flat against the hard planes of his stomach and chest. He hardened instantly.

Cherry broke away, inhaling sharply. Luke opened his eyes, surprised by the blush crawling up her cheeks, yet aware of the heat firing in his own face.

Suddenly the tangy scent surrounding them morphed into something . . . pungent.

"Oh no." Cherry grimaced and dropped back away from him. "Skunk."

Luke followed her gaze to where a pink poodle raced out of the underbrush, headed straight for them.

"Lucky!" Cherry gestured at the dog. "Patio. Do not come near us."

The poodle stopped in his tracks, tipping his

ridiculously fluffy head as if he wondered who Luke was and whether he could make it past Cherry to find out. The stench thickened, and Luke's eyes began to water.

Cherry squeezed her own eyes shut for a moment. "I'm afraid I'll have to owe you a rain check on dinner."

Luke pointed to the dog. "This yours, I take it?"

She nodded and frowned. "Lucky. He's a bit smitten with the neighborhood skunk who, quite obviously, wants nothing to do with him."

Luke couldn't help but laugh. "Sorry. But I can't help noticing your dog is pink."

"Tomato juice." She pointed toward the patio and the dog immediately marched toward an outside shower, obviously well practiced in what was to come.

Cherry shrugged and shook her head. "Don't take this the wrong way, but you probably want to leave now. This gets kind of ugly."

"I'll drop your car off in the morning."

"Thanks."

Relief and disappointment battled in Luke's gut as he headed around the house and back toward his car. Talk about saved by the bell.

Hell, he'd been saved by the skunk.

Any longer, and he'd have lost complete control. Once he'd experienced the taste and feel of Cherry's mouth against his own, he'd realized just how hungry he'd become.

But suddenly it hadn't been food he craved.

His getaway couldn't come a moment too soon.

CHAPTER 5

The next morning, Cherry did her best to focus on the messages on her answering service and not on the remembered feel of kissing Luke.

She glared at Lucky where he snoozed in the corner of her office. Talk about packaging issues. The dog didn't even know he was a dog. He was a rich shade of pink this morning, last night's fiasco having required a vat of tomato juice.

She listened as her financial advisor rattled off his latest suggestions for investing her wealth. If the man had any smarts at all, he'd suggest buying stock in the tomato-juice industry. Heaven knew Lucky alone ensured its value would continue to climb.

As if sensing her thoughts, the dog sighed and rolled over onto his back, all four paws in the air. That's probably how she'd find him someday—keeled over in the wooded area next to the house, fatally doused by the skunk.

She jotted down the names of her other callers. Only one was unfamiliar, and this one had called three times.

Moose Buck.

What kind of a person went by the name Moose Buck? Good grief. It sounded like something an adult film star would make up. And who was he? While his first two messages were cryptic, his third sent chills up her spine.

Wanted to know if you were able to get your car started.

Was this person watching her?

Great.

One of the joys of being a lottery winner was that every crackpot came out of the woodwork. Maybe Liz's practice of wearing a different wig every day wasn't such a crazy idea after all.

Cherry rubbed her tired eyes, exhausted from her lousy night's sleep. Between Lucky getting skunked and the burning desire meeting Luke had set into motion, she'd done nothing but toss and turn once she went to bed. Finally, it had been less stressful to get up and scrub the floors.

She might be tired this morning, but she had the cleanest tile around.

The worst thing was her damned tattoo hadn't stopped itching since the moment just before Lucky had made his odiferous entrance. The itch had never failed to signify a major life change. And she'd never had a false alarm. But she refused to accept that's what Luke represented. A pleasant fling? Maybe. A life change? *No way.*

What they'd shared had been nothing more than a kiss brought on by the stresses of the day. A scorching, sizzling, knock-your-chastity-belt-off kiss.

Cherry lowered her head to her hands. How could she have let her guard down like that? Even worse, she'd been disappointed when he'd left. *Disappointed.* Pathetic.

She squeezed her eyes shut and concentrated on ignoring the ache in her chest. The thing was, Luke Chance represented the one anomaly she had yet to encounter since she moved to Mystic Beach. The man wasn't attracted to her money; he was repelled by it. She had to admit that little twist on reality was sexy all in itself.

When Monique's recorded voice sounded on the line, Cherry refocused, not wanting to miss anything in the woman's message. Apparently the Development Commission had selected two finalists. The Women's League . . . and the Youth Center.

Marvelous.

Now Cherry couldn't avoid Luke even if she'd wanted to. They'd be forced to attend the same functions—as head-to-head competitors for the one thing they each wanted most.

Monique signed off with a reminder to be at the county offices tonight at seven for finalist photos.

Cherry's heart sank. And her tattoo itched.

"Come on, Lucky." She hung up the phone and waited for the dog to scramble to his feet before she headed for the kitchen. "I'm not letting you out of my sight."

Maybe that would keep the little Romeo out of trouble. As if she were capable of keeping her dog away from inappropriate sexual temptation.

Just look how beautifully she'd done for herself.

Gramps pulled his elbow free of Luke's steadying grip as the pair walked across the parking lot toward the garage. The morning sun reflected sharply off the shop windows. "I can walk on my own two feet."

"Yes, sir."

Luke smiled. One minute, his grandfather was sure he was dying. The next, he was bucking for independence. At least Luke knew the confusion tendency ran in the family.

For Luke, the inner turmoil had started the moment he pulled away from Cherry's villa the night before. The hot buzz of desire that still lingered today was a tangible reminder of just how deeply the woman had gotten under his skin— and in just one day. That was a first.

The realization had been sobering—and frustrating. Even worse, the Youth Center director had called early that morning to let Luke know their project had made the final cut. They'd be competing one-on-one with the Women's League and their little plant center.

He wouldn't be able to steer clear of Cherry Harte now if he tried.

"I should probably be resting." His grandfather's voice interrupted Luke's train of thought. Thankfully.

"Doc said you're better off up and around. You can watch me work." He pointed toward a stool in the office. "Grab a seat and I'll get you a soda."

"Pepsi?" His grandfather's white brows arched over hopeful blue eyes.

"Doc said no caffeine." Luke frowned. "Remember?"

Luke shook his head as he pulled open the refrigerator and grabbed a ginger ale from the bottom shelf. Gramps took the offered can, scowling first at Luke, then at the unopened lid.

"What? You too weak to open a flip top?" Luke reached for the can, popped the tab, and handed it back.

"What happened to Cherry last night?" Gramps nodded toward the Jaguar, still parked in one of the service bays.

"Nothing," Luke lied. "I dropped her at home. End of story."

"End of story, my foot. I may have a bum ticker, but I don't have a bum brain." Gramps tapped the top of his white-haired head.

"There's nothing wrong with your ticker."

"Don't change the subject." Gramps narrowed his eyes. "It's gonna be a long, lonely life if you avoid romance forever, son. You know, some people really do stay together all their lives."

That came from out of left field.

Luke stopped, measuring the bittersweet expression on his grandfather's face.

"Your grandma and I would have," Gramps continued.

"I know." Luke's heart ached for the older man's loss.

A massive stroke had stolen away Luke's grandmother long before her time. His parents' fatal car wreck had followed just a week later.

"I'm thankful for every day I had with your grandmother." Gramps waggled a wrinkled finger in Luke's direction. "I'll tell you one thing, though. I didn't waste any time when I met her. I knew the second we met she was my soul mate."

Luke blew out a frustrated breath. "Cherry Harte is not my soul mate." His gut caught at the thought of how close he'd come to making an irreversible mistake with the woman. "Stop playing match-maker."

"Then stop playing games."

"I don't play games." Luke stiffened, tension mounting at the base of his skull.

His grandfather shrugged. "I call 'em like I see 'em."

"Gramps." Luke patted his grandfather's knee. "You met her once."

"But I saw the sparks."

Sparks. There had been plenty of those.

"Do you know who she is?" Luke's traitorous pulse quickened. His body might be screaming out for more—much more—of Cherry Harte, but his brain knew better.

He'd hit the Internet as soon as he'd gotten home. What could he say? You could take the reporter out of the field, but you could never take away his need to dig. Luke had discovered exactly when Ms. Harte had settled in Mystic Beach and with how much money—right down to the number of zeros on her multimillion-dollar lottery check.

New money. A *ton* of new money. Getting involved with her would be his worst nightmare. He needed to remember to send Lucky a box of bones. The pooch had saved him from a round of romantic suicide.

What he hadn't been able to figure out was who might be interested in tinkering with her car. He wasn't ready to let that trail go. He could chalk up his interest to customer service. Nothing more.

His grandfather nodded. "One lucky lady."

"So you know about the lottery?" Luke shot a glare at the older man, who nodded.

"The widow's a whiz on that computer."

"Why didn't you tell me?"

"I know how you are about money." Gramps shrugged and took a sip of his soda. "True love's a funny thing, though. Can overcome even the hardest head."

Luke pinched the bridge of his nose, then fumbled around on the desk for a pack of gum. There had to be one somewhere. Hell, the rate things were going, he should probably stockpile the stuff. "Your Ms. Harte is the last thing I want. Been there, done that. Remember?"

Gramps's tone dropped low, intent. "This is different. She's just a normal gal who hit the numbers. Just because other people change with a new financial status doesn't mean this one will."

Luke flashed on the memory of his high school sweetheart—the one who'd left him high and dry when she'd inherited her father's wealth. Then a second image blew through his mind—that of his friend Jimmy.

Jimmy had dipped his hand into company profits and chosen a new life for himself. New clothes. New house. New car. The icing on the cake had come the day Jimmy vanished—apparently under a new identity.

The problem there was that when he'd skipped town, Jimmy had taken Luke's career down in flames.

Luke thought about the insipid CD in Cherry's car—some positive mumbo jumbo about self-improvement.

He'd vowed never to be taken for a fool again, and he sure as hell wasn't going to bend that rule now, especially not for a woman apparently *intent* on changing with her new financial status.

Luke shook his head, annoyance beginning to edge out the sympathy he'd felt moments earlier. "I like my life just as it is. Let it go."

Amusement danced in Gramps's eyes. "You can't deny the little lady turned your head."

"Oh, she turned it," Luke agreed. "But I don't need her complicating my life. Things are fine just as they are."

A fluffy white brow arched. "You can't hide forever in that apartment over the garage."

"I'm not hiding." A knot of dread twisted in Luke's stomach as he sensed his grandfather's favorite lecture was about to begin.

"You've been hiding since the day you came home from Miami with your tail between your legs."

Luke winced. Not this. Not now.

"So you blew a story." Gramps clucked his tongue. "People make mistakes."

"I blew a story, an investigation, *and* my career." Luke bristled, his pulse beginning to pound in his ears. "I chose a personal relationship over the facts. I won't make that mistake twice."

"Jimmy was your friend. You believed him when he said he'd make good."

"Yeah." A bitter laugh slipped from Luke's mouth. "Guess he's making good now, wherever it is he's hiding with all the money he embezzled."

"You really believe that?"

The question stopped Luke cold. His gut told him Jimmy might have never had the chance to get away, even if he'd wanted to. But the facts pointed to a complete betrayal by the man he'd once thought of as his closest friend.

Luke shook his head. "I'm still not entirely sure what to believe, but some day I'll figure the whole thing out."

"Time to move on." His grandfather's features tensed. "Life's too short."

Luke forced a smile, hoping to defuse the mood. "All the more reason to avoid our little lottery winner."

His grandfather's pale gaze narrowed. "That sweet girl cared enough to drive you to the hospital to visit your poor, sick grandpappy, and you didn't care enough to give her a chance."

Oh, brother.

Luke blew out a tired breath. "Give it a rest."

"You two would make a nice pair. She's got a—"

"Light in her eyes." Luke opened his desk drawers one after another, searching for gum. He slammed the last one shut, then patted his shirt pocket again. Still empty. "We've established that."

"Well, she does." Gramps frowned.

Luke met his grandfather's intent gaze. "Look at me. This isn't up for discussion. I know you mean well, but let it go."

His grandfather tapped a finger against Luke's chest. "You've got a big heart, son. Any woman would be lucky to have you."

Luke swallowed, leaning against a second stool. He might have a big heart, but he'd save it for his grandfather and the kids at the Youth Center. They were a whole lot safer than a tempting blonde with millions in the bank.

Gramps lowered his voice. "Never knew I raised a coward."

Luke scowled. "You didn't."

He remembered the feel of Cherry's lush curves pressed against his chest and the way her full lips had parted under the pressure of his own.

Heat coiled low and tight inside him.

Shoving the memory far into the recesses of his brain, he straightened, heading toward the Jaguar. "I've got work to do." The sooner he got this over with, the sooner he'd be free of Cherry Harte. Sure, he'd have to see her between now and the final awarding of the Framingham Estate, but he could handle that.

"You'll be sorry, son." Gramps's disappointed voice trailed him across the garage floor.

Somehow, Luke couldn't help but think if he gave in to the woman's temptation, sorry was exactly what he'd be.

Cherry stared at the coffeepot, letting the chugging sound soothe her as she repeated her daily affirmations.

"Every day in every way, I'm getting better and better. Better and better. Better and better."

The sound of Liz's footsteps on the back staircase broke her trance and she turned. Today's wig was a spiky red number, a cross between punk and *I Love Lucy.* The beauty mark, interestingly enough, had shifted from the left to the right corner of her mouth.

Liz wrinkled her nose as she reached the bottom step. "Eau de love?"

"Unfortunately." Cherry shot a look at Lucky, who returned a sheepish glare.

"And to think," Liz snickered, "we named him for the lottery, never knowing we'd be predicting his sex life."

She settled at the kitchen island, flipping the newspaper open to the puzzle page. The woman was unable to begin her day without completing the hidden-word puzzle. Cherry always figured the quirk fit her otherwise disguise-oriented life.

"You haven't taken any calls on the house line about the Jaguar, have you?" Cherry asked.

Her sister shook her head without looking up from the paper.

As if on cue, the phone rang.

Liz waggled her brows. "Maybe you two have a psychic connection."

"Hardly." Cherry snapped the receiver from its base and paced toward the hall. Selfishly, she didn't want Liz hanging on her every word with Luke.

When Bart Matthews's voice sounded confidently over the phone line, the anticipation in her stomach morphed to full-out, somersaulting disbelief.

"We need to talk."

"No." Cherry scrubbed a palm across her eyes. "We don't." She hadn't spoken to the man since the night before their planned wedding. Why start now?

"Your silence is affecting my campaign."

"It's all about you, isn't it?"

Bart had announced his state senate campaign just after their engagement. He'd capped off his successful career in the district attorney's office by sending a bounty hunter after Cherry's mother in the middle of their rehearsal dinner.

If she'd been smart, Cherry would have been the one to leave him standing at the altar. But no, she'd stuck to the plan they'd agreed upon. Of course, Bart hadn't shown up at all. Minor detail.

"No," Bart answered. "It's all about the truth."

"The truth is that I asked you to let me handle things, and you chose your career over my wishes— and my family."

"The family you've disowned?"

"That's my choice." She flinched at the defensive tone of her own voice.

"And what I did was *my* choice."

"Well then, you're an idiot, Bart."

Liz had emerged from the kitchen, eyeing Cherry with curiosity. At the sound of Bart's name, her baby blues popped wide.

"Cherry, we've been friends our whole lives. We need to deal with this."

"You probably should have thought that through before you picked your job over everything else."

"I did it for you. Your mother needed to get help."

Cherry snorted. Loudly. "Don't even try to pretend you care about my mother."

Liz's eyes were the size of small saucers now. Not knowing Bart's side of the conversation must be killing her. If Cherry knew her at all, she was calculating how quickly—and how quietly—she could snap up the extension in the den.

"I'm hanging up now. Don't call me again."

Liz mouthed the word, "No."

Cherry narrowed her eyes at her sister, hoping her dismay was transmitting loud and clear.

"Cherry, I—"

"Good-bye, Bart." Cherry punched the Off button and tossed the phone onto the bench in the hall.

"You were a little harsh." Liz fisted one hand on her hip.

Cherry burst into disbelieving laughter. "You have got to be kidding me."

Liz shook her head. "It's been four months. The three of us have been friends our whole lives. We need to deal with this."

Almost the exact words Bart had spoken. Suspicion whipped to life in Cherry's belly. She spun on her sister, pointing a finger. "Have you two been talking?"

Liz's brow crumpled, and if Cherry wasn't mistaken, she could hear the wheels turning in her sister's brain. Liz shook her head, the spiky shoots of red snapping with the move.

"What? No zippy comeback?" Cherry pursed her lips.

Liz shrugged, but Cherry couldn't help but notice her expression turned a bit sad. "I'm done with your hand-me-downs. Why would I talk to Bart?"

With that the doorbell rang.

"Now what?" Cherry snapped, realizing her tired nerves had been stripped bare by the sound of Bart's voice. Darn the man.

"I'll get it." Liz crossed quickly away from Cherry toward the front door. "Maybe it's Picasso."

Her sister had refused to call the artist by his right name ever since Cherry had told her about this morning's consultation. She squeezed her eyes shut, praying for patience. "His name is Yogi."

Liz gave another quick shrug as she reached for the doorknob. When she yanked open the front door, the man on the threshold was nothing short of a vision. A vision of what, Cherry wasn't quite sure, but definitely a vision.

He sucked in his tanned cheeks as if he were a male runway model about to step out. His retro paisley shirt hung open to his waist, exposing sleek, lean abdominal muscles just above the spot where the gaudy material disappeared into the waistband of a pair of expertly faded blue jeans. He reached to tuck a silken strand of chin-length raven hair behind his ear.

For a fleeting moment, Cherry wondered if he and Monique shared the same hair stylist along with their taste in art.

With a snap of his fingers, a young woman appeared at his side, looking suspiciously like Velma from *Scooby-Doo*. She wore her bobbed brunette hair in a wide, pink headband. Pushing up her glasses, she squinted, nervously drumming a pen against a notebook.

Liz's eyes sparkled, and Cherry was quite sure her sister was taking mental notes on new costume ideas.

The man dramatically arched one brow as he spoke. "This . . . is Greta. She will be taking notes today. And Yogi is ready for your consultation." The words purred from his lips. He snapped his fingers again. "Let the magic begin."

Cherry could only stare, slack-jawed, wondering how much more surreal her day could get.

With that, the man's perfect nostrils wrinkled. "What is that . . . odor?"

"Skunk," Liz snapped.

Yogi frowned. "Yogi cannot work with skunks on the premises."

Cherry shot a lethal glare at Liz, then nodded reassuringly at the man. "No skunks, just one unfortunate pup who had a run-in."

As if on cue, Lucky trotted down the hall in all of his pink glory.

"Magnifique," Yogi exclaimed. "He is a vision in pink." He snapped his fingers in his assistant's direction. "The odor kit, s'il vous plait."

Greta reached inside her briefcase and extracted a small white object and handed it to Yogi. He snapped the surgical mask into place over his nose and mouth, then clapped his hands.

"Yogi is ready to begin."

"And you thought I was a freak," Liz muttered.

"Freak?" The mask muffled Yogi's clipped tone. Cherry bit back the urge to laugh—or cry. At this point she wasn't sure which way she was leaning.

"Magnifique." She repeated his earlier term, hoping he might believe he'd misunderstood Liz's mumbling.

Relief eased through her as smile lines crinkled Yogi's cheeks just above the mask's elastic band.

A madman was about to paint her foyer. Her ex-fiancé had reappeared. Her dog stank. Her *house* stank. And she couldn't get the image of Luke Chance out of her head.

So far, the reinvention of her life was proceeding perfectly. *Just perfectly.*

CHAPTER 6

Luke shoved a hand through his hair as he pulled the tow truck into Cherry's development. The guard waved him past, and he twisted the rearview mirror in order to check his reflection.

The reality of what he'd done clicked like a slap. He shoved the mirror back as it had been. He didn't care how he looked. He didn't care what Cherry thought of how he looked. The woman's packaging issues were rubbing off.

All I need is within me now.

Luke grimaced. When he'd taken Cherry's car out for a test drive, he should have never listened to the CD she'd left in the dash. Some kind of positive-thinking brainwashing. Unfortunately, one phrase had cemented itself in his brain—a lot like the blonde had cemented herself in his every waking thought.

He had no time for Cherry Harte, her brain-washing, or his grandfather's matchmaking.

He'd been delayed in leaving the shop by an emergency call from the Youth Center director.

Apparently, the center's landlord had dropped a bomb. There would be no renewal of the lease. Instead, Mystic Beach was in for yet another strip mall. Tanning salons. Tile shops. Just what southwest Florida needed.

If the Youth Center failed in its bid to win the Framingham Estate, the kids would be out of a facility in three months.

Luke blew out a frustrated breath. In Mystic Beach, success boiled down to who you knew, not who you were trying to help, but he was sure of one thing. He'd do whatever it took to make sure the group didn't lose out to a bunch of plants. If that put the lovely Ms. Harte on his bad side, so be it.

He pulled in front of her villa, easing his tow truck to a stop.

Damn.

He shook his head in disbelief. Had the woman's house grown overnight? In broad daylight, the place was huge. If he hadn't believed her to be a multimillionaire before, he'd believe so now. The house screamed money. Hell. The house screamed *loaded.*

Disappointment nagged at the base of his skull. Much as he'd like to think he'd seen the real Cherry when she'd driven him to the hospital, truth was he'd probably pegged her correctly from the beginning. Women like her didn't care about kids who needed a recreational facility.

They cared about tea parties, cocktails . . . and plants.

Just look at the claptrap she listened to. Her millions weren't enough for her. She craved more. And once Monique Goodall and the Women's

League sank in their talons, Cherry's transformation to high society would be complete.

His only goal now was to deliver her keys, find out who might have done the number on the Jag's wiring, and run like hell.

Yogi breezed into the house, not gracing Liz with so much as a glance. Cherry's sister leaned against the wall, pressing one hand over her mouth. At least she had the good sense to hold back whatever biting remark she'd formulated in response to the man's entrance.

Suddenly, the hideous mural in Monique's office seemed tame compared to what Cherry imagined Yogi capable of.

"I wanted to tell you what I had in mind." She stepped toward where he stood, staring at the wall they'd discussed.

He held up one long-fingered hand and sucked in his cheeks. The mask puckered in, then released with a snap as he blew out the breath. "You must not interrupt Yogi when he's trying to read the space."

Liz snorted, hurrying past them toward the kitchen, short red spikes bouncing all over her head. "Excuse me."

Cherry fought the urge to trip her sister as she fled, choosing instead to force the issue with Yogi.

"It's important to me that the piece be soothing. I don't want anything . . . anything . . . disturbing." There. Nondisturbing was exactly what she needed. No hallucinogenic visions of superheroes floating over the city.

Yogi paused, gracing her with an annoyed

sideways glare. Okay. She could see they were off to a great start.

"Something tasteful. Calm." Cherry gave a quick shake of her head, unable to rid herself of the vision of Monique's frightening mural. "No pink."

Yogi froze, slowly pivoting to face her. He'd sucked in his cheeks so severely he looked like a surprised ghoul. "No pink?" His dark eyes thinned to tiny slits. The surgical mask puffed in and out, in and out.

Cherry steeled herself. She was perfectly capable of handling this. She could stand up to . . . Yogi. She had hired *him*, for crying out loud. Narrowing her gaze, she shook her head. "No pink."

They stood facing each other for several long seconds, like two gunslingers in the Old West.

Yogi broke first, which filled Cherry with immense satisfaction. One raven brow arched as he pressed his lithe fingers to his lips through the mask. "Interesting."

With that, he spun away, consumed once again with developing his vision. Greta shrugged, then scampered after her boss.

"Tell me again why you commissioned this guy?" Liz sidestepped to where Cherry stood.

Unease tumbled through Cherry's stomach like a runaway roller coaster. "Monique says he's all the rage." She hugged herself, trying to hide her doubt as the man paced wildly around the house. "Everyone who's anyone has his art in their home. He's brilliant . . . supposedly. Don't forget, we've got the *Mystic Living* photo shoot coming up."

Liz squinted, then shook her head. "Have you actually seen any of his work?"

Sadly, yes. Cherry nodded but had zero intention of describing *what* she'd seen to Liz. Better to keep her comments brief. "Inspiring."

Yogi breezed past, mumbling incoherently. Greta scampered behind, scribbling furiously into her notebook. She shot Cherry and Liz a nervous smile. Lucky trailed along, a tight third in the space-evaluation procession. He'd apparently decided Yogi was worthy of his attention—and aroma.

The two sisters turned to follow the trio's frenzied moves. Liz clucked her tongue. "I actually remember a time when you were capable of independent thought."

Cherry scowled. "I know what I'm doing. It's part of my plan."

"Remind me to put that on your tombstone." Liz tossed the parting shot over her shoulder as she sashayed away.

"Our financial planner agreed this was a wise investment," Cherry called after her sister, refusing to be intimidated by Liz's doubt.

"Yeah?" Liz snorted and stopped short. "What are his thoughts on swampland? Heaven knows there's plenty of that around here."

"Not funny." Cherry pivoted back toward where Yogi and Greta measured the entryway. "You understand the look I'm going for, right?"

Yogi turned his superior stare in her direction. "I"—he splayed one hand flat across his exposed chest—"know what you need."

A second snort sounded from Liz's end of the hall. "I'm going to grab a stool," she said. "This is one show I don't want to miss."

A knock sounded just as Liz disappeared into the

kitchen. Cherry turned, her breath catching at the sight of Luke filling the still-open doorway.

He'd obviously run a hand through his jet-black hair. Bright color flushed his cheeks, no doubt from the scorching-hot temperature outside. He'd rolled up the sleeves of his denim work shirt, and his well-worn jeans fit him in all the right places. Her gaze fell to his tan work boots and she inhaled sharply.

There was no doubt about it. He was one fine specimen of the male species.

"Dropped off your car." His deep voice rumbled across the space between them, snapping Cherry's focus away from his feet. "Need to go over what I found with you, though."

"Come on in." Cherry forced the words past the unwanted—yet undeniable—lump of attraction in her throat. "Want something to drink?"

He shook his head. "Got to get back. I'm trying to keep an eye on Gramps."

"How is he?" She mentally scolded herself. How could she have forgotten to ask?

Luke nodded, his eyes darkening as he focused on her mouth. "Ornery as usual. He'll be fine."

Awkwardness danced between them, as if the ghost of last night's kiss hovered just above them in the hall. Cherry realized she hadn't felt this uncomfortable since she'd worn her Brownie uniform a day too early in first grade.

She admitted she was no ace at small talk, but this was ridiculous. "Heard the Youth Center was named a finalist." The words rushed out in a jumble. "Congratulations."

"You, too." Luke nodded, a crooked grin toying with his lips.

Those lips. Those tempting, firm, blood-sizzling, heart-pounding lips. Cherry blinked.

Down, girl.

"When Monique told me you were the second selection, I was so happy for you. Your group, I mean. Your kids. The group's kids."

Lord help her. Had she been this inept back in high school?

"Thanks." His grin broke into a wide smile, lighting his handsome features and sending her insides spiraling into a tight ball of tension.

Cherry breathed in through her nose, hoping it would fend off the feeling of impending hyperventilation.

Yogi zipped past again, this time drawing maniacally on a small sketch pad.

Cherry pointed as he passed. "Yogi, this is Luke, my . . . mechanic. Luke . . . Yogi. An artist I've commissioned."

Amusement glimmered in Luke's dark gaze, and the grin returned to his face, this time spreading even wider. He gestured toward the mask. "And I thought you had packaging issues."

Cherry shot him a warning glance just as Greta scampered past, rushing to keep up with Yogi.

Luke tipped his head toward Greta's back, dropping his voice low. "That must be Boo Boo?"

"Not funny," Cherry muttered under her breath.

Luke swiveled to study the dynamic duo, then refocused on Cherry. Her pulse quickened, blood humming through her veins.

"Really?" He chuckled softly. "Because I thought it was pretty good."

Yogi's arrogant gaze narrowed as he gestured toward his helper. "This is Greta."

Luke's surprised expression sent a ripple of desire washing over Cherry. "Let's hope he paints as well as he hears," he whispered.

The sound of a feminine throat clearing captured both Cherry's and Luke's attention. Liz stood just behind Cherry, fists on hips, taking in their exchange.

"You must be Luke."

He nodded and gave her extended hand a quick shake.

"I'm Liz."

As Liz stepped back, she tossed Cherry an all-knowing smirk that spelled nothing but trouble.

"How about some coffee?" Liz asked. She nodded toward Yogi and Greta. "I was just about to pull up a stool to take in the show. Want one?"

"Tempting." Luke smiled warmly. "But I need to get back to work."

Liz tipped her head to one side. "Promises to be some performance."

"He's obviously *not* your average bear," Luke added.

Liz's baby blues grew wide. "A sense of humor and drop-dead gorgeous. Imagine that."

Cherry winced as a blush fired in Luke's cheeks.

Yogi and Greta suddenly appeared in their midst, sparing them any additional deep thoughts from Liz.

The masked artist stopped so abruptly in front of Cherry, his heels snapped together. "My work here is done. Yogi will return tomorrow to start on your sketches." He waved one hand through the air like a magician waving an invisible wand. "Prepare to be dazzled."

Cherry opened her mouth but was unable to formulate an intelligent response. Luke and Liz both discreetly averted their faces, no doubt hiding matching grins.

"We've already discussed my fee, yes?" Yogi sucked his cheeks in expectantly.

"Yes." Cherry nodded, wondering briefly how much dictating into her little recorder Monique would do if Cherry sent Yogi packing.

"Marvelous." Yogi lowered the mask to his neck, gripped her shoulders, and brushed an air kiss past each of her cheeks. "Yogi accepts cash only. No checks."

With that, he straightened, snapped his fingers, and was gone, his assistant, Greta, close behind.

"You don't see that every day," Liz muttered.

Luke nodded. "Thank goodness."

The focus of his dark gaze returned to Cherry, pinning her where she stood. "About your car—"

No sooner had the front door closed behind Yogi than the doorbell rang.

"Da Vinci must have forgotten part of his ego." Liz crossed the foyer, waving a dismissive hand at Cherry and Luke. "I'll get it. Don't let this momentary interruption stop whatever it was you two were doing."

Cherry pressed against the vein that had started to throb over her temple, but when she turned to see who was at the door, she dropped her hand from her head to her chest.

Beyond the visitor, a yellow cab sat in the driveway, its driver working feverishly to pull a large steamer trunk from the backseat. The dapper passenger stood at the threshold, beaming at Liz, who had instantly crossed her arms in a defensive pose and taken a backward step.

His mustache was trimmed to perfection. His dark blond waves fell into impeccable rows. His charcoal suit fit to a tee. Yet the one accessory Cherry couldn't take her eyes from was the simple gold chain around the man's neck. The chain her mother had given her father many, many years before.

Monty Harte.

"Expecting company?" a deep voice rumbled close to her ear.

Luke. Good grief, she'd forgotten he was still here. She had to get rid of him before he realized this man was her father. The last thing she needed was for the news of Monty's arrival to spread.

"Yes." The word sounded of its own volition. "Right on time."

Luke pursed his lips and squinted. She could tell he wasn't buying a word. "Listen, I need to talk to you about your car."

Cherry glanced from her sister to her father to Luke. One of them had to go, and the easiest target was the last. She gripped his elbow and dragged him toward the door. "I'll send you a check."

Luke planted his heels, and Cherry's forward progress ground to a standstill. Luke's expression grew even more serious.

"Really. You can trust me. I'm good for the money." She pushed against his arm.

He shook his head. "Someone tampered with the wiring. Are you in some kind of trouble?" One dark brow arched as he looked from Cherry to Monty and back.

"I knew it," Monty called out. "I got here just in time. That Moose is nothing but bad news."

"Moose?" Cherry snapped her focus to Monty. "How did you know about Moose?"

"Who's Moose?" Luke interrupted. "Why would he tamper with the wiring in your car?"

Monty slapped Cherry on the shoulder and she staggered sideways. "My arrival is not a moment too soon."

"Does somebody want to tell me what the hell is going on?" Luke asked.

Liz dragged her stool closer. "Told you this was going to be good."

"I've got it all under control now," Monty said.

"Who are you?" Luke's brows had snapped together, forming a puzzled streak across his forehead.

"Monty." Cherry's father tipped his head toward Luke. "I'm the girls'—"

"Butler," Cherry interrupted before Monty could say anything more.

"Butler?" Luke swore softly under his breath. He reached into his shirt pocket and pulled out a pack of gum. Without speaking, he shoved a stick in his mouth, followed by a second and then a third. "Keys are in your car," he said as he spun toward the door. "No charge."

Cherry followed him outside, pulling the front door closed as he headed for his tow truck. The cabbie had managed to hoist her father's trunk to the drive and now stood staring at the monstrosity, hands on hips. From the size of the thing, they were going to need a backhoe.

Monty sure as hell hadn't packed for a short visit.

"Sorry about the confusion," she called out to Luke.

He stilled as he slid into the driver's seat. "About last night."

He hesitated for a beat and Cherry's thoughts flew from her father's arrival back to the scorching heat that had spread between her and Luke when they'd kissed.

"It can't happen again." He pulled the driver's door shut, then barreled out of sight.

Her heart hit her toes. Never kissing Luke again was for the best, but the hollow regret that swelled inside her defied all rational thought.

When he was safely gone, she shoved open the front door and pinned her father with a glare. "How much do you need?"

He blanched. "Is that why you think I'm here?"

"Please." She scrubbed a hand across her eyes. "We haven't heard a peep out of you in ten years and suddenly you show up? Or are you going to try to tell us you haven't heard we hit the lottery?"

His brilliant blue eyes widened. "You hit the lottery?"

Liz snorted and kicked him in the shin. She'd been doing so ever since she'd been a toddler. Cherry imagined the move packed far more of a punch these days.

"I'm here to protect you," Monty said as he moved away from Liz and reached down to rub his leg.

"Protect us? We did just fine without you all these

years." Cherry planted her fists on her hips. "And we don't need your protection now."

Hurt flickered across her father's face, and Cherry winced internally. She was fairly certain her words had stung far more sharply than Liz's kick.

"Trust me, you do." Monty straightened and flashed a wide smile. "But I'm here now, so your worries are over." He tipped his head toward the staircase. "My room up that way?"

"Your room?" Cherry laughed in disbelief.

She had a Women's League membership to secure, a mural to supervise, and a photo shoot to prepare for. Giving Monty Harte a room didn't fit that equation no matter how she looked at it.

"Can't protect you unless I'm under the same roof."

"Protect us from what?" Liz asked. She stepped toward Monty and he took a matching step in reverse.

"Moose," he answered.

Cherry thought about her messages from Moose. The remembered sound of the man's voice made her shiver. "Is this one of your scams?"

He screwed up his features. "Cherry. Baby. Would I scam my own daughters?"

"Wouldn't be the first time," Liz grumbled, obviously still bitter about the fact Monty had emptied out their piggy banks before his final departure.

The dog chose that moment to race through the front door, reeking of a fresh spray.

"What in the hell is that?" Monty cried out, whipping a handkerchief from his pocket and pressing it over his nose and mouth.

"Your first assignment," Cherry answered, heading for the steps.

Her father narrowed his eyes.

Cherry shrugged. "You want to protect us? You can start by bathing the dog. Tomato juice is in the pantry. Shower's out on the patio." She started her ascent, not stopping to look back.

"Don't you want to know who Moose is?" her father's voice called out after her.

"Not now," she answered. "I've had enough excitement for one day."

Once in her room, she sank to the floor, staring at the carefully crafted goal poster she'd made the day after she and Liz won the lottery.

From her hair to her shoes to her house, she'd carefully chosen every piece of her new life. And every piece had been intended to lock away the old life for good.

Only now, her past had moved in, complete with his steamer trunk. Worse, some guy named Moose had apparently sabotaged her car.

Then there was the issue of Luke, who probably thought she was completely insane. What he thought really shouldn't matter, but the sad fact was, it did.

Cherry stared again at her poster.

Luke Chance.

Not on the poster.

Not in her plan.

Yet somehow, in the course of twenty-four hours, he'd taken over most of her conscious thought.

Damn it all to hell.

CHAPTER 7

Back at the garage, Luke's shop had become a shrine to Cherry Harte. Photocopied newspaper and magazine articles covered every inch of his bulletin board and most of his desk.

Gramps.

For some reason, the little lottery winner had kicked his grandfather's matchmaking game into overtime.

Luke leaned toward the largest photo—a shot of Cherry smiling at a table full of men at a local shelter. He skimmed the caption. Apparently the shot had been taken during one of her outings with the Women's League.

He scrutinized the photocopy more carefully. If a newspaper photographer had been anywhere near the Women's League, good old Monique would have wormed her way into the picture somehow. And there she was.

Behind Cherry. In the shot. Subtly appearing uninterested in being immortalized. What a joke.

As if there had ever been anything subtle or un-planned about a single move the woman made.

He glanced back at Cherry, studying the soft curve of her jaw and the way she'd tucked her hair behind one ear. Fresh-faced. Sincere. But sooner or later she'd be just like Monique. The thought sobered him, saddened him.

Damn his heart for the way it had let the woman in, and damn Gramps for the reminder.

He let his gaze wander from article to article, from shot to shot. He settled on a grainy black and white of Cherry and Liz surrounded by a group of children in hospital gowns. In the shot, Liz wore what appeared to be a clown wig as she painted a young girl's face. The child was bald, and Luke's gut caught in sympathy.

No other adults were in the group, and Cherry and Liz appeared to be acting alone—without the Women's League.

Cherry sat cross-legged, a picture book open in her lap. She smiled as he'd never seen her smile. If he didn't know better, he'd swear the children in the photograph had captured her heart and mind, making her forget about how she appeared to anyone who might be watching.

The photographed Cherry Harte looked com-pletely happy and at ease, and that was a combi-nation he had yet to see on the actual woman's face.

As he scooped up the articles strewn across his desk, a third photograph caught his eye. In it, Cherry and Liz each held a corner of a huge check. Their lottery winnings.

The two women looked nothing like the pair he'd left back at Cherry's house. Liz's hair fell long and blond, well past her shoulders. Cherry looked drunk with excitement, her short hair mussed and sexy as hell. She sported no fancy shoes or flirty dress, just a pair of jeans, a white T-shirt and a trim black blazer.

He'd never seen her look more beautiful.

Why had she traded it all for flash? Why had she wanted to? And who the hell was Monty? And Moose?

The woman definitely had one hell of a story—and it went far deeper than her lottery win.

No.

Luke shook his head and willed his curiosity to the far recesses of his mind.

He gathered the photocopies one by one, not stopping to remove pushpins. Corners ripped, photos crinkled. He balled the collection between his hands and shoved it far down in the trash can.

His investigating days were over. He didn't care about Cherry Harte and her present. He didn't care about Cherry Harte and her past. All he needed to worry about was surviving the Development Commission events between now and the final selection for the Framingham Estate.

Then Cherry Harte would be out of his life. For good.

When Cherry emerged from her master suite, dressed for the finalist announcement, she'd selected a tailored suit that skimmed her legs at mid-calf. She'd chosen an olive green, figuring it to be subdued. Proper. Appropriate.

She'd slicked her hair behind her ears after using

a temporary dark blond rinse to tone down her color. She'd added a strand of pearls at her throat as a finishing touch.

"Who died?" Liz asked as Cherry neared the bottom of the steps.

"Very funny."

Liz, apparently, had undergone a personality change. She'd traded in her short, red spikes for long, flowing chestnut curls. The beauty mark had disappeared altogether.

Cherry had asked her to attend the photo session, and she'd met her halfway on her outfit. Instead of Liz's normal animal-print leggings, she'd donned black leggings and a zebra-print blazer. It was a start.

Monty emerged from the kitchen, crystal cocktail glass in hand. He acted and looked as though he'd lived in the villa all his life. "You two going out?"

"Don't get too comfortable." Cherry nodded toward his cocktail. "I still haven't decided if you're staying."

"Of course he's not staying," Liz added. "He never stayed before. Why would he start now?"

"I was talking about the short-term." Cherry glared at her sister. "You're not helping."

Monty tipped his head toward Liz. "Wasn't your hair short and red last time I saw you?"

He spoke the phrase as if he were talking in years instead of hours.

Liz stared at him without saying a word. At least she hadn't kicked him in the shin. *Yet.*

"She likes wigs." Cherry peeked into her office, wanting to make sure Lucky was securely confined inside the house. He was sound asleep, pink belly up, pink paws sprawled—apparently exhausted from his latest excursion and his first shower with his grandpa.

"Why do you wear wigs?" Monty's voice turned Cherry's attention back to her family in the foyer. "Are you sick?"

Cherry rolled her eyes. He just couldn't let it go, could he?

Monty reached toward the long, chestnut curls and Liz planted a hand on top of her head.

"Do not touch my hair." She stepped sideways, out of reach of her father's grasp. "No one touches my hair."

"So, you're not sick?" Monty tipped his head and scratched his chin. "You have your own hair underneath?"

"Lots of it," Cherry chimed in, but shut her mouth when hurt flashed across Liz's baby blues.

"Show me," their father urged.

Liz slipped the wig off, then shook out her tumbling blond waves. Her hair fell to her shoulders and, other than the fact that the silky strands had spent the last four months shoved up under whatever wig had suited Liz's daily moods, they shone.

"Why?" Monty's voice had gone soft. The gentle tone caught Cherry by surprise, summoning back a long-lost memory of her family gathered together on a snowy day—all soft voices and happy innocence.

Liz stepped up onto the first riser of the staircase, turning to keep her back to Monty.

"Why?" he repeated.

Liz pivoted, meeting his questioning gaze. "Because you never came home." With that, she ran up the steps and disappeared toward her bedroom suite.

Leave it to Liz to cut right through the bullshit.

Monty stared at the empty staircase. Uncomfortable silence filled the foyer. Cherry cleared her throat. "Soda, Monty? Coffee?" Maybe if she distracted him with hospitality, Liz's awkward departure wouldn't hang like a black hole in the center hall.

No such luck.

"What did she mean?"

When Monty switched focus from the steps to Cherry, sadness played at the corners of his eyes. Cherry's heart caught. The man might not be Ward Cleaver, but he still had feelings.

"She likes to dress up." Cherry gave a quick shrug.

Monty shook his head. "That's not what she said."

Cherry sighed and hugged herself. "The way she explained it to me was that she'd worn my hand-me-downs all her life. When we won the lottery, it was her chance to buy and wear whatever she wanted. She's playing dress-up." She gave another quick lift and drop of her shoulders. "She might be a grown woman, but she likes nice things. New things."

Her father narrowed his eyes, obviously wanting the connection between Cherry's explanation and Liz's biting comment.

"Things were tough after you left. They got tougher when Mom got into trouble." Cherry hoisted her chin. "Liz and I did the best we could."

Her father dropped his gaze to the floor as if counting the colors in the intricate tile design.

Cherry waited. Waited for his response. For his

apology. For anything. Anything that might explain the reason he'd left them for a life of running.

When he straightened, brandishing a broad smile, a lump of expectation caught in her throat.

"Did you say coffee?"

Disappointment edged out the expectation, and Cherry jerked her thumb in the direction of the kitchen. "Come on. I'll put on a pot before I leave."

Her father pointed to her head as they headed down the hall. "What's your excuse for this mousy color?"

"Packaging issues."

CHAPTER 8

The crowd waiting inside the Development Commission's meeting room was growing restless. Cherry stole periodic glances at Luke where he stood gathered with other Youth Center board members. Even though she'd spent the entire afternoon positively affirming him out of her head, she couldn't bring herself to walk over to him. If she were a brave woman, she would.

Isn't that what every great female lead would have done? What about Katharine Hepburn? Good old Kate would have waltzed over, dazzled him with witty prose, then left him standing there with his tongue hanging out.

But not Cherry. She stood fingering the strap of her purse, trying to focus on Monique's pratterings about the challenges of running the Women's League and shouldering the weight of her responsibilities to the community.

Liz's fingers gripped Cherry's elbow. She leaned close, brushing her lips against Cherry's ear. "Stop fidgeting. Social goddesses do not squirm."

She'd dragged Liz along for moral support. After the morning's multiple fiascos, she'd figured backup couldn't hurt. Of course, she should have known Liz would be anything but quiet backup.

Once Liz had peeled off the chestnut wig for Monty's benefit, she'd apparently been uninterested in putting it back on. Instead she wore a raven-black bob, eerily similar to Monique's cut. The beauty mark had reappeared, this time a bit higher on her left cheek.

"Did you see Luke?" Liz whispered. "That man looks finger-licking good in a suit. If you don't get your act together soon, I might have to make a move."

An unfamiliar flicker of jealousy ignited deep in Cherry's belly. "You're not his type." She dropped her voice low, below Monique Goodall's radar screen. "He's got a thing against women with money."

"Honey, there are ways to make a man forget all about money." Liz dropped her hold on Cherry's arm and moved as if she were going to cross to where Luke stood.

"No." Cherry grabbed the strap of Liz's purse, jerking her to a standstill.

Monique and the other Women's League members turned in unison to glare at Cherry's outburst.

Cherry tipped up her chin. "No . . . wonder this whole process has taken so much time. Just look how long it's taking them to make tonight's announcement." She pasted on a phony smile and hoped for the best.

The women offered Cherry nods and smiles,

then returned to their conversations. Monique lifted her tiny voice recorder to her lips and uttered something, no doubt a permanent recording of Cherry's social ineptitude.

Liz bit her lip, showing uncharacteristic restraint for the second time that day. "Nice save."

Cherry sidestepped away from the group, dragging her sister with her. "Where were you going?"

Liz's eyes twinkled. "To say hello to your new stud muffin."

Heat flushed Cherry's cheeks. "He's not my stud muffin."

"So you keep saying." Liz's brows lifted in unison. "You'd never know it by your little purse snatching."

Cherry squeezed her eyes shut, then refocused on her meddling sister. "I was afraid you'd make a scene." She shot Liz a frown. "You're driving me insane."

"Puhlease." Liz gave an exaggerated eye roll. "I live to make you insane."

With that, the chatter in the room died away to a murmur as the Development Commission members filed into the room. Cherry gave Liz's purse strap another yank for good measure, then focused on the impending announcement.

Luke listened to the Youth Center director in total disbelief. Here they stood, moments away from being named a finalist for use of the estate, and their lead funding source had fallen through—brought up on fraud charges. He shook his head, not wanting to believe his ears. The project didn't stand a chance.

They'd worked months to secure that funding. Where in the hell were they going to get a half million dollars to show good faith, let alone the other half million to meet the finalist requirements?

Only one person he knew had that kind of money, and he sure as hell wouldn't be asking her.

"No." Cherry's voice cut through the din of the crowded room. He looked over just in time to see her explaining something to the other plant aficionados gathered around her. Apparently her campaign for permanent membership was going well. It seemed she had the rapt attention of every Women's League member in attendance.

He stared at the way her hair curled around her ears where she'd tucked it back. The look would be ridiculous on some women—more of a boy's cut than a female's—yet on Cherry it suited. The feathery look matched the usually frilly dresses she wore and the ridiculous excuses for shoes she pranced around in. Yet, unless his eyes deceived him, she'd darkened her hair. The change made her appear less vibrant, less alive. He shifted positions to get a better look. Maybe it was just the lighting in the room.

Nope. He'd been right. What had she done?

Women.

To make things worse, she'd shown up in a drab, tailored suit. She'd obviously caved to the will of Monique, wearing a skirt that was far too long for her—not to mention the fact it hid her knees. Her transformation to Women's League clone was proceeding just as planned.

Luke's heart sank.

As he watched, she grabbed her sister, Liz, and dragged her away from the others.

Spunk. That was one thing the woman couldn't hide. Even today when she'd been lying to him about whoever the man had been at her front door, she'd been glowing with vitality. He wondered if she had any idea at all of how sexy she was when she felt cornered. Or frustrated.

Hell.

When she breathed.

Luke flinched at the thought, willing himself to look away. She might be sexy no matter what she wore and no matter what color she dyed her hair, but Cherry was from the other side of the room, so to speak. He contemplated the well-coifed women around her, then glanced back toward his own group. Real people. Real mission. Kids in need.

Yes, sir. His grandfather's attempt at blinding him with newspaper photographs and articles had been just what the doctor ordered. Seeing Cherry's transformation from hometown girl to Monique Goodall wannabe had cured him of any lingering urges he had of kissing her.

Luke caught himself staring again at the curve of her ankles where they peeked out from beneath the long skirt. He reached to loosen his tie, forcing his gaze away from her. The sooner he mastered the fine art of ignoring Cherry Harte, the better off he'd be.

"This meeting will come to order." The Development Commission chair rapped a gavel against the podium, and the room fell silent.

Five minutes later the announcement had been

made, just as expected. Additionally, both groups were mandated to tour each other's facilities, starting in two days with the existing Youth Center.

Luke remained off to one side, avoiding any possibility of meeting Cherry's gaze, or worse, bumping into her. Monique Goodall and the Youth Center director posed with the Development Commission chair for photographs.

Surprise blew through Luke when the director crooked his finger in his direction. He moved toward where the man stood, his mood morphing to unease when he realized Cherry walked next to him, moving in the same direction.

"Luke." Her soft voice tickled his ear.

"Ms. Harte."

Her features fell momentarily, but she quickly recovered. "I'm sorry about the craziness earlier today."

"I trust your butler got settled in?"

She nodded and opened her mouth to speak. Before she could say anything, they had reached the small gathering at the front of the room.

"We need two volunteers to pose shaking hands," the chair explained to Luke. "Do you mind?"

"No."

The chair turned to Cherry. "How about you, Ms. Harte? We'll have you represent the Women's League."

Monique emitted a small choking sound, then cleared her throat. "Cherry is merely a provisional member."

Luke hated the shadow that passed across Cherry's face, like that of a child who'd been scolded. Leave it to Monique to try to steal the spotlight. His gaze locked with hers, but he quickly looked away. She was one person he had no intention of engaging in a staring match.

"Seems to me you already got the bigwigs in a photo," he said to the chair. "Ms. Harte would be perfect for a volunteer shot."

"Wonderful," the chair agreed.

Monique made a snapping noise with her mouth, then turned away. "I need to check on something," she offered as she hurried off.

The photographer rushed forward from his tripod, positioning Cherry and Luke facing each other, uncomfortably close. Cherry's pale eyes, full of surprise, never left Luke's.

"Thank you." Her voice sounded like a lover's whisper. Soft. Alluring. Nerve-wracking.

"No problem." Luke looked down at his shoes, unable to take another second of the emotion emanating from her gaze.

Cherry shifted closer, turning toward the photographer. "This okay?"

"Perfect." The man held a hand up over his head. "If you'd shake hands and look this way, I'll check the lighting."

Luke straightened his tie, then clasped Cherry's small hand inside his. He couldn't deny the charge that spun outward from the spot where their fingers met, up his arm, through his heart, and straight to his groin. Damn his body's reaction to this woman.

He pinned her with a stare, surprised to find a mix of uncertainty and desire waiting for him in her answering look.

"It'll be just a second," the photographer explained. "Hold that pose."

A second couldn't come soon enough.

Cherry fought the heat licking up her arm from the spot where Luke's fingers clasped hers. She avoided meeting his gaze, afraid of what unwanted thoughts might race through her brain—afraid of what she might do or say.

"Hold it for just another moment, please." The photographer fumbled with his tripod. "My settings are off, but your pose is perfect."

"Unbelievable," Luke grumbled beneath his breath.

Cherry lifted her eyes to his, her breath catching at the unmistakable tension simmering between them.

His voice dropped to a whisper, perceptible only to her ears. "Too much packaging, by the way."

She directed her gaze to their joined hands, willing away the pleasurable sensations his calloused grip sent to the southern regions of her body.

What in the hell was wrong with her? Maybe she was attracted to him merely because he wanted absolutely nothing to do with her money. Maybe it was the old reverse psychology working. She should sleep with him and put herself out of her misery. Perhaps that was the only way to get this tension out of her system.

A tiny moan sounded deep in her throat at the thought. She lifted her gaze to Luke's once more, heat flooding her face as his dark brow lifted.

"Problem?"

She shook her head. "Tickle in my throat."

He shifted uncomfortably, and the photographer clucked his tongue. "Surely it can't be that much of a burden to hold the young woman's hand?"

"Surely," Luke muttered, the deep timbre of his voice kicking Cherry's discomfort to a fevered pitch.

"Ready now," the photographer called out.

Luke turned to face the camera, and Cherry followed his move, smiling brightly, hoping against hope her exaggerated smile hid the turmoil tumbling through her. Darn, but the man played havoc with her resolve—and the last thing her resolve needed was more havoc.

"All done." The photographer tipped the beak of his cap. "Thank you."

Luke dropped their posed handshake so abruptly Cherry stumbled backward. He stepped quickly across the room, thanking the photographer as he passed and bidding farewell to those gathered. He was out of the hall and gone from sight before she knew what hit her.

"Your mouth is hanging open." Liz's voice sounded sharply from beside her.

Cherry snapped her jaw shut and hugged herself.

"Yeah." Liz nodded, then shot Cherry a wink. "I can see why you'd pick your goal poster over him. Man looks dreadful in a suit. And those eyes." Liz faked a shudder. "Why would any woman want to be the object of their attention?"

Cherry pressed past her sister, plucking her purse from the chair where she'd left it. She needed fresh air to shake the odd tingling sensation Luke Chance had left zipping through her veins.

"I'll be outside. Meet me at the car when you're ready to leave."

She'd no sooner reached her car and leaned against the driver's door than a male voice sounded—close and threatening.

"I'm sure those society types inside would love to know how much time your mother's in for and how much your old man owes the casino."

CHAPTER 9

Cherry recognized the voice instantly from her answering service.

Moose.

Damn. She should have listened to Monty when he'd wanted to fill her in over coffee.

She swallowed, then turned to face the man her father had vowed to protect her from.

She looked straight into darkness. *Empty* darkness. Where in the hell was he?

"Don't be put off by my lack of height." The voice sounded from the level of her waist, and she looked down into the most ferocious face she'd ever seen. "I'm one mean son of a bitch."

Maybe, but if Liz hadn't still been inside, they probably could have kicked him in his shins and run for their lives.

The dreaded Moose looked like a bad—but short—caricature of every gangster movie she'd ever seen.

"Moose?"

"At your service." He tipped his hat quickly.

Cherry thought about his first words. "What do you mean Monty owes the casino? He said this wasn't about money."

"Honey, it's always about money."

Cherry nodded with resignation. For Monty Harte, it had always been about money. And now he'd come home, in a manner of speaking, because of money.

Cherry and Liz had it, and he needed it.

The old, familiar hurt tugged at her heart. It was funny how all of her millions did nothing to take away the sting. She'd moved across seven states, changed her address, changed the car she drove, changed the shoes on her feet, but she hadn't been able to change how empty she felt whenever she thought about her father.

For Monty Harte, it would always be about the money. It was time she faced facts once and for all.

"How much?"

"Two hundred and fifty grand." Moose chewed on a toothpick that had somehow appeared from one of his pockets while Cherry had been lost in her mini pity party.

She let the number rattle around in her brain before she spoke. She wasn't too familiar with casinos, or bosses, but she was fairly certain people had been killed for far less than two hundred and fifty thousand dollars. Monty might not be the ideal father, but he was the only one she had.

"So, what are you? Some kind of loan shark?"

"I prefer the term *reimbursement specialist*." He nodded.

Cherry frowned. "If I write you a check, you'll go away, correct?"

Moose wiggled the toothpick between his teeth as he grinned. "Not so easy, sweetheart. Your old man insulted the boss. Lucky for him, they go way back. That's the only reason your pop's still alive. Boss wants to avenge his reputation, so to speak. This is personal."

Great. A thug with honor.

"Meaning what?"

"Meaning there's going to be one more game. Double or nothing."

"With my father?" Holy cow. Double or nothing added up to half a million dollars if Monty lost again. "And all's forgiven if Monty wins?"

"As long as he never shows his face in Reno again."

Yeah, like that could happen. That was about as likely as Lucky leaving the neighborhood skunk alone.

"And if he loses, I pay you half a million dollars?"

He shook his head. "Not so easy. If you lose, someone in your family pays."

Cherry swallowed. "What?"

"Not what. *Who.* Your old man will understand."

"All right." Cherry straightened. She might be scared spitless, but she had no intention of showing it. "Double or nothing at what?"

"Poker." The toothpick now rolled from side to side on Moose's slimy tongue. Cherry sincerely hoped he didn't harbor delusions of the move being attractive, because it was anything but.

"My father wouldn't know a poker face if it jumped up and bit him. Is that how he lost the money?"

Moose shook his head, obviously enjoying himself. "Craps. And the boss doesn't want to play Monty."

She didn't like the direction their conversation was taking. "Who does he want to play?"

Moose jabbed a chubby little finger in her direction. "He wants to play you."

Cherry stepped back, unable to wrap her brain around Moose's last sentence. "I don't gamble."

The little man shrugged. "You won the lottery, didn't you?"

"I bought one ticket." Cherry grimaced at the sound of her high-pitched, tight voice. "Once," she whined softly.

"Well, if you want to see all of your family members stay in one piece, you better hope your luck holds out." He turned to walk away.

"Why me?"

"You seem like the most rational one in the family."

If that wasn't a vote of confidence, she didn't know what was.

"What about my car?" She patted the hood. "Did you mess with the wiring?"

He chuckled as he walked away. "I'm very good at what I do."

"Did you mess with it again tonight?"

He hoisted his tiny shoulders in another shrug. "Maybe I did. Maybe I didn't. You might want to give your mechanic a call."

Then he was gone. Vanished into the darkness of the parking lot, leaving Cherry and her whirling thoughts behind.

Luke ripped off his tie and shrugged out of his jacket as he stood in front of the restroom mirror.

He'd headed straight for the sink and a face full of cold water as soon as he'd dropped Cherry's hand.

His restraint couldn't take much more. Maybe the attraction he felt could be written off as the result of having gone so long without enjoying the company of a lovely female, but he doubted it. With his luck, he was one of those guys who were secretly attracted to his polar opposite. Lord knew Cherry personified that in spades—or at least she tried.

The one thing he had no doubt about was that he couldn't get away from the woman or the damned light in her eyes fast enough.

He stepped out of the men's room and had no sooner rounded the corner toward the exit sign than Monique's voice stopped him cold.

"Fancy meeting you here, Luke."

The familiar dread crawled up his neck. Even the woman's voice dripped with insincerity. He pivoted to face her. "Monique."

"I wouldn't expect your little photo to show up in the local paper." She tipped her head to one side. "As I understand it, the subscribers prefer to see upstanding citizens, not lottery winners . . ." She hesitated as if searching for the perfect insult. "Or reporter wannabes fallen from grace."

Bull's-eye.

Luke took the insult in silence, having learned long ago not to provide Monique with the satisfaction of turning defensive.

He studied her instead. As usual, her hair hung in smooth perfection, each strand brushed to a shine. Her make-up was classic. Not too much, yet just enough to make it known she could afford the best. Her jewelry was another matter. There she showed absolutely no restraint.

His stomach turned sour.

"Congratulations on the Youth Center's selection." She moved toward him slowly, no doubt calculating each step before she took it.

"Same to you." He nodded. "May the best program win."

She chortled. "Really? You know your little center doesn't stand a chance, don't you?"

He bit back the first response that came to mind, choosing the high road instead. Anger seethed just below the surface of his restraint. "Actually, Monique, I happen to feel the Youth Center is the best program. So I think we stand a good chance."

Luke held his ground, determination surging through him as he faced the woman he'd once thought he'd spend the rest of his life with.

What a fool he'd been.

"We're competitors." Monique clapped her hands together. "Isn't fate a funny thing?"

"A regular riot." Frustration swirled in his gut.

He turned one last time for the exit, this time not stopping until he was outside in the parking lot. When he reached his Karmann Ghia, he leaned heavily against the door.

Competitors.

It appeared fate had not only tossed him back into Monique's world, but it also wasn't going to allow a clean getaway from Cherry Harte. Hell. Fate had put the two head-to-head as finalists for the Framingham Estate. Worse, he'd have to see her again the day after tomorrow, and the day after that.

He scrubbed a hand across his face and shook off

the buzz still zinging through his veins just from holding the woman's hand, amazed his encounter with Monique hadn't erased any of Cherry's lingering heat.

Luke yanked open the driver's door, sank into the seat, and twisted the key in the ignition.

It would take a lot more than fate to make him let his guard down again. He was done with Cherry and the way she made him feel. Hell, he should thank Monique for the reminder of why. Tangling with Cherry Harte would be nothing but trouble.

Nothing.

After all, history had a funny way of repeating itself.

That's when he saw her leaning against the roof of her Jaguar, her face buried in the crook of her arm.

He should drive past. He should resist the urge to see if she was all right . . . to see if she needed help . . . to see if she needed *him*.

If he pressed the accelerator and sped away now, he'd only have to endure two more encounters with her before the final announcement. Then he'd be able to walk out of her life forever.

Luke pulled a stick of gum out of his coat pocket and began to chew. This time, the sweet juice did nothing to soothe his frazzled nerves. Nothing to numb the urge to check on Cherry.

He turned off the ignition and climbed out from behind the wheel of his car, headed straight for the woman who was sure to be his undoing.

Heaven help him.

"Problem?"

Yes, Cherry thought as Luke's voice sounded across the darkness of the parking lot. She had several, not the least of which was the man asking the question.

Her tattoo itched.

Great.

Did that mean Luke was the messenger for her impending life change, or Moose? She shuddered.

"Cherry?"

Luke's hand grazed her shoulder, sending a wave of heat and want spreading across her back. She jerked away, straightening as she took a backward step.

"Hey." His voice dropped low, soft. "You looked like you needed help. I didn't mean to startle you." He pointed across the lot. "I can go if—"

"No." She interrupted him. "I mean . . . do what you want." Confusion swirled through her. Luke. Monty. Moose. None of it made sense, and now she had to win a poker game to set it all right again.

A laugh burst through her lips.

A poker game. Definitely not on her goal poster.

"Have you been drinking?" Luke's inquisitive gaze narrowed.

She wished. "No." Cherry shook her head.

She had to find Liz and get out of here. She planned to pin Monty under the brightest light she could find and make him fill her in on just exactly how much trouble he'd put them all in.

"I thought maybe your car wouldn't start again." Luke stepped closer. "When I saw you leaning over it like that."

Her car. "Yes," she sputtered. "I mean, no. I mean, I'm not sure."

He nodded, taking the ever-present pack of gum from his pocket and unwrapping a piece. "Gum?"

She extended her hand. What the hell. It certainly seemed to do something for him. "Thanks."

His eyes widened when she took the offered stick. He unwrapped a second for himself and popped it into his mouth.

The soothing sweetness that spread through Cherry's mouth surprised her. She and Luke stood companionably for a few seconds, chewing in silence, savoring their gum.

"Want me to check under your hood?"

Luke's words made her stomach catch.

Did she ever.

Cherry sighed inwardly as she watched the strong lines of his jaw work his gum. Letting him touch more than her car would only further complicate her perfectly planned life. She swallowed, smoothing her hair behind her ears. "Just to be safe. Would you mind?"

Luke shook his head. "Give me your keys."

Cherry handed them over and stepped aside.

She admired his physique as he worked. The width of his shoulders. The sureness of his moves. The way the hair at the nape of his neck broke into the slightest of curls. She watched as concentration strengthened his already strong features.

She sighed. Then she chewed faster.

Maybe Luke was on to something with the whole gum-chewing habit.

A few minutes later he was done and slipped the tiny flashlight she kept in her glove compartment back into place. "Everything's fine." He stared at her, and she fought the urge to squirm. "What really happened out here?"

She shook her head. "Nothing. I just thought I'd

take you up on your offer to check." She shrugged and pasted on a smile. "Since you asked."

One dark brow lifted, kissing his hairline. "I'm not buying it. I might be able to help, if you'd let me know what's going on."

Should she ask for his help? She actually considered the option until the reality of her genealogy gave her a mental wake-up slap.

No.

She was better off keeping her family secrets to herself. The last thing she needed was Luke Chance telling anyone involved with the Development Commission or the Women's League about her family tree. A scandal like that might very well knock the Horticultural Center out of the running for the estate, not to mention what it would do for Cherry's reinvention plan.

Good old Monique would have a thing or two for her little recorder then.

"Thanks anyway, but no."

He stepped close, clasping one firm hand on her shoulder. Panic and need battled inside her.

"I don't want to worry about you, Cherry. I don't want to think about you. I don't want to dream about you. I don't even want to see you after this week, but if you needed help, I'd help you."

Cherry's breath hitched and her eyes locked with Luke's. For a split second, she let herself remember how it had felt to have his lips on her lips, his hands on her body, his—

"There you are," Liz's bright voice sang out, breaking the spell. "You missed all the sweets inside."

Her spiked heels clicked across the drive, and

Luke dropped his hand to his side. He turned toward Liz, obviously surprised when he spotted her bobbed black hair.

"She has a thing for wigs," Cherry whispered. "In case you were wondering."

"So the packaging issues are genetic?"

If only he knew.

Liz's gaze widened and she waggled her brows, shooting a knowing look at Cherry. "Maybe you didn't miss the sweets after all."

"We need to go." Cherry grabbed for the driver's door. "Thanks for checking under the hood, Luke."

Liz slapped her thigh. "Maybe *I* missed all the sweets."

"Get in." Cherry jerked her chin toward the opposite side of the car. "Please."

Liz ran a finger along Luke's jaw as she passed. "Nice to see you again, Mr. Chance."

Cherry watched as Luke's gaze followed Liz around the car. The unwanted whisper of jealousy made a second showing deep in the pit of her belly.

She jumped when his focus snapped back to her.

"I meant what I said." His tone was more intense than it had been a few moments earlier.

If only. "I'll keep it in mind."

Cherry slammed the door and said a silent prayer before she turned the ignition key. With her luck, Moose had rigged the car to blow up. Heaven knew the thug was small enough to shimmy under the belly of the thing. She had never thought to have Luke check there.

She held her breath and turned the key. The engine hummed to life uneventfully, and Luke gave her the thumbs-up.

"Why do I feel like I missed something?" Liz asked.

Cherry didn't speak until they were halfway home. "Do you know how to play poker?"

"Luke wants you to play poker?"

"No." Cherry took a deep breath. *All I need is within me now.* "Never mind."

She punched the Play button on the CD player, waiting for the affirmation to soothe her spirit. *Every day, in every way, I'm getting better and better. Better and better.*

What a load of crap.

She pressed the Eject button, grasped the disc, and hurled it like a Frisbee into the backseat.

"You know, you could have killed someone with that thing." Liz frowned. "Namely me."

Cherry ignored her. She was too busy trying to make sense of the past few days.

"Want something else on?" her sister asked.

Cherry shook her head. "You wouldn't happen to have any gum, would you?" Lord knew, she could use another stick . . . or two . . . or three.

Liz made a face, then turned to the window.

Cherry's resolve had begun to crack, and the crack was beginning to spread.

Cherry burst through the front door of the villa only to find Monty and Lucky settled in front of the wide-screen television watching celebrity poker.

"Poker!" She stood between the screen and her father. "Why didn't you tell me?"

"You said you didn't want to know." Monty lifted his brows and she'd be damned if Lucky didn't deliver a matching expression.

They did have a point.

Quite frankly, she'd wanted to clasp her hands over her ears and run screaming when her father tried to talk to her earlier, but now he had her interest. Him and his quarter-of-a-million-dollar debt.

"Moose was waiting for me outside of my meeting. You want to tell me how in the hell you managed to lose so much money playing craps?"

Liz held up a finger. "Wait a minute. Let me get a beer. I don't want to miss anything else." She took off for the kitchen. Lucky scrambled close on her heels, probably hoping he'd have a chance to head out back for a late-night rendezvous.

Monty didn't wait for Liz's return. "I've never been very good when it comes to gambling."

Cherry grabbed the wall to hold herself steady. "Dad. You've spent your life gambling. That's why you left us, remember?"

A shadow passed across her father's classic features and Cherry couldn't help but wonder if he didn't feel regret somewhere deep inside—*somewhere*.

"You can believe whatever you want, honey."

"Don't honey me. There isn't going to be any honeying me. All I want from you is the truth." She clapped her hands together. "Spill it."

Liz slid around the corner, a bag of chips in one hand and a beer bottle in the other. She fell into an overstuffed chair and made room for Lucky. The dog catapulted his little pink body into the seat next to her. Both sets of eager eyes moved from Cherry to Monty, Monty to Cherry.

"Did your sister meet Moose?" Monty tipped his head to where Liz and Lucky waited for the show to begin.

Liz rolled her eyes. "Would somebody *please* explain what's going on?"

"I'll fill you in later." Cherry pointed a finger at her dad. "Don't try to change the subject. I want to know how you lost a quarter of a million dollars."

Liz choked midsip. She jumped out of the chair and nailed Monty midshin before she settled back in next to Lucky.

"Damn it," Monty yelled as he rubbed his leg. "Aren't you getting too old for that?"

Cherry held up both hands, her patience stretched far beyond its breaking point. "Please. Tell me what you did."

Monty directed one last glare at Liz, then faced Cherry. "The boss and I go way back."

"To where?" Liz snorted. "Juvenile hall?"

Cherry shot her a look and she fell silent. Lucky, on the other hand, had moved to the front door and was scratching the wall.

"Forget it, Romeo."

He sneered at Cherry as he pranced back toward her office, pink puffed head held high.

Luke was right. The entire family had packaging issues.

"We've been friends a long time, but this was the first time I ever gambled at his club."

She turned back toward her dad. "And that didn't go so well, did it?" Cherry asked.

"I made a mistake. I offered to work off the debt, but he said no."

"So"—she planted her hands on her hips—"this has nothing to do with protecting me or protecting Liz. Moose said if I lose, someone in this family is going to pay. The only reason you showed up is to get me to save your ass. Right?"

"Not exactly." The shadow had returned to Monty's face.

"Well?" Cherry was beginning to think Liz had the right idea. Kicking Monty held great appeal at the moment.

"It's not my ass I need you to save." He looked from Cherry to her sister and back again. "It's your mother's fingers."

Cherry's annoyance had morphed to full-blown disbelief. While cutting off Fran Harte's fingers would certainly put a damper on the woman's stealing, it wasn't something you typically wished upon a parent.

"It's personal." Monty shrugged.

No kidding.

Liz thrust her half-full beer bottle in Cherry's direction. Cherry grabbed it, hoisting the cool glass to her lips and swallowing until she drained the bottle.

It seemed the perfectly orchestrated reinvention of her life was about to go straight down the toilet.

CHAPTER 10

Luke sat at his desk the next morning and rubbed the corners of his jaw. He'd chewed so much gum over the last few days he'd probably sprained something. Not to mention the fact his nights were getting progressively more restless.

Last night, for example, he hadn't slept a wink. It was bad enough he couldn't shake the desire Cherry had kicked to life, but his reporter's instincts were driving him insane.

The woman's problems ran deeper than the Women's League, and he wanted to know more. Whoever Monty and Moose really were, they spelled trouble.

He should be focusing his energies on the Youth Center and the quest for new funding, but the little lottery winner had managed to capture his every thought. He needed to snap out of the spell she'd cast and shift his attention back to the kids.

He had no intention of losing out to a bunch of plants. Monique Goodall could kiss his ass before he'd let her group win the Framingham Estate. If the past had taught him anything, it was that she only cared about one thing.

Money.

Luke shook his head. Make that two things.

Money and prestige.

Monique cherished her precious reputation— the reputation he hadn't been good enough to be part of.

It would be a cold day in hell before he'd allow the woman get the best of him again. And he sure as hell wouldn't let it be at the expense of the Youth Center.

He slammed a fist against the desk.

"Problem?" Gramps said over his shoulder.

"Plants," Luke growled.

"Speak up, son. Did you say plants?"

"As in Horticultural Center."

"Ah." Gramps patted Luke's shoulder as he pulled up a stool. "Cherry Harte."

Cherry Harte.

A woman equally obsessed with image and money, yet with some sort of complication tossed into the mix. Luke pinched the bridge of his nose. "That woman is a non-issue." He'd be darned if he'd give his grandfather any room for hope. "It's her project I'm worried about."

"Can't fool me, son." Gramps winked. "You always did have a strong reaction to cherries."

"Very funny." Luke frowned. "I learned to avoid them like the plague. Remember?"

Gramps put down the business section of the paper and stooped toward the trash can. He blew out a breath. "The widow and I spent a lot of time on these copies."

Luke rolled his eyes. Next time, he'd shove his grandfather's matchmaking efforts even farther out of sight. He tapped the paper. "Since when do you read the business section?"

"I was thinking about playing the stock market." Gramps pulled the wad of photocopies out of the can and began to flatten them against the corner of Luke's desk.

"With what?" Luke studied the older man. "Your good looks?"

Gramps grinned and smoothed a hand over his hair. "How much do you think I'd get?"

"Hard to tell," Luke teased. "Maybe you should ask the widow what she thinks."

Color flared in his grandfather's cheeks. He pointed to the now-smooth copies. "We thought you'd appreciate these."

"I appreciate them." Luke pulled down the shop's pending work orders, hoping his grandfather would drop the subject if he didn't make eye contact. "I'm just not interested."

"Worked mighty hard," the older man reiterated.

Gramps never had been able to drop a topic midconversation. Luke patted his pocket. He'd changed his mind on the gum. Empty. He'd have to deal with his grandfather without sugar.

"I have no intention of falling for Cherry."

Gramps placed a hand on top of the work orders, blocking Luke's view. Luke raised his chin to meet the older man's gaze.

"You're making a mistake, son."

"No." Luke shook his head. "The woman's not just rich, she's in some sort of trouble. The only mistake would be getting involved with her."

His grandfather clucked his tongue. "You used to live for trouble. Couldn't keep you out of it back at the paper."

"Those days are over." Luke gave his temples another rub. "I left them behind in Miami."

What was it Monique had called him? A reporter wannabe fallen from grace?

"Can't hide forever," Gramps muttered.

Here they went again. "I'm . . . not . . . hiding."

"Could have fooled me." His grandfather sighed. "I could go any minute. Then you'd be all alone."

"So you keep telling me." Luke tamped down the battling emotions swirling through his gut, straightening to meet the elder Chance's scrutiny. "You're healthy as a horse, and you're not fooling anyone. Least of all me."

It was time to change the conversation's direction. "Our lead grant fell through yesterday," Luke continued. "We've got to line up new funding or we'll be dropped from consideration. I've got more important things to worry about than your favorite lottery winner."

Gramps's bushy white brows snapped together. "You can't tell me that puss on your face isn't because of Cherry. The girl's getting to you, isn't she?"

And how.

Luke eyed his grandfather's expectant gaze, wanting nothing more than to end this discussion. "I'll admit she's got a light in her eyes, but she's no better than Monique. I'm not going down that road again." No matter how amazing it had felt to hold Cherry in his arms.

Gramps reached for the stack of photocopies and shoved the photo of Cherry and Liz at the children's hospital under Luke's nose. "I don't see Monique Goodall anywhere in that picture. Do you?"

"No." Luke thumbed through the rescued stack of papers until he found the one he wanted. He pointed to the shelter photo. "But she's big as life there. They belong to the same women's group, for crying out loud. Let it go."

"The widow's going to be disappointed. She's got her heart set on fixing you two up."

Luke forced a smile. He had to admit if he'd seen the Cherry captured in the lottery picture first, he'd have pursued her in a heartbeat. But that would never happen now. She'd become one of *them*—the elite of Mystic Beach. He wanted no part of her or her money.

The time had come to play hardball. "You seem to be spending a lot of time with the widow."

Color fired in Gramps's cheeks, and he smoothed a hand over his wavy hair for a second time. "I'm just using her for her DSL."

Luke bit back a grin. "I'm sure."

Gramps gathered the photocopies from the corner of the desk, opened a file drawer, and dropped them inside. He turned, white eyebrows lifting to a pair of inverted vees. "In case you want to rethink your decision."

"Never. Not going to happen."

Gramps leaned close, tapping a finger to Luke's chest. "Never say never, son."

Luke pushed back his chair and walked to the filing cabinet. He slid open the drawer and hoisted the pile of newspaper and magazine articles from inside.

Gramps twisted up one corner of his mouth. "Don't know where you get your stubborn streak."

Luke chuckled, holding the photocopies over the trash can. "Now that's the pot calling the kettle black." He released his grip, letting the papers flutter into the waste container below.

"You're a damned fool," Gramps mumbled. He straightened from the stool, pausing to pat Luke's shoulder. He pointed at the trash. "Someday you'll wish you kept those pictures as a reminder of the one that got away."

Luke stared at the container for a long time after his grandfather walked out into the shop. Finally, he kicked the can, sending it back behind the filing cabinet—out of sight.

Out of sight. Out of mind. Just like the woman herself.

As soon as Luke disappeared under the belly of a Volvo, Eugene dialed Cassie's number. She snapped up the phone on the second ring.

"Eugene," she answered, impatience blatant in her tone. "Did it work? I've been on pins and needles all night."

Confusion swirled in his gut. "How did you know it was me?"

Cassie muffled a sigh. "Caller ID, Eugene. Caller ID."

Right. She'd explained that to him about a dozen times. "You're a whiz, woman. A real whiz."

"Cherry? Luke?" She clucked her tongue. "Honestly, you've got me so caught up in the two of them it's worse than watching my shows."

"Well." He moved the phone tight to his mouth, as if the walls had ears. "Seems he's too stubborn to admit he's got feelings for the girl. Don't know where he gets it from."

She mumbled something that sounded suspiciously like, "Runs in the family."

"What did you say?"

"Nothing. What shall we do next?"

He shrugged. "Guess I need your keen intellect to help me out on this one."

"I'll start the tea."

Eugene puffed out his chest. "I'll be right over."

He shot a glance toward the shop. Luke was nowhere in sight. "There is a new wrinkle." He dropped his voice to barely more than a whisper.

A moment of silence beat between them.

"Seems the Youth Center's run into a little funding problem."

"Oh, Eugene." Cassie's exasperated tone made him step back. "Why don't you just tell the boy the truth?"

He considered her question for a moment, then shook his head as if she could see it through the line. This was one thing he wouldn't rush. "Not until he's ready."

"Well, if he needs the money now, don't you think he's ready now?"

Eugene pictured the grim set of his grandson's face as he'd talked about avoiding Cherry—heck, as he'd talked about avoiding life. The man was more stubborn than a mule at the edge of a cliff.

"Not yet."

Cassie's sigh filtered across the phone line loud and clear. "You're an old fool, Eugene."

He bristled, scowling into the phone.

"What time shall I expect you?" Cassie asked.

A strange warmth bubbled to life deep inside Eugene's gut. "Give me ten minutes."

The woman might be more opinionated than he liked, but he was growing fond of her cucumber sandwiches.

Cherry and Liz sat in the sun-filled kitchen nursing their second pot of coffee. Cherry's head ached from the previous night's two-beer drinking binge.

What a lightweight.

Bart Matthews had called again. Twice. She'd hung up on him both times and had finally turned off the ringer on the phone. She hadn't heard a peep from the man in four months, and now he wanted to be her best friend.

Yogi had arrived in grand fashion and stood sketching in the foyer. She'd always thought most artists preferred to work in their own studios, but Yogi explained he needed to paint in the space where the finished piece would hang. Apparently his creative juices were inspired by the energy of the wall.

She winced, wondering once again just how huge a mistake hiring the man had been.

He appeared to have a fondness for whistling show tunes and was currently stuck on a loop of "All That Jazz."

If Cherry thought the outfit Yogi wore yesterday had been interesting, today's defined a whole new fashion standard. Skintight black pants and a too-small black and white striped T-shirt sheathed his lean body. He'd pulled his dark hair into a short knot of a ponytail and had topped the entire look with a hot pink beret.

Liz sat at the counter, tipping her head from one side to the other, measuring the artist as he worked. She took a sip of coffee, then muttered beneath her breath. "I'm thinking Pepe Le Pew." She snapped her focus to Cherry. "Maybe he's trying to get Lucky." She snickered at her own joke. "Get it?"

Cherry nodded, thinking the cold, harsh reality was she'd commissioned a lunatic. "You know how those artistic types are."

"Insane?" Liz offered.

"Eccentric." Cherry countered. "This is a good sign. A *creative* sign."

Liz shook her head, covered today in short platinum curls. She shot Cherry her I'm-on-to-you face. "Nah. That man's just plain nuts."

At that, Yogi's whistling stopped. Liz's blue eyes rounded to saucers.

"You think he heard me?"

Cherry slouched down on her stool, willing her velour robe to swallow her up. She'd had enough turmoil the past few days to last a lifetime. "He does have very good ears."

"Yogi has *very* good ears." The man's none-too-pleased velvet tone sounded from the archway to the kitchen. He nodded toward Cherry, ignoring Liz's presence. "Yogi is ready for you to review his sketches."

"Yogi needs to stop talking in the third person," Liz mumbled into her coffee mug.

"Yogi prefers it," he replied.

Bright red fired in Liz's cheeks, and she offered an apologetic smile to the man.

"That mouth of yours should be declared a national hazard." Cherry slid from her stool, yanking her robe tightly around her waist.

She padded behind Yogi as he returned to the hall. Three sketches sat propped against the wall. She followed the lines etched on each and frowned.

The first featured sharks doing what Cherry was quite sure could be considered an ancient mating ritual. The second sported a gaggle of angry-looking flamingos picketing a golf outing, and the third displayed what appeared to be alligators donning tennis visors.

Good grief. Yogi wasn't simply insane, he was insane with issues.

"None of them look very soothing." The dull ache of Cherry's hangover tightened, pulsing cruelly above her left eye.

Yogi sucked in his cheeks, planting one fist on his hip and gesturing with his bony finger to the sketches. "But they *are*. This is Mystic Beach. A portrait of paradise."

If this was Mystic Beach, she planned to run screaming all the way back to New Jersey.

Yogi turned to face her, looking scarily like Joan Crawford.

Cherry winced, then let out a tired breath. "How about some nice palm trees? Maybe a beach?"

He pushed back his pink beret and scowled. "But why?"

"Because I've been threatened by the world's smallest hit man and I'm too hungover to face anything with teeth or beaks today. Please?"

Yogi took a step backward. Cherry wasn't sure which part of the sentence had stunned him into submission, but she was thrilled something had.

He narrowed his dark eyes, never letting his scrutiny of her features waver. "Very well." He finally looked away, returning to his work. "I'll give you soothing, if you give me pink."

"She's paying *you*, Rembrandt," Liz's voice bellowed from the kitchen.

Cherry grimaced. "Sorry. She's not a morning person."

One dark brow lifted. "Evidently."

She shook her head, the image of Monique's mural all too fresh in her mind. "No pink." She pivoted and headed for the kitchen before he could argue.

Her chest swelled with pride. It felt good to stand up to the great Yogi. Heck, it felt damned good. His whistling had resumed by the time she hit the kitchen doorway.

"Maybe there's still a spine in you yet." Liz winked as Cherry leaned against the island. "So. What is the newly created Cherry Harte going to wear to the Youth Center tomorrow?"

Cherry turned to her sister, her gaze scanning Liz's leopard-print leggings, high, backless black sandals, and white crepe wrapped blouse.

"Certainly not that." She laughed.

Liz shook her short platinum curls and glanced down at her clothes. "What's wrong with my outfit?" She looked up at Cherry and frowned. "These are my lucky pants."

Yogi's whistling switched from "New York, New York" to "The Lady Is a Tramp."

Liz turned to face him, gracing him with her most threatening glare. He never so much as flinched.

Cherry broke into a smile, the first since she'd encountered Moose in the parking lot the night before. "Lucky for what?"

"I had them on under my bridesmaid gown the night we won the lotto."

Cherry shook her head, fighting the image that popped into her mind. "I so did not need to know that."

"I'll let you wear them for the big game."

Dread pooled in Cherry's belly. *The big game.* All she had to do now was wait for Moose's call and learn how to play poker.

She was doomed.

"Where on earth am I going to learn how to play poker?" She lowered her face to her hands.

"Yogi is the Mystic Beach poker champ." The artist's voice chirped from the hall. "For the last three years running."

Cherry pinched herself. Honestly. She couldn't make this stuff up if she tried.

She lifted her head and squinted in his direction. He'd donned his surgical mask sometime after her plea for new artwork, and he now sashayed toward the kitchen, lowering the mask beneath his chin as he approached.

When he reached the island, he stopped, dramatically raising a finger to his lips.

"You wish to learn poker?"

His voice climbed so high on his last word that he squeaked.

"Desperately," Cherry answered.

He sucked in his cheeks and Cherry held her breath.

"Will you let Yogi paint whatever he wants?" he asked. "In whatever color he chooses?"

Damn. An insane artist with issues *and* blackmail tendencies.

Cherry looked from Yogi to Liz. Her sister's eyes widened and she shook her head. "You're screwed either way."

Truer words had never been spoken.

Cherry straightened and thrust her hand in Yogi's direction. "You're on."

CHAPTER 11

Eugene made himself comfortable on Cassie's lanai as she prepared lunch. He realized he'd been here just yesterday, but he had a legitimate reason. There had to be a way to force Luke to admit his feelings for Cherry, and he needed Cassie's help.

Her standard poodle shoved her head into Eugene's lap and whined. He rubbed behind the dog's ears, smiling as the animal's eyes winked shut with pleasure.

"Be right out." Cassie's voice sounded brightly from the kitchen.

"Take your time. Fifi and I were just relaxing." He glanced about the widow's landscaped backyard and sighed. Beautiful. The woman had a definite talent for making a home comfortable. Heck, she had a definite talent for making a man feel comfortable.

That's when it hit him.

He'd been so caught up in scheming to get Luke and Cherry together that he'd let the widow under his skin. He looked down at the dog's happy expression.

The widow *and* her dog.

Tarnation.

He dropped his hands from Fifi's head and sat up straight. The dog leaned back, tipping her fluff-topped head to one side, apparently confused by the sudden move.

Comfortable.

Eugene's plan had been to utilize the widow's research skills to encourage the romance between Cherry and Luke. Instead, he was on his third straight day of cucumber sandwiches. Even worse, he liked them. And he liked Cassie's company.

He blew out a stunned breath.

The woman had sucked him into her web like a spider reeling in a moth. A foolish, old moth.

He climbed to his feet just as Cassie appeared at the door, a serving tray balanced in her arms.

"What is it, Eugene?" Concern twisted her features. "Is it your heart?"

It just might be, and that was the problem. He hadn't been with a woman since his beloved wife had died. He wasn't about to two-time her now.

Eugene stepped a wide path around Cassie and her tray. "I've got to go."

Her features crumpled. "But you haven't touched lunch. We haven't had a chance to talk. I thought you were going to fill me in on the latest developments. What about Luke and Cherry?" She tipped her head toward the food. "I made your favorite."

Guilt tapped at the back of Eugene's brain. She

had gone to a lot of trouble. It might be only proper to eat a sandwich or two and then flee.

He met her worried gaze and felt his stomach tighten, fighting the urge to smooth his hair like a suitor prepping for a courting call.

She'd gotten to him. How had he missed the warning signs? He had to get out and he had to get out *now*.

"Eugene?" Cassie stepped closer. "You're scaring me. Should I call Luke? Or an ambulance?"

Maybe she should call a shrink, because what he needed was his head examined.

"I'm fine, Cassie. Just forgot something back at the shop." He tipped his chin toward the tray of food. "Sorry for your trouble."

He hurried around her and headed for the door, pausing for a brief second to look back.

Cassie stood with her head tipped in perfect synchrony with Fifi's. Reality shuddered through him. He liked her . . . really liked her. Hell, he even liked her dog.

He needed to beat a path back to the shop and stay there. Maybe Luke had the right idea about avoiding life, after all.

Eugene knew one thing. He'd only ever loved one woman. When she died, he'd sworn he'd never love another. He wasn't about to break his promise now.

Cherry and Yogi were halfway home from Barnes and Noble—a copy of *Poker for Dummies* clutched in the artist's hands—when Yogi swore under his breath.

"What?" Cherry shot him a quick glance, but Yogi continued to stare intently at the side mirror.

"Make a turn." He spoke sharply, the note of excitement in his voice unmistakable.

"Why? Weren't you in a rush to get started on our first lesson?"

"Just do it." Yogi drew the words out like an impatient Nike commercial.

Cherry flipped on the right signal and cut down a side street. "Now what?"

Yogi held up a hand, shushed her, then swore softly again.

Now she was just plain getting annoyed. The man was completely insane. "Don't shush me."

He shushed her again. "There is a perp on our tail."

"A what?"

Cherry studied the rearview mirror, taking note of a dark blue SUV behind them.

"A perp," Yogi repeated. "It's what they say on all the cop shows." He gestured impatiently toward the rear window. "A perp."

Cherry made another turn and watched as the SUV smoothly followed. Her pulse quickened. "We're being followed?"

"Yes." Yogi drew the word into a hiss. "This is what Yogi has been trying to tell you."

"Then Yogi should have gotten right to the point."

She turned again, realizing she'd succeeded in heading deep into a wooded area that grew more and more deserted as they drove. "What do I do now?"

Yogi planted his fists on his hips, staring again at his mirror. "Pull over."

"What?" Cherry winced when her voice squeaked. So much for calm, collected elegance. At this point she was scared spitless. What if Moose was behind the wheel of the SUV? The man might be tiny, but he was mean. "Are you insane?"

"Yogi does not appreciate that word. Please refrain from using it in Yogi's presence."

Cherry counted to three, concentrating on calming her pounding heartbeat. "You wouldn't happen to have any gum, would you?"

Her future poker teacher scowled at her, twisting up his already frightening features into a mask of disgust. "Gum is bourgeois."

Oh brother. She was being tailed through the backwoods of Mystic Beach by heaven knew who and her only protection was an insane artist with an attitude.

Cherry glanced at the Barnes and Noble bag. Maybe she could beat whoever was in the SUV senseless with the poker book.

"Pull over." Yogi slapped one slender-fingered palm against the dash.

"No way."

"Just do it."

Cherry jerked her Jag to the side of the road, dread tightening her throat as the SUV pulled in behind her. When Bart Matthews appeared from behind the driver's door, her fear morphed quickly into disbelief.

"Damn," she muttered. What the hell was Bart doing in Mystic Beach?

Yogi had twisted in his seat to scrutinize the approaching perp. "You recognize him?"

"I haven't seen him since he left me at the altar, but yes."

Yogi gasped. "He did what?" He gripped the book in his hand and reached for the door handle. "Yogi will take care of him. The brute."

Cherry smiled then, just a little bit, unable to ignore the warm feeling Yogi's protectiveness sent through her. He might be completely insane, but somewhere beneath the dramatics and the attitude lurked a heart of gold. The glimmer she'd just witnessed had been unmistakable.

"It's okay." Cherry patted the hand that clutched the book. "I don't love him anymore."

A vision of Luke danced through her head and she blinked it away.

"I'm not sure I ever did."

Yogi shot her a frown. "Yogi does not understand."

She shook her head. "Sometimes, neither does Cherry."

A few moments later, the standoff had begun. Cherry faced Bart, several paces separating them, as Yogi circled, *Poker for Dummies* held high.

"Who the hell is this?" Bart jerked a thumb in Yogi's direction.

"My bodyguard," Cherry quickly answered.

Yogi's chest puffed out and he smiled.

Bart frowned, then refocused on Cherry. "What did you do to your hair?"

Cherry lifted a hand to the darkened strands, then straightened. She owed this man no explanations. "It's none of your business."

He stared at her for a moment before he spoke. "Why won't you take my calls?"

Cherry lost herself for a moment in the dark blue shade of his eyes, remembering how fascinating she used to find the color. But that had been years ago, before the planned wedding, before his arrest of her mother. Before her new life had kicked in.

Bart Matthews represented the old life. The life she wanted no part of.

All she wanted now was to send him away before he could bring everything she'd worked for crashing down around her ears.

"I don't want to speak to you," she answered.

"That was evident the fourth time you hung up on me." He stepped closer and Yogi cleared his throat. Bart took a step back to his original position. "I just want us to work through this."

Cherry weakened momentarily at the pleading tone of his voice. Then she remembered their rehearsal dinner and the way the bounty hunter had hauled her mother out of the restaurant.

"No way." She narrowed her eyes and took a deep breath. "What are you doing in Mystic Beach?"

"There's a conference, but I wanted to see you. I need to talk to you."

She shook her head. "Why are you really here, Bart? Admit it. You want me to do something that will help your campaign, right? Didn't you say that on the phone?"

He nodded. "I did say that. But I thought maybe we could patch things up—be friends again."

Even Yogi clucked his tongue at that one.

Cherry shook her head. "I'm not going to stand here and listen to this." She eyed Yogi and pointed to the Jag. "Let's go."

Yogi arched one dramatic brow. "Yes?"

"Yes," she answered as she retreated toward her car.

"But Yogi didn't even get to use the book on him."

Great. An insane artist with an attitude, an agenda, *and* a longing for violence.

"Cherry," Bart called after her.

She spun on one heel, wondering for a brief second if she was being unfair. But she wasn't. Reconciling with Bart served no purpose.

Old life.

New life.

Bart reached out a hand as if Cherry might weaken and run right back to him. "We're not through here."

"The thing is, Bart, we are."

She and Yogi climbed into the Jag, pulled a quick three-point turn, and never looked back.

Luke stared at the scrapbook Gramps had left on his desk. The older man must be playing hardball. Maybe he thought he could knock his grandson out of his self-imposed life of seclusion by challenging him with the past.

Not likely.

He flipped open the padded leather cover just the same. He remembered his amazement the first time he'd seen the collection of clippings. Amazement that he'd covered so many stories during his reporter days, and amazement that his grandfather cared enough to save every single clipping.

Luke's heart gave a little squeeze as he looked at the documentation of his career.

Reporter wannabe fallen from grace.

Damn Monique Goodall and her snide remarks. Hell. He should be damning himself for letting the woman get to him after all this time.

But she did.

Possibly because she was right.

He was a reporter wannabe fallen from grace. He'd been close to breaking the largest story of his career—a story that would have taken him to the top. A story that would have made his name synonymous with hard-nosed investigation.

Instead, he'd succeeded in making his name synonymous with being soft—with letting a friend get away with embezzlement and fraud.

Luke turned the pages of the scrapbook one by one, scanning each headline, remembering each story, each interview. He missed his old life sometimes. Hell. He missed it all the time. But life was good here.

He glanced at the garage, a touch of pride swelling inside him. He and Gramps had a successful business. They had each other. He had his work for the Youth Center.

Life was good and he had no intention of changing a single thing.

Cherry's image flashed through his mind, and his stomach tightened traitorously.

Nope.

He wasn't about to let her any further under his

skin than she'd already gotten. Status quo. He needed to remember those words, even though the light in her eyes and the story he knew she hid beckoned him to do anything but.

Later that evening, Cherry curled up on her back patio, flipping through the copy of *Poker for Dummies*. She'd been a bit distracted after her encounter with Bart, and her first lesson with Yogi had been less than successful.

When she'd confused a flush with a straight three times in a row, the temperamental teacher had taken his surgical mask and gone home. He'd left her with strict instructions to study the book before their next session.

So here she sat, doing her best to concentrate on terms like *pairs* and *straights* and *five-card stud* while her brain tossed around the faces of Luke and Bart and Moose and Monty. Suddenly, Monique and her little voice recorder had become the least intimidating part of her life.

"Thought you could use a break."

Her father's voice captured her attention and she turned to watch him approach. He set two steaming mugs of coffee on the small end table and lowered himself into a chair.

Cherry gladly closed the book and sighed. "This is more difficult than I thought."

"Always is."

The now-familiar shadow passed across his features and Cherry couldn't help wondering what he referred to. She was fairly certain it wasn't poker.

Monty picked up one of the mugs and tilted his chin toward the Gulf. "You've done well for yourself. You should be proud."

She chuckled. "It's not as if I earned it. I bought a winning ticket, that's all."

He shrugged. "Sometimes good people attract luck." He took a sip of his coffee and swallowed before he spoke again. "I've never been very lucky."

Cherry watched him silently. How could she respond to that? If she agreed, she might as well confirm his fears that he hadn't been a good person or a good father. But the reality was, he hadn't been, and somehow, she didn't have it in her to lie and tell him anything different.

After several moments of quiet, Monty shifted the subject. "Why did you ruin your hair?"

"I told you." She took a swallow of coffee. "Packaging issues."

"I have no idea what that means." He squinted.

"I want to make a new life for myself—a new identity. Maybe I wanted a new hair color to go along with everything else."

Monty shook his head. "You were full of light before. Now you just look a little . . . dim."

Cherry frowned. "Are you talking about my hair color? Or something else?"

"Sometimes . . ." He breathed in deeply and hesitated, as if choosing his words carefully. "Sometimes, life gets complicated and it's tempting to do something drastic."

"Like run away?" She wished she could take the words back as soon as they slipped from between her lips, but the damage had been done.

Monty looked as if she'd slapped him. "Like run away." He nodded, then reached over to pat her hand. "But some people do the opposite. They hide. And others try to change their identity. They might even change their hair color." He shifted back against his seat. "It takes all types."

"So Mommy always said." Cherry shifted back against her own chair and watched as the sun began its nightly descent behind the waters of the Gulf.

"Your mother is an astute woman."

"When she's not shoplifting."

Monty snapped his tongue. "There is that."

A commotion from the bushes at the far end of the property caught their attention. Someone or something yipped, and the sound was almost human.

Cherry hit the patio running. "Lucky!" If he'd run into the skunk again, she'd have his little fluffy head on a platter.

But it wasn't a skunk that hustled out from between the foliage. Not hardly.

It was Moose.

The little man hit the yard in a full-out sprint, trailed closely by Lucky, who gripped a piece of pin-striped material in his front teeth.

"Serves you right, you little bastard," Monty yelled and shook his fist as the tiny thug dashed past.

Cherry stood, her feet frozen to the spot, unable to believe her eyes. It wasn't every day you saw a pink poodle chasing off a reimbursement specialist.

A few moments later, an engine rumbled to life and the squeal of quickly departing tires could be heard from out front. Lucky returned a few seconds later, still clutching the piece of Moose's suit in his mouth.

The poodle sashayed onto the patio, then made a dash for the bushes, apparently intent on showing off his souvenir. *Great.* She might as well get the dog's tomato-juice shower ready now.

"I'll go check your wiring." Monty headed toward the driveway.

"Thanks." Cherry returned to her poker book, trying to shake the realization Moose had been lurking in her own backyard.

The little thug was ever present. Ever threatening. And if she didn't memorize this book inside out, the wiring on her car was going to be the least of her worries.

CHAPTER 12

Luke glanced across the gym from the bleachers, where he and several other board volunteers sat listening to the center director's latest plans. His young basketball team practiced lay-ups on the far half-court. At least, they were supposed to be practicing.

One boy bounced a ball off a second's back. A third spun his ball on the tip of his finger as the rest of the boys cheered him on, their laughter growing louder with each passing second.

Luke chuckled inwardly. Kids. He cupped his hands around his mouth. "Lay-ups, guys. Lay-ups!"

The boys sprang into action, falling into the familiar practice formation as if they'd never been distracted.

Luke settled back against the bleachers, realizing the others present had been staring at his outburst.

"Sorry." He shrugged quickly. "You can take the coach out of practice, but you can't take practice out of the coach."

"No problem." The center director handed a

single sheet of paper to each volunteer. "This is a list of major givers in our area who are sympathetic to causes such as ours."

The members of the Development Commission and the Women's League were due any minute, and the Youth Center volunteers had a lot of ground to cover before the others arrived. The last thing they wanted was for their current funding shortage to become public knowledge.

Luke took a sheet, glancing at the short list of banks, corporate foundations, and private individuals. His gut caught when his gaze landed on Cherry's name. The woman and her sister definitely had the resources to help, but apparently their support had been promised to the competition.

"We have less than three days to identify a new lead funding source and a match." The director shook his head. "Or we can forget about the Framingham Estate. Ideas?"

Raucous laughter sounded from the opposite side of the gym, and warmth swelled inside Luke as he watched the kids practice. His moment of pleasure was quickly replaced by the reality of the situation.

Now that the current building's owner had announced his demolition plans, the Youth Center was truly running out of time. He'd been a fool to waste so much time thinking about Cherry and his past when he should have been worrying about the kids and what would happen to them if the campaign efforts failed.

"The trick," the director continued, when no one else offered suggestions, "would be to identify people on this list with the ability to make a quick decision and back it up with major financial support."

Luke's heart started a slow sink toward the pit of his stomach. He didn't like the director's line of thinking.

"Anyone like that on this list?" another volunteer asked.

The director nodded his head, his features serious. "Cherry Harte. She's a private individual and as such has the ability to make her own decisions. She and her sister both have money, but apparently Cherry controls the purse strings."

Luke's throat constricted, and he choked.

"Luke?" All eyes focused on him. "Something to add?"

Not if he could help it. He shook his head.

The director clasped his hands together. "When she and the other Women's League members arrive today, I'd like each of you to watch how she reacts to our programs. If any of you can strike up a conversation, all the better."

The Development Commission members started to trickle in through the side door, and the director lowered his voice. "Let's be honest, the woman and her sister have more than enough money to support both projects."

The director headed across the gym floor to greet their guests, but Luke sat tight, trying to ignore the coffee he'd chugged on the way to the meeting as it gnawed its way into the lining of his stomach.

A man who truly didn't care what Cherry Harte thought would ask her for the money. He wouldn't care if she thought him a gold digger. He wouldn't care if she thought him beneath her.

His stomach flipped and he grimaced.

As much as he wanted to prove he'd been worthy of his board appointment, the director would have to find another patsy to woo Ms. Harte. He couldn't do it. Not after he'd gone on and on about her *type*.

He glanced back toward the boys on the far court, his stomach somersaulting into a full roll. Damn. There had to be another way to find funding in time. Some way that didn't involve Cherry.

One of the administrative assistants scurried around the edge of the gymnasium floor. "The rest of our visitors just arrived. The director would like you all over in the administrative hall."

The group of volunteers descended from the bleachers, heading off toward the spot where their tour would begin.

Luke waited, unable to deny he wanted a glimpse of Cherry. He bit back a laugh as the members of the Women's League entered the gymnasium and stopped short. Led by Monique herself, they piled up behind each other, little carbon copies in their beige suits. Wearing their beige shoes. Smiling their beige smiles.

With one exception.

Cherry Harte came racing in behind them. "Am I late?" Luke couldn't help but pick out her voice across the huge space of the gym. "Sorry."

She also wore a suit, but in a brilliant shade of red. It hugged each luscious curve like a glove—a glove he'd like to run his hands all over.

Down, boy.

Her hair, still darker, had been mussed—as if tossed and tumbled by the wind—and he couldn't help but think this was how she'd look after making love. The high-heeled shoes she wore covered her toes but appeared to be held on by nothing but a pair of skinny red straps.

He hadn't set eyes on her in two days, but if it were possible, she affected his senses even more now than she had on previous occasions.

He reached for his shirt pocket, relieved to find a fresh pack of gum waiting.

Monique shook her head and dug into her purse. She lifted her tiny recorder to her lips as she turned and waved across the gym to where the rest of the group waited.

"Let's have some fun," Luke said to no one in particular as he set out across the gymnasium floor.

Cherry didn't notice his approach. Instead she stood, mesmerized, watching the boys practice. The brightest smile Luke had ever seen spread wide across her lovely face. As he drew near, he realized his grandfather had been right all along. The light in Cherry's eyes shone like a beacon.

A sudden realization hit him, and he stopped midstride.

In Cherry's smile, Luke saw what he'd been craving all along—a glimpse of the real her. A glimpse of Cherry happy and at ease, not focused on what others thought. As she watched the kids play, she beamed, lit from within.

Luke's glimpse came to an abrupt stop when she turned and caught his eye. Her features stiffened, and she straightened.

Did he make her that uncomfortable?

Well—he bit back a smile—he had just the solution.

"Ladies." He pointed to the women's feet. "I'm afraid you'll have to take your heels off to cross the gym." He shook his head, trying for a sincere expression. He was having a devil of a time hiding his grin. And Cherry was on to him.

Her smile had returned, and he heard her hushed laugh as she slipped first out of one shoe and then the other. The rest of the Women's Leaguers fussed and fumed, but Cherry merely stood there barefoot, waiting for Luke's next direction.

He'd never seen anyone so beautiful. And he was quite sure he never would again.

Luke gestured toward the opposite side of the gym, and the Women's League, with Monique at the helm, began their barefoot walk across.

"Psst." Cherry crooked her finger.

"What?"

She stepped back outside and returned with a shiny black, rhinestone-studded dog carrier. Lucky stuck his pink head out of the opening, a black velvet bow on each ear.

Luke groaned. "Why do you do this to the poor dog?"

"It's part of my skunk-avoidance plan." She planted one fist on her hip and glared at Lucky.

The dog smelled faintly of a recent spray.

"You might need a new plan."

"You have no idea."

The poor dog's beady eyes pleaded with Luke to help him make a break for it.

"I was talking about the bows. And the carrier." Luke scowled. "Lucky probably isn't trying to mate with the skunk, he's probably trying to commit doggicide."

"That," Cherry's eyes popped wide, "is not funny."

Luke pointed to the carrier. "Would you blame him?"

"I can't carry him around." She met Luke's gaze, eyes twinkling. "Heaven knows Monique has already got enough on her recorder to write a book. This would get her started on the sequel."

"We can leave him here with the boys." Luke nodded toward the gang in the corner. "They'll keep an eye on him. You can trust them."

He watched as she padded barefoot toward the basketball practice, Lucky's container in one hand, her shoes dangling seductively from the other. He'd have to be dead not to appreciate the sway of her red-clad rear end as she crossed the floor.

And judging by the sensations coming from the lower half of his body, he had absolutely nothing to fear in the mortality department.

Cherry hurried as she crossed back to where Luke waited. He looked like a million bucks in his collared T-shirt and khaki shorts. Much as she hated to admit it, the man made her want to strip right out of her ridiculous suit.

Right here. Right now.

In the middle of the gymnasium floor.

She needed to get a grip.

"Do you have any gum?" she asked once she was within earshot.

He smiled and handed her a stick. "I take it your trip home was uneventful the other night?"

She warmed at the genuine concern in his expression. "Totally." It had been the arrival home that had been something else.

"Car running all right?"

She sank her teeth into the gum and sighed as the sweet flavor filled her mouth. "Dead again. I had Liz drop me off."

She had no intention of telling him about Moose's latest visit. Goodness knew the man already suspected she was up to something. If he ever found out what, he'd probably blow her little cover sky-high.

Luke frowned. "I'll run you home and take a look."

"Isn't that above and beyond your usual services?" She waggled her brows, satisfaction easing through her as his throat worked.

All she needed was *not* within her now. It was standing right in front of her.

She *really* needed to get a grip.

"Mr. Chance. Ms. Harte," the Development Commission chair barked out across the gym. "We're ready to begin."

Luke gripped her elbow to guide her toward the group, and Cherry savored the heat that spread outward from the light pressure of his fingers through her suit jacket.

"Speaking of packaging . . ."

He spoke in a low tone, undetectable to anyone but her as they neared the group. Her mutinous heart caught for a split second.

"Thought you were on the beige plan?"

She shot him a look and gave a quick shrug. "I must have missed today's lesson."

She had no intention of telling him her poker lesson had run long and she'd had to grab the first suit in her closet. When her car hadn't started,

Monty had wanted to go on a Moose hunt. While Liz had raced Cherry and Lucky across town, Yogi had stayed behind to teach her father relaxation techniques.

Talk about the blind leading the blind.

"Well, between you and me," Luke's voice was now a mere whisper—a deep, husky, blood-boiling whisper, "the beige team ought to be taking lessons from you."

He dropped his hand from her arm and moved into the hall, disappearing into the crowd.

Cherry did her best to focus on the Youth Center director's voice and not on the rapid pulse thrumming in her ears—or the way her tattoo itched.

Again.

An hour later, the group had finished its tour of the facility and listened to the director's plans for the Framingham Estate.

Humbled, Cherry had to admit the needs of the Youth Center made those of the Horticultural Center pale in comparison, especially with the kids' current facility scheduled for demolition.

As the group scattered, Luke reappeared at her side, car keys jangling from his hand. "I'll go grab Lucky and meet you outside."

She nodded. Her tattoo had gone berserk when she'd caught a second glimpse of him during the tour, and she gave in now to the temptation, scratching with abandon. Of course, she'd thought all eyes were focused elsewhere until she saw Monique shake her head and reach for her recorder.

Great.

Cherry waved good-bye and headed for the parking lot. Maybe once the Horticultural Center won the estate, she'd be able to locate a replacement facility for the Youth Center. She smiled to herself as she headed outside.

Wouldn't that give Monique cause for commentary.

Five minutes later, Luke broke the awkward silence in his small car. He crooked a dark brow. "Want to tell me why someone named Moose is tampering with your car?"

If only he knew.

"Who said he tampered with my car?"

"Your butler."

"He's heavily medicated." Cherry shook her head and crossed her arms. "I wouldn't believe a word he said, if I were you."

"Well." Luke gave her a glance that meant all business. "Someone messed with your wiring, and you need to take this seriously. Any reason why? Or who?"

She had two hundred and fifty thousand reasons, but she wasn't going to share them with Luke. No way. The man might be giving her fantasies about ripping her goal poster to shreds, but her willpower was stronger than his pull.

She sneaked a glance at his bare thigh.

Yup. Definitely stronger than his pull.

"You know." Luke's voice broke into her thoughts—thankfully. "You'd have no reason to know this, but I used to be a reporter. I have a nose for a story, and I sense one in you."

Whoa. Luke's words evaporated any thoughts of desire. Reporter? Story?

Holy exposure. This guy had the ability to do more than blow her carefully created identity sky-high. He had the ability to obliterate it.

Cherry laughed, working to sound uninterested when she was anything but. "No story here. Nope. Nothing."

"Right." He sat silent for a minute before he continued. "Just know that if you ever change your mind, I might be able to help you out."

"I thought you didn't like me. You didn't want to think about me." She spat back his words from the night of the photo session.

Luke shrugged. "I've been thinking I might have been too harsh."

Cherry inhaled and blew out a slow breath. The man was making her head hurt. "Have any more gum?"

"Glove compartment."

Cherry reached for the pack and held it out to him. They unwrapped their pieces simultaneously and chewed.

"Let's change the subject." Luke reached behind the seats and flipped open the latches on Lucky's carrier. "Why don't you let the poor dog be a dog?"

"Because he's from a select line of champions. He needs to act like it."

Lucky scampered up onto Luke's lap. As the light turned green, Luke helped his front paws up onto the door so Lucky could see outside.

Cherry's heart jumped to her throat. "What if he falls?"

"He won't fall."

Lucky shot her a victorious sneer.

Luke fumbled with the black bows until he had

them out of the poodle's fur. The wind kicked in through the window and Lucky's pink ears lifted, like carefree sails on the warm breeze.

Luke laughed as he accelerated into traffic. "Happy now, buddy?"

Lucky turned and planted a sloppy kiss on Luke's chin, then turned back to the window.

Cherry tensed. "Are you sure he can't fall? Won't that dry out his eyes? This can't be good for him."

Luke reached over and squeezed her knee. Her jaw froze midchew and she lifted her eyes to his. His features had gone slack and for one brief moment, Cherry wanted to throw her new identity out the window and jump into the man's lap.

After all, look how happy sitting in his lap had made the dog.

"You can't plan everything, Cherry." He put his hand back on the gearshift and focused on the traffic ahead. "Sometimes life throws you a curveball."

Tell her about it. Hers was sitting in the next seat over. She was beginning to think her obsession with planning was far overrated.

"Want to tell me why you're so anxious to join the Women's League?"

She bristled. "I thought we'd changed the subject to the dog?"

"We did." He nodded. "Now we're changing it back." He tipped his chin toward Lucky. "See that carefree smile on his face?"

"Dogs don't smile." Cherry leaned over to look anyway, and she'd be damned if Lucky's pink puss didn't look a whole lot happier than normal.

"You had that same look today at the gym. Just for a moment." One dark brow lifted.

Cherry chewed faster. "You're comparing me to a tomato-juice-stained dog?"

"No." Luke laughed.

The sound caught her by surprise. It was a nice sound—a *wonderful* sound.

"You smiled." He shot her a lopsided grin. "When you were watching the kids."

She remembered the exact moment. The boys had looked so happy playing basketball. Footloose. Without a care in the world. "They seemed like great kids."

"They are great kids. That's why we're working to make sure they always have a place to go." His tone dropped low. "I have no intention of letting them lose that estate to a bunch of socialites with a fondness for plants and cocktail parties. I'd like to think you understand that."

What was the man doing? Trying to guilt the crack in her resolve into a chasm? She popped open the glove compartment. "Mind if I take another piece?"

"Go right ahead."

The security guard waved them through the gate to her community. Neither of them said another word until he pulled into her drive.

Cherry gathered Lucky and secured him in his carrier before he could make a break for it. Luke climbed out and headed for Cherry's car, but stopped partway across the drive.

"What would you say to a truce?"

Cherry froze in her tracks. "With you?" She choked on her wad of gum. When she turned to face him, he looked as surprised by what he'd said as she was to hear it.

"I want to show you something."

That's exactly what she was afraid of—that he'd show her something that would upend all of her carefully made plans.

His dark brows lifted, as if issuing a dare.

"Show me what?" She gripped Lucky's container and stood her ground.

"Meet me at the fishing pier at seven and you'll find out. We'll grab some dinner."

Much to her dismay, her head nodded yes before her brain had a chance to kick in.

What the hell.

A girl had to eat.

CHAPTER 13

A few hours later, Cherry walked the length of the pier, scouring the crowd for any sign of Luke. Why on earth had he asked her to meet him here? As far as she knew, the closest restaurant was several blocks away.

She cupped one hand above her eyes to peer into the setting sun. Rich violet hues streaked across the horizon as the large orb slipped beyond the point where the sky met the Gulf.

Her breath caught. Had he invited her to watch the sunset? Surely not. He had said truce, but he'd made it clear she wasn't his type.

As she neared the end of the pier, a cluster of small boys and one towering, dark-haired man captured her attention. The man bent to bait the hook of a fishing line and Cherry squinted to see his profile more clearly.

Her belly tightened, her body recognizing Luke's manly features an instant before her brain clicked in. Warmth blossomed deep inside her.

Ignoring the way the man affected her was

hopeless. She'd listened to her CD on the drive over, but the calming effects were lost the moment Luke came into view.

"Me next, Coach!"

One small voice sounded above the crowd. Cherry watched Luke's face break into a wide grin. What was he up to now?

"Hold your britches." His rich voice rumbled with amusement. "Everyone gets a turn. Save some bait for Miss Cherry when she gets here."

Cherry wrinkled her nose. Bait? Fishing? When he'd said they'd grab dinner, she hadn't taken him literally. She stood motionless, deciding to watch for a few moments before she made her arrival known.

Luke worked patiently with each young boy—baiting hooks, casting lines, offering encouragement. Each small face lit with excitement. Enthusiasm. Happiness.

The cool evening air rippled the skirt of Cherry's dress, unable to chill her bare legs as warmth continued to spread through her.

Luke oozed vitality, tempting her closer and closer still. This was where he belonged—getting his hands dirty with a bunch of children who adored him, not stuffed into a suit in front of the Development Commission.

She smiled at the happy expression plastered across his face. If only they weren't competitors. At this moment, she'd buy him the Framingham Estate outright—no questions asked—just to bask in the heat of his grin.

One freckle-faced lad reeled in a flip-flop sandal, and a symphony of giggles filled the air. Luke's rich, male laughter boomed across the pier, wrapping itself around Cherry like a worn, favorite blanket. Damn, but he was . . . real.

And he was nowhere on her goal poster.

She let out a deep sigh, stepped away from the railing, and headed straight for Luke and his gang of fishermen.

"Hey." The soft timbre of Cherry's voice tickled Luke's ear just as he freed the fished-out sandal from Kevin's hook.

Luke trained his gaze on her as she approached, fighting the urge to shake his head. As usual, she was breathtaking. One of her soft, filmy dresses hung loose around her curvy frame, fluttering around her damn knees. Bright blue sandals trimmed with some kind of sparkly dots covered her feet. Actually, *covered* wasn't the most accurate term. Instead, the straps slipped in and out between her toes—her toenails painted a matching, vivid blue.

He raised his gaze to meet hers, and her pale eyes widened. "You don't approve of my footwear?"

"Packaging."

"You said dinner." Cherry nodded toward the boys draped over the railing, dangling their fishing poles. "You didn't mention we were catching it first."

"Builds character." He narrowed his eyes. "Something you could use."

He'd shocked himself when he'd invited her, but on the drive home he'd got to thinking. What could it hurt? If anything, she might offer to fund the Youth Center of her own free will.

She opened her mouth to argue with his last

statement, but he turned toward the boys before she could utter a word. "Guys? Where's that fishing rod we brought for Miss Cherry?"

"Fishing rod?" Cherry's voice squeaked.

Luke stole a glance at her startled expression, quickly looking away. He hadn't been prepared for the way his body would respond to seeing her again so soon. It was far safer to focus on the boys— and the fish.

"Is this what you wanted to show me?" Disbelief tinged her words.

He crooked a finger in her direction, finding great satisfaction as she glanced from the railing to the fishing pole to him. Palpable tension sizzled between them as their eyes locked. "Come see how the other half live."

She planted a fist on one hip. "You treat me as if I've never gone fishing."

Luke arched his brows, doing his best to ignore the raw, hot desire pooling in his gut. "Have you?"

Cherry glared at him. He could almost see the smoke pouring from her ears.

Damn, but the woman was breathtaking.

"No." She reached for the pole. "Give me that."

Her fingers brushed against his as she snatched the pole from his grip. Each of his nerve endings sprang to life.

"Careful with that," he muttered as she stepped to the rail. "There's a hook at the end of that line."

She pinned him with a vivid look, the familiar fire twinkling in her eyes. "Then you'd better make sure you stand clear."

Luke held his hands in the air, stepping backward from where she stood. "Let 'er rip."

Cherry glanced behind her, double-checking that none of the boys were in her path. She swung the rod back over her shoulder, then forward, casting the line effortlessly out onto the water. A throaty laugh tumbled from her lips. "Yowza."

A brilliant, carefree smile spread across her face. *Jackpot.*

The gathering of boys whooped and clapped, obviously enjoying the fun Cherry was having with Luke. Luke narrowed his gaze in their direction and they quickly busied themselves with their own fishing rods and buckets.

He moved back toward Cherry, leaving only a few inches between his chest and her shoulder. Her throat worked visibly as he stood beside her silently.

Heat fired in his cheeks. *Odd.* The breeze must have stopped. Without warning, Cherry's spicy scent enveloped him, sending a shock wave crashing through his system. He refocused on her line, hanging slack over the side of the pier.

"Where'd you learn to do that?" he asked.

"I read."

Her full lips pressed together coyly, her eyes softening as she turned to toss him a smug look. He was suddenly filled with the urge to kiss her, remembering how their one kiss had rocked him straight through.

He increased the space between them, leaning his elbows on the railing. Safer. Farther away from her flimsy dress and her intoxicating scent. "You read about fishing?"

She tipped her head, measuring him with her bright gaze. "I do many things that might surprise you."

Luke swallowed. Hard.

Her line suddenly tugged taut, and she let out a cry of surprise.

"Reel it in." Luke stepped behind her, placing his hands over her smooth arms. "Gently. Don't lose it."

"It might be the matching flip-flop," one of the boys joked.

Cherry laughed, her body soft and warm beneath Luke's touch.

This was the Cherry he'd seen at the hospital with his grandfather and then again in the photo and at the gym. Why on earth did she want to hide who she was beneath the beige veil of the Women's League?

Cherry worked to slowly reel in the line. Whatever was at the other end gave her a solid tug in return. "Wahoo," she whooped freely, uninhibited.

This was the Cherry that had gotten under Luke's skin. The *real* Cherry.

If he wasn't careful, he might not be able to get her out.

An hour later, Cherry watched Luke say good-bye to the last of the boys. She waited next to the driveway, savoring the relaxed, peaceful sensation that filled her. Amazing.

Who'd have thought she'd be capable of casting a line, let alone catching a fish? Or three? The remembered feel of being enveloped in Luke's arms overcame her momentarily, washing her in a flash of heat and need. She cleared her throat, doing her best to tamp down the desire puddling at her core.

She wiggled her toes into the light coating of sand

covering the brick walk, her sandals dangling from her fingers. She smiled at Luke's broad back as he patted a young boy's shoulder and spoke to his foster mother.

Such a good man. *Such a real man.* He would definitely play havoc with her plans if she let him. The trick was to resist, no matter what.

As the car drove away, Luke turned to face her, gesturing for her to catch up. She snapped herself from the trance, quickly closing the gap between them.

The evening breeze ruffled his dark locks and Cherry worked to keep herself focused, to resist the urge to entwine her fingers in the silky strands. To fight the desire to press her lips to his.

For the briefest moment, his warm, strong hand pressed against the small of her back, guiding her toward the parking lot. She longed to lean into him, to let go of their differences, to relish the heat of his palm through the soft cotton of her dress.

She longed to forget about her goals, about her new identity, about Monty and Moose and poker. She longed to forget about everything—except the man standing next to her.

As if he'd read her thoughts, Luke dropped his hand, moving a step ahead, putting distance between them.

"Come on." Luke tipped his head toward their cars. "I know a place that serves a mean snook."

Luke pulled alongside the garage and climbed from his car, reaching for the bucket of fish. He waited as Cherry parked her Jaguar and climbed out, watching closely for her reaction.

"We're having dinner here?" She pointed to the sign. Chance Auto.

"Home-cooked meal," Luke answered, scrutinizing her every move.

Cherry's forehead wrinkled. "I didn't realize you lived here. Where?"

He pointed to a set of stairs. Cherry's gaze followed, green eyes widening as she spied the entrance door and the windows framing either side.

"Gramps has one just like it around back. You have a problem with that?"

A soft laugh escaped her lips, her focus returning to him. "What happened to our truce? Did you run out of gum?"

Cherry's words challenged his expectations, not that she'd done anything but since she'd clicked across his garage a few days ago.

She pointed toward the bucket. "Need help?"

He shook his head. "After you."

Luke dropped his gaze to the curve of Cherry's calves as she climbed the wooden steps. She skimmed one hand seductively along the railing as she climbed, and he couldn't help but wonder how it would feel to have those fingers on his arm . . . on his cheek . . . on his chest.

The heat that had been simmering in his gut all night began to boil, and he fought to regain his willpower.

"This reminds me of my old apartment." Cherry hit the landing, then turned to wait for him, eyes sparkling. "Liz and I had one just like this over a pizza parlor back home."

He cleared the top step, setting down the bucket to dig his keys out of his pocket. "You lived in an apartment like this?"

"And you wonder why I'm so focused on a new identity."

Her eyes widened as soon as the words slipped from her lips. "Luke. I'm sorry. I didn't mean it."

The fire in his belly cooled to a slow simmer. He shouldn't be surprised by her words. After all, he hadn't heard anything on her affirmation CDs about striving to move lower on the economic ladder.

People with money were different. And Cherry was definitely people with money—just as Monique had been. And was.

Cherry ruffled a hand through her short hair. The spicy scent of her shampoo enveloped Luke as she held out her hand. "Truce? Again?"

He shook her hand, cleared his throat, then pushed open the door. "Welcome to my humble abode."

She stood on the threshold for what seemed like an eternity. When she spoke, her voice had gone thick with emotion.

"I love it." She turned to face him, raw desire blatant in her eyes. "It feels like you."

Hell. How could he stay upset with the woman when she looked liked *that*? He wanted her so badly he could taste it.

"Thanks." He ground out the words as he moved in a wide arc around her. "I'll just take these fish to the deck."

"Luke." The intense tone of Cherry's voice stopped him cold. "I'm just an average girl who hit the lottery. I'm no different than you are."

"Yes . . . you are." He spoke the words slowly and deliberately as he headed for his fish-cleaning utensils. She was millions different and he needed to remember that. Money changed people.

Even if she had been an average girl once, it seemed to him she was fighting with all her might to lock the average girl far, far away.

Her heels clicked across the wooden floor, and the traitorous longing inside him anchored his feet to where he stood.

"You're the first person I've met since Liz and I won the lottery who actually has contempt for my money. Most people are looking for a handout."

He turned to face her and she moved in close—toe-to-toe. So close, he could feel her heat.

"I wish you'd tell me why."

Luke shook his head. "Ancient history." He lifted a brow. "Trust me. A handout from you would be the last thing on earth I'd ever want."

Unless of course it was for the kids, and he sincerely did not want to make that request. Not from Cherry.

Her pale gaze narrowed, a spark flashing from deep inside. Of what? Anger? Frustration? Desire? Confusion?

Join the club, honey.

Maybe she found him just as perplexing as he found her. Their chemistry was undeniable, but one thing was guaranteed. If they gave in to temptation, theirs would be a lethal combination.

He steeled himself, doing his best to remember she stood for everything he'd sworn off, truce or no truce. "I've got fish to clean."

Cherry's intense stare never wavered from his

eyes. She wrapped her soft fingers around his on the handle of the bucket. "Wait."

His willpower started to crack, the sultry tone of her voice reigniting the low, heavy heat inside his gut. Her touch burned into his skin.

Luke set down the bucket, his gaze locked on hers. Cherry's pale focus bore into his, determination shining, sending his senses reeling.

"I need to thank you." She straightened, pulling herself taller.

"For what?" He could barely form the words, let alone speak them. His brain seemed capable of only one thing. Wanting her. *Badly.*

"For giving me a night off from my plan. For taking me fishing with you and the boys."

The heat building inside him bubbled to a boil at the memory of her laughter on the pier. The way she'd fit in. How right it had felt having her at his side.

Cherry's spicy fragrance wrapped itself around him, reaching deep, tapping at the door of restraint he'd fought so hard to keep locked.

"You didn't feel like you were too good to be there?"

"No." Her soft breath brushed against his face. "I was proud to be there."

Her features softened, her full lips open, inviting.

"Proud?" He covered her shoulders with his hands, pulling her body to his.

She swallowed and nodded.

Luke's restraint snapped. He brought his mouth down over hers, thrilling to the feel of her lips parting beneath his. He deepened the kiss, drinking her in, encircling her waist and pulling her body tight against his own.

Her soft breasts pressed against his chest. Her luscious curves complemented his sharp edges. She fit. They fit. Together.

Cherry wrapped her arms around him, her fingers tangling in the hair at the nape of his neck, exploring, touching, stroking.

Red-hot fire scorched through Luke's body, searing his blood with an urgent need for her. She was like no one he'd ever met, and his body's response to her was like nothing he'd ever known.

He eased his hands along her sides, up from the curve of her waist, gently stroking his thumbs over the swells of her breasts.

Cherry inhaled sharply, pulling her lips from his.

"Too fast?" he asked.

Her wide, hungry stare met his. Liquid heat simmered in the depths of her eyes. She shook her head, then dropped her mouth to his neck, trailing kisses along his jaw.

Luke's erection pressed uncomfortably against the zipper of his shorts, his desire growing more urgent as Cherry nipped lightly at his earlobe. He caressed her breasts, gently rubbing her swollen nipples between his thumbs and forefingers.

His pulse roared in his ears, the room around him fading until all he knew and felt was Cherry. The rest of the world fell away.

The Framingham Estate. Their competition. Her money. All of it.

Gone.

In that moment, the sole focus of his existence

was this complicated, yet simply amazing woman who'd stolen his heart.

He longed to run his hungry touch over her flushed, naked flesh, making love to her until she moaned and cried out in pleasure.

Differences be damned.

Restraint be damned.

Sanity be damned.

Cherry's tattoo had never itched with such fervor. Stick a fork in it. Hell, stick a fork in *her*. She was done. She couldn't deny what she felt for Luke a moment longer.

Hot moisture pooled between her legs as his hands moved over her body like no other man's had. Her nerve endings responded, snapping to a frenzy of blatant lust and need.

Lord, how she wanted him—and wanted him now.

She tipped back her head, allowing him access to her neck as he lowered kisses to the soft hollow at the base of her throat. His fingers roughly unbuttoned the front of her sundress, unclasping the closure of her bra before she realized what had happened.

Luke leaned away for a moment, gazing at her, half-naked before him. "So beautiful," he murmured, before closing his lips over one nipple, sucking until she thought her knees would give way. His strong palm pressed hot against her back, pulling her fully against his hungry mouth.

Cherry held his shoulders, surrendering her body to his hands, his lips, his touch. With his free hand he worked the material of her skirt higher and higher until his fingers connected with the bare skin of her thigh. Cherry's heart hammered against her rib cage, threatening to burst from her chest.

Luke cupped her bottom, pressing her against his arousal, then slipping his hand between their bodies, sliding his fingers against her moist panties. Hot, sexual desire ripped through her. Her body tensed with a coiled, crazed need she'd never felt before.

She had never wanted anyone as she wanted Luke. Even more than sexual desire, she longed to tell him everything—to purge herself of the half-truths and the secrets. She'd tell him about Monty . . . and Fran . . . and Moose . . . and her poker lessons. She'd come clean. She'd trust him, just as he'd asked her to.

Then her carefully reinvented life would be exposed. *Completely.*

Cherry's heart caught in her chest, twisting in defiance of the hunger rippling through every fiber of her being.

What on earth was she thinking?

Her eyes flew open.

Luke Chance was a former newspaper reporter. *A reporter.*

Hell. If she told him the truth about her family, she'd be handing him the story of the year.

She couldn't fall for this man—couldn't trust this man.

To top it all off, his beloved Youth Center was her competition, for crying out loud. If she lost control now, it would lead only to one thing—a total derailment of all she'd worked for over the past four months.

She had to stop. They had to stop. *Now.*

"Stop." Panic clutched at Cherry's throat. "I can't do this."

She scrambled free of Luke's embrace, pulling the straps of her sundress up to her shoulders, fumbling to fasten her bra and buttons.

My God, she'd almost caved completely. Hot tears stung at her eyes, but she frantically blinked them back.

Luke stepped toward her, but Cherry held up a hand to keep him away. "Did I hurt you?" he asked, concern shining brightly in his stunned gaze.

Not yet.

"No." Her voice cracked with her tortured emotions. "This was a mistake."

She met Luke's glare. Disbelief and frustration battled in the depths of his dark brown eyes.

Cherry turned and grabbed for her purse where she'd left it next to the front door. She reached for the doorknob, but Luke's firm fingers gripped her elbow.

She had to get out of here, had to get away from him, before she lost control. Before he saw how much she wanted him, how much she needed him.

"Please let me go," she whispered.

"Not until you tell me what just happened."

"This can never work. It's too complicated." She straightened, pulling her elbow free of his grasp. "You know I'm right."

"Until tonight, I would have agreed with you." His features tensed, as if she'd caused him pain. "Didn't you feel anything on that pier tonight? I sure as hell did." He winced. "I still do."

"It's only chemistry," Cherry lied, slapping away the images of him with his grandfather, on the pier with the kids, laughing with Liz about Yogi. She had to leave—now, while her heart still stood a chance of surviving. "The Women's League is my top priority. Coming here was a mistake."

Luke pulled back, shoving a hand through his hair. A cloud passed across his features. She'd hit the target with those two words.

"That's really all you care about? The Women's League?"

Cherry nodded, seeing her way out. "I'll help you find another location for the Youth Center." She twisted the knob, pulling open the door to her escape. *Coward.*

"I'm talking about what's happening between *us*." The harsh anger in Luke's voice stopped her cold. "My grandfather thinks your money hasn't changed you as a person. But he's wrong, isn't he?"

Cherry blinked. All she'd wanted to do since the moment she won the lottery was change. Why not? Just look at the crazy life she'd left behind. For once in her life, she had a chance to reach the top of the heap. Finally.

But meeting Luke had made her question it all. Her goals. Her decisions. Her packaging.

The man had turned her vision on its ear, and quite frankly, it was easier to walk away from him than it was to question everything she'd done over the past four months. No matter how much it hurt.

"What do you do, Cherry?" Hurt and confusion

shimmered in his stare. "Flip a switch? One minute you're one of them. Next minute you're human. Tonight I actually wanted to win your heart, but I think you've forgotten how to use it."

Her heart hurt. Her head spun. She had to get away before the pain in his eyes pulled her back. She couldn't give in. She *wouldn't*.

Every day, in every way, I'm getting better and better.

"Better watch out," Luke continued. "You keep denying who you really are and that heart will turn to stone."

Cold resignation settled in her belly. He knew nothing about the life she'd endured thanks to her parents. Even if he did, he'd never understand.

She was doing the right thing.

She turned away, pulling the door open.

"Do you have any idea of the good you could do?" He'd moved so close his breath brushed the back of her neck. "Without the Women's League."

His words halted her forward motion.

"You say people only want your money," he growled. "What do you think the Women's League wants? Do you really think they're any different?"

His words hit hard, tapping into the seed of doubt that Liz had planted after Cherry first applied for membership. "You're wrong," she said flatly. "They want to help me. They're making me a lifetime member."

"Well"—he chuckled, a cold, bitter laugh—"I hope you and your new beige friends will be very happy together."

Cherry launched herself into motion, hurrying down the steps and across the parking lot. She dropped inside her car and slammed the door before Luke could say anything else.

As she pulled out of the lot, the Jaguar's head-lights slashed through the darkness, lighting her way back to her plans for acceptance.

She pressed the Play button on the CD deck, want-ing to affirm Luke's parting shot out of her head.

Silence followed.

Damn.

She'd completely forgotten she'd tossed the disc into the backseat of the car.

Do you have any idea of the good you could do? With-out the Women's League?

His words echoed in her mind, battling with the image she'd so carefully cultivated, tangling with the desire she'd seen burning in his eyes.

Damn.

Where was a pack of gum when you needed it?

CHAPTER 14

Luke opened the door to the deck and hurled the bucket of fish out into the darkness. The bucket landed with a dull thud. Good riddance. He didn't want a single reminder of Cherry anywhere in sight.

How could he have been so stupid? Luke slammed the door, slapping his palm against the doorframe. He crossed to the kitchen, yanked a cold beer from the fridge, and slammed the door closed. He twisted off the cap and drained half the bottle in three gulps.

A truce.

What a fool he'd become. He'd been ready to make love to the woman. Not sex. *Love.*

How could he have let himself feel anything for her? She ran more hot and cold than the plumbing in this damned apartment. One thing was for certain. He wouldn't let himself be sucked into her sexy little web again.

No way.

The phone rang and he snatched the receiver from the wall.

"What?" he barked out.

"Luke?"

He flinched, instantly recognizing the Youth Center director's voice. "Sorry. Thought you might be someone else. What's going on?"

"We got turned down by two more funding sources tonight. I need you to step to the plate."

Luke set the beer bottle on the kitchen counter, fighting the dread clawing its way up his throat. "Such as?"

"Cherry Harte." The director paused. "I saw you leaving with her today. She's our only hope of getting the money we need in time."

Luke leaned hard against the counter, drawing in a slow, steadying breath. Tonight he'd let himself be derailed by the temptation of Cherry, and in doing so he'd forgotten the real reason he'd invited her to the pier. He'd planned to use the occasion to demonstrate how important the Youth Center project was. He'd hoped to persuade her to offer funding without having to ask for it.

Their angry parting exchange flashed through his mind. "I might have blown that already. Sorry."

"Did she say no?" The director's palpable disappointment echoed through the phone.

Luke thought about saying she had. Maybe then he could avoid seeing her again, but he'd never been much for speaking anything but the truth. "Not exactly."

"Luke. The entire project depends on this."

Luke swallowed, closing his eyes and pinching the bridge of his nose. "Damn it," he muttered.

"What was that?"

"Nothing." He shook his head. His life had been

so . . . easy . . . before the blond package from hell had pranced into his shop in her ridiculous little shoes.

"So you'll make the request?"

"Let me think about it."

"There's nothing to think about." The director's stern tone rattled Luke's head, and he reached for his beer. "If you don't do this, the Youth Center project will fail. Come see me tomorrow and we can go over your pitch."

What choice did Luke have? He couldn't let down the board, and he sure as hell wasn't going to let down the kids. He patted his pocket, hoping to find some gum. Empty. Just like the pit of his stomach.

"I'll be there after lunch."

As he hung up the phone, he drained the last of his beer.

He'd just gotten done telling Cherry he'd never ask for a handout. If he made this pitch, she'd think he'd been lying from the start, when that couldn't be further from the truth.

Luke sank onto a kitchen chair, letting his head fall back against the seat. She'd probably hate him.

He shouldn't care if she hated him or not—especially after tonight. But he did.

That fact alone bothered him more than anything else.

He spotted a pack of gum on top of a stack of napkins, reached for it, but then hurled it across the room. He could stick twenty pieces in his mouth but it wouldn't cure what ailed him.

No.

This time, he was in deep. And he had only himself to blame.

When Cherry arrived home, a dark blue SUV sat bathed in the glow of the house's spotlights, parked off to the side of the drive.

She held her breath as she squinted toward the front door, sighing when she zeroed in on just who it was that had come to visit. Just as she'd suspected.

Bart Matthews sat smack in the center of the villa's front steps.

The thought of throwing her car in reverse and heading anywhere else was tempting, but she had a feeling the man wasn't going to give up until she talked to him.

Well . . . she'd show him.

"I have nothing to say to you," she hollered as she scrambled from the Jaguar. "And what the hell are you doing in Florida?"

"I told you. I'm here for a conference." He straightened, smoothing the front of his jacket.

"You could have warned me."

Cherry's heels snapped across the driveway. Maybe if she breezed past him quickly enough, she could make it inside without having to actually converse with the man.

"I tried to tell you I was coming."

"You didn't try very hard."

"You hang up on me every time I call." His voice tightened two octaves, something that had happened for as long as she'd known him. He'd been incapable of hiding frustration, even as a kid. Cherry slapped away the unwanted memory.

"Okay. I'll give you that."

Bart was halfway across the drive to meet her before she realized he was in motion. His chestnut hair had broken into waves from the tropical humidity. His navy eyes danced expressively, even in the dark of night.

Darn the man.

His expression softened. "I need your help."

Cherry's heart tightened in her chest, her stomach roiling sour. "That's a joke." She waved a hand in the air as she skirted around him. "I needed your help the night you sent your little bounty-hunter buddies after my mother, but that didn't stop you."

"I had a job to do. I had a plan."

Bart's words stopped her cold, and she spun to face him.

A plan. Was this how she sounded to Luke? She forced the thought out of her head.

"Your only *plan* was to humiliate my family the night before our wedding. You didn't trust me. I told you I'd make things right. She would have turned herself in after the wedding, but *no.*"

Cherry gestured wildly, fighting the desire to wrap her hands around his throat. "You had to grab all the headlines you could for your stupid little state senate campaign."

She closed the space between them and pounded her index finger into his chest with her last few words.

He captured her hand in his fist and scowled. "You done yet?"

"For now."

Damn. That had felt good. Maybe she should have taken his calls after all.

"I made a mistake. This whole thing hasn't been exactly great for my image."

Cherry extracted her hand from his and hugged herself. "No kidding." She let out a tight laugh. "You jilted your fiancée, remember?"

He reached for her arms, but she twisted away.

"Listen." He shoved a hand through his hair. "You were only marrying me to get away from your family, and I was only marrying you to help the campaign, right?"

Well, when he put it like that . . .

They'd concocted the scheme together, having been friends their whole life. So what if they didn't share passion. They got along. Wasn't that more than most married couples could say?

"Wait a minute." Cherry shook her head. "*You had my mother arrested.* At our rehearsal dinner. After I'd asked you not to."

"She broke the law."

Cherry snorted.

Good grief, she was turning into Liz.

"Bart, my mother's been breaking the law since we were in junior high. This is not news."

"It was time someone stopped her."

"No." She shook her head. "Your opponent was getting more press than you, so you went for a fresh scandal. At my family's expense."

"You hypocrite."

His harsh tone hit her like a slap.

"What did you call me?" She stepped toward him, and he instinctively backed away.

"Hypocrite." He straightened. "You've spent your whole life trying to disown your family. Don't play high-and-mighty with me." He jerked his thumb toward the huge house. "Nice crib, by the way."

Cherry frowned, looking from Bart to the house, then back to Bart. He was right.

She backed away, unwilling to listen to anything else he had to say. Quite frankly, she was running on emotional overload and she was about to snap.

"If you need a campaign contribution, I'll write you a check. Go away, Bart." She scampered toward the steps, hoping she'd reach the door before he spoke another word.

"I don't want your money." His voice had risen again, slicing sharply through the otherwise still night air. "I want your help."

She'd been a fool to think she could recreate her life. The past was never more than a few steps behind, always at the ready to jump up and bite her in the derriere.

What a prize she was. Luke would thank her for running away if he ever heard the full story.

"I'm in love with Liz."

She hadn't seen that one coming. She spun to face him. "What?"

Bart's features fell slack, and he shook his head. "The closer our wedding got, the more I realized I've been in love with your sister my whole life."

His statement hit Cherry like an anvil between the eyes. Her knees gave way and she sank to the bottom step.

"You love Liz?" The words were difficult to force past the disbelief knotted in her throat, but maybe if she said them often enough they'd be easier to understand.

She lifted her gaze to his. "As in *love* Liz?"

Bart closed the space between them, standing so close the toes of his well-worn loafers kissed the brick next to her feet. He nodded.

"Does she know?" Tears choked Cherry's voice, and she hated herself for letting him see her raw emotion.

He shook his head. "I didn't know until you and I put our plan into motion."

Cherry grimaced. Her and her damned plans.

"You know, she's got the same parents I do. You're going to have to overcome the whole arresting-her-mother thing before you work this out."

Bart nodded. "I know. It's taken me four months to gather my courage to face her."

"And you want *me* to help *you?*"

He knelt in front of Cherry, his stare locking with hers. "Please."

She chuckled, the sound strangled and tight.

He reached for her chin, but Cherry jerked away, dodging his touch.

"We both deserve someone who drives us crazy— someone who's wild about us."

A sudden image of Luke flashed through Cherry's mind and she shoved it down. Way down.

Bart stood, taking a step backward. "We were wrong to think a plan could make us happy."

She stared at him for several long moments, considering his statement. Luke's face flashed again. His eyes. His touch. His lips.

None of them part of her plan.

Suddenly the evening air closed in, making it difficult to breathe. "I think crazy may be seriously overrated."

She stood, reaching for the front door. "I need to go now."

Bart started toward his car, stopping to turn back. "I'm staying at the Mystic Diamond. Please help me, Cherry. Do it for true love."

She shut the door and leaned her head against the cold, smooth surface.

Crazy. Everyone deserved someone who drove them crazy.

Cherry relived the feel of Luke's lips on her shoulder, her neck, her breast. Her breath caught as she remembered his rough fingers caressing her bare skin. The man definitely drove her crazy.

I actually wanted to win your heart, but I think you've forgotten how to use it.

His words still stung, and she rubbed her tattoo through her dress, even though it had stopped itching.

It had stopped itching.

Good grief. What had she done?

She headed for the living room and slipped a backup affirmation CD into the stereo. She selected a track and cranked the volume as high as it would go. As she headed for the kitchen, the soothing words blared, kicking up the determination in her veins.

Every day, in every way, I'm getting better and better. Better and better. Better and better.

She paused in the hall just long enough to peek at Yogi's work. The large canvas sat untouched against the wall. What did she expect? She'd occupied all of his time with bodyguard duty and poker lessons. At this rate, she'd be lucky if he had anything done in time for the *Mystic Living* photo shoot.

And to think, a few days ago that had been the most important thing in her life. Now she needed to beat a casino boss at poker, decide whether or not she wanted to help her ex-fiancé win her sister's love, and pretend she wasn't falling in love with her mechanic—who also happened to be her competition.

We were wrong to think a plan could make us happy.

Bart's words echoed in her brain. She'd always hated it when he'd been right.

"Monty?" She called out into the house, but no one answered. She grabbed an iced coffee from the fridge and stepped back into the hall. The affirmation CD continued to play in the background. "Lucky?"

Silence.

Great. Just what she needed—Lucky and Monty missing and probably together. She might as well set out the tomato juice now.

She flicked off the CD and headed upstairs, pausing outside the door to the guest bedroom. "Dad?"

She knocked lightly and waited several seconds. When he didn't answer, she pushed the door open, peeking inside.

Her breath caught at the sight of his steamer trunk, closed, every inch of its surface covered with mementos of Monty's life.

Of their life.

As a family.

She dropped to her knees and stared at each item, taking them in one by one. The photo of Liz the day they'd brought her home from the hospital. Her own first-grade picture. The picture she'd drawn for one of his birthdays. A small copy of her parent's wedding portrait.

Tears swam in her vision. Her mother and father smiled back. So young. So happy. What had gone wrong?

A gold chain draped over the edge of the frame, and Cherry reached out to touch it, running a finger along its length. When she plucked it from where it hung, a plain gold wedding band dangled from the length of gold.

A sob caught in her throat.

"What are you doing?" Liz's voice sounded from the doorway, nothing more than a whisper.

"You'll never believe it." Cherry gestured for her to come in, and her sister dropped next to her, onto her knees.

They sat there in silence for a long time, each studying every precious object her father had carried with him through the years—each carefully transported, displayed, cherished.

"I always thought he left because he didn't love us," Liz said. "I shouldn't have kicked him so hard."

Cherry nodded, unable to answer.

"Should we tell him we found it?" Liz asked.

Cherry's heart hurt, a little bit for the two daughters sitting there, questioning all of their beliefs about their dad, but a whole lot for Monty, who had obviously been living in the past for a long, long time.

She shook her head. "He'll tell us when he's ready." At least she hoped he would.

She pulled herself to her feet and held out her hand for Liz. Her sister took it, and they stood side by side, holding hands like they hadn't done in years.

Sometimes the surprises in life didn't hit you head-on; sometimes they hit you from the past.

As Cherry stood there staring down at the shrine her father had created for the life he'd left behind, she realized those were the surprises that rocked you the hardest.

CHAPTER 15

The next morning, Luke stared at the work schedule tacked to his bulletin board. Somehow, he couldn't make his brain focus on anything but Cherry.

How could he ask her for money after all she'd said? Making the request would be the one thing guaranteed to chase her off for good.

He scrubbed his hands across his exhausted eyes and into his hair. Damn. He really did care what she thought.

Gramps dragged a stool next to the desk and set down a half-eaten pack of crackers. "What in tarnation is that smell, son? Somebody leave a body in a trunk?"

No, Luke thought. But it was a tempting thought. Maybe if he tossed the little beige wannabe in the trunk of her Jag for a little while, she'd realize life was too short to be living by other people's rules.

"Snook." He stretched toward the bulletin board, scribbling a note on one of the work orders.

"The fish?" His grandfather's tone rose. "Where?"

"On my deck."

Gramps's palm closed over Luke's shoulder. "You going to explain? I could go—"

"Any minute." Luke shook his head. "I know."

He patted his grandfather's hand and let out a long breath. "It's symbolic. I swore off Cherry Harte." *Again.*

One of Gramps's white brows rose in an amused arch. "You won't have to swear off her. She won't come within a mile of the stench."

"Even better." Luke scowled.

He eyed the pack of crackers his grandfather had set down on the desk. "Not dining on cucumber sandwiches with the widow today?"

Gramps shook his head and screwed up his mouth. "Nah. I've had enough. Figure that must be how she killed off her first husband."

The sad edge to his eyes betrayed his tough talk.

"I'm not buying it." Luke propped his chin on his fist. "You want to talk?"

The second white brow lifted. "Nothing to talk about."

Luke shook his head. "You're not fooling me, old man." He pushed back to fully face his grandfather. "Let me see if I've got this straight. Cassie Pettigrew has wormed her way under your skin, right?"

And he should know the signs. They were staring back at him every time he glanced in a mirror.

A soft flush played along Gramps's neck. "Tarnation." He plucked a cracker from the pack, popped it into his mouth, and chewed.

"You can't avoid the topic by shoving food in your mouth." Luke crossed an ankle to his knee. "I can wait all day to have this conversation." He pointed to his grandfather's wide eyes. "I learned from the best."

His grandfather chewed the cracker more slowly than a cow working its way across a field. Luke grinned, amusement welling inside him for the first time since Cherry had fled into the night.

When Gramps swallowed, Luke reached for the cracker package, sliding it out of his reach before the older man could repeat the avoidance tactic. "I could go any minute," he teased.

Gramps's eyes narrowed. "She's . . . she's . . ."

Luke chuckled. "You can't even come up with an excuse, can you?" He reached out to pat his grandfather's knee. "You're not getting any younger. Aren't you always nagging me about life being short? Or are you going to hide in this garage forever?"

A shadow flickered across his grandfather's face. Luke's heart ached as the older man looked down, studying the concrete floor.

Gramps was a man who prided himself on loyalty. When his wife had died, he'd closed the emotional door on romance. If the widow had cracked a window to the possibility of new love in his grandfather's life, Luke had every intention of encouraging him to take a chance.

"Nana would have wanted you to move on a long time ago, you know."

Gramps nodded without looking up.

"Just because you care for Cassandra Pettigrew doesn't mean she's going to die and leave you. It also doesn't mean you love Nana any less."

That got the older man's attention. His white head snapped up, his gaze locking with Luke's. "I miss your grandmother every day."

A knot tightened in Luke's throat. "I know you do. I do, too."

He thought of his grandmother and his parents, all gone before their time. Maybe there was something to be said about Gramps's constant warning that he could go at any minute. Truth was, he could. They all could.

Luke pushed back his chair and reached for his grandfather, wrapping his arms around the man's slender shoulders. "Maybe it's time we *both* stop hiding in this garage. What do you say?"

Gramps pushed free of Luke's embrace, gripping his shoulders. "You finally going after Cherry?"

Luke measured his grandfather's expectant expression, not wanting to get the man's hopes up. After the woman's Jekyll-and-Hyde moment the night before, Luke would have to be a fool to go after her again. But maybe a fool was exactly what he needed to be.

"I have to speak to her tonight." *About the little matter of a million dollars.* "We'll see how that goes."

He reached for his keys where they hung on the pegboard. "I have a meeting over at the Youth Center, but I'll make you a deal."

"Name it." Gramps straightened on the stool, looking more vital than he had in years.

"I'll try living if you will."

His grandfather extended his hand and they shook, eyes locked.

Luke could only hope holding up his end of the bargain wouldn't be as painful as he expected it would be.

* * *

Eugene stared at the phone as he slowly ate the rest of his crackers. He had to admit the lunch menu had been more attractive at Cassie's house. Nothing against Luke, but so was the company.

He let out a deep sigh, contemplating his grandson's words about moving on. The boy had a point. Eugene's sweet wife had told him in their youth she'd want him to love again if anything ever happened to her.

His heart twisted, aching in his chest. Of course, they'd never imagined she'd die so young.

The widow had snagged his affections after all his years of carefully avoiding women. He grimaced. No wonder Luke was so cautious in matters of the heart. Just look at the example he'd been given.

Eugene reached for the phone, juggling the receiver in one hand as he dialed Cassie's number from heart. She answered on the third ring, her sweet voice drifting across the telephone line to tease his senses.

He swallowed, saying nothing.

"Hello. Is anyone there?" Impatience mixed with something else in her tone. Sadness?

Eugene lowered the receiver back to its base, hanging up. No matter what Luke said, he couldn't do this. He wasn't willing to put his heart back on the line. At his age, he ought to be planning for a happy death, not thinking about courting the widow Pettigrew and her poodle.

Coward.

He'd used the word on Luke, and now he was forced to use it on himself. He'd become a coward.

He sucked in a fortifying breath, lifted the receiver once more, and hit the phone's redial button.

Cassie answered almost immediately.

Eugene slammed down the receiver as soon as he heard her voice.

Maybe he could tell Luke the widow had rejected his advances. Then he'd never have to admit he'd been full of hot air.

Cherry sat at the kitchen island, nursing yet another cup of coffee. She was into her third day of poker lessons with Yogi and, quite frankly, her brain hurt. Of course, the mask he wore did nothing to make his instruction any easier to understand.

The mystery of where Monty and Lucky had been the night before was no longer a mystery at all. Apparently, Monty had decided he'd like a moonlit stroll, and he'd taken his new buddy, Lucky, along—without a leash. The smell of skunk permeating the house today proved what a brilliant idea that had been.

If Cherry couldn't get the pungent aroma out before the *Mystic Living* photo shoot, her father wouldn't have to worry about Moose's boss. She'd gladly hand the man Monty's head on a platter.

"I really ought to wring your neck," she muttered in her father's direction.

He sat, supervising her training. The wayward— and very pink—poodle sat obediently at his feet.

Monty shrugged. "You need to let the dog be a dog." He looked down at Lucky, who returned a loving gaze. "Look at him. He's pink, for crying out loud. You keep it up, you'll turn him into a girl."

Cherry frowned. "He wouldn't be pink if he didn't keep humping the skunk."

"Atta boy, Lucky." Monty hoisted his coffee cup in a toast to the dog, who acknowledged the honor by rolling over onto his back, hoisting his pink paws into the air.

"Yogi needs quiet, please." The artist-slash-poker-teacher's eyes squinted above his surgical mask.

"Sorry," Monty muttered. He shook his head. "You know, the smell's really not that bad once you get used to it."

"Silence."

Cherry smiled. Her life might be spiraling out of control, but no one could say it was boring. Not by a long shot. Moose had called earlier that morning and wanted to meet her that night to set the details for the game. She hadn't mentioned the little thug's run-in with Lucky, thinking it best to pretend the entire incident had never happened.

She wondered momentarily if Yogi would be available for bodyguard duty. She was fairly certain the ponytail-wearing painter would have no problem kicking Moose's ass if he got out of line.

She glanced at her father with an entirely different perspective this morning. Sure, he'd gotten the dog skunked again on his watch, but how could she be angry with a man who'd carried his family treasures around in his steamer trunk for the past ten years?

"Today, we're focusing on seven-card stud," Yogi said as he dealt the cards.

Two hours later, her father and the dog had grown bored. They'd left her high and dry—alone with Yogi—and her head was spinning.

Her sole hope for extracting her carefully planned life intact from the chaos that was her father, her mother, Moose, and Luke sat across the kitchen island from her, staring over the top of his surgical mask.

She carefully studied the hand he'd dealt and tried not to make a face. The sides of Yogi's mask puffed out and in, out and in.

She glanced up at his expression, trying to decide on her strategy. "You aren't making this easy for me."

"No?" The mask muffled his voice, making him even more difficult to understand than usual.

"You look ridiculous." She pointed to the lower half of his face.

"There's no accounting for taste."

No kidding.

"How am I supposed to judge your poker face when I can't see half of it?"

He lifted and lowered his bony shoulders, covered today by a glossy, checkered shirt. "You must learn to read your opponent's eyes."

"'You must learn to read your opponent's eyes,'" Cherry repeated in a mumble. "You sound like a broken record."

"You should not mock Yogi. Yogi will make you a champ."

"I don't need to be champ." She blew out a deep breath. "I just need to win one match." She met his gaze, hoping he'd understand how serious she was. "It's a matter of life or . . . fingers."

"There is no need for dramatics." He rolled his eyes.

This, from the king himself.

She studied the five cards in front of her, lined up in a tidy row. Two tens. One three. A queen. One four. Unless Yogi had a royal or straight flush, she had him. And based on the cards he was showing, there was no way.

"I'll raise you another twenty," she said, hoping she'd finally gotten the terminology down pat.

He studied her face, and she concentrated on keeping her features steady. Confident. Strong.

"Yogi folds." He tapped the top of the island. "Show your cards."

She turned over her hold cards, splaying them on the table as he'd taught her. Two more tens. Four of a kind.

"Ah." Pride shone in his expression—at least the part of his expression visible above his mask. "You're going to make Yogi very proud."

She should be so lucky.

Luke measured the enthusiasm on the director's face, unease churning in his gut.

This time last week, he'd never heard of Cherry Harte or her millions. Now, he'd become the chosen one in the quest to help her part with one of those millions in order to save the Youth Center.

Even worse than the anticipation of how she'd react when he made the request was the fear he'd experience another total restraint meltdown.

There was no denying the truth. The spunky blond socialite rendered useless every defense mechanism he'd worked so hard to perfect.

The director launched into an explanation of needs-assessment pitching, excitement beaming from his expression. "The key is to identify what need the Youth Center fulfills for Ms. Harte. Does she want recognition? We can give her that. Does she want to sleep well at night, knowing she's helped children? We can give her that, too."

Luke nodded, pretending to listen, yet unable to wrench his thoughts from which of Cherry's needs he'd like to assess. Unfortunately, none of them had a thing to do with money—or kids.

He bit back a groan, wondering how in the hell he could get himself out of this one.

"I've done extensive research on her," the director continued, sliding a stack of articles and reports toward Luke. "Make sure you thoroughly familiarize yourself with everything here."

Luke stared at the pile, amazed at its thickness.

The director patted the papers. "Here you have a printout of every organization she's supported over the past four months, her employment history before that, the purchase and tax information on her home, a report on her family and background. Oh."

He snapped his fingers, as if he'd forgotten the most important thing. "We also know what restaurants and shops she frequents. Try to utilize that in your approach."

Damn. The man had better sources than Luke had back in Miami.

The director narrowed his eyes, apparently trying to stress his final point. "Use tonight's cocktail party to your advantage. Assess her likes and dislikes. Figure out the best way to approach her."

Her likes and dislikes.

Luke was fairly sure she liked the press of his lips against the soft spot at the base of her throat. And she'd responded quite positively to his hand snaking up beneath her dress.

Damn it. Why couldn't he get the woman out of his head? After the way she'd left last night, he had no doubt she'd shoved him out of hers.

"Are you listening?" The director's impatience was palpable in his tone.

Luke blew out a breath. "Absolutely."

The director's chair scraped back as he stood. "I'll leave you alone to go through this. You've got a lot here to digest, but I'll check back in a half hour to see if you have any questions."

"Sure thing."

Luke waited until the man's footsteps faded down the hall before he started flipping through the stack.

At first he found nothing that he hadn't seen before. The same photocopied article about her lottery win. The same shot of her and Liz at a children's hospital. A list of previous employers.

That caught his attention. It seemed Cherry Harte had been a hard worker—a very hard worker—holding down two jobs at all times, and over the course of a few months, three.

He sat back, letting that knowledge sink in. Not exactly what he expected. The woman really *had* transformed herself. Without seeing these papers, he wouldn't have guessed she'd so much as broken a nail in her past life.

He continued to flip, not finding a whole lot his grandfather and the widow Pettigrew hadn't already given him, until he reached her family information.

Sister: Liz Harte.

Mother: Fran Harte.

Father: Monty Harte.

Whoa.

Luke pushed back from the table. Monty was

her *father*? Why on earth would she have said the man was her butler? Was she that ashamed of where she'd come from that she'd lied?

He skimmed the printouts on Monty but came up with nothing more than the fact the man had been a resident of Reno, Nevada, for the past ten years—and a casino employee.

Her mother, apparently, had a record of shoplifting—although nowhere in the paperwork did Luke find information on the woman's current situation or residence.

He sat back against the chair and crossed his arms over his chest, thinking. The family history hinted at here was not the typically spotless lineage the Women's League required.

No wonder Cherry worked so hard to keep her old life out of her new one. Her past held secrets that would toss her carefully crafted identity on its ass.

Packaging issues.

Understatement of the century.

He flipped through the rest of the reports but was unable to find any additional information that might explain why someone had tampered with her car. Not that it mattered. What he'd found was intriguing as hell.

For a fleeting moment, he thought about holding his new findings over Cherry's head when he made the funding request, but blackmail had never been his style. But just because he didn't believe in blackmail didn't mean he wasn't going to press for the full truth.

Luke pushed back from the table and gathered the paperwork. He'd assess Cherry's needs, all right. Right after he got the woman to explain her family tree.

"Anything you can use?" The director's voice sounded behind him.

Had it been a half hour already?

Luke nodded toward the pile of paperwork. He needed to find out how much the man knew. "Have you gone through these already?"

"No." The director patted him on the shoulder. "I trust you to use them to your full advantage."

As Luke walked out of the building and back toward his car, clutching the bundle of printouts in his arms, that's exactly what he intended to do.

Maybe then, he'd finally understand what made Cherry Harte tick.

CHAPTER 16

Cherry sipped her sparkling water and watched the cocktail party from a dark corner of the room. Her brain hurt from playing so much poker, and the risk of making a fool of herself by slipping the words *straight* or *fold* or *flush* into conversation with the beautiful people of Mystic Beach made it safer to keep to herself.

Plus, this made it easier to avoid Luke.

She took another sip of her water and studied the room.

Cocktail-party guests mingled as caterers circulated trays loaded with high-end finger food suited for the social elite of Mystic Beach. A scale replica of the proposed Horticultural Center sat off to one side, surrounded by no one. Monique held court in the center of the room, bemoaning the difficulties of running a charitable women's group.

A longtime Women's Leaguer sidled up to Cherry, holding her wineglass lip-high. "That woman would stick a knife in her gut if it would get her attention."

Cherry sputtered on her water. "Pardon?"

She'd never heard a single member say an unkind thing about Monique. The admission was shocking, startling, out of left field—and funny.

Cherry blinked at the woman, who winked in return.

Cherry laughed, then steadied herself. She raised her own glass in front of her lips and talked out of the side of her mouth. "What I'd like to know is, what's the deal with the little voice recorder?"

The woman smiled and tipped her head. "Honey, there are more than a few of us who'd like to stick that thing where the sun doesn't shine." She tipped her head toward Monique. "Be careful of that one."

As the woman stepped away, she looked back at Cherry and winked again.

Cherry, on the other hand, concentrated furiously on giving the mental signal to her brain to snap her jaw shut. The woman's remarks might have been wine induced, but apparently things at the Women's League weren't as rosy—or as beige—as they appeared.

When she realized she'd stepped out into a bright area of the room, she pressed back into the dim corner, scanning the crowd for Luke.

He hadn't said a word to her all night, not that she'd expected him to. He and the other representatives of the Youth Center stood in a pack, huddled like a school of fish seeking protection from the sharks and their queen.

The contrast between this meeting and yesterday's Youth Center tour was striking. Having spent the evening fishing with Luke and the boys, Cherry couldn't help but wonder if she wasn't supporting the wrong cause.

Sure, her contribution to the Horticultural Center secured her Women's League membership, but wouldn't she rather be helping kids? Liz would love that. Heck, her sister spent every free minute over at the children's hospital and had been urging Cherry to start their own foundation.

Maybe Luke had been right. Perhaps Cherry needed to stop staring at her goal poster and start following her heart.

As she watched, the handsome mechanic shifted in her direction. Cherry moved away, sliding along the wall. She wasn't quite ready to face his music. Memories of her exit last night had made her cringe this morning.

She'd thought about trusting him and spilling the beans about Monty and his debt. Who knew? Perhaps Luke and his Miami resources could help her beat Moose and his boss at their own game.

Luke shifted closer still, now meeting her eye. She smiled, but his gaze only narrowed into a glare. Cherry twisted to look behind her. No one there. Luke's lethal look had been intended solely for her.

She might have softened in her position overnight, but apparently Mr. Chance had not. Cherry pivoted and headed toward Monique's private bathroom.

He'd never find her there.

If Cherry thought she was getting away that easily, she'd better think again. Luke still hadn't decided whether or not he'd be hitting her up for the Youth

Center money tonight, though based on what the group had spent on this little shindig, they had money to burn.

Hell, they could buy their own estate for their Horticultural Center. If they were truly charitable, they'd drop from the running and let the Youth Center have the land they needed.

Cherry slipped out into the hall and disappeared around the corner. Luke quickly checked to make sure he wasn't being watched, then beelined straight for her. He no sooner cleared the first wall than he spotted the frilly hem of her black dress as she made a second turn.

There was only one office down that hall— Monique's.

Luke's stomach turned.

The last place he wanted to be was in that woman's space, but he was determined to get to Cherry. If he had to track her to Monique's office, so be it.

Since he'd left the director's office, he'd tried to talk himself out of confronting her about her family, but it had done him no good. His reporter days might be a part of his past, but he couldn't ignore Cherry's hidden story. The fact she ignited sexual cravings he'd thought long dead made it all the more compelling to find out exactly who she was— and if her past had anything to do with the tampered wiring he'd discovered in her car.

Luke reached Monique's office just as the bathroom light flicked on and Cherry started to pull the door shut behind her. He crossed the room in three strides and blocked the door's closure with his foot.

He hated to break it to Cherry, but she'd have to

hold her business a little longer. He had business of his own.

The door snapped open and Cherry glared at him, wide-eyed, her expression a mix of surprise and anger. "Why, Mr. Chance, if you had to use the facilities, all you had to do was knock."

He stepped into the small space with her, clicked the door shut, and flipped the lock. When he backed her toward the sink, her look changed to one of panic.

"I know I left rather abruptly last night, but don't you think you're overreacting?"

He shook his head. "I'm not here about last night."

"You're not?"

"No."

He gripped her elbows and she stiffened beneath his touch, a sharp contrast to her pliable body the night before. A twinge of regret pulsed through him.

He'd been intent on squeezing the truth out of her, yet when he looked into her eyes—when he felt her warmth and smelled her spicy scent—he only wanted . . . her. Suddenly, understanding her family took a backseat to the heat burning in his gut for the woman before him.

Cherry's throat worked and her expression softened. "Are you all right?"

No. He wasn't.

Luke shook his head.

"Is there anything I can do?"

The kindness in her voice broke his restraint, and his need for her poured through. It made no difference how she'd left last night—or who her parents were—he desired the woman standing before him like he'd desired no other.

Cherry's eyes grew huge as he lowered his face to hers.

"Luke?"

The whispered word brushed against his lips just before he closed his mouth over hers. A tiny protest sounded in her throat, but her lips opened to his kiss as if welcoming him home.

Suddenly he couldn't move his hands over her luscious body quickly enough. He needed her. Wanted her. Hungered for her.

Luke pushed against her, pressing his erection against the smooth plane of her stomach. Let there be no doubt as to how she made him feel.

Cherry offered no protest, instead plunging her fingers through his hair, pulling his face tightly against hers. Her mouth moved hot on his. Her body pressed against his with all of her glorious peaks and valleys, twists and turns.

He was lost in her completely, and at that moment, there wasn't a story in the world worth pulling himself back for.

What was it Bart had said? Maybe she'd been wrong to think a plan could make her happy?

Amen to that. For the first time in a long time, Cherry didn't give a damn about her plan or about the women out in the other room pretending to care about the Horticultural Center.

For the first time in a long time, she planned to do what felt right. And at that moment, nothing felt more right than Luke Chance.

After what she'd seen in her father's room last night, she'd tossed and turned, questioning everything, including how she'd walked away from Luke. Maybe there was a way to have it all—her new life, her acceptance, love.

Maybe all she needed was Luke to help her figure it all out.

"Luke?"

His hot mouth had moved to her neck, trailing kisses down the soft hollow at the base of her throat.

Cherry's knees buckled, but she fought through the fog of her desire to tell him her decision. "Luke?"

"What?" He lifted his face to hers, his eyes wild with desire, his cheeks flushed.

"I've decided to tell you about Monty."

Luke shook his head, pressing a kiss to the curve of her jaw. "I know all about Monty."

Her breath hitched as she yielded to his touch. "What do you mean, you know all about Monty?"

"He's not your butler." His lips pressed to her neck now, her earlobe, her cheek. "He's your father."

How in the hell did Luke know Monty was her father?

She pushed him away, holding him at arm's length when every nerve ending in her body begged her to strip naked and let his amazing lips explore her from head to toe.

"What did you just say?"

Luke's eyes appeared to be out of focus, his expression a lusty blur of blatant sexual want. "I said I know Monty's your dad. I read it in the report."

Hot anger blazed in her cheeks and Luke straightened, as if suddenly realizing what he'd said.

"What *report*?" Cherry asked, pushing Luke as far away as the small bathroom would allow.

"The report I . . . found."

Sad resignation edged out any remaining lust that had flowed through Cherry's veins. He'd smelled a story and gone after it, instead of backing off. "You wanted a story, right? And I just happened to be the most convenient one. Me and my family."

Luke shook his head. "It's not like that. I just want to understand you."

"I'm sure."

Cherry smoothed her dress, then checked her make-up in the mirror. She held her features straight, not wanting to show the fear tangling with the anger inside her. If Luke had found out about Monty, it wouldn't be long before he put the other pieces together.

She moved toward the door. "If you'll excuse me, I have another meeting tonight."

Luke's features tensed. "For your precious Horticultural Center?"

Cherry reached around him, grabbing for the doorknob. "Yes," she lied. She sure as hell wasn't about to tell him she was meeting Moose.

"What do you think Monique would say into her recorder if she knew about your family?" He grasped her elbow, trying to block her from leaving.

Anger flashed through Cherry. "You wouldn't dare."

He arched one brow and her stomach flipped.

If Luke exposed her parents' true identities, she'd be out of the Women's League so fast her head would spin. Even more important, she couldn't risk him discovering anything that might jeopardize the poker game.

"Leave my family alone." She pulled the bathroom door open and stepped out into Monique's office. "And you and I"—she jabbed a finger into his chest—"we're done meeting like this."

She hurried toward the hallway but stopped to look back at him one last time. Her head hurt with the turmoil of emotions that battled inside. "There's your story."

Then she turned and fled for the parking lot, unable to believe that at least part of her carefully kept secret was out, and she was at Luke's mercy as to how far out it got.

The director ambushed Luke as soon as he reentered the main room. "Did you make the request?"

The request? Not hardly. He'd been too busy blowing what little restraint he'd had left. "She was in a rush. I'll have to ask her later."

"She left?" The director glanced around the room, then his gaze settled back on Luke.

Luke nodded, trying to focus on the director's line of questioning when all he could think about was how badly he'd screwed up his planned interrogation of Cherry.

That was the downside to being male. When presented with the woman of your lust-filled dreams in a small, enclosed space, you tended to forget why you were there in the first place.

"She had a meeting," he said, willing the director to leave him alone so that he could go after Cherry. He reached into the pocket of his jacket but came up empty. "You wouldn't happen to have any gum, would you?"

The director shot him a puzzled look and frowned. "Who was she meeting with?"

Luke shook his head. "Something about the Horticultural Center. I'm not sure."

"Do you think it was an additional funding source?" The director squinted, steepling his fingers. "We can't seem to secure one, yet I've heard rumblings they're on their way to a second."

He patted Luke's arm as he turned away. "Keep at her. We can't afford to lose this campaign. We've got to do whatever it takes."

Whatever it takes. The man's words bounced around Luke's brain as he headed for his car. As much as he wanted the Framingham Estate for the Youth Center, he was not about to let the director find out about whatever had gone on in Cherry's past—at least not until he'd figured it out himself.

When he reached the parking lot, her car was nowhere to be found.

Damn.

He scrubbed a hand across his tired eyes and let out a frustrated breath. One thing was certain. The woman might run, but he was not about to let her get away.

When Cherry walked back into the house, Monty, Yogi, and Lucky sat like three peas in a pod eating popcorn and watching television.

Yogi had donned a fresh mask, which he lifted for each morsel of popcorn he slipped into his mouth.

"Cherry," her father called out. "You're just in time. Where's your sister?"

"She should be back any minute." At least, she'd better be.

Liz had promised to put Cherry in full disguise for her meeting with Moose. The last thing she needed was anyone spotting her having drinks with a three-foot thug. "What's going on?"

Her father patted the sofa cushion next to him and punched up the volume on the Food Network. He pressed a finger to his lips. "Quiet down, now. I promised your mother I'd have you watch this."

"Mom? You talked to Mom?"

"Every Sunday night." He waved her over. "Hurry, before you miss it."

Cherry sank onto the sofa next to him. Lucky blinked and sneered as if she'd interrupted boys' night. She stuck her tongue out at the curly, pink fur ball, then focused on the television screen.

A title appeared on the screen. *Cooking Behind Bars.*

She nodded toward the screen. "What's this?"

"Your mother's taken up baking."

Cherry swallowed. Hard. "What?" Dread danced at the pit of her belly.

"Just watch."

The camera panned across an industrial-looking kitchen, then zoomed in on the petite, well-coifed Fran Harte in her best jailhouse blues. Her rinse had faded, and her once-blond curls had turned more silver than anything else. The gleam in her eyes, however, shone more brightly than ever.

"Why . . . is Mommy . . . on TV?" Cherry jumped to her feet.

"Isn't it great?" Monty's voice had gone all chipper and light. "They picked her coffee cake recipe out of hundreds. Hundreds!"

Her mother waved to the camera. "I want to give a big shout out to my husband, Monty, and my daughters, Cherry and Liz, down in Mystic Beach, Florida. My parole hearing's coming up in a few months. Hang in there, gang."

Cherry sank to her knees and shuffled closer to the screen. Surely, she must be dreaming. There was no way Fran Harte could be on television, outing Cherry and her false heritage to the world. Yet there she was.

It was bad enough that Luke had apparently uncovered something on Monty, but this . . . this was incomprehensible.

"Is this a local New Jersey show you're picking up on satellite?" Cherry's voice squeaked, it had grown so tight with dread.

"National cable." Monty beamed. "I'm so proud."

"Proud," Cherry whispered. And busted. Cherry could only hope the members of the Women's League hadn't gotten home from the party, and if they had, they weren't big into cooking. Luke she wasn't worried about. The man screamed anything but domestic.

She watched her mother flit about the women's correctional kitchen—sifting, mixing, chatting as if she owned the joint.

One thing was certain. Her mother's less-than-subtle appearance added a whole new twist to her family problems. She might be able to keep Monty and the poker game a secret, but if Monique

Goodall caught wind of Fran Harte's cable-television debut, Cherry could kiss her society ass good-bye.

"Would you turn that off?" Luke called out to Gramps. "How can you watch those shows hour after hour?"

He'd been so frustrated with Cherry and his own lack of willpower that he'd gone back to the shop to work. While hard labor usually helped his state of mind, right now he waffled between wanting to throttle the woman and wanting to make love to her until he fell unconscious. Not to mention the fact he'd crammed so much gum in his mouth, his jaw hurt.

"I could go any second, son. Show some respect."

"Gramps." Luke stepped close, eyeing the screen. The Food Network. Just what he needed. A talking head who sounded gratingly familiar—like an older Cherry Harte. "Number one, you're healthy as a horse. Number two, what in the hell are you watching the Food Network for?"

"I was thinking about whipping up a dinner for the widow sometime." His voice dropped low. "In case I ever see her again."

"You haven't called her?" Luke asked.

"I left a message," Gramps mumbled.

Luke couldn't help but notice that the older man's fingers were crossed. Just then, his grandfather pointed excitedly at the screen. "This show's a doozy. There are some serious gourmet cooks behind bars in this country."

Luke bit back a laugh. He had no doubt. His thoughts were interrupted, however, when the convict on screen shouted out a greeting to her family. Her family in Mystic Beach, Florida—including her daughter Cherry.

Luke dropped the wrench he'd been holding, and it clattered against the concrete floor.

"Well, I'll be," Gramps mumbled. "That's some coincidence."

"That is no coincidence." Luke headed for his car.

So that explained the missing whereabouts of Cherry's mother. No wonder she'd panicked and run when she'd found out he knew about her father. Monty Harte appeared to be only the tip of the family iceberg.

And suddenly, Luke had no plans to wait until morning to get the full story on the rest of her family tree.

CHAPTER 17

Liz pranced into the house just after Fran's segment had ended. She eyed the group gathered in the living room. "Did I miss something?"

Cherry turned to face her, blinking at the curly pink wig her sister sported. Her entire family had gone insane. What other explanation could there be for the events of the past week?

"Yogi has just witnessed a genius at work," the artist proclaimed. "Your mother has magic fingers."

Liz squinted at Cherry. "I'm afraid to ask."

Cherry climbed to her feet and ran a hand over her exhausted face. All this, and now she had to go meet with Moose. "Mom just made her Food Network debut."

Liz snorted. "Bet that wasn't on your goal poster."

Hardly. Cherry frowned at her sister but turned on her father.

"Do you want to explain why you vanished from our lives but carry around every memory you could possibly pack into your steamer trunk?"

"So much for letting him come to us." Liz kicked off her shoes and dropped into a chair.

Lucky jumped out of Monty's lap and catapulted into Liz's. Cherry couldn't help but notice that Liz's curls matched Lucky's juice-stained fur.

She refocused on their father, noticing he'd gone a bit pale.

"I didn't want to leave you two behind, but she'd have been lost without you. Hell." He took a swig from his crystal tumbler, then rubbed his mustache. "I was lost without you girls, but your mother wanted me out."

Liz gasped and Cherry frowned. Not exactly the story Fran Harte had weaned them on. "What do you mean, she wanted you out?"

"She wanted better *things*." He emphasized the word as if it were evil. "Wait until she gets a load of this place." He gestured toward the cathedral ceiling and the foyer, then blew out a dramatic breath. "You'll never be able to get her to leave."

Cherry eyed Monty and Yogi, side by side on the sofa, looking awfully comfortable with their popcorn bowl between them. He was probably right. Her picture-perfect paradise villa had morphed into a commune for wayward relatives—and poker teachers.

"Anyway," Monty continued, "your mother thought that if I went out west, I'd make better money. I lied and told her I was scamming the casinos because it fed into her dreams of adventure."

He scratched his chin and shook his head. "Would you believe she used to have a poster in our bedroom of all the things she wanted? All the places she wanted to see? She said she had to visualize things to make them come true."

Cherry flashed on her own goal poster, plastered to the wall of the master suite, and winced. She stole a peek at Liz, who met her gaze and grimaced sympathetically.

"I was never good enough," Monty added. "No matter what I sent home, no matter what I bought her, I couldn't give her what she needed."

"So what did you really do?" Liz asked.

"Room service." He shrugged.

"Room service?" Cherry couldn't believe it. All these years, she and Liz had thought their father was a con man who'd deserted them for a life of scams. In the course of twenty-four hours, they'd learned he'd worked an honest job on the other side of the country, trying only to earn his way back into their mother's heart.

Then she remembered his huge debt. "So how did you lose two hundred and fifty thousand playing craps?"

"An old friend of mine said he knew someone who could get your mother out of jail. His son." He stared at the floor, apparently no longer able to face his daughters' amazed expressions. "I didn't have any money, so he let me borrow against the house."

Everyone had fallen silent. Except Lucky. The pink fur ball had lost interest early on and snored loudly, belly-up in the chair.

"I made a mistake." Monty's voice cut through the quiet room. "And I should have come home when she started stealing. I never thought it would get so bad."

"But why did this guy threaten to hurt Mom?" Cherry asked. "That seems a bit extreme."

"That wasn't my buddy." Monty shook his head. "That was his son. The guy who's coming here to play you." He pointed at Cherry. "He believes lessons are important."

Great.

She frowned. "I thought I was playing the boss?"

"The son is the boss now." Her father took another hit of his cocktail. "Next generation. Not so nice."

"Surely he can't get away with hurting Mom in jail?" Liz asked. "He'd never be able to pull it off."

"He's done it before." Monty shrugged. "You'd be amazed what this guy's gotten away with. He's got casino and real estate investments in five states and takes his success—and his pride—seriously. When I couldn't pay my debt to his family, he took it personally."

"Then why did you do it?" The vein over Cherry's left eye had begun a steady drumming. It seemed the more she thought she understood the people in her life, the more confusing they became.

"I love Frannie." Monty's voice took on a defeated note and he dropped his face into his hands.

Cherry's heart broke for the man she realized she didn't know at all.

"I'd do anything for her," her father added softly.

Cherry straightened and took a deep breath. "Don't worry, Dad. I won't let you down."

Liz jumped to her feet. "Neither will I."

Yogi lowered his mask and the elastic snapped against his neck. He crossed to where Cherry stood, sucked in his cheeks, and planted his palms firmly on her shoulders. "All you need is within you now."

Did the man know no boundaries? First her popcorn, now her affirmation CDs.

She rolled her eyes, stepped free of Yogi's grip, and headed for the staircase. She had to get ready for her meeting with Moose.

She'd always resented being named for a slot-machine symbol, but right now Cherry needed all the luck she could get. If she played her cards right—literally—maybe this time she could fix things so they'd all come out on top.

Luke reached the gated entrance to Cherry's community just as her Jag zipped onto the street. He pulled a U-turn and followed, determined to get to the bottom of whatever was going on.

Five minutes later, her car pulled to a stop in front of the Mystic Grille. Liz hopped to the curb, sporting a long pink wig.

Packaging issues.

He pulled his car around the side of the restaurant, watching as Cherry parked her car and climbed out. His gut twisted as he stared into his rearview mirror. She wore a long black wig, the tightest spotted pants he'd ever seen, and her high-heeled red shoes.

Just what in the hell kind of meeting was she headed to?

He waited until she'd disappeared through the Grille's front doors before he climbed out of his car. At least locating her inside wouldn't be a problem. The woman was bound to stick out like a sore thumb.

Suddenly, understanding Cherry's family paled

in comparison to figuring out just what the woman herself was up to. And he was fairly certain her meeting had nothing to do with the Horticultural Center.

Cherry grimaced as Moose leaned across the small round table to squeeze her hand. "Maybe after the poker game, you and I can head out to Reno, sweet cheeks. Love the hair, by the way."

Her stomach rolled sour and she extracted her hand from his grubby little mitt, glancing over to where Liz sat at the bar. Liz had agreed to step in if needed. All Cherry had to do was give the signal.

She turned back to face Moose, straightened in her seat, and pasted on a phony expression of confidence. Truth was, he was the scariest little man she'd ever set eyes on.

"Let's cut to the chase, Mr. Buck. I plan to kick your boss's ass, so all we need to do is set the time and place for the game and I'll be on my way."

His raspy laugh started low in his belly and worked its way higher, growing louder and louder. Cherry slouched in her stool, hoping no one she knew was in the bar. The wig wasn't a foolproof disguise, and she certainly hadn't counted on Moose drawing attention, for crying out loud.

"Can you try to be a little more discreet." She leaned toward him. "Some of us have to live in this town."

The little man pulled a toothpick from the breast pocket of his suit jacket and stuck it between his lips. "Sweet cheeks, if you don't mind me saying so, you look like you've never had a discreet day in your life."

Cherry narrowed her eyes, fighting the urge to kick his stool out from under him.

Every day, in every way, I'm getting better and better. All I need is within me now.

Who was she kidding? "Oh, screw it."

The little man waggled his brows. "Honey, I thought you'd never ask."

"No." Cherry leaned back on her stool and waved off his sexual delusions. "I wasn't talking to you." She tapped her watch. "It's late. What's the plan?"

"Four o'clock. Day after tomorrow."

She shook her head. "That's no good for me." Her mind raced. She had the *Mystic Living* photo shoot at five and the final Development Commission announcement at six. She'd never be able to pull off a poker game at four o'clock.

Moose let loose with another stare-inviting laugh. "The boss said four o'clock. Day after tomorrow."

"Well, it's not good for—"

"Hey!"

The sharp tone of his voice stopped Cherry's head midshake. "All right. I'll deal with it." How, she had no idea, but she'd think of something. "What type of game?"

"Poker." He shot her a how-dumb-can-you-be sort of look.

"No." Cherry rolled her eyes. "Seven-card stud? Texas hold 'em? What?"

"You'll find out when the boss tells you."

She narrowed her glare. She didn't stand a chance if she couldn't practice. "Look, I need to know what—"

Moose leaned forward and dropped his voice menacingly. "You'd better put on your big-girl panties and deal with not knowing, 'cause that's the way it's going to be. Understood?"

Oh, she understood all right. She understood it was time to get away from the tiny man—before she wrapped her fingers around his little nasty neck and squeezed.

Cherry reached up for a lock of the wig's hair and began to twist it around one finger.

Moose rolled his toothpick from one side of his mouth to the other. "You know," he pointed toward her head, "I read in *Cosmo* where that's a sign of sexual frustration." He puffed out his chest. "Trust me when I tell you it's not the size of the package, but what you do with it."

Good grief.

Cherry scowled at him and twirled her hair faster.

Did *everyone* have packaging issues?

And where in the hell was Liz?

"Hey, sailor." Liz slid onto the bar stool next to Luke. "Come here often?"

Luke choked on his beer. Damn. He should have anticipated one of the sisters spotting him in the crowd. Oh well. If nothing else, he might be able to get some information about exactly what it was they were up to.

He eyed today's wig. "Nice package."

"What's that?" Liz's pert nose wrinkled.

"Inside joke." He took a drag on his beer and tipped his head toward Cherry's table. "Want to tell me what's going on over there?"

Liz made a snapping noise with her mouth. "Not for me to say, is it?" She patted him on the shoulder. "Nice try, though. Very smooth delivery."

Luke couldn't help but grin. "I do my best." He refocused on Cherry. "Isn't it a little early for trick-or-treat?"

Liz scowled. "There's nothing wrong with dressing up."

He glanced at her pink wig and shook his head.

Maybe the Harte family was in some sort of trouble. It would explain the secrets—and the outfits. The next time he tried to force Cherry into full disclosure, he'd stand firm against the seductive pull she had over him.

He stole another look at Liz and had a thought. Maybe he'd start with the Harte at hand.

"So that must be the wire-tampering Moose?" he bluffed.

"Oh." Liz turned to face him, surprise painting her features. "I didn't know she'd told you that. Yeah." She nodded.

If bluffing had worked once, it was worth trying twice. "So who's this guy after? Monty?"

Liz frowned and shook her head. "No. This guy's setting everything up."

She jumped down from her stool before Luke could get any more information out of her. "Gotta go. That's my sign."

Luke snapped his attention to Cherry. She sat twirling a long, black curl around one finger. The seductive move ignited a traitorous longing deep in his core. Damn, but the woman made him weak.

He needed to find out exactly who Moose was, and this time he wasn't about to let Cherry and their shared sexual chemistry throw him off course. He slapped a ten on the bar and headed for the back door.

The only way to avoid Cherry was to seek another source for information. It was time to call some old friends.

"Ready to go?" Liz asked, leaning across the table.

Cherry took full advantage of the way Moose had zeroed in on her sister's cleavage. She grabbed her purse and slid down from her stool. "See you the day after tomorrow."

Moose laughed again and the sound boiled Cherry's blood. "You dumb broads better guess again if you think you can beat the boss at his own game." He struggled down from his stool and stood there, hands on hips, shaking his head, belly laughing. "My money's on the two of you being losers—just like your old man."

Cherry inhaled sharply, struggling for a way to control her murderous urge. Liz, on the other hand, must have left her restraint at home. She glared down at Moose and kicked him, right in the knee.

He went down like a house of cards.

"Shit. You kicked me."

"Sorry." Liz grabbed Cherry's arm and hurried her toward the door. "I slipped."

"Nice hit."

"Thanks." Liz giggled. "I think my technique's improving. Hey." She came to an abrupt stop, yanking on Cherry's arm. "Did you see your boyfriend?"

"Who?"

"You know who." Liz scanned the bar, frowning. "That's funny, he was right over there." Her features fell. "I figured he came to protect you. He was watching your every move. That man has it bad, I'm telling you."

Cherry suddenly felt ill, and it wasn't just from spending time with Moose. "Who?" she repeated, not sure she really wanted to hear the answer.

"Luke." Liz's forehead puckered. "You mean he didn't tell you he was going to be here? I thought you two had it planned." She gave a quick shrug. "He knows Moose was the one who messed with your car."

Cherry's heart hit her toes. He knew about Moose as well as Monty? Why was the man so determined to figure out her life?

As much as she wanted to believe he was concerned for her well-being, she couldn't help but face facts. If Luke exposed her now, his Youth Center would be a shoo-in for the Framingham Estate. The scandal alone would rock the Women's League—and their Horticultural Center.

What the hell was he up to? And why did he care?

She had her answer the next morning when Liz tossed the morning paper on top of her bed. Cherry threw back the covers and followed the line of Liz's finger to the headline.

Local Socialite Leads Double Life.

"Son of a bitch." Cherry rubbed her tired eyes and stared at the front-page photo of Moose leering at her across the table.

"The good news," Liz said as she handed Cherry a steaming cup of coffee, "is they pegged you for a hooker." She tipped her still-pink-wigged head from side to side and wrinkled her nose. "The bad news is Monique already called and said she expects you at the office as soon as you're awake."

Cherry sagged, unable to believe her eyes.

There was only one person who could have done this. One person with the newspaper contacts, the nose for news, and the front-row seat.

Luke Chance.

Her tattoo itched and she groaned.

He'd proven to be a major life change, all right, but certainly in no way she'd ever imagined.

CHAPTER 18

Gramps slapped the morning paper on top of Luke's desk, and Luke growled.

He'd been in the zone for hours, making calls and doing research on the Hartes. His notes and printouts lay scattered wide across the work surface, and the last thing he needed was a newspaper in his face.

"Hey." He stopped midprotest when his focus landed on the front-page headline.

Local Socialite Leads Double Life.

"What the—?"

He recognized the shot instantly as having been taken last night in the bar. Whoever had snapped the photo must have been operating without a flash, but how could Luke have missed a photographer? Maybe he *had* been in hibernation too long. His razor-sharp instincts back in Miami would have picked up a fellow journalist a mile away.

Luke studied the photo of Cherry in her sky-high red heels, her spotted, skintight pants and the long, black curly wig.

Was it any wonder he'd lost his edge? Just look

at the bombshell who'd turned his status quo on its ear.

"Says our Cherry's a nightwalker," Gramps said, hurt palpable in his voice.

"A vampire?" Luke couldn't help but tease, but felt guilty instantly. His grandfather had been genuinely upset by the article. He could only imagine how seeing the article had affected Cherry.

"A hooker, son."

"Gramps." Luke reached out to pat the older man's arm, trying to soothe the distress painted across his face. "Even Cherry doesn't have that many issues." Though heaven knew the woman had plenty.

Not the least of which was this article. Who'd snapped the shot? And why?

"It's probably just some freelancer out for a few bucks." He pointed at the trash can. "Just look at all the articles you found on her. She's a big lottery winner. Everyone wants a story."

And he should know. He planned to be first in line when the woman explained just what in the hell was going on in her life.

He scanned the text but came up with nothing more than speculation and circumstantial evidence. Heck, the reporter hadn't cited a single source.

"This is garbage." He tapped the newsprint.

Although if he knew Monique, her little recorder would blow a fuse over this piece of so-called news. He seriously doubted front-page hooker-costume photos fell under the approved activities column in the Women's League handbook.

Chances were pretty good this was not going to help the Horticultural Center in the final selection, nor was it going to help Cherry in her quest to package her life.

His gut caught and twisted. He didn't want to care how this would impact her plans, but he did.

Luke squinted at the newspaper photo. If he could figure out the exact identity and employer of the little man with Cherry, perhaps he could help her find a way out of the mess she was in.

Of course, if she'd trust him enough to confide in him, it would save everyone a whole lot of time.

Luke shook his head. She'd made it clear that wasn't going to happen.

No. He tapped his pencil to the newspaper, then circled the image of Moose. He'd fax this photo to some of his old newspaper buddies. After all, you never knew what interesting tidbits might turn up.

The basic questions still remained the same, but now there was a new wrinkle. Who had tipped the newspaper, and why? Luke shook his head. The puzzle had gotten more complex, but one thing seemed obvious.

Cherry Harte had far more to worry about than packaging issues.

Partway through Monique's diatribe on social responsibility and appearance, Cherry began to fantasize about how far down the woman's throat she could shove the little recorder.

Maybe Luke had been right. The only reason the Women's League had considered Cherry for membership was her money. She'd been kidding herself to think she'd ever be a full-fledged member of the beige people.

Hell. Just look at the last week of her life. There was nothing beige about her.

She glanced back at Monique, who continued to make suggestions into her recorder. Surely, there would always be another hoity-toity organization more than happy to welcome her checkbook balance with open arms.

Cherry's heart gave a disappointed flip. It wouldn't be the Women's League—the crème de la crème—but maybe that wasn't the worst thing that could happen in her life.

Hell. She knew it wasn't.

Liz had never been very good with money, but she had made an interesting suggestion. Maybe the two of them should start their own foundation. They could both get little recorders and play constructive criticism just like the big boys.

She winced. So not their style. But the whole foundation concept had merit.

Cherry pulled her focus back to the verbal thrashing at hand. Any time now, Monique was bound to get to her point, and Cherry had no doubt about what that point would be. Her membership application was about to be stamped *NO* in big red letters.

She wasn't worried, though. Right after she murdered Luke for setting her up, got the paper to print a retraction, and let Monique finish recording her shortcomings for the permanent membership record, she'd simply revamp her goal poster.

Check that. Right after she won the poker game, she'd revamp her goal poster. First things first.

"I just can't imagine what you were thinking." Monique clucked her tongue as she snapped off the recorder.

Finally.

"Why were you dressed like that in the first place?"

"Family joke." Cherry shrugged.

What the hell, it wasn't a complete stretch of the truth. These days, her family *was* the joke.

"And that *hair.*" Monique splayed a perfectly polished hand across her chest. "What were you thinking?"

"Well," Cherry leaned forward and waggled her brows, "you did once suggest I go a few shades darker."

Monique's eyes narrowed to angry slits. "Have you been drinking?"

Cherry frowned. "Not an entirely unappealing idea, but no."

Maybe she should tell Monique the truth.

She'd been at a clandestine meeting with a tiny thug who'd been charged with planning the poker game that would help her clear her father's gambling debt and save her jailed mother's fingers.

Cherry started to giggle. She just couldn't help herself. The whole situation was utterly, totally, preposterously unbelievable.

Her giggle morphed into full-blown laughter. The laughter took on a life of its own, shaking her so hard she hugged herself and held on as tears streamed down her cheeks.

"Are you quite sure you're not drunk?"

"Quite," Cherry sputtered. She stood and grabbed her purse from the floor, wiping the tears from beneath her eyelashes. "Are we through?"

"Quite." The chill in Monique's tone was palpable. "All I need is your check."

Check? "For what? I'm sure I'm no longer a provisional member, right?"

"For the Horticultural Center." Monique straightened and stared directly into Cherry's eyes. "Surely you know a pledge is a pledge."

"I don't think so." Cherry took two steps toward the door.

"Ms. Harte."

Uh-oh. Formal name. The woman meant business.

"Can you imagine the field day the paper will have with you once they learn you've jeopardized the entire Horticultural Center campaign?"

Cherry blinked. Maybe Liz had the right idea from day one. She *should* be rolling around on a beach somewhere with the cabana boy. This socialite crap was for the birds.

"I was only giving you money to improve my status and reputation." She shook her head. "I don't think that plan has gone well so far, do you?"

"Well, if you want to save what little reputation you've got left, you'll ante up. Otherwise, I'll make sure the paper does a full-page story that will run you out of town."

Ante up. Hell. The poker game.

She needed to keep up appearances just long enough to avoid drawing any more attention to herself—or her family.

"Do you watch the Food Network?"

Monique screwed up her face. "The what?"

Well, that was one encouraging sign in the fiasco that had become her life. She might be plastered all over the front page of the paper, but her mother's television debut seemed to have flown under the radar.

Cherry grabbed the door and cracked it open. "I'll think about what you said."

"I'll expect you at the announcement, check in hand." Monique had retaken her seat and clicked on her recorder. "Maybe we'll list you as an anonymous donor. That way you and your sordid family jokes won't taint our reputation. Once the buzz over your little photo has died down, we'll reconsider your membership."

Cherry hated to admit Monique's final words gave her goal poster a tiny glimmer of hope, but it was the final click of the recorder that sent her over the edge.

She'd moved from the door to Monique's desk before she realized what she'd done.

Cherry snatched the recorder from Monique's hand and held it to the woman's neck like a switchblade. "I'll write you a check if I feel like writing you a check. Got it?"

Monique paled and nodded, very gently.

"Good." Cherry crossed to the door and yanked it open, recorder in hand. "And I'm taking *this* with me."

As she drove away, she watched the image of her perfect life as a Women's League lifetime member dissolve before her eyes. The parties. The magazine photo spreads. The acceptance.

The funny thing was, the loss didn't hurt half as badly as she had thought it would. Actually, the weight on her shoulders felt lighter than it had in months.

Cherry pulled her car into the Mystic Diamond parking lot, cut the ignition, and sat in stunned silence.

What a difference a week made.

Bart's words about plans not making people happy had never rung more true. So here she sat, staring at the hotel where he'd said she could find him.

She had two questions for the man whose diamond ring she'd once worn. If he answered to her liking, she'd help him win Liz's heart. After all, one Harte sister deserved to find true love.

Her heart gave a pang and she let out a sigh.

True love.

She waited for her tattoo to itch. Nothing.

Her window of opportunity with Luke Chance had slammed shut right after he'd set her up with the local press. Damn the man. She'd expected so much . . . more.

Cherry swallowed down her disappointment and set out for the hotel entrance.

A few moments later she stood at the marble-topped registration desk, oddly unsettled at the thought of the conversation she was about to have with Bart.

"Yes, can I help you?" The middle-aged gentleman eyed her with a kind expression, but Cherry found herself completely unable to speak.

"Miss?"

"Bart Matthews," she sputtered out. "I believe he's a guest at your hotel."

The man consulted the computer screen on the counter before him, then pinched his mouth into a tight line. "He's got the do-not-disturb on his phone."

Probably buried in some campaign strategy session. "Could you deliver a note?" She leaned against the counter, trying her best to convey urgency

through her eyes. "It's a matter of life and death."
Sort of.

The man narrowed his gaze at Cherry, then slid a slip of paper and a pen across the counter.

Fifteen minutes later, as she paced back and forth across the length of the piano lounge, Bart appeared. His hair looked as though he'd been shoving frustrated hands through it for most of the day, but his navy blue eyes sparkled with genuine delight.

"You came." He stepped near, then stopped, as if considering a hug but thinking better of the move.

Cherry's heart slapped against her ribs. She wiped her clammy palms against her dress and struggled to remember the words she'd practiced while she'd waited.

Bart's expectant gaze only added to her frustration. He stepped close, reaching out to touch her elbow. She didn't pull away, drawn to the comfort of the familiar move. He'd been her friend since grade school, after all, and despite the whole jilted-at-the-altar fiasco, she had missed him from time to time.

Yes, they'd screwed up by trying to plan a marriage without love, but surely they could get past that—for Liz.

A soft smile tugged at the corners of Cherry's mouth at just the thought of Liz and Bart together. The amazing thing was the combination wasn't difficult to picture. Why hadn't she envisioned the pairing before?

Maybe she had been too busy making plans.

"You know." She chose her words carefully, slowly.

"I'd find it a lot easier to help you win my sister's heart if you'd work on getting Mom some help."

A lopsided grin spread across his face. "Already in the works. Did you know she's been cooking?"

Cherry fought back a laugh, remembering her mother's national television debut. "I've heard that rumor."

"Apparently the cooking therapy offers her the same release the stealing did."

There was no accounting for taste in obsessions— especially among the Hartes.

Bart shook his head, his gaze softening. "I know we really screwed up, but I've missed you. And Liz."

Thus bringing her back to the reason for her visit. Cherry straightened, blowing out a breath to steady herself. "I came here to ask you two questions."

A dark brow lifted.

"One." She held up a finger. "What makes you think you love Liz?"

The light that came into his eyes before he answered was all Cherry needed to see. For all intents and purposes, he could have saved his breath, but she let him speak.

"I haven't gone a minute since the rehearsal dinner without wondering where she is. What she's doing. If she's happy. If she's sad. If she needs someone to talk to."

An image of Liz's daily wig parade flashed into Cherry's mind and she bit back a smirk. Oh, Liz definitely needed someone to talk to.

Based on the way Bart had sent himself into a starry-eyed daydream, she'd put money on him being just the guy.

"Pretty good." She nodded. "Not bad at all." She held up a second finger. "One more thing."

He nodded, eyes still bright, and refocused on her face.

"If Fran were paroled and Monty moved back home, and you and Liz settled in New Jersey, what would you do?"

He shrugged as if the answer was a no-brainer. "Buy a bigger house."

Jackpot. Maybe she'd even let him have Yogi. Maybe.

"How'd I do?"

"You're in."

"Okay." An ornery glint sparkled in his eyes. "I've got a question for *you*."

"Shoot."

"Have you stopped making your crazy plans?"

She blinked. Had she? Could she? "I'm not sure."

"Did I ever tell you what my mother used to say?" Bart tightened his grip on her elbow and gave her a quick shake.

Cherry shook her head.

"She always said that life is what happens when you're busy making other plans."

No kidding. Too bad Bart's mother hadn't let her in on that little secret a long time ago.

"Then why did you go along with the whole marriage scheme?"

"You can be very persuasive," he teased.

A laugh burst from between Cherry's lips and Bart smiled. Her tattoo itched just at that moment, ever so slightly. *What in the heck?*

Bart frowned. "You okay?"

"I think so."

The tattoo itched again. She slapped a hand over her belly, willing it to stop. There was no life-changing conversation going on here—except for the whole no-plan concept, and she wasn't 100 percent sold on that one.

Cherry looked up at Bart. "Think you can come by the house tomorrow? Around three?"

He nodded. "I might be a little late. I've got a conference session that could run long, but I'll get there as soon as I can."

Worry prickled at the base of Cherry's skull. She needed him in and out before four, but what was she going to say? *You need to be gone before the casino boss and I play poker to see whether or not he takes out a hit on Mom's hands?*

No. Somehow she didn't think she'd be able to slip that one past his law-enforcement tendencies.

She'd have to trust fate on this one.

Heaven help her.

CHAPTER 19

The sun was high overhead as Cherry crossed the hotel courtyard toward the beachside bar. She slipped off her suit jacket and draped it over her arm, tipping her face skyward to let the hot afternoon rays soak into her skin.

Since everyone seemed to think she'd been drinking, she might as well deliver on the expectation. Besides, Liz's words about umbrella-laden drinks had cemented themselves in her brain.

"Miss?" A waiter spoke up from beside her. "I asked if you needed assistance."

"Sorry," she murmured. "Table for one, please. Facing the Gulf."

"Right this way."

She followed him to a secluded corner table. A royal palm's fronds cast jagged shadows, and he wordlessly cranked the umbrella open, providing Cherry with additional shade and privacy.

"Thanks." She settled onto a stool facing the glistening waters, sighing inwardly as an odd, yet comforting, sense of peace eased through her.

Her socialite aspirations might have hit a little speed bump, but Bart and Liz suddenly had a shot at a future and so did her parents—assuming Cherry won the game.

She glanced down at her watch. Damn. She'd been supposed to meet Yogi for another lesson. Oh well, maybe he'd actually get some work done on the mural instead. Not that there'd be any *Mystic Living* photo spread now.

She let loose with a long exhale, and the waiter positioned himself between Cherry and the view. "You look like you could use a drink."

Could she ever.

"Something with an umbrella, please." She spread her fingers across the smooth teak tabletop and tipped her head to meet the waiter's gaze. "What do you recommend?"

His dark eyes bored into hers and he paused before he answered. "Sex on the Beach."

Cherry's stool wobbled beneath her and she clutched the edge of the table to steady herself.

The waiter burst into laughter, a warm smile spreading across his face. "Sorry. You looked like you needed a laugh. That one gets them every time."

Maybe she didn't belong out here, slogging back an umbrella-laden drink. Perhaps she really was safer back in her bedroom with her goal poster. Though the thought of sex on the beach definitely held an appeal—with the right guy.

Luke.

She willed her tattoo to itch. Nothing. Why had the stubborn tattoo itched when she and Bart had talked about giving up plans, but not now?

Her heart sank. Probably because Luke had ratted her out to the local paper.

The waiter continued talking. "You'll like it. I'll bring you one."

Cherry propped her chin on her fist and stared at the Gulf. Off-season tourists sat scattered across the pristine white sand, and countless couples walked hand in hand next to the water's edge.

She closed her eyes and tried to imagine strolling along the surf with Luke. The mental picture her brain sent back had nothing to do with long walks along the beach and everything to do with hot sex in a small space.

Shivers of awareness heated her every nerve ending, and the remembered feel of his calloused fingers against her skin ignited a heavy longing deep in her core.

She blinked her eyes open, shaking off the image. The man had tipped the newspaper, for crying out loud. It had to have been him. So why was her brain still conjuring up sexual fantasies in which she and Luke played starring roles?

Dread whispered through her. If Luke did figure out her family secrets, the paper would not only give him the front page, they'd probably give him the whole edition.

Cherry reached into her purse and plucked out Monique's recorder, studying it in her hand. She pressed the red button marked Dictation and watched as the tiny screen displayed ascending numbers. Cool.

She held the tiny object to her lips and spoke. "Note to self. Find a new mechanic." She stole another glance at the silken sands of the beach. "Then find a cabana boy to roll around with."

She studied the little contraption again, giving the red button another press to make the recording process stop, then pressing an arrow to repeat what she'd said.

Her recorded voice rang out crystal clear.

". . . find a cabana boy to roll around with."

What did you know? The possibilities were endless.

"You know, I'm also the part-time cabana boy." The waiter nodded toward a small hut on the beach as he slipped Cherry's drink onto the table. "Let me know if I can get you anything else." He shot her a wink before he headed toward another table.

Cherry winced, then pressed the red button on the recorder again. "Note to self. Make sure no one's listening before making notes to self."

She took a sip of her drink, choking on the unexpected sweetness. She plucked the umbrella from her glass, twirling it between her fingers.

As she stared at the colors of the paper umbrella, she sucked on the straw, startling herself when she hit the bottom of the glass with a slurp.

Wow.

Maybe she *had* really needed a drink. Perhaps Monique was more insightful than Cherry gave her credit for.

As she turned to order another, the waiter approached, a fresh drink on his tray.

"You must have read my mind." Cherry pasted a bright smile across her face, suddenly feeling warm and fuzzy. Her little drinking excursion had been a brilliant idea.

"First one always goes down easy." He set down

the drink and widened his gaze. "Can I get you anything else? Anything at all."

Embarrassed heat seeped into Cherry's cheeks. She took a quick sip of the drink as she vigorously shook her head. "No, thanks."

After he'd left, she took another long swig and relaxed against the table. Her knees and elbows felt like jelly, and suddenly she couldn't have cared less that all of Mystic Beach thought she was a hooker.

Suddenly all of her troubles seemed . . . *fuzzy*.

She pressed the tiny red button one more time. "Note to self. Drink more often."

Her waiter plunked another glass onto the table.

"Oh, no." She shook her head again, noticing her brain seemed to slosh from side to side. "No more for me."

Cherry reached for her purse, and the surroundings spun. *Uh-oh*. She glanced at the second drink, realizing she'd downed it as quickly as the first.

"No charge. Drinks are on the guy over there."

Her waiter pointed toward the entrance, and Cherry squinted, trying to focus on the spot. Blurry, but empty.

"Where?"

"There." The waiter pointed again. Lower.

It was when Cherry lowered the target of her focus that she saw him.

Moose.

Her heart hit her stomach.

The tiny thug bowed at the waist, then turned and walked away.

Cherry dropped her forehead to the tabletop. She was going to need a ride home. Again.

"He said to tell you he looked forward to your meeting tomorrow." The waiter's voice interrupted her mental wallowing.

"Great."

"Anything else I can get you? Anything at all?"

A tow truck.

"No. You've done quite enough."

Cherry's knees wobbled beneath her as she stood. She gripped the table, inhaling a steadying breath. Damn it. She'd meant to let loose, not get looped.

The waiter's warm palm cupped her elbow. "I could see you home."

Definitely not on her goal poster.

She shook her head, uneasiness flitting through her belly as she pointed to her feet. "First day with my new shoes."

Cherry pulled her elbow free from his grip, focusing on walking a straight line from the bar to her Jaguar. Maybe Moose had shown her some uncharacteristic mercy and left the wiring alone for once.

When she slipped into the driver's seat a few moments later and turned the ignition key, nothing happened. She slouched, leaning her head against the steering wheel. She tried the ignition again.

No response.

The reality was she had no business being behind the wheel in the first place. Moose's fixation on tampering with cars was a blessing in disguise.

Cherry leaned back against the seat, thinking through her options.

Her new waiter friend would be happy to see her home. She shuddered, not at all interested in what he seemed to have in mind. She tried Liz's cell phone, but the call clicked instantly into voice mail. Probably out charming sick kids.

She tried the house line but got no answer. With her luck, Monty and Yogi were probably out getting Lucky skunked.

That left Luke.

Cherry fished his business card from her wallet, eyeing the phone number for several long seconds. The last thing she wanted was for him to see her like this.

Hell, the last thing she wanted was to see him— period. Her belly tightened defiantly.

She grimaced and dialed.

A gruff voice answered on the third ring. "Chance Auto."

"Gramps?" Hope swelled in Cherry's heart. Perhaps she wouldn't have to see Luke after all.

"Yes, ma'am. Who's this?"

"Cherry Harte."

"Miss Cherry." He virtually sang her name and she grinned, warming to the recognition in his voice. "Saw your picture in the paper today."

She winced and rubbed a hand across her partially numb face.

"Luke was mighty upset about it."

Disbelief surged through her. "He was?" *Why?* Had he wanted a tighter shot? A better story?

She couldn't do this. She couldn't face Luke or his grandfather right now.

Cherry gave the ignition key one more turn.

Zilch.

She let her forehead drop to the steering wheel again. It seemed her neck had lost the ability to hold up her head.

"Mr. Chance, I hate to bother you, but I need another tow."

"Let me get Luke."

"Wait!" Her voice jumped three octaves. She concentrated on sounding calm, not wanting to alarm Luke's grandfather. "Could we keep this between us? Please."

If she had to face one of them, she'd much rather it be the elder Chance.

Silence stretched for several beats and then he spoke, his voice dropping lower than before. "Tell me where you are. I'll be right over."

Luke had heard the phone ringing as he'd rounded the corner from his apartment into the shop. "Was that the fax?"

He'd sent the photo from the paper to a few of his old reporter buddies, hoping to get a lead on the identity of the guy who'd been with Cherry. He'd been upstairs ever since, poring over his notes.

The one thing he could say for Cherry Harte was that she'd stumped his ability to piece together a story. It was as if she'd jammed his signal—in more ways than one.

"Phone," Gramps answered as he pulled on his baseball cap. "Someone needs a tow."

Luke eyed his grandfather's expression carefully. "You feeling all right? You look flushed."

Gramps scowled. "I was just thinking. Maybe you

should call Cherry for your answers instead of all this sleuthing you're doing."

Just the sound of the woman's name kicked Luke's gut into a tight knot. The last thing he needed to do was talk to her. Much as he wanted to check on her, to make sure she'd been all right after she'd seen the article, he'd probably take one look at her stubborn face and pick up where he'd left off last night—with her pinned against the nearest hard surface.

He swallowed down the fire building inside him.

"Trust me when I tell you she doesn't want to talk to me," he answered, thinking back on their last encounter in Monique's bathroom.

To complicate matters, the Youth Center director had called to follow up on Cherry's donation. Apparently the little piece in the paper hadn't fazed him one bit.

Luke did a mental eye roll. Up until the day Cherry had clicked into his shop, the kids had been his top priority. He had no plans of letting them down now. Sooner or later, he was going to have to face her. And when he did, he'd have to ask her for a million dollars.

He squeezed his eyes shut and fought the urge to bang his head against the wall.

Gramps cleared his throat and slid the cap off his head. He sank onto a stool with a moan and clasped a hand across his chest.

Luke's heart jumped to his throat. "Gramps!" He crossed to his grandfather in one stride. "Is it your heart?"

His grandfather's brows snapped together and he

shook his head. "Could be. Just think I need to rest a bit."

"I'll call the doctor."

Luke's pulse kicked up a notch. Maybe he shouldn't have teased his grandfather all this time about milking the angina episode. What if the hospital had missed something?

Gramps shook his head. "I'm okay. Just upset about Miss Cherry." He waved a hand in the air. "It's gone already. Probably something I ate."

Luke stood his ground, ready to dial 911.

"Go on, son." Gramps tipped his head toward the tow truck. "False alarm."

"You sure?"

His grandfather nodded. "Never been more sure in my life."

Luke held out his hand. "Give me the address. I'll handle this and be right back." He pointed toward his grandfather's apartment in the back. "I want you to go lie down. And if you feel funny at all, you call me. Or you call Cassie. Understood?"

His grandfather fished a scrap of paper from his pocket and handed it over. Luke read the scribble. *Mystic Diamond.* He wasn't one to turn down a job, but there had to be closer shops to the Gulf-front hotel than his.

He frowned. "You sure you're all right?"

Gramps nodded. "Just being prudent." He pointed to the paper, and Luke couldn't help but wonder at the glint that came into his grandfather's eyes. "Didn't catch her name, but I reckon you'll know her when you get there."

* * *

As soon as Luke and the tow truck cleared the lot, Eugene dialed Cassie's number.

Whoa boy, wait until the widow heard the latest. Not only had the boy spent the entire day researching Cherry's life, but her car's breakdown had been heaven sent.

Maybe Cassie was right. Sometimes you just needed to let true love take its course.

She answered on the third ring, her voice full of hope.

Reality slapped Eugene like a cold shower.

He hadn't spoken to the woman since he'd run from their last lunch. Here he sat reaching out to her at the first sign of news regarding Luke and Cherry.

"Hello?" Cassie's bright voice rose as if she'd been expecting his call.

Eugene opened his mouth to speak, but lowered the phone to its cradle instead.

Disappointment and regret whispered through him.

Old fool.

Calling the widow to share good news.

He'd never planned to take a second chance on love in this lifetime, and he wasn't about to start now.

CHAPTER 20

Cherry had decided she'd better walk to sober up, but as usual, her plan had fallen flat on its face.

Strike that. She'd fallen flat on her face—the moment she'd wedged her heel into a crack in the wooden promenade that ran between the parking lot and the beach.

She studied the lazy glide of a pelican overhead as the waiter struggled to free her shoe from the planks.

"Any tools in your car?" The man's face had gone beet red, and if she wasn't mistaken, his urge to bed her had been replaced by an urge to throttle her.

She shook her head.

He stood and let out a frustrated breath. "I'll be right back." He frowned. "You really ought to carry tools."

Cherry glowered at his retreating back. Liz didn't know what she'd been talking about. These cabana boys were moody.

She pulled out the recorder and pressed the button. "Note to self. Buy tools." She clicked the recorder off, then on again quickly. "Second note to self. Rethink the entire cabana-boy thing."

Her surroundings spun, and she hiccuped. Not good.

She clicked the recorder off again and closed her eyes, sinking down onto her rump and tucking her knees up under her skirt. She wrapped her hands around her legs.

"Another one bites the dust." The rich rumbling voice sent a jolt of awareness straight to her core. She snapped open her eyes and scrutinized the pair of work boots positioned next to her on the walk. Definitely not the waiter. And definitely not Gramps.

Her gaze climbed the front of the soft, worn jeans, skimming past the narrow hips to the broad chest, the crossed arms, and the smug, crooked grin. Her breath caught—and her tattoo itched.

Thank goodness.

"Just my Luke . . . er . . . luck."

He kneeled next to her, fingering the trapped sandal. "You know, it's true what they say." He gave a firm yank and the sandal sprang free, the leather heel deeply scarred from the ordeal. Luke dangled the dainty sandal from his finger and grinned. "The camera adds ten pounds. Your package looks much thinner in person."

Cherry bristled. "You son of a—"

"Watch your language." He extended a hand. "You never know who's listening."

Anger rushed through her. "How dare you tip the newspaper like that. I've been banned from the Women's League and probably everywhere else by now."

He crooked a brow. "Well, then I wish I could take the credit, but I can't."

She frowned, confusion whirling in her brain. "You can't take the credit?"

Luke shook his head. "I'd like to understand what you've gotten yourself into, but I sure as hell wouldn't sell you out to do it. I wouldn't mind knowing who did, though, so I could give them a piece of my mind."

Cherry waggled a finger at him. "Why were you there?"

"Looking for you."

Her tattoo itched again, and relief pulsed through her.

"And I was looking for answers," Luke added.

"Did you find any?" She squinted at him and held her hand up. He shook his head and reached for her, letting her slip her fingers into his.

For the first time that day, Cherry felt at ease, and she was fairly sure it wasn't from her blood alcohol level.

"What were your questions?" Her traitorous pulse had quickened, but she was too tipsy to care.

Luke wrapped an arm around her waist and tugged her close to his side. "Well, my first would have been to ask you what temperature I should set the oven to if I want to bake coffee cake."

Cherry did her best to ignore the loud, steady hum singing in her belly as she studied the way the man's denim shirt stretched across his chest. "Didn't figure you to be a Food Network aficionado."

His dark gaze locked on hers and her insides did a somersault. "Not me. Gramps." His expression morphed from charmed to tense. "Want to tell me what your mother's doing behind bars?"

Cherry shook her head, never taking her eyes from his. "Not really."

Tiny frown lines formed to either side of his eyes. "Why won't you trust me?"

She thought about that one for a moment. She wanted to trust him, but right now she had all the challenges in her life she could handle.

"Complicated," she answered. "Let's just say this goes way beyond packaging issues."

"Will you at least tell me who this Moose really is?"

She waggled her brows, suddenly realizing her knees weren't going to hold her much longer. "If I told you that, I'd have to kill you."

Luke opened his mouth to respond just as the waiter reappeared. "I'll take it from here, Skippy."

Cherry couldn't help but notice the relief on the waiter's face as he scurried away.

"All right." Luke hoisted her into his arms, and Cherry happily settled against his chest. "Let's get you home. I'll worry about your car later."

Luke focused on the road, trying not to stare at Cherry's flushed profile. She ran a hand through her hair and grinned sheepishly. "Sorry you had to see me like this. I might be a little tipsy."

And a whole lot sexy.

Now he knew why Gramps had suddenly developed chest pains. Luke should have known his matchmaking grandfather was up to something.

"Want to tell me why you decided to go drinking? Were you that upset about the article?"

Cherry snorted uncharacteristically. "Liz always thought I should be drinking on the beach with the cabana boy instead of sucking up to the Women's League." She shrugged. "I thought I'd give it a try."

"And how'd that work out for you?"

"Not too well."

"And the Women's League?"

A sly grin spread across her face as she dug in her purse. When she hoisted a tiny recorder in the air, he laughed. "You didn't?"

"I did." She fumbled with the object, then pressed her lips to the microphone. "Note to self. Send Monique a thank-you note for the recorder."

She snapped off the recorder and dropped it back into her purse. "Manners, you know."

Manners, however, were the last thing on Luke's mind. The sight of Cherry's mouth speaking softly into the recorder had reignited the hot need he'd felt the night before.

He'd known seeing the woman would throw off his focus, but he'd underestimated just by how much. He needed to shift the conversation back to the issue of her family—and Moose—before he lost his train of thought completely.

"I thought you'd be upset about the picture."

"Please." She waved a hand dismissively. "Telling the world I'm a hooker is so far off the truth it's funny. Hell, turning a trick or two would be a piece of cake compared to what I have to do."

She slapped a hand across her mouth when she realized she'd offered too much information.

"Which you won't tell me."

"Nope."

"Not even if I could help you?"

She stared at him and her eyes narrowed as if she might actually be considering the idea. "Why do you suddenly care so much about my life?"

Luke's pulse picked up a beat. He shrugged. "It's funny. I've been asking myself that same question."

Cherry breathed in deeply through her mouth, then hugged herself. Her forehead crinkled. "I thought you didn't want to care for me, or worry about me, or think about me, or whatever it was you said."

He met her green stare, and his gut clenched. He more than cared for her. He'd passed that marker a long way back.

"I was wrong."

Her pale brows lifted. "You don't say."

They rode the rest of the way in silence. Luke wondered why on earth he'd felt the need to be honest when she was obviously being anything but.

He stole periodic glances at Cherry's profile as he drove. Her eyes were shut, long lashes feathering her cheeks. A soft grin tugged at the corners of her mouth.

If she thought he was done questioning her, she was wrong.

Then he remembered the Youth Center, and the fact he still had to ask the woman sitting next to him for a million-dollar donation.

All he had to do now was figure out how.

Her catnap had taken the edge off of Cherry's buzz by the time Luke pulled the truck into her neighborhood.

So Luke *cared.* Awareness shot through her veins. *Very interesting, indeed.*

Maybe there was a way to tell him just enough to see if he meant what he said. Perhaps she could offer the basic family information and watch for a reaction.

After all, he'd been the one to question her packaging. She might as well show him a small piece of what she'd been hiding.

Neither of them said a word until she pushed the front door open. The house sat blessedly quiet.

"Monty? Lucky?"

She waited. No answer.

Her heart began a steady tapping against her ribs. She placed her palm on her abdomen as she pushed the front door closed. When she lifted her chin to meet Luke's gaze, his brow furrowed.

"Did I ever tell you how I got my name?"

He shook his head.

She could stop here and he'd never know. Maybe she should. Maybe this was just the Sex on the Beach talking—make that Sexes on the Beach.

Hmm. Not a bad thought.

Focus, Cherry. Focus.

"I told Monique I was named for my mother's favorite dessert, Cherries Jubilee."

"But?"

Luke took a step closer and Cherry's tattoo itched, right on cue.

"I wasn't named after a sophisticated dessert." She unbuttoned her dress just enough to expose her belly button and the tattooed patch of skin next to it. "I was named after a slot-machine symbol."

The small mark peeked from between the parted

fabric—a single cherry dangling from its stem. "Got it when I was eighteen. I'm still not sure why."

"What is it?" Luke squinted, stepping closer. "A tattoo?"

Cherry nodded. "A cherry." She lowered her gaze to her belly, running her finger around the stained skin. She couldn't believe she was exposing her tattoo to Luke. Now, he'd have no doubt she had packaging issues.

She looked up to check his expression, and her breath caught at the blatant desire smoldering in his eyes.

Carnal need pooled in Luke's gut. Good Lord, the woman was going to be the death of him.

"Why?" He forced his brain to form the question, which was difficult considering there was no blood in any part of his body north of his waist.

Did the woman have any idea what she was doing to him?

She raised and dropped one shoulder. Her stare met his once more, the fire in her eyes burning hotter than anything he'd ever seen.

She knew.

Luke gripped her shoulders, unable to hold back any longer. His questions could wait.

Cherry softened beneath his touch, her hungry eyes locking with his. He brushed his lips lightly against hers, then drank deeply as she parted her lips, her tongue dancing with his.

She pulled back. "I think I'm ready to tell you about my family."

He hoisted her into his arms, taking the steps as quickly as he could. "Typical woman. Lousy timing."

Cherry's laughter tickled his ear as her fingers explored the nape of his neck and the skin beneath his collar, sending his internal temperature skyrocketing.

"Which room?"

She pointed with her foot, and he carried her through the open door and lowered her to the quilt-covered bed.

Luke dropped to his knees next to the bed, slipping his fingers into the opening of her dress. He eased the fabric aside to expose her creamy flesh and the small cherry. How could he have missed this at his apartment? Of course, he had been focused on points farther north.

Cherry visibly shivered as he trailed his finger across the small tattoo. She propped herself up on one elbow, a devilish grin spreading across her face. "Gotta like a man who appreciates fine art."

He laughed, dropping a kiss on the fruit tattoo, letting his lips linger against Cherry's warm flesh. His arousal pressed against his jeans, urging him to hurry when all he wanted to do was take his time.

"Why did they name you after a slot-machine symbol?" He raised his gaze to meet Cherry's.

Desire burned in her stare, sending a jolt of need straight to Luke's groin. She reached for him, trailing her fingers along his cheek. "Maybe they wanted me to be luckier than they had been."

Luke turned his face into her touch, losing himself momentarily in the feel of her soft caress against his skin.

"I had a father who left us, trying to please a

mother who apparently couldn't be pleased. She always wanted what she didn't have but never stopped to realize how good she already had it."

Cherry bit down on her lip, the move kicking Luke's libido into overdrive. He traced the outline of the tattoo, pressing down onto the ripe red flesh. "And winning the lottery let you get away from all that?"

"I thought I could reinvent my life."

Luke reversed the direction of his finger, tracing the outline once more. "And?"

"I think I was wrong." Cherry's words came in ragged bursts, as if pushed through the fog of her desire.

Luke turned to kiss the soft flesh of her hand. He captured her wrist in his fingers, running his lips from her palm to the inside of her wrist, then to the inside of her forearm.

Cherry swallowed, her eyes now closed, her features slack. "Sooner or later, you have to deal with who you really are."

Luke forced himself to look at her, lifting his mouth from her skin when a hint of sadness slipped into her tone.

Cherry's pale eyes snapped open, their corners serious.

At that moment, he would have done whatever it took to erase the sadness and the worry from her face. He would have done anything to see her smile like she had that night on the fishing pier.

Sudden tears glimmered in Cherry's eyes and he pulled himself up onto his knees, stretching to press a kiss to her cheek. He traced one eyebrow and then the other with his lips, willing away her heartache.

Luke hoisted himself up onto the bed and gathered her into his arms, pulling her tight against his body, pressing her curves against the front of his denim shirt. He hooked his fingers beneath her chin, pulling up her watery gaze to meet his.

"I think who you are is pretty amazing."

A lone tear slipped over her lower lashes.

Luke reached to brush away the moisture, and Cherry's hand closed over his fingers. She tugged his hand toward her mouth, pressing her lips to his fingertips.

Hot desire scorched through him.

Cherry's eyes locked with his, need shining in their pale depths. Her lips parted, wrapping their silken sensuality first around one finger, then a second. Every fiber of his being screamed to kiss her mouth, to slip off her dress, to make love to her.

She teased her lips slowly, devilishly over his fingers, one after the other. A flash of life glimmered in her stare, and Luke wanted her as he'd never wanted another woman.

Angling his mouth over hers, he lowered Cherry against the pillows, drawing his fingers down the soft expanse of her neck, unbuttoning her dress and tracing the lacy edge of her bra. Cherry's sharp intake of breath only ratcheted up his desire.

His heart screamed to possess her fully, to experience the promise of her body. He willed his brain to control his need long enough to make love to her slowly, carefully.

Luke slipped off her clothes, then flicked open the simple clasp of her bra, cupping the fleshy mound of one breast, caressing the velvet skin. He circled his thumb around her taut nipple, tightening his arm around her body as she arched against him.

Slow, he coached himself. *Slow.*

It seemed he'd waited a lifetime to be with her, and he wasn't going to rush loving her now.

Hurry, Cherry screamed silently. She needed Luke inside her before she exploded.

She'd never been the aggressor during sex, but there was a first for everything. She shimmied out of her underwear, shifted positions, rolled on top of Luke and reached for the button of his jeans. She freed the button and unzipped the placket, pushing the well-worn denim out of the way.

She caressed his hard, hot length through his cotton boxers, smiling when the touch elicited Luke's throaty moan. For once, one of her plans seemed to be working.

Cherry slipped her fingers inside Luke's boxers, encircling his thick, smooth shaft and stroking slowly, tightening her grip as she did so. Luke's kisses fell away from her neck, his breath coming in ragged gasps.

She pushed away from the pillows, bending to kiss the tip of his arousal. She devilishly flicked her tongue against his moist flesh, opening her mouth to taste him.

"I can't last." The words rushed from Luke's mouth.

"That's the idea." Cherry moved her lips and tongue in a slow dance against Luke's rock-hard length. The heaviness between her own thighs

threatened to explode, her body's awareness of
Luke having kicked to a frenzy.

"No more," he growled.

In one smooth motion, he peeled his jeans from
his legs and stripped off his shirt. Cherry traced her
fingertip over the soft hair encircling one of his nipples. Strong hands closed around her waist, lifting
her to straddle him.

"I don't have protection." His words came out in
a groan.

Cherry smiled. The man wanted her—badly—
and she liked the heady feeling. Who was she kidding? She *loved* it.

"I'm on the pill." She pressed a kiss to his chest,
flicking his nipple with her tongue, then blowing
on the damp trail her lips had left behind.

She was the seductress in her own erotic tale
and the thought thrilled her, filling her with a sensual heat she hadn't thought possible.

She lowered herself onto Luke, her breath catching as his erection pressed, then pushed inside
her, filling her slowly at first, then quickly, fully. A
myriad of emotions flooded her—fear, excitement,
and unbridled pleasure.

Luke cupped her breasts, gently caressing them
with his strong, calloused fingers. The amazing
sensation scattered any remnants of worry from her
mind.

Their bodies moved as one in a slow, sensual
rhythm.

Luke's gaze locked with hers, his eyes dark and
hungry. His touch trailed from her breasts over
the curve of her waist, his fingers pressing hard into
the flesh of her hips and buttocks.

He pulled her tight against him, deepening his thrusts, sending her spiraling deeper into a cavern of mind-numbing sensations.

She closed her eyes, losing herself to the pressure coiling inside her.

"Look at me." Luke's gruff voice shocked her and she snapped open her gaze.

The white-hot need mirrored in his eyes sent the first pulse of Cherry's release rushing toward the edge. Suddenly he slowed his movements, rolling to position himself above her. She raised her hips to meet him, opening her body and her heart to all he had to offer.

"Do you trust me, Cherry?" His soft words surprised her.

The certainty of her response eased any doubt lingering in her mind. "Yes."

He filled her then. Cherry's orgasm was immediate, waves of joy and release flooding through her. She closed her eyes momentarily, but opened them to watch Luke, smiling as his eyes closed, his features twisting, then smoothing as he groaned and shuddered, rocking their bodies together until they both lay spent, sexually and emotionally.

Cherry smiled, savoring the feel of his damp body molded to her own as she drifted off to sleep.

Luke woke a bit before three in the morning, blinking at the bright red numbers glowing on Cherry's bedside clock. He slipped from the bed without waking her, pulling the quilt over her naked body.

His gut tightened, responding to the sight of

her slender shoulder lit by pale moonlight. Regret tangled with relief.

What had he done?

Actually, he'd done exactly what he'd wanted to do since the day she'd walked into his life. But making love to Cherry hadn't answered any of the questions still lingering between them.

And more importantly, making love to Cherry hadn't erased the fact he needed to ask her for a million dollars if he planned to save the Youth Center.

Luke dragged a hand across his face as he stared down at her sleeping form. Regret welled up inside him, but he shoved it away. He'd find a way to make things right between them.

Somehow.

He pulled on his jeans, then shrugged his shirt up over his shoulders, leaving it unbuttoned. In Cherry's bathroom, he found a small glass and a bottle of aspirin. He shook two pills into his hand and filled the glass with cool tap water. She'd need them first thing, even though he knew she'd sobered up enough to know exactly what they'd done last night.

His belly gave another twist, nerve endings humming to life. He needed to leave now before he woke her for round two. Hopefully, there'd be plenty of time for that later on.

Right now, he had to get back to the shop in case any faxes had come in. If Cherry wasn't willing to tell him what was going on, he'd figure it out himself.

He set the water and the tablets quietly on the nightstand next to Cherry's sleeping head, then pressed a soft kiss into her tousled hair, breathing deeply of her spicy scent.

When he came back with her car, he'd make the funding request.

As he turned toward the door, his gaze fell on the handmade poster hanging on her wall, a jumble of photos and magazine prints. He ran a finger over the edges of the life—the plans—Cherry had captured on paper.

Was she really ready to give up on the Women's League and everything she'd worked so hard for? Or would she wake up in the morning recommitted to creating a life of privilege and status?

Dread tangled with the regret inside him.

He turned to steal one last glimpse of Cherry asleep in the moonlight and patted his shirt pocket. Empty. Not that it mattered.

Cherry Harte had pulled him back into the land of the living and everything he'd worked for two years to avoid.

He had a feeling there wasn't a stick of gum in the world that could help him now.

CHAPTER 21

Cherry pried open her eyes and peeked at the other side of the bed. Empty. Her heart caught and twisted, instant regret slicing through her.

How could he be gone after the night they'd shared? After she'd told him the truth about her parents . . . well, some of the truth.

She tamped down her disappointment and stared up at her goal poster, brightly displayed in the sun filtering through the bedroom curtains. What had she done?

She'd *slept* with him. And she'd liked it—a lot.

Desire rippled through her, reawakening pleasure points she'd forgotten she owned.

Crazy.

Bart had been right. There was something to be said for spontaneity.

She flashed back on her meeting with Monique, wincing at the memory of holding the recorder to her throat. And to think, that had been *before* the drinks.

Well, one thing was certain. Monique would never let her get away scot-free with a stunt like that.

The amazing thing was that the thought didn't strike terror into Cherry's heart. Not in the least.

A week ago, all she'd cared about had been securing her permanent Women's League membership—and falsifying her family's identity to do so. This morning, that same family sat first and foremost on her mind—right after Luke.

From Liz's crazy wig fetish to her father's traveling memorabilia trunk, Cherry finally understood her identity couldn't be hidden by her possessions or her status. No, her identity screamed loud and clear in the people she loved. They defined her.

Luke's face flashed through her mind, sending hot desire pulsing between her thighs at her memories of their night together—a mind-numbing tangle of sheets and caresses, lips and words. Passion.

They'd fit together perfectly, as if he should have been front and center on her goal poster all along.

So where had he gone?

Cherry flipped back the covers and squinted toward the foot of the mattress. Nothing. Not a trace of Luke Chance remained. The last thing she'd expected from him had been a quick hit-and-run.

Fresh regret eased through her, edging out the heat in her veins.

"Lose something?"

Liz's overly bright voice reverberated off Cherry's now-aching temples, shattering her silent torture. She peeked from beneath the covers at her sister's smug expression, willing away the blush on her traitorous face.

"My sock."

"Well"—Liz shot her a devious wink—"your sock

left a note in the kitchen. Said he'd stop back later on with your car."

Cherry snuggled down into the covers and smiled, relief flooding through her.

Liz sat on the edge of the bed and gloated. She wore a shorter version of the pink wig, looking eerily more like Lucky every day. The beauty mark perched on her top lip now, looking very much like an angry mole.

"I think you need professional help," Cherry mumbled into the pillow.

"Me?" Liz poked her in the shoulder. "I'm not the one who has a pissed-off man with an eye patch waiting for her downstairs, shuffling cards."

Cherry's heart jumped to her throat. "Is the boss early?"

Liz frowned. "No. Yogi."

"With an eye patch?"

Liz rolled her eyes as she rose to her feet. "Apparently he and Monty got into a scuffle last night at bingo."

The dull throbbing next to Cherry's eyes morphed to a drum corps. "Bingo?"

Liz shrugged. "This family is well on its way to the funny farm."

Cherry eyed her sister's outfit and giggled. Well on their way? Hell, they had a lifetime pass.

"Are those your lucky pants?" She pointed to the leopard-print leggings sheathing Liz's slender legs.

Her sister nodded. "Figured we'd need all the luck we could get today." Liz gestured to Cherry's poster as she walked past. "Ready to burn this thing?"

Cherry sat up, wrapping the sheet around her. "Almost."

"Well," Liz shot her a wink and headed for the hall, "better hurry it up and get with the program." She jerked a thumb toward the staircase. "Angry man with an eye patch shuffling cards. Remember?"

Cherry glanced at the clock on her nightstand after Liz had left, and adrenaline spiked to life in her veins. Bart would be there in three hours, and Moose and his boss in four.

As she pulled herself to her feet, she spotted the aspirin on the nightstand. *Luke.*

Cherry smiled, swallowing the tablets down, then stopped to stare at her goal poster. Sooner or later, someone was bound to figure out who you really were, no matter how well you thought you had your true self hidden—or your fake self planned.

She pulled the jumble of photos and magazine prints from the wall, slowly tearing it into long, multicolored strips. As they fell to the floor, she quietly repeated her favorite affirmation.

"Every day, in every way, I'm getting better and better."

Maybe it had taken a good, solid man to make her realize that sometimes a dog was just a dog. And sometimes, a simple girl from New Jersey was merely a simple girl from New Jersey, no matter what her checkbook said.

Luke stared at Cherry's car and scrubbed a hand across his face. To think, a week ago the Youth Center had been the only thing in his life that mattered—except for his grandfather. Now, the identity-challenged Cherry Harte had taken center stage.

And he still had to ask her for a million dollars.

Gramps cleared his throat. "Problem, son?"

"Problems," Luke answered. "Multiple."

"Cherry?"

The concern in his grandfather's voice tugged at Luke's conscience. "Could be." He smiled at the older man. "How's your heart today, by the way?"

The corners of his grandfather's mouth twisted into a wry grin. "Better." He nodded toward the parking lot. "Couldn't help but notice you were out late. Must have been a tough job. Good thing you went in my place."

Luke shook his head and whistled. "Let's just say your ticker would have never survived."

Gramps's smile turned serious. "Will yours?"

Luke nodded, ignoring the tiny voice inside his head that said things were going to get a whole lot worse before they got better. "It might. If I play my cards right."

He pushed back from his desk and tucked his notes and papers into a folder. No new faxes had come in overnight, so he remained clueless as to the identity and background of the elusive Moose.

Oh well, Cherry would tell him when she was ready. In the meantime, he had to face the music or watch the Youth Center dream evaporate before his eyes.

"I've got to run Cherry's car back and ask her to help the Youth Center win the estate."

His grandfather's forehead puckered, surprise flashing through his features. "Thought you didn't trust people with money. Didn't want to be indebted to them."

Luke patted the older man's arm as he brushed

past. "I still don't, but my stubborn pride isn't going to help those kids secure a place of their own. I guess sometimes you have to accept your weaknesses and move past them."

He paused when he got to the door, looking back at Gramps's puzzled expression. "You might have been right about Cherry, though. Maybe money doesn't change everyone."

He laughed at the way his grandfather's eyes popped wide, then he turned and headed toward Cherry's car.

If Cherry had to look at another hand of cards, she'd scream. Okay, so she might be a bit hungover, but this was ridiculous. She stared at Yogi and tried not to laugh. Between the mask and the eye patch, the man had only two inches of skin visible on his face.

"You want to tell me one more time what happened?"

"Bingo accident." He continued to shuffle the cards without looking up.

Cherry narrowed her gaze. "Like what? Your little marker flew up and hit you in the eye?"

"No." Her father's voice answered. He'd come in from walking Lucky, who, by the way, had a definite gleam in his beady little eyes today. "That would have been a finger."

Cherry's headache began to pulse anew, only this time she was fairly certain it had nothing to do with last night's alcohol consumption. She frowned at Yogi, who refused to look up from the deck of cards. "Yogi. A *finger* hit you in the eye?"

"That is correct," he mumbled through the mask.

Cherry fought the urge to snap him with his own elastic.

She looked from Yogi to Monty to Lucky, then back. Dread began to uncoil from the pit of her stomach. "One of you had better start talking."

Monty and Yogi glanced at each other, at the dog, and finally back at Cherry.

"You aren't going to be happy," her father said.

She blinked.

Exactly the words she hadn't wanted to hear.

"Moose showed up."

"At bingo?" Cherry squinted at her father.

Monty nodded. "He got angry because he didn't win once." He shook his head. "Horrible temper. And he threatened to kick Fifi."

Cherry tipped her head toward the ceiling. None of this was helping her headache. "Who's Fifi?"

"The poodle," Yogi mumbled through the mask.

"What poodle?" Cherry had begun to rub her temples, secretly wishing they'd all disappear.

"The poodle Lucky defended," Monty answered.

Cherry studied Lucky, wide-eyed with amazement. "He defended another *dog*?" Lucky wagged his fluffy pink nub in return.

She shook her head and refocused on Yogi, pointing to the patch. "So tell me again how this happened."

"That would have occurred when he was trying to pry Lucky's teeth out of Moose's leg." Monty grimaced, as if remembering the moment. "Index finger. Direct hit."

Yogi pressed a hand to his eye patch. "Then Monty sat on the angry little man until he passed out."

Cherry lowered her face to the table and folded her arms over her head.

"Told you you weren't going to be happy," her father said.

As soon as Luke lowered Cherry's car to her driveway, he headed toward her front door. He walked confidently, having made the decision to tell her about his past. Why not? Perhaps if he confided in her, it would make his change of heart about asking for a handout easier to swallow. Maybe she'd consider it a show of good faith.

He'd no sooner rung the doorbell than she snapped it open, a bright smile spreading across her lovely face. She pressed a quick kiss to his lips and urged him inside.

His gut tightened instantly with hunger for her, but he ignored it, knowing there was no time to spare. Beyond her, Monty and Yogi flitted in and out of Cherry's office—two men on an apparent mission.

Yogi wore an eye patch above his surgical mask, and Cherry's father hummed something that sounded suspiciously like "Jail House Rock."

"I'd invite you to stay." A shadow passed across Cherry's eyes. "But we're . . . cleaning. Big *Mystic Living* photo shoot later today."

Suddenly all thoughts of honesty flew out of his head, and frustration edged out the warmth he'd felt upon seeing her. "You're lying."

She frowned, taking a step backward. "I beg your pardon."

He gestured at the frenzied activity down the hall. "What's going on?"

A forced smile spread across her face. "I told

you. *Mystic Living* is coming today to do the photo shoot before the final announcement. There's a lot to prepare. The office. Yogi's mural. My outfit. The decorations."

She ticked the points off on her fingers and Luke moved to push past her. Cherry blocked him, sidestepping into his path. The corners of her eyes had softened, and her lips pressed into a tight line.

"Luke."

The soft sound of his name on her lips brought back memories of their lovemaking in hot, distracting flashes.

Luke squeezed his eyes shut and willed the images away. "Why don't you trust me?" he asked. "Why do you continue to feel you have to lie to me?"

She reached for his chin, her soft fingers brushing against the line of his jaw. "I'm asking *you* to trust *me* this time. Please."

He narrowed his gaze on her. "Are you in trouble?"

"More than I can explain to you in the time I've got right now." She pulled herself to her tiptoes and pressed a soft kiss to his lips. "Trust me. After I make things right, I'll tell you every juicy detail."

She nodded, her forced smile not reaching her eyes. "I've got it all under control." She shrugged. "There's not a thing for you to worry about."

But he was worried. About whatever it was she and her family had gotten themselves into and about how he was going to ask her for the Youth Center funding.

Luke reached for Cherry, gripping her elbows and pulling her close. Her pale gaze scrutinized his, the color fading from her cheeks.

"What is it?" Confusion wove its way into her expression.

A knot tightened in Luke's throat, but he swallowed it down. As much as he wanted to know exactly what she and her family were up to, he'd run out of time. "Remember last night when I asked if you trusted me?"

She nodded.

"Well, I'm going to trust you now because I need to ask you a difficult question and I want you to know I'm serious. All right?"

She stood silent, searching his face.

"Remember how I told you money changes people?"

She nodded.

"I still believe that, but not for all people. Not for you."

She smiled, this time the expression genuine, lighting up her face.

"I was once engaged to someone, my high school sweetheart. When her father died unexpectedly and made her very wealthy, she dropped me so fast my head spun. Money changed her."

Cherry bit down on her lip and Luke fought the longing the simple move kicked to life.

He continued. "Then I had a story back in Miami. I found out a good friend of mine, Jimmy Doran, had gotten involved with a developer—a crooked developer—named Hoyer. Michael Hoyer."

Just saying the name brought a bitter taste to Luke's mouth. Monty crossed the hall, going back into Cherry's office, and Luke dropped his voice lower, hoping to avoid being overheard.

"I was about to break a huge story on Hoyer, but

it involved my buddy. He admitted he was guilty, but he asked me for time to take care of some personal business before I went public. I gave him twenty-four hours and then I never saw him again."

Cherry splayed her hand against Luke's chest, and the tender move eased the tension building inside him.

"He disappeared with a whole lot of money, and my story was lost. It ended my career and my credibility. Hoyer got away scot-free."

"I'm sorry." Her throat worked. "Luke?"

"Yeah?" He pulled her closer to him, wanting nothing more than to skip his next question and take her upstairs to lose himself in the peaks and valleys of her body. He longed to make love to her while the Youth Center took care of itself.

But he couldn't.

Cherry's eyes had gone huge, and she looked at him so intently he could have sworn she must be able to see what he had to say next.

"Why are you telling me all of this now?"

"Because of what I have to ask you. I want you to understand how much you've helped me move beyond my past where money is concerned. Thanks to you, I'm ready to reenter the land of the living."

"Phone." Monty's voice rang out from the office, shattering the intimacy of the moment. "Says it's urgent, Cherry."

Cherry winced, and Luke nodded. "I'll wait."

After all, this time he wasn't leaving without Cherry's answer—whatever that answer might be.

CHAPTER 22

"Hello."

Cherry waited for the other party to speak, all the while staring at Luke. His admissions had stunned her *and* touched her deeply. But what on earth was he leading up to that he felt he had to confide his secrets?

"Cherry, darling. Do you have your check all ready for the meeting?" Monique's voice rang out across the line.

If Cherry didn't know better, she'd say the woman sounded chipper—and delusional. Did she really think Cherry was going to show up in her beige suit, close-toed shoes, and dull hair with her check in hand?

Hell. She planned to strip out the dark blond color the second Luke walked out the door.

Cherry studied the man, unable to shake the feeling that whatever he was about to say couldn't be good. "I don't have time to talk to you, Monique. I'm in the middle of something."

At the mention of Monique's name, Luke flinched.

He truly did loathe the Women's League. That was without question.

"Who could you possibly be talking to who's more important than me?" Monique's curt voice snapped Cherry's attention back to the conversation.

"Luke Chance," Cherry answered responsively, without thinking of how Monique would react.

"And what does he want? Money?"

Okay, now the woman was just pissing her off. "No, Monique, he does not want money. He and I have a personal relationship, for your information. Not that it's any of your business."

"Really?" Monique's tone dropped low and intent. "Well, let me warn you about Mr. Chance before you go any further with your *relationship*."

Luke's cheeks had flushed with hot color thanks to Cherry's side of the conversation, and she couldn't imagine why, unless he was worried his being in her home might somehow impact the Youth Center campaign.

"Luke Chance and I were once engaged to be married."

Monique's words might as well have been a brick aimed dead-on between Cherry's eyes. The room spun and she leaned her back against the wall to hold herself steady.

Luke and *Monique*?

"Why, Cherry," Monique continued. "I do believe you've finally been rendered speechless."

"Go on," Cherry said softly.

"Dear Luke went into a bad spell a little while back and I had to break things off. You see, I came into a lot of money and, quite frankly, I felt that was the only reason he was with me. I can't be with a man who's only after my wealth."

A soft chuckle filtered across the line. "You'll learn. Spotting gold diggers comes with experience. Now, let's get back to tonight's meeting, shall we?"

Cherry had turned her back on Luke, unable to face him at that moment. Her mind raced in a jumbled mess of his words, Monique's words, and her own doubts.

Didn't she have enough to worry about without new additions to the equation?

"You're going to show up at the meeting, check in hand," Monique continued. "Then you'll smile for the press. Understood?"

Cherry's blood began to boil. She'd had just about enough of Monique for one conversation. "Quite frankly, I have no intention of doing any such thing."

"But you will." A short burst of laughter carried across the line, filling Cherry with the urge to reach through the phone and strangle the woman.

"I have a lovely tape of your mother's appearance on the Food Network, and I seem to have developed a bruise on my neck from your assault." She sighed, and Cherry realized she'd come to despise the woman she'd once wanted to emulate.

Monique launched back into her threat, never missing a beat. "Unless you want the authorities and the press on your doorstep, I'd suggest you do as I request."

Request? The woman's idea of a request was nothing short of blackmail.

"Do you understand me?" Monique asked.

"Most definitely."

Cherry ended the call and turned to face Luke. She understood, all right, but she still hadn't decided whether or not Monique scared her enough to comply.

Her father's worried face caught the edge of her focus, and her anger with Monique began to crumble. She couldn't risk the press or the police crashing their little poker party.

If everything went as planned and she won, her father's debt would be cleared and her mother would be safe. If things went any other way . . . well . . . she refused to let her thoughts go there.

She inhaled sharply and focused on Luke, the full impact of Monique's disclosure suddenly hitting her as she faced him. "Sorry for the interruption." She forced the words through the lump in her throat. "What were you saying?"

"Who was that?" Luke's eyes had gone dark.

Cherry shook her head. "No one who matters."

His gaze narrowed as if he wasn't sure she was telling the truth. The fact the man could read her every emotion didn't bode well for her upcoming poker match.

"Monique Goodall?"

Cherry nodded, shifting the phone from one hand to the other, tempted by the urge to throw it at him. How could he have not told her? Not once?

"It's ancient history, Cherry. She's the one who dropped me as soon as she inherited her father's millions." He took a step closer and Cherry backed away. "Money changes people. It changed her."

"But not me, right?" Sadness had begun to edge

out the confusion in Cherry's heart, settling with a heavy weight in her chest.

"The Youth Center needs your financial support before tonight." He blurted out the sentence without warning, and Cherry took a backward step.

Disbelief surged through her. His statement came from so far out in left field she almost laughed.

"You once said you'd never ask me for a handout." Her incredulity morphed to anger. "Would you believe I thought that was the sexiest thing I'd ever heard anyone say?" She shook her head. "I'll never learn."

Luke looked as if he'd been slapped. "I don't want to ask you. I have no choice."

"But you *are* asking?"

He nodded. "For the kids."

For the kids.

She flashed back to the night on the pier and her subsequent thoughts about how much more deserving the Youth Center was than the Women's League. Had he been setting her up even back then? Had every move been made to soften her up for this very moment?

Cherry corralled her anger, working not to take out all of her fears and doubts on the man who stood before her. "If I don't support the Horticultural Center tonight, she's going to expose my family."

Disappointment flashed across his face. "I thought you were done worrying about appearances."

She stared at him, wordlessly, suddenly unable to sort out exactly what she was feeling. Was Luke really who she'd believed him to be? Or had Monique been the one speaking the truth?

Had every one of Luke's actions been calculated to earn her trust? To get her to sway her funding to his cause?

To win?

"You need to leave." Her voice sounded flat, as if the events of the past week had finally sucked the last drop of life out of her.

Now Luke was the one who appeared to be filled with anger. His neck and face had blossomed into angry splotches of red. "Don't let her sway you, Cherry. You're better than that." He pointed at the phone. "You're better than *her*."

Cherry closed the space between them, reaching up to place a hand along his cheek, her throat tightening at her need for this man. Yet her heart broke at the thought he might have used her for her money—like all of the other gold diggers in her life.

She dropped her hand to his chest. "How long have you known you had to ask me this?"

He faltered, her question obviously taking him by surprise. "Since the night we went fishing."

Sudden tears swam in Cherry's vision, but she blinked them back. She would not let him see her cry. "Is that why you spent last night with me?"

"No." Luke shook his head and reached for her, but she backed out of his reach, turning away.

Her heart twisted and caught. She'd believed in him. Trusted him. Made love to him. And now he was asking her for money?

"I'd never ask for help if there was any other way," Luke continued, each word ratcheting up the confusion and pain swirling through her. "The last thing I want you to think is that I'm after your money."

She forced herself to speak. "How much of my money are you not after?"

The ensuing silence wrapped itself around her fragile spirit, squeezing tight.

"A million dollars."

Cherry flinched, then steeled herself. She turned, facing him head-on. Enough was enough. "I need you to leave."

"Cherry." His voice was tight, pained. "This has nothing to do with last night."

"Give me some credit, Luke." A bitter laugh slipped from between her lips. "I should have seen this coming. I've had enough practice over the past four months."

His expression darkened. "Do you think I've been after your money all this time?"

She stared, not sure of anything at that moment except the crushing ache in her chest—the one that meant her heart was slowly breaking.

"Cherry." His eyes narrowed, a furrow digging into his proud forehead. "I made love to you last night because I wanted *you*. I still want you. That has nothing to do with what I'm asking you now."

She squeezed her eyes shut, not wanting to see his face. How could he lie to her? How could he say his request had nothing to do with all the attention he'd given her? The man would probably earn an Academy Award nomination for this performance.

"Leave." The dull pain spread outward from her chest, making its way into every muscle, every bone. She'd given herself to him. Completely.

And now she needed him out of her house and out of her sight. She pointed toward the door.

"Not like this." Luke's fingers grazed her arm but she twisted free. "I've given you no reason to distrust me. I'm asking you because I need help. Do you think this is easy for me?

"What did last night mean to you?" he asked. "Nothing more than another night off from your plan? Like fishing?" He pointed to the phone she still clasped in her fingers. "I never thought you'd rush right back to socialite lessons today. What was all that talk last night? Lip service?"

Cherry shook her head. "Just go."

Luke crossed to the door. She drank in the way his jet-black hair curved against the nape of his neck. For one crazy moment she thought of reaching for him, telling him it didn't matter. He could have his money as long as she could have him.

He stopped in the door, gripping the wall. "I'm not like the others. And I didn't think you were, either."

With those words, he released his hold on the doorjamb and walked out of Cherry's life.

Not like the others. No. He was nothing like the others. He'd not only asked for her money, he'd claimed her heart.

As Cherry stood and stared at the space where he'd been, Monty approached and wrapped his arm around her shoulder. She leaned into the father's touch she'd missed for so many years.

"You okay?" he asked.

"Yes." But just then, she felt anything but.

"Cherry?"

She nodded, unable to speak for fear she'd cry.

"I couldn't help but hear Luke mention Michael Hoyer. How does he know him?"

Cherry pushed away from his embrace, turning to face him. "Why?"

When Monty gave his answer, the day she'd thought couldn't get any worse, did.

CHAPTER 23

An hour later, the office setup was complete. Monty and Yogi had disappeared to do who knew what, and Bart had arrived. Cherry left him standing in the foyer while she went in search of Liz.

As she climbed the stairs, she relived her earlier confrontation with Luke.

I'm asking you because I need help. Do you think this is easy for me?

His words haunted her. She'd assumed the worst, sending him away, certain all they'd shared had been an act. Had she been wrong?

Her gaze fell to the blue toenail polish she wore, the same polish she'd worn to the pier when she'd gone fishing with Luke and the boys. He'd kissed her that night for the second time, and she'd panicked and run.

Luke Chance had told her he wanted to win her heart.

Cherry hesitated at the top of the stairs, suddenly feeling very ashamed. She hugged herself. Why had she let Monique's words sway her opinion?

The man had never given her any reason to doubt his sincerity. The woman, however, had done nothing but.

Cherry cringed, nearly overwhelmed by the conflicting emotions battling inside her.

Hadn't she once thought sleeping with Luke would ease the tension between them? What a fool she was then.

What a fool she was now.

Luke had asked her for money because of his love for the Youth Center. He'd stepped out of his comfort zone, risking the possibility she'd react just as she had. He'd put himself on the line for what he believed in, and she'd jumped down his throat.

Luke Chance was the real deal, and that scared the hell out of her.

She found Liz in the master suite, elbow deep in Cherry's closet, trying to pick out the perfect poker-playing outfit to bring the Hartes luck.

Cherry refocused on Liz—and Bart.

She could either soften up her sister, taking time to tell Liz about her recent conversations with Bart, or she could spring the news of his arrival in one fell swoop.

Cherry glanced at the clock. Three-thirty. Moose and his boss were due in half an hour.

Fell swoop it was.

"Bart's here to see you."

Liz dropped Cherry's bright red suit to the floor. Her breath visibly caught, the emotion on her face morphing from shock to disbelief, from happiness to trepidation and back again.

Okay, so perhaps a subtle announcement might have been called for, but time *was* running short.

Liz reached up and patted her pink wig, sheer panic emblazoned across her features. Her lips mouthed the word, "What?" But she made no sound.

"He's here to talk to you." Cherry gripped her elbow and dragged her toward the hall. "And I want you to listen to everything he has to say. With an open mind."

"Sh . . . sh . . . shouldn't he be talking to you?" Liz's voice squeaked like a first-grader's and she dug the heels of her stilettos into a groove on the tile floor.

Cherry yanked harder. "I already talked to him."

She grasped both of Liz's shoulders, positioning her face so close to her sister's their eyelashes touched. "You know how I like to make plans?"

Liz nodded, baby blues huge.

"Well, Bart and I planned our wedding."

Liz blinked. "Don't most people plan their wedding?"

"Not like this." Cherry shook her head. "We planned it to make us both look better."

Liz squinted and Cherry barreled ahead. "He thought being married would make him a stronger candidate for state senate, and I thought being married would help me get the hell away from our life."

Who had she been kidding?

"Well," she continued, "let's just say that was the first plan to backfire in my face."

"But he had Mommy apprehended as soon as we finished dessert." Liz sounded as though someone had slipped her a helium-filled balloon at some point between the bedroom and the hall.

Cherry nodded. "I know. But he's sorry. And he's working on getting her help."

"Really?" Liz brightened. "And he's downstairs?"

"Waiting for you."

"For me?" Liz's tone had continued to climb, and she now sounded like a chipmunk on speed.

Cherry nodded. "Listen, I know you have a thing about my hand-me-downs, but trust me on this one. Bart was never mine to hand down."

Sheer confusion played across Liz's pretty face. Cherry eased her sister to the top of the steps, enjoying the way Liz's body language relaxed the instant she spotted Bart.

"Go ahead." Cherry dropped her voice to nothing more than a whisper.

She held her breath as Liz descended, not sure if she was more afraid Liz might fall off her towering heels or that she would impale Bart with one swift kick should he say something not to her liking.

A few minutes later, Cherry realized she had nothing to worry about.

Liz and Bart stood in close conversation—voices low, eyes locked.

Cherry wondered how she'd never noticed the spark that arced between them. Maybe she'd spent too much time making plans instead of paying attention to those she loved.

She glanced down at her watch and gasped. Ten to four. Moose and his boss would be here any second.

"Liz," she called out. "Make sure Yogi and Monty are ready. Ten minutes to showtime."

Bart planted a kiss on Liz's cheek, then looked up to where Cherry stood, meeting her gaze. He mouthed the words, "Thank you."

Cherry's pulse skipped—ever so slightly—but

she nodded back. She'd thought this moment might break her, but instead she felt as if her heart had grown inside her chest.

She'd loved these two people all of her life. What better ending than for them to find their way to each other?

She cleared her throat when her sister continued to stare into Bart's eyes. "Liz? Honey? Poker. Moose. Monty. Let's move." She clapped her hands.

She spotted the questioning look on Bart's face and laughed. "Remember when you wanted crazy?"

He nodded.

"Well, you're about to get it in spades."

Luke sat in the parking lot of the Youth Center, not wanting to go inside. Hell. He didn't want to do anything but find a quiet, dark place in which to hole up and figure out how to prove his feelings for Cherry had nothing to do with her wealth.

He ached as if she'd ripped the heart from his chest. A quiet voice deep inside the recesses of his brain told him he'd done the right thing—told him Cherry would understand eventually—but the rest of him didn't seem to agree.

Luke shoved away the frustration boomeranging around inside him and pushed himself from the driver's seat, launching his body toward the entrance.

He'd driven around Mystic Beach longer than he'd thought, and if he didn't soon break the news to the director that they'd get no funding from Cherry, there would be no time to prepare a contingency plan.

He patted his shirt pocket but found no pack of gum. He suddenly realized it didn't matter. It was time for him to stop hiding behind a sugar rush.

As Luke crossed through the gym, the decrepit condition of the facility hit him full force. The rickety bleachers. The damp cinder-block walls. The cracked linoleum hallways. *Lord, what a mess.*

He fought to tug his focus from thoughts of Cherry back to today. The Development Commission announcement was fast approaching and the Youth Center's future hung in the balance. If they failed in their bid to land the Framingham Estate, the kids would have nowhere to go when the current facility was demolished.

When he reached the long, dark hallway on the far side of the gym, a jumble of voices bubbled from the open administrative office door. Inside, employees and volunteers buzzed with activity. Luke stopped at the doorway, centering himself before he let them down with his news.

"Luke." The director's voice boomed across the din.

Luke's stomach pitched, then tightened. A dozen excited faces cast quick greetings, yet there he stood, about to bring their hopes and plans crashing down.

The noise of copiers, printers, and chatter was next to unbearable. On top of it all, someone had microwaved popcorn, and the smell hung thick in the air.

The director approached Luke, clasping a hand on his shoulder. "Great news about the funding."

"She didn't say yes." Luke forced the words past the lump of disappointment in his throat.

The director shook his head, grinning wide.

"Doesn't matter. Once the two funding sources that turned us down saw Cherry's photo in the paper, they reconsidered. We're in. It worked like a charm."

Luke zeroed in on the director's words. "What worked like a charm?"

"The article. Sheer genius." He slapped Luke on the shoulder. "Thanks to you."

The director stopped to sign a paper an assistant foisted into his hand, then refocused on Luke. "Matter of fact, there's been so much uproar about that photo that the Horticultural Center will probably have to withdraw."

Luke's mental fog lifted, and he focused solely on the director and what the man had done, anger beginning to percolate deep inside his chest. "You had her followed?"

The director nodded. "Couldn't have done it without you. I thought she was meeting with a funding source, but when the guy I sent saw her outfit and the man she was with, he clicked off the shot."

He laughed, and the sound made the small hairs at the nape of Luke's neck bristle.

"Sheer genius." The director repeated, stopping to skim a handout for tonight's meeting. "After all, once the story's out there, it doesn't matter whether it's true or not. It's all about first impressions."

Luke's anger surged, threatening to explode from his chest. He narrowed the space between himself and the director, doing his best not to draw attention to their conversation. "You purposely had her followed?"

"Hey." The director shrugged. "I didn't dress her.

We're talking about the center, Luke. This is our chance to knock the competition out of the race."

Luke gripped the man's collar, not caring who saw their exchange. "We're talking about Cherry Harte's reputation. What about that?"

The director peeled Luke's fingers from the front of his shirt. "What the hell is your problem? She can *buy* a new reputation."

But she couldn't. She'd already learned that lesson.

Luke wanted to throttle the man for what he'd done. "You risked the Youth Center by doing this. Do you realize that?"

The man shook his head. "Not if no one finds out." He stepped so close his warm breath brushed Luke's face. "No one's going to find out, are they?"

Luke stilled, frozen by the director's words. He'd told Cherry he had nothing to do with the photo, when in reality he had.

"What you did was unethical."

"Ethics?" The director scowled. "We're talking about helping the kids. Ethics can be bent."

"Ethics." Luke spoke the word slowly, wanting to convey exactly how serious he was. "Ethics are something the kids look to us for." He pointed a finger at the director. "And you've just let them down."

Luke turned to leave, not quite sure where he was headed. He realized then that all activity had stopped. All eyes focused on him—and the director.

He slammed the office door as he escaped the small space, determined to make the right decision. He'd do anything for the kids but lie.

They deserved better.

They deserved much, much better.

* * *

Cherry had just finished fluffing her once-again blond hair and buttoning her red suit when Yogi yelled, "Showtime!"

All the stress and confusion of the previous week settled into a knot in her stomach—a living, breathing, pulsating knot.

She glanced to where her goal poster lay in shreds against the wall. Calm assurance suddenly smashed the tangle in her stomach to bits. She was through making plans to hide from her identity.

She was Fran Harte's daughter—from her goal poster to her desire to become something she wasn't. So what? She was only human. And so was her mother.

She was also Monty's daughter, yet she had no plan to lose today's bet. Hell, maybe by the time all was said and done, each of them would have learned their lesson.

As she rounded the top of the steps, Moose's little figure came through the door on crutches. A striking man, not much older than Luke, followed, his stance so powerful that for a moment Cherry couldn't find her breath.

She forced herself to walk down the steps slowly, regally, owning the space—*her* space.

When she hit the tile floor of the foyer, she endured the handshakes and the introductions, all the while holding her chin high.

Cherry studied her opponent, Michael Hoyer, as he situated himself at the table. The same Michael Hoyer who had played a role in the end of Luke's career.

Her family's past had not only crashed into her present, but it had dragged Luke's past along for the ride.

Cherry nonchalantly fingered the recorder in her pocket. Maybe by the time the afternoon was over, she'd be able to hand Luke a story that would answer all of his questions—a small gesture to make up for how horribly she'd behaved.

She took a steadying breath, then turned to Liz. "Take off your pants."

CHAPTER 24

Luke stood in front of the shop's ancient mirror, fighting with his tie. He hated this damned suit but had to look the part for the Development Commission.

The chair had agreed to meet him early, and Luke planned to tell the truth about the article and the Youth Center director's role. He had to.

The Youth Center would survive.

Somehow.

Maybe the commission would grant an extension to identify new funding, or maybe he'd be able to negotiate a delay in the scheduled demolition. Luke's heart sank, defeat seeping into his tired muscles.

There was a very real chance he'd fail, leaving the kids with no place to gather. No place to belong. He straightened, giving his tie another yank.

"Will you let me fix that fool thing?" Gramps slapped Luke's hand away from the silk. "You're twisting it. What's the matter with you today, son?"

Luke shook his head and looked toward the ceiling as his grandfather wrestled with the tie.

What was the matter? He was about to blow the campaign and he'd probably already blown his chances with Cherry. Adding to his frustration, his fax machine still sat empty. Apparently none of his sources recognized Moose, or if they did, they had no intention of sharing information.

"Thought you had your funding." Gramps finished his adjustment of the tie and patted Luke's shoulder. "You should be happy."

"I asked Cherry to help before I found out about the bank funding."

"So?" Gramps's bushy brows pulled together.

"I asked her for no reason. We'd already gotten the money."

Crookedly.

Gramps shrugged. "At least you asked her. That took gumption."

Or stupidity. "Fat lot of good it did." Luke shrugged into his suit jacket. "I'm telling the commission the truth about the article. We'll probably be kicked out of the running."

Gramps stared at him long and hard. "You're going to let a bunch of hoity-toity plant lovers win? Thought you'd jump at the chance to let them lose."

"Cherry deserves the truth." Luke shrugged, waiting for a response.

Gramps only nodded.

"The kids deserve the truth." Now Luke nodded as well, meeting his grandfather's serious gaze.

Gramps continued to nod, his eyes narrowing.

"Women," Luke grumbled.

His grandfather's expression softened. "Got a light in her eyes."

Luke winced. "So you keep telling me." He pinched the bridge of his nose. "The last time I saw her, that light looked more like an oncoming train."

Gramps raised a fluffy brow. "You going to fight for her?"

Luke remained silent for several long beats. *Fight for her?* He'd chosen saving her reputation over saving the Youth Center, even after she'd accused him of being a no-good gold digger.

She really didn't deserve to be fought for. Did she?

He envisioned the light in her eyes, the cherry on her belly, and the uninhibited joy in her smile after they'd made love. His gut clenched.

As far as his heart was concerned, there was no choice.

Luke looked at his grandfather and nodded. "I think I might."

A bright smile spread across his grandfather's face. "I wouldn't worry about the money, son. For all you know, the funding you need has been right under your nose all along."

Luke shook his head, turning for the parking lot. Maybe Gramps was right, but Luke couldn't see how. All he knew was he had a Youth Center to save and Cherry to fight for.

Damn.

Whatever happened to his safe and boring life?

Eugene waited until Luke's car had cleared the lot before he picked up the phone and dialed

Cassie's number. The time had come to tell Luke the truth about exactly who he was.

His hopes sank when there was no answer at the widow's house. *Fool.* What if he'd waited too long? What if she'd moved on to the next eligible bachelor on the Mystic Beach Senior Center list?

His gut twisted at the thought.

He was still staring at the phone in his hand when a large standard poodle shoved her nose into his lap. His heart lurched in his chest, and he jumped at least a foot.

"Land's sake, Fifi." He patted the dog's head. "You near gave me a heart attack."

"There's nothing wrong with your heart that I can't fix, Eugene Chance."

His attention snapped to the sound of Cassie's voice. She stood in the doorway, lips pursed, looking as though she might kill him.

"Cassie."

"Don't you Cassie me, old man." She stomped over to where he sat, peering down at him. "Were you ever going to speak when I answered the phone? Or were you just going to continue to hang up?"

Busted.

He flinched, still patting the dog's fluffy head. "How did you know?"

"Caller ID, you old fool." She rolled her eyes. "I've told you a million times."

Warm embarrassment fired in his cheeks. She was right.

Cassie let out a sigh. "What was so important that you kept calling? Or were you finally ready to admit you've got a little crush on me?"

Eugene puffed out his chest, then exhaled slowly.

"You know you do." Cassie shook her head. "Listen. At our age we can't dilly dally with this stuff. Either you're with me, or you're not."

He stared at her, measuring the flush of color in her cheeks and the determination in her gaze. Her eyes flashed and he blinked.

Cassie Pettigrew had a light in *her* eyes. He should have known all along. His heart swelled with quiet contentment and he knew he'd finally found his match.

Again.

"Can you ever forgive me for being such an old fool?" He reached for her hand, cradling it between his own.

Cassie smiled. "Pish posh." She leaned down to press a soft kiss to his forehead.

Eugene swallowed, his blood pressure soaring to the stratosphere.

She tipped her head sideways, her eyes bright with affection. "Now bring me up to date on Luke and Cherry. I've been dying of curiosity."

Five minutes later she frowned at him. "Eugene Chance." Her sharp tone startled him. "You'd better march over to that county office and tell Luke about the money."

Eugene planted a kiss on her bright pink lips, then stood back, savoring the happy surprise in her pale eyes. He held up a finger as he pushed the office door closed.

"I will, but first, you and I have got some lost time to make up for."

* * *

Things at the poker game were going downhill fast. Yogi had taken off his surgical mask and was using it to pat the beads of sweat from his upper lip.

Monty had borrowed a toothpick from Moose and chomped on it so loudly Cherry could have sworn Luke was in the room chewing a wad of gum.

As for her, full-blown panic had set in.

Everything Yogi taught her hinged on reading her opponent's face, and since Hoyer had insisted on a game of old-fashioned basic poker, there were no cards visible on the table. Her read on the hand he held had to come from his eyes.

The thing was, the man wore huge sunglasses. Not sleek, sophisticated I'm-a-badass-poker-player glasses, but huge I-just-had-my-cataracts-done glasses.

"Isn't there a rule against those?" She blurted the words out loud before she could censor herself.

Hoyer never spoke. Hell, he hadn't spoken yet.

"What?" Moose asked.

Cherry tipped her chin toward the boss. "The glasses. How am I supposed to read his expression?"

The little man only laughed. Cherry couldn't help but notice Lucky had begun to growl.

Moose hobbled to the far side of the room, as far from the pink poodle as he could get.

Suddenly, Cherry had a brainstorm.

"May we take an intermission?" she asked.

Again, Hoyer said nothing, but Moose snorted. "Sweet cheeks, there are no intermissions in poker."

Think fast, Cherry. Fast. "Female troubles." She faked a pained expression.

"Five minutes." Hoyer's voice filled the room for

the first time, and she shuddered. It wasn't that the man's voice was striking. It was terrifying.

Cherry scrambled from her chair and hooked Liz's arm. She nodded to Bart, Monty, and Yogi to follow.

"I thought you said female troubles?" Moose asked.

"I did." She stopped in her tracks and rolled her eyes. "*Big* female troubles."

She dragged her family into the kitchen and planted her fists on her hips. "Lucky needs to get skunked."

Three and one-half pairs of eyes frowned back.

"Think about it," she continued. "If we can get that guy's eyes to water, maybe he'll take off his glasses."

Monty's gaze popped wide. "Brilliant."

"But what about the photo shoot?" Liz asked.

Cherry shook her head. "I don't think they're coming and even if they do, this is more important."

Yogi bit his lip.

"Spill it," Cherry said.

"Yogi thinks Lucky has a new girlfriend."

Monty nodded. "You're right."

"Why?" Cherry's voice tightened.

"He hasn't been the same since the bingo incident." Yogi shrugged.

Cherry glared at the man's good eye. "Because?"

"The dog he was protecting was a striking young pedigree named *Fifi*."

Disbelief swept through Cherry. Of all the times for her dog to realize he was a dog. "Well, somebody needs to get skunked."

The five of them looked at each other, poor Bart's face one of total puzzlement.

Suddenly, Cherry, Monty, and Yogi focused on Liz's curly pink wig—the wig that looked frighteningly similar to Lucky's fur.

She clasped a hand on top of her head. "No."

"We have no other choice," Cherry said.

Liz gripped the wig in both hands and held on tight. She shook her head. "No."

"For your mother, Lizzie."

Cherry couldn't help but notice her sister's features soften at Monty's use of the pet name.

Bart stepped forward and wrapped his fingers around Liz's hands, lowering them to her sides. He stood close, looking only into her eyes.

"Don't take this the wrong way, but I can't imagine why you'd want to cover up your beautiful, blond hair."

Liz's pale brows lifted. "Really?"

Bart nodded.

"You *really* think so?"

He nodded again.

"Take it." Liz yanked the wig from her head and tossed it to Cherry, who tossed it to Monty.

Bart, however, apparently wasn't done with his plan to free Liz's package. He pointed to her upper lip. "When did you get a mole?"

A pink blush fired in Liz's cheeks. "It's a beauty mark."

"Why would you *ever* need a beauty mark?"

The question was such a simple one, yet the way Bart asked it made everyone sigh. Loudly. Yogi actually gasped.

Cherry tried to remember a time she'd heard a

voice so full of raw admiration and, dared she say, love.

A memory of Luke's voice passed through her mind.

I don't want to like you, Cherry. I don't want to think about you. I don't even want to dream about you. But if you needed help, I'd help you.

Lord. She'd been a fool not to pick up on that same tone in Luke's voice. It had been there all the time.

Monty handed the wig to Bart, and the couple dashed out back in search of a skunk.

Cherry returned to the table and settled in her chair. She warily eyed her shrinking pile of chips and prayed she could hold on until the wig got back.

Maybe she could run a diversion. Hell, it was worth a shot.

Her gaze fell to the wrapped canvas leaning against the wall. The masterpiece Yogi refused to unveil until the people from *Mystic Living* arrived.

She cut her eyes at Yogi, then back to the canvas.

He shook his head.

She shot him a death glare, cut her eyes to the canvas, then back to him.

He frowned.

"We forgot to present you with your gift, Mr. Hoyer."

The man gave no response, not that she'd have been able to see it if he had.

Yogi's frown had turned into a pout, but he followed Cherry's lead, slowly walking toward the canvas. To Cherry's amazement, Hoyer had lowered his glasses, revealing the coldest eyes she'd ever seen.

Her heart hit her toes. Even if the skunk stench

worked and he took the glasses off for good, she found it difficult to believe his eyes would show emotion. Matter of fact, she doubted the man had shown an ounce of emotion a single day in his life.

Yogi flipped the cover off the canvas at the precise moment Bart and Liz reappeared. Liz gave Cherry the thumbs-up signal, but Michael Hoyer began to laugh.

The sound started low in his gut and traveled up and out, booming across the table.

Moose laughed.

Yogi laughed.

Even the dealer Hoyer had brought with him from Reno laughed.

Cherry turned to take in the painting and pressed her fingers to her lips.

Yogi had gotten his pink.

In the painting, five pink poodles sat around a card table, playing poker—a brilliant tribute to the old classic.

"Magnificent," Hoyer said. But his one-word admiration was followed shortly by his question. "What, for the love of money, is that stench?"

Cherry's eyes had begun to water, but she blinked the moisture back. "What do you mean?"

Monty and Yogi followed her lead, both shrugging.

"I don't smell a thing," Liz said, and Bart agreed.

Hoyer pulled a handkerchief from his pocket and began to mop his eyes.

The game belonged to Cherry from that point forward. Apparently Hoyer was a man who liked control, and when anything moved beyond his

control, like the forces of a nature—or a coopera-
tive skunk—he floundered.

She beat him on a straight flush. Yogi said he'd
never seen anything like it.

Hoyer was livid, but he'd lost fair and square—
relatively speaking. As the dealer gathered the
chips and cards, Hoyer graced them with one parting shot, directed to Monty.

"You got lucky, old friend." He pointed an elegant
finger directly at Monty's nose. "If it weren't for my
father, you'd have never gotten this break." He
laughed. "I don't like people taking advantage of
my money."

Excitement tingled in Cherry's stomach and she
reached into her suit pocket, praying she'd pressed
the right button.

"You're all talk, Hoyer." Monty frowned and
Cherry secretly thanked him. His one short phrase
had sent color firing in Hoyer's cheeks.

"I could have taken your wife's fingers—one by
one." Hoyer laughed. "Hell, I could have taken
her out. A hit on the inside is cake. I should know,
I've orchestrated plenty."

Monty rolled his eyes, and Cherry thought Hoyer
would explode.

"What about the guy from Miami?" Monty prod-
ded, going for exactly what Cherry wanted. "I heard
he's on an island somewhere, living large on your
money."

Hoyer closed the space between himself and
Monty, and Cherry held her breath. She beamed
with pride as her father stood strong against the
man's menacing figure.

Hoyer spoke softly, yet clearly. "Jimmy wasn't as

smart as he thought he was." He gave a small chuckle. "Now, he's just plain dead."

Lucky had moved in on one side of Monty, and Liz stood tight on the other.

"Careful, boss." Moose pointed his crutch at the dog. "That one bites." Then he gestured to Liz. "And that one kicks."

"Cars," Bart called out from the foyer. "You expecting the press?"

Cherry's stomach tilted sideways.

Monique. That bitch.

Hoyer and his little band of thugs moved faster than a group of roaches in a spotlight. They were in the hall and out the back door before the doorbell rang.

When Bart pulled the front door open, a lone woman stood on the top step, a camera around her neck and a notepad in her hand. "Hi. I'm here to shoot your spread for *Mystic Living.* May I come in?"

Cherry looked at the shambles of her house and down at Liz's lucky pants she'd pulled on beneath her skirt. Then she realized she reeked of skunk.

Hell. The entire place reeked of skunk, but suddenly she didn't care. She extended her hand to the woman, looking past her as she issued a greeting.

"I thought you said cars? Plural." She squinted at Bart.

He shrugged. "I always did have a problem with exaggeration."

Cherry pivoted on one heel, reaching to grab her purse. She had some unfinished business to take care of, and she was running out of time.

"My sister would be happy to answer any of your questions. She's really the brains behind the whole"—she glanced at the mess of their house and laughed—"decorating scheme."

Liz gave her a lethal glare but smiled, waving her toward the door.

The woman from *Mystic Living* raised her camera. "How about one shot before you leave. Of your family."

The thought warmed Cherry deep down, in a way that only the word *family* could.

So they gathered—next to Yogi's poker masterpiece. Cherry and her father. Liz and Bart. Yogi and Lucky.

The eccentric, irresistible, amazing group of people that had taught Cherry to say good-bye to packaging issues forever.

Monty caught her by the elbow just as she reached the front door. "I won't be here when you get back."

Her heart fell to the depths of her stomach. "You're leaving again?"

He smiled. "Only for a few days." He pressed a kiss to her nose. "I have to see a woman in New Jersey about a coffee cake."

Cherry beamed as she dashed for her car.

Such joy and certainty filled her about what she was going to do, she didn't care how ridiculous she might look or how bad she might smell.

Liz's leopard-print leggings peeked from beneath her classic red suit, but they'd brought her such luck today, she didn't dare take them off.

Hell. If nothing else, the outfit spoke volumes about the many—and proud—faces of Cherry Harte.

CHAPTER 25

When Cherry barged into Monique Goodall's office, the assistant chased her across the outer foyer but never had a chance of catching her.

An amazingly calm assurance filled Cherry. She didn't care what she might be interrupting. She didn't care that her visit might be unwelcome or that she might be breaking some unwritten socialite rule.

She was acting on impulse and she'd never felt so empowered in her life.

Monique's head snapped up from her date book as Cherry careened into the office. "Have you brought the check?" The woman's perfectly lined lips pressed together in obvious disapproval of Cherry's entrance—and her outfit.

Cherry shook her head, no longer a player in the approval game. "You want your funding?" She stepped close to the desk, tapping the sleek surface. "I've got some conditions for you to meet."

"Conditions?" Monique's shocked gaze widened. Cherry held a finger in the air, excitement tingling to her extremities. "One. You withdraw your proposal to the Development Commission."

Monique's mouth gaped open.

Perfect.

Another finger. "Two. You identify a new location for the Horticultural Center."

Monique's mouth snapped shut.

Even better.

A third finger. "Three. You present me with plans for a recreational program to benefit area children. I'm sure the kids at the new Mystic Beach Youth Center would love learning about horticulture."

Monique shot daggers from her glare. She splayed her fingers on the desktop, taking a deep breath before she spoke. "I'll crucify you at the meeting."

Cherry felt her chest swell with satisfaction, not caring if Monique Goodall burned her at the stake. "Go for it."

"Do you know what the media will do to you?"

Cherry laughed. "Do you know what they'll do to *you* when they find out I've offered you a million dollars and you *still* plan to squeeze out the Youth Center? Kids, Monique."

She held up her hands like weights on a scale. "Kids. Plants. Which do you think the public will have more sympathy for?"

Monique's cheeks puffed out and in. "You will *never* be a member of the Women's League."

"Puhlease." Cherry rolled her eyes and fingered her abdomen where the tattoo lay hidden, itching out of control. "Is that the best you can do?"

She spun on her heel, turning for the door. "I'll expect your withdrawal at the meeting."

She dashed into the hall without waiting for the woman's response, frantic to catch Luke before he left the garage. If she had her way, the Youth Center was about to land its new home.

Luke shifted in his seat, waiting for the Development Commission chair to speak. He'd come clean about the article and its origins, realizing he'd not only implicated the Youth Center director, but also the program itself.

The regal gentleman took a deep breath, then leaned forward. "You realize you leave me with no choice."

Luke nodded. "I knew that coming in, sir, but I refuse to let the program be tainted by something this unethical."

"Word of this might still leak out." The man pressed his lips to a thin line. "What then?"

Luke thought for a moment, realizing the man had spoken the truth. "Hopefully the public appreciates the good the Youth Center does for the Mystic Beach community. We'll have to hope they'll forgive us."

The chair nodded his head, rubbing his chin. "What would you do if you were in my position?"

This question Luke had prepared for. "I'd allow the Youth Center to withdraw, sir. No questions asked. On the grounds of funding issues."

"And what about your director? Will he remain

on staff?" The man ran a hand through his silver hair.

Luke shook his head. "No, sir. He'll be removed. You have my assurance as a member of the board of trustees."

"Very well, Mr. Chance." The gentleman pushed to his feet, extending a hand. "I'm sorry to accept the Youth Center's withdrawal. I wish your organization much luck in identifying another property for construction."

"Thank you, sir."

As he turned for the main meeting room, cold resignation settled on Luke's shoulders. He'd just single-handedly destroyed the Youth Center's last chance at the Framingham Estate.

Short of a flat-out miracle, they'd lost all hope.

A very large, very bored-looking poodle greeted Cherry as she walked into Luke's shop. The dog lazed next to the closed office door but scrambled to its feet when she approached.

Cherry's stomach lurched reflexively. This particular poodle was five times the size of Lucky, and she'd seen what those tiny fangs could do. "Good girl . . . er . . . boy." She smiled. "Nice doggie."

The office blinds had been pulled tight, and a soft giggle filtered from the other side of the glass.

Cherry froze with a sudden image of Luke in a lovers' clinch. Her insides pitched, nausea washing over her. Oh God. Maybe it all *had* been an act. Maybe he didn't care for her at all.

The poodle nuzzled Cherry's feet, its whiskers

tickling her exposed toes. *Poodle.* A connection clicked in Cherry's mind and she let out a relieved sigh. *Cassandra Pettigrew and her derned dog.*

If Gramps and the widow Pettigrew were sequestered behind closed doors, Cherry had no intention of interrupting. She tiptoed backward, away from the office.

The poodle followed, stopping suddenly to yap. Loudly.

Cripes. "Not now. I'm leaving."

"Who's there?" Gramps's voice called out from behind the closed door. "Fifi, what's all the racket?"

"Thanks a lot." Cherry dropped her tone to a whisper, frowning at the dog. "Fifi?" She tipped her head from side to side. *Couldn't be. Could it?*

"It's Cherry." She raised her voice enough to be heard through the door. "I was looking for Luke, but I can see I came at a bad time."

The office door snapped open and a red-faced Gramps stepped from behind it. A splotch of bright pink lipstick smudged his upper lip.

Cherry wiped at her own lip. "You've got a little—"

Gramps's blush deepened as he dragged the back of his hand across his mouth.

"Customer service." He winked.

A laugh slipped from Cherry's lips.

Gramps's expression grew serious and he glanced at the clock on the wall. "He headed over to the meeting a while ago. Shouldn't you be on your way?"

Cherry pulled her thoughts back into focus. Gramps was right. She didn't have much time, but why had Luke gone so early? "How long ago did he leave?"

Gramps stepped closer, glancing back toward the office door. "Half hour, maybe."

Perfect. Cherry's heart caught and twisted. She'd come up with a plan to make things up to him, but she had to hurry.

She started to turn away. "I've got to catch him."

"Smart money says you've already done that."

Gramps's soft words stopped her in her tracks. She met his gaze, her insides warming when his features broke into a wide grin. "I hope so."

Gramps placed a finger to his lips, giving a quick nod. "You know, if you look closely enough, he's got a light in his eyes."

Cherry's heart tilted inside her chest. Gramps was right. Luke *did* have a light in his eyes, especially anytime he'd been looking at her.

She closed the space between herself and Luke's grandfather, planting a quick kiss on his cheek.

His already flushed cheeks darkened. "Better get going."

Cassandra Pettigrew peeked around the door, her tightly permed hair seriously askew, her bright pink lipstick smeared.

Cherry smiled. "Nice to see you again, Cassandra. How kind of you to check in on Luke's grandfather."

Cassandra brightened. "I wanted to see how his heart was working."

Cherry stifled a giggle. "I have a feeling it's working just fine."

Cassandra beamed, and Gramps shot Cherry another wink.

Wasn't love grand?

"As you were." Cherry broke into a run, headed for her Jaguar.

Even though Gramps said she'd already caught Luke, Cherry wasn't so sure. She was certain of one thing, however. She planned to do whatever it took to reel in the man.

Permanently.

CHAPTER 26

Cherry screeched the Jaguar to a stop outside the entrance to the county offices. There wasn't time to park. Who'd ever heard of traffic during June in Mystic Beach?

She sprang from the car, racing up the steps to the entrance. She glanced at her watch. Fifteen minutes late. Her heart caught, nervousness flickering through her. She'd never slip in unnoticed, but she swallowed down her fear. It didn't matter. She was Cherry Harte, damn it, and she was on a mission.

A deserted hallway greeted her. Great. They couldn't have started late, for once. She paused at the meeting room door, fingers on the handle, heart slapping a crazy beat against her ribs. *I can do this.*

Her eyes flew open, eyeing her target. *No, I can't.*

Voices sounded from inside. Good grief. She really was late. Cherry pressed against her tattoo through the fabric of her suit. The next few minutes were dedicated to everyone who'd ever been ashamed of who they were.

Even more important, what she was about to do

was for Luke, the man who'd taught her to trust her heart—as well as her heritage.

She swallowed, reached for the handle, and yanked.

A sudden urge to throw darts filled Luke as Monique took the podium. Just once he'd like to see her flawless ice-princess mouth at a loss for words.

"Members of the commission," she began.

Luke groaned. *Just once.*

He lowered his face to his palms as the woman droned on about the planned Horticultural Center. *Plants.* He'd let the kids down by losing to plants. How would he ever face them?

"The Women's League is delighted to announce a one-million-dollar funding pledge from Cherry Harte."

Luke snapped his head up from out of his hands, glaring at the podium. Polite applause smattered throughout the room as members of the Women's League smiled their bright, holier-than-thou, beige smiles.

Monique couldn't be telling the truth, could she? Had Cherry really gone back to the—

"Excuse me." Cherry's voice rose above the applause.

Luke turned, straining to see her. His heart stopped at the sight of her in her fitted red suit and spotted . . . leggings?

She winked as she passed his seat, and he grinned in spite of himself. What was she up to?

Cherry waved her hand in the air. "May I approach, please?"

Monique's mouth gaped open as Cherry edged her away from the microphone.

"You are?" the commission chair asked.

"Cherry Harte." She glanced at Monique, giving her a look that would have frozen fire. Luke's belly warmed. Looked like good old Monique was at a loss for words after all.

"There's been a misunderstanding." Cherry leaned into the microphone. "I made my pledge to the Women's League on the condition they find an alternate location for the Horticultural Center."

A collective gasp rose from the others in attendance, and Monique made a bold move to wrestle the microphone from Cherry's hand. She stopped abruptly, and Luke could have sworn he saw Cherry plant a quick elbow to her ribs.

He propped his chin on his fist, leaning around the gentleman blocking part of his view. This was one show he had zero intention of missing.

"Are you saying you will not fund development of the Horticultural Center on the Framingham Estate?" The chair's voice rose above the din.

"That's correct." Cherry glanced over her shoulder to where Luke sat, her fiery green gaze locking momentarily with his. She turned to refocus on the commission. "I will be funding the Youth Center, however, in whatever amount they need. I'm confident their program is the wisest choice for the estate."

Cameras flashed and reporters scribbled frantically in their notebooks. Luke shook his head, a disbelieving laugh slipping between his lips. Son of a gun. The girl had more heart than even he'd given her credit for.

"The Youth Center had to withdraw their application," the chair said solemnly into his microphone.

Cherry shrugged. "That's my fault, I'm afraid. I didn't give them my answer quickly enough."

She leaned forward, sending the commission what Luke was sure must be one of her dazzling smiles. "Surely you aren't going to hold my mistake against the children."

The commissioners glanced from one to the other, murmuring amongst themselves. All color had blanched from Monique's face. She sank, defeated, onto an empty chair. Cherry never flinched, holding her ground, standing tall and confident.

"You also should know"—Cherry's voice grew even stronger—"my family and I will be establishing the Harte Foundation to support projects like the Youth Center. You can rest assured the construction phase of their project will receive whatever funding it needs."

Luke's chest swelled with pride. He leaned out into the aisle to get a clear view of her legs. *Damn.* The woman and her knees looked even sexier in leggings. Who'd have thought it possible?

"In light of this unexpected funding reversal"— the chair tapped his microphone to regain the room's attention—"the Mystic Beach Development Commission is pleased to award ownership of the historic Framingham Estate to the Mystic Beach

Youth Center, pending approval of all construction and financial documents."

Luke jumped to his feet. Cherry shook hands with each commissioner, then spun to face him, her brilliant smile lighting up her face.

He closed the space between them, stopping short of reaching for her. He nodded toward her outfit. "Excellent choice in packaging."

She grinned, turning one foot to display the full leg. "Liz's lucky pants. Aren't they cute?"

"How'd they work out for you?"

She smiled at him and his stomach caught. "Beautifully."

He sent up a silent prayer and asked, "Are we all right?"

Cherry brushed her finger along his chin, sending a jolt straight to his heart. "If you'll forgive me."

He shook his head. "I should have asked you as soon as I knew we were in trouble."

"Puhlease." She pressed her finger to his lips, ratcheting up his pulse. "You told me yourself how you felt about people with money. No wonder you hesitated to ask." She rolled her eyes. "And when you did ask, I acted like a fool."

Luke arched a brow. "You *were* rather harsh."

She pulled Monique's recorder from her suit pocket, waved it in the air, then handed the tiny device to him. "A little something to make things up to you."

He pressed the Play button and her voice rang out in the crowded room. "Note to self. Find a new mechanic."

He grimaced and she snatched the recorder away. "Not that one." She adjusted a button and pressed Play again. Michael Hoyer's voice sounded, confessing what he'd done to Jimmy.

Disbelief and sadness battled inside Luke. "So he never got the chance to come back?"

Cherry shook her head.

Luke frowned. "How in the hell did you get this?"

"I promise to tell you every juicy detail. Trust me. This just might be the story of your career." She winked and warm laughter bubbled from her lips. Luke's restraint didn't stand a snowball's chance in hell.

He studied her leggings again and grinned. "I've got some issues with this particular packaging, like how quickly we can get you out of those. Any bathrooms around?"

A sexy smile tugged at the corners of her mouth. "I'm sure there must be."

He leaned close, gripping her arms and brushing her ear with his lips. "I have been craving cherries, you know."

What the hell. Maybe it was time he faced his allergy head-on.

Cherry sputtered, then stepped back, biting down on her lower lip. His poor, tortured libido threatened to explode. He angled his mouth down over hers, not caring that they stood in the middle of the meeting room or that a camera flashed, followed by a second and a third.

"Ahem." A gruff voice sounded just below Luke's ear. *Gramps*? It couldn't be.

"You two want to break it up? I could go any time."

Cherry opened one eye, then pushed away from Luke. His grandfather stood arms crossed, bushy brows meeting in an amused peak.

"What are you doing here?" Utter disbelief tinged Luke's voice.

"Heard you needed some money."

Cherry bit back her surprise as Gramps pulled an envelope from his shirt pocket, handing it over to Luke.

Luke hesitated, then took the envelope and slipped a single sheet of paper from inside. His eyes grew huge, then zeroed in on his grandfather, intense and dark.

"What is it?" Curiosity filled Cherry.

Luke handed her the paper, and her gaze fell to the letterhead. An investment firm. She scanned the statement for the name on the account. *Luke's name.* She read further until she found the current balance, inhaling sharply when she saw the figure.

Eight and one-half million dollars.

"You're loaded, son." Gramps clasped a hand on Luke's shoulder.

Poor Luke had gone pale and stared wordlessly at his grandfather.

"How did you do this?" Cherry asked.

Gramps puffed out his chest. "I bought Microsoft in 1986. I wanted to make sure my boy never wanted for anything."

Cherry's insides warmed as she measured the man who had raised Luke, loving him enough to secure his future.

"Luke?" She placed her palm on his back. He relaxed beneath her touch.

"Why didn't you tell me?" Luke's tone had gone soft, shocked.

"I wanted to wait until you were ready."

Luke laughed. "And?"

"Seems to me, you and Cherry are on your way to happily ever after." Gramps winked. "That's all I needed to see."

Cherry waved one hand. "Aren't we rushing things a bit?"

"Cherry's right. You might be jumping the gun, Gramps." Luke's color returned, flushing his cheeks a rosy red.

"It's not that." Cherry dropped her hand from Luke's back, crossing her arms in mock annoyance. She shook her head. "I make it a rule not to date wealthy men. You know how money changes people, and they're always worried about appearances."

Gramps grinned, clearly understanding her teasing tone, but Luke spun to face her, his expression serious and dark. "I don't want you to date me, Cherry."

Her heart caught, anxiousness twisting in her belly.

"I want you to love me."

His words filled her with warm relief and sent her tattoo into an itching frenzy.

Gramps clapped and let out a whoop, the sound echoing into the now-empty meeting room.

Cherry clasped a hand just below her neck, willing her heart to slow down before it burst from her chest. "I do love you, Luke. Very much."

He kissed her then, long and deep. Cherry's toes curled as his lips pressed to hers. The promise of her future with Luke filled her with a security she'd never known.

When they came up for air, Gramps had disappeared.

"Come on." Cherry tugged on Luke's hand and pulled him toward the nearest restroom. "I've got an itch I need you to scratch."

ABOUT THE AUTHOR

After a career spent spinning words for clients ranging from corporate CEOs to talking fruits and vegetables, Kathleen Long now finds great joy spinning a world of fictional characters, places, and plots. She shares her life with her husband and their neurotic Sheltie, dividing her time between suburban Philadelphia and the New Jersey seashore. There she can often be found—hands on keyboard, bare toes in sand—lost in thought and time. After all, life doesn't get much better than that. Please visit Kathleen at www.kathleenlong.com.

Contemporary Romance By
Kasey Michaels

For my agent, Deidre Knight, with thanks. I hope this is only the first of many projects we'll see through together.

CHAPTER ONE

AFTER TWENTY YEARS fifteen minutes more or less didn't matter much.

Jimmy Falcon pulled his shirtsleeve down over his watch, leaned an elbow on the bar and picked up his glass. If he had to wait for a woman, he didn't know of a better way to pass the time than standing in his own club, sipping old whiskey while listening to hot jazz.

When he checked the time again, discovering that only fifteen minutes more had passed, he realized even waiting with jazz had its limits. Where was she? Had she decided not to show up after all?

Finally, he decided to wait outside, by the entrance to the club. Maybe she'd had trouble finding the place. He could flag her down when she drove by.

Then again, would she even recognize him, after twenty years? Would he recognize her?

The answer to that question hit him right between the eyes as he stepped through the door. In a night full of people, he couldn't help but notice the woman on the other side of the street. She was tall, generous through the hips and long in the legs under her jeans. She could be anyone, from anywhere, but something about the set of her shoulders inside a soft pink T-shirt, the tumble of gold-red curls clipped on top of her head, created a vibration deep inside him.

Barely noticing the traffic, he got across as fast as he

could and put a hand on her arm. "Emma? Emma Garrett? Why the hell are you standing here in the dark?"

As she turned toward him, her blue eyes widened, first with caution, then surprise, finally, laughter. "Jimmy! I was coming in to find you!"

Just like that, with a street full of people gaping at them, Emma Garrett took hold of him. Again.

She flung her arms around his neck, and Jimmy returned the embrace, cautiously at first, then with more enthusiasm. Twenty years since he'd last held her, but the fit felt like it was yesterday. They were nearly the same height; her full breasts pressed into his chest as she hugged him tight, then tighter still. She wore a different perfume than he remembered, but he liked it. He liked everything about having Emma Mae Garrett this close.

When he finally forced himself to ease back, Emma let him go until just their hands touched. He searched her face in the streetlight's glare, seeing again the clear, pale skin, dusted with freckles, the deep peach of her mouth, the bright blue eyes. For a second he was seventeen again, starting the best summer of his life.

But the past was…just the past. With a wrench, Jimmy pulled his thoughts to the present. "This isn't the safest part of town to stand around in after dark. Come inside." Taking her hand, noticing its softness, he led Emma across the street and into The Indigo.

One of the edgier jazz bands was playing tonight, the music hard and loud. Smoke hovered in the air and he heard Emma cough as the fog caught her by the throat. The place was full, especially for a Tuesday. He threaded his way through the crowd without letting go of her hand, stopped at the bar long enough to order them both a drink, then headed for his office.

"Sorry about that." He leaned back against the closed

door. All they could hear now was the pulse of the bass and the drums. "Things get kind of loud out there."

Smiling, Emma shook her head, and a curl of red-gold hair escaped to bounce on her neck. "It's wonderful music." Her English accent was as elegant as he remembered.

"You still like jazz?"

"I dropped it for a few years. Then came to my senses."

"Nothing's quite the same, is it?"

"Nothing." They looked at each other for a second, while the air got tighter, harder to breathe. Jimmy thought about the beat-up truck he'd owned that summer two decades ago, about popping an Ellington tape into the player and sitting with his arm around Emma, watching the sun disappear behind the mountains. About the things they'd learned together in that truck, in the dark...

"Have a seat," he said abruptly. Looking relieved, Emma sank into the recliner in the corner while he rounded his desk. Before he could sit down, there was a knock on the door.

"Drinks, boss." Darren McGuire, the club's server, set a tonic water on the table beside Emma and a whiskey at Jimmy's right hand. "Anything else?"

Jimmy consulted Emma. "Would you like a sandwich? Nachos? The variety's not great, but we can feed you."

She leaned forward to pick up the tonic. "Actually, I haven't eaten since my flight left New York at nine this morning. I'd love a bite—something simple."

He nodded at Darren. "Ask Hank to give us the best he's got."

The young man raised an eyebrow. "That's not much." He caught sight of Jimmy's frown. "I'm going. I'm going."

Shaking his head, Jimmy dropped into his chair. "God save me from wisecracking waiters." He took a drink of whiskey, just for something to do. After twenty years, after anticipating this meeting for five long days, he suddenly didn't know how to act.

The direct approach usually worked best. "So...your e-mail was kinda mysterious. You said when you were coming here, but not why."

After a pause, while she stared into her glass and he stared at her, Jimmy said, "Emma? Do you want some gin with the tonic? Vodka?"

She jumped a little. "Oh. No. This is fine. I'm simply trying to decide how to begin."

"Sounds bad."

"It is, in a way." Her gaze came to his face. "My father had prostate cancer. He died three months ago at home in England."

The ground dropped out from beneath Jimmy's feet for a minute. It was always a shock when someone you knew—and liked—was gone. "That's... I'm sorry. He was a really good man."

"Yes." She looked at her hands, set down the glass of tonic.

Another long silence. "Are you here because of your dad?"

"Yes. I don't know why I'm making this so difficult." She drew a deep breath. "Before he died, my father asked me to find you. And when I found you, he wanted me to bring you a bequest."

"He shouldn't have bothered." Jimmy resisted the urge to loosen his tie, though his collar felt a little tight all at once.

"But he did." She reached into her large leather purse and drew out a polished wooden box, four inches square, two inches deep. "The gift is inside. I don't know what it is—there's a seal I didn't want to break." She showed him the blob of gold wax over the catch on the side.

"Emma, I don't need—"

She got to her feet and crossed to the desk, picked up his hand and placed the box on his palm. "It's yours. He wanted you to have it."

He felt her touch deep in his chest. "Okay, okay. We'll see what's inside."

"This isn't any of my business." She backed toward the door. "I'll leave you alone."

"No way." He reached across and caught her wrist. "We're doing this together. Sit down."

He waited until she took the straight-backed chair on the other side of the desk, then pulled out his pocketknife and flipped open the blade. The sharp tip slipped easily underneath the seal and pried it off in one piece.

He closed the knife and set it aside, then sat staring at the box. Walnut, he thought, inlaid with two lighter woods in an angular, mazelike pattern. "Well, here goes." He thumbed the hook free and eased the top back on its hinges.

Clean, soft sheepskin filled the shallow cavity, cushioning a silver disk as wide as the box. He picked up the medallion for a closer look. Inlaid with gold and silver and different shades of turquoise, the piece felt heavy in his hand.

"What is it?" Emma asked softly.

Jimmy shook his head. "Hell if I know." Fine engraving combined with the inlay to create a sunrise over mountains.

Emma stirred. "There's something in the lid."

Laying the disk on its nest, Jimmy pulled the folded sheet of paper out of the box's top and spread it open. Bold handwriting in fountain-pen ink covered the page.

Jimmy,
   You may remember Joseph Hobson, an elder of your tribe on the reservation in South Dakota. After a chance meeting in Africa as college students, he and I corresponded for many years; my work with the

Sioux language and traditions owed much to the friendship between us. When I left the United States and returned to England the last time, he knew we would not see each other again in this life. This medallion was his parting gift to me. He did not know where or by whom it was made, only that he'd received it from his father, who got it from his grandmother.

I've been unable, over the years, to pursue any useful research on this amazing work of art. And now I've run out of time. I feel strongly that the medallion has a purpose in the lives of those who hold it, and equally strongly that I must convey the purpose to you. I would be pleased to think you and Emma worked together to discover its significance. May your effort bring you what you most desire.

Until we meet again, I remain your friend,

Aubrey Garrett

Without a word, Jimmy passed the note across the desk to Emma. She read silently, then sat for a minute with her fingertips against the letters, as if she could connect with the writer. Her lips trembled slightly, and her blue eyes were bright with tears.

His own throat tightened. "I know you miss him."

"Oh, yes." She pressed her lips together. "That's why I felt compelled to deliver the gift as he asked."

"Did you know about—" he pointed to the medallion "—this?"

Emma shook her head. "Dad didn't mention it to me. I was studying in France during his last trip to the reservation, about six years ago. And I never noticed it when I visited. His house was always such a jumble of books and papers and artifacts..." She took a deep breath. "It's taken me this long to get the place orderly enough to sell."

Jimmy refolded the note and put it back in the top of the box, which he closed and latched. Then he covered Emma's hand with his own. "I'm grateful your dad thought about me. And I'm really glad for the chance to see you again. Can we spend some time together? How long will you be in Denver?"

"I...don't have any definite plans for the next few weeks. I'd be glad to stay for a bit and help you with the research."

A warning bell sounded in his brain, just as a knock shook the door. "Food, boss."

He welcomed the interruption. "Come in."

Darren set a paper plate on the small table beside Emma's drink. "Hope you're not vegetarian. It's ham and cheese."

Her smile was a gift. "That's perfect. Thank you."

Backing out into the hall, Darren looked a little starstruck, the way he did when he met one of the jazz players he idolized. "Any time." He left the room without a single smart remark.

Emma returned to the recliner and picked up half of the sandwich. "I don't have to be back in England until just before the Michaelmas term starts. October," she explained at his puzzled look. "And this is August. We should be able to check out a number of reliable sources and references in that length of time." She bit into the sandwich and began to chew. Hard.

Jimmy took hold of his drink, then leaned back in his chair. "That's not how I define seeing each other. We've got twenty years to catch up on. We'll need quite a few dinners together, lunches, maybe a trip into the mountains..."

After a silent minute Emma put down her sandwich. "You do intend to discover the history of the medallion, don't you?"

He shrugged, trying for detachment. Staying cool had always been hard with Emma around. "I don't need to know any more than that it came from your dad."

Despite his attempt to be gentle, her eyes flashed with indignation. "But he wanted us to find out the rest!"

"He was dying, Emma, and probably in a good deal of pain. Did you never think he might not have been... rational?"

"He was completely rational until the very end." She squared her shoulders and lifted her chin. "Certainly he was sound of mind when he wrote that letter."

She'd backed him up against the wall, with words if not in fact. But Jimmy fought on. "If it didn't matter enough for him to have done something in six years, why does it matter now?"

"What reason could there possibly be to avoid learning everything we can?" On her feet again, she came to the desk and leaned forward, her graceful, long-fingered hands pressed flat against the oak-paneled top.

"Because—" Jimmy took a couple of seconds to get his voice and his feelings under control "—researching that piece won't involve just reading books and museum catalogs."

"I've been involved in historic research professionally for fifteen years. I know what kind of investigating is required. We'll need to talk to people, perhaps visit the reservation."

"Exactly." He pulled in a deep breath. "And I'm not going back. Ever."

Of all the reactions Emma had anticipated from Jimmy Falcon, this was not one. She stared at him in confusion, until the words began to make sense in her brain. "You won't go back to the reservation?"

"No." He sipped his drink, avoiding her eyes.

"When were you there last?"

Under the rich golden tone of his skin, his cheeks flushed a dull red. "The day after high-school graduation."

She needed another moment to fully understand. "You haven't seen your family since then?"

"There wasn't all that much family to begin with. My aunt died just a couple of years later and my cousins left the rez for I don't know where."

The flaw in his argument was obvious. "If no one is there that you know, then where's the threat in going back?"

"I didn't say there was a threat." Now he looked directly into her face. His gaze, so warm and welcoming only a few minutes before, had cooled. "I said I won't go back. I don't want to go back. I left that part of my life behind when I left the rez, and that's where I want it to stay."

She straightened and surveyed the man across the desk. From his well-cut black hair to his gray shirt and midnight-blue tie, he was the picture of success. There seemed to be nothing left of the wild Indian youth she'd known. The picture she'd retained in her mind all these years showed him balanced barefoot on the edge of a cliff, his hair long and straight and gleaming black under the midday sun, his brown chest bare and his muscular arms widespread like the wings of a hawk. Newly emerged into manhood, his energy and courage and mystery had enthralled her completely. They'd had one summer together, the kind of romantic interlude every teenage girl dreams of.

But that summer belonged to the past, and perhaps the Jimmy Falcon she'd loved did, too. After all, twenty years apart would make strangers out of anyone. This Jimmy certainly seemed like someone she didn't know.

And Emma was suddenly too tired to push the issue further. However they spent their time together, she might find a way to change his mind about the medallion. Or perhaps she would pursue the research by herself. If that was all she could do for her dad now, then she would.

"I didn't come here to argue with you," she told Jimmy. "Let me call a cab to take me to the hotel and you can get back to work."

He locked the box and medallion in a desk drawer, then got to his feet with a kind of controlled jerk. "I'll drive you."

Their trip to his office through the crowd in the club had been erratic and distracting. She hadn't noticed his gait then, but she did now. As he came around the desk, he limped. Badly.

"What happened to your leg?"

Jimmy choked out a laugh. "Don't beat around the bush, Emma. Let's cut to the chase." Resting some of his weight on his hands, he leaned back against the desk. "I was a cop a few years ago, and I showed up in the wrong place at the wrong time, during a gang fight." His tone was casual, but the disability obviously bothered him.

"That must have been very difficult to deal with."

"It's okay." He shrugged. "I found something new to do."

She tilted her head toward the door and the main room of the club. "Successfully, judging by the crowd."

He glanced at the plate the server had left. "But not by the food. You didn't eat more than a bite of your sandwich."

Emma hesitated, and he nodded ruefully. "It wasn't very good, was it?"

An apologetic smile didn't soften the truth. "Not very."

"Hard to ruin a ham sandwich and chips. But decent cooks won't stay in this part of town."

"So the music must be fantastic."

Now he grinned, with pride. "Yeah."

"And you have a responsibility to be here." She turned

to pick up her now practically weightless purse. "I think I should take a taxi back to the hotel."

He shook his head. "I think not." That seemed to settle the issue, for Jimmy, at least. "So, can we have dinner together tomorrow night? About seven?"

Her annoyance at his attitude regarding the medallion leaked away. "I'd like that."

"Good." Music flooded into the office as he opened the door. "After you."

There was—always had been—an air of command about him she couldn't ignore. "Thank you."

"My pleasure." He returned her smile with the same appreciative grin that had snared her when she was eighteen. And did so again now.

On their way through the crush of people in the main room, he stopped at the bar and exchanged words with the woman making drinks, a pretty blonde with a figure Emma envied. What she wouldn't give to be five foot five with a waist that small!

When they stepped outside, Jimmy touched her lightly on the shoulder. "I'm parked down here." Emma turned obediently to the left, trying to ignore how she reacted to that simple, impersonal contact.

Under a street lamp only a few yards away, he stopped beside a sleek, black Jaguar XJE. Emma paused at the front bumper. "Very nice. But..." She glanced down the street. "Don't you worry that such an expensive car will be stolen or damaged?"

"I've got a loud burglar alarm, and a steering-wheel lock." Jimmy opened the passenger door. "Besides, it's just a car. Expensive, but easy to—"

The sound of garbage cans crashing and voices yelling interrupted him. A writhing mass of bodies tumbled out of the blackness of a nearby alley, almost under Emma's feet.

Obscenities and curses drowned all the other night noises. Something flashed in the streetlight. The blade of a knife.

Jimmy opened the car door and pushed her inside. "Lock the door. Use the phone and dial 911."

Hands shaking, she did as he said. But being locked in the car didn't prevent her from witnessing the brawl. Time seemed to stop, though the whole episode lasted a minute at most. The violence broke into two battles—in the nearest, a thin man in black had hold of a younger man around the knees while the other assailant tried to get a grip on the victim's throat. Unnoticed in the fury, Jimmy stepped in and grabbed the neck of the would-be strangler's T-shirt, pulling backward, diverting his attention from his prisoner. Freeing one leg, the youth kicked out at the face of the man in black. The blow connected and the man fell back against a wall, blood spurting from his nose.

Thanks to Jimmy's interference, the young man also managed to escape from the hold on his throat. He swung at his attacker and fell to his knees, breathing hard, only to be hit from behind by the man he'd just kicked. Face pushed into the pavement, he flailed his arms and legs, but the weight on his back didn't budge.

The second man turned on Jimmy just as the other fight came apart. One of that struggling pair ducked, rolled away from his assailant—the one with the knife—and came to his feet right outside Emma's window. The entire scene froze at that instant, went completely quiet. No one moved, except for the boy lying facedown. He couldn't see the gun now trained on everyone involved in the confrontation.

Everyone…including Jimmy.

CHAPTER TWO

JIMMY STRAIGHTENED, dropped his hands to his sides and took a few breaths to get control of his voice. "Lose the gun, Tomas. The police are on their way."

A siren in the distance backed him up. Some of the regulars on the street had noticed the commotion and were coming to investigate. Just what they needed—more targets.

"Go to hell," the boy snarled. "These bastards were gonna kill us." He pointed the gun at the guy sitting on his friend's back. "Get off him. Now." The man hesitated, then jerked at the sound of the hammer being pulled back. "Or I'll blow you off."

With a final shove at his captive's shoulders, the creep scrabbled onto the sidewalk and backed up, crabwise, against the building.

Tomas nodded his approval. "Good idea. Now you—" he turned to the man with the knife "—drop the friggin' knife before I friggin' shoot your hand off. Good. You okay, Harlow?"

The other boy staggered to his feet, wiping blood off his face. "I'm okay."

Jimmy could see Emma staring out the car window behind Tomas, her eyes wide with shock and, probably, terror. He started to sweat, thinking what a bullet could do to the thin shield of glass. "Nothing's going to happen now, Tomas. Put the weapon away."

As Harlow limped up beside the Indian boy, blue lights

flashed at the corner. "Come on, Tommy. You want to keep that piece, you'd better stash it before the cops see you carrying." He glanced at Jimmy, his eyebrow quirked. "Mr. Falcon's not gonna give us away, right?"

"I didn't see a gun...unless I count to five and it's still in his hand."

Tomas dropped the pistol into a pocket of his camouflage jacket just as a department vehicle pulled up behind the Jag. A couple of uniforms Jimmy didn't know got out, each with a hand on his weapon and the other hand holding his stick.

Great. This explanation would have gone down easier with somebody he'd worked beside. "Evening, Officers."

The taller one just looked him over. "What's going on?"

"These guys jumped us in the alley." Tomas spoke before anybody else could. "Practically killed us with that knife there." He kicked the weapon with his toe.

"Sure." The cop looked back at Jimmy. "Who are you?"

"Jimmy Falcon. I own The Indigo." He nodded toward the nightclub. "I was about to take a friend home when these guys rolled out of the alley. I stayed to keep the numbers even."

Finally the outlaws on the ground got their share of attention. The shorter cop glanced at Harlow. "You say these three attacked you?"

"Yeah."

"You didn't, like, attack first?" He began to sound bored. "What were you doing in the alley, anyway?"

Both Harlow and Tomas cut their gazes Jimmy's way. "Just hanging out," Harlow said in his Texas-flavored accent. "That ain't a crime."

"Uh-huh. You buying or selling?"

"Dunno what you're talking about."

The shorter cop pushed at one of the thugs with the toe

of his boot. "This one's out cold." Bending over, he patted down the body. "Don't think he's carrying anything besides a pack of gum."

"Check out the rest of them," his partner ordered.

The other two dealers gave up bags of coke and weed, and a couple of dimes of heroin. Jimmy saw Harlow swallow hard as the small plastic sacks dropped into an evidence container.

Two minutes later the Saturday-night special was out in the open again. The short cop balanced it on his palm. "Nice toy. You got a permit, son?"

Tomas told the cop what he could do with the permit.

Using a speed and expertise Jimmy remembered from his days on the force, the cops slammed Harlow and Tomas up against the side of the police cruiser, patted them down again and cuffed them.

Emma sprang out of the Jag like a lioness in the African bush. "Don't be so rough! They're only boys!"

Jimmy caught her arm and pulled her back. "Stay out of it, Emma. These guys know what they're dealing with. You don't." Another police car pulled up, and the three pushers, who—Jimmy had reason to know—had been in and out of jail for years, got their own sets of bracelets.

Emma turned on Jimmy. "I saw them earlier tonight as I was coming to see you. They were hungry. They're young and homeless. They need help, not more violence."

The cops exchanged derisive grins.

"They're drug addicts." With a hand on each of her arms, Jimmy pulled her farther away from the scene. "The whole mess is about selling and buying drugs. Let the police sort it out."

She struggled against his grip. "How do you know that?"

"Because they hang around here a lot. Because they hit

on me and my customers..." He watched her cheeks flush. "Damn. You gave them money."

"I told them to get something to eat!"

"We did, too," Harlow called. "Meat loaf and potatoes and corn. Thanks, lady." A cop shoved him into the cruiser and closed the door before he could say anything else.

Yet a third cop strolled over. "You're Falcon?"

"Yeah. This is Emma Garrett." He released her, reluctantly. "She called in the incident from the car."

"What's going to be done with those boys?" Emma wanted to know. "Where are you taking them?"

"Detention." The officer—his name tag said Havers—made a note on his pad.

"Jail?" Her voice squeaked on the single syllable.

Jimmy put a hand on her back, trying to give comfort. "They'll have a bed for the night, Emma. And a decent breakfast. They'll be okay."

She gazed at him, disbelief written in the lines between her eyebrows. "Does this happen often?"

"It's a tough neighborhood," Havers said. "We're taking your word for what happened, Mr. Falcon, mostly because we ran you through the computer and found out you're an ex-cop."

"Gee, thanks."

"You'll want to be available in case we have more questions."

Jimmy shrugged. "I'm not going anywhere."

Havers nodded. "Thanks for the help."

In another few minutes, the cruisers took off and the sight-seers went back to their regular business, whatever it was. Jimmy put a hand to Emma's jaw. Under smooth skin, the muscles were tight. "Let me take you to your hotel." With a sigh, she slipped past him into the seat, and he caught a whisper of that new scent—some kind of flower he didn't recognize, but wanted more of. While he buckled his seat belt, her fingers stroked the curve of the dash, her skin pale against the black leather and dark wood.

He blew out a short tense breath. "Where are you staying?"

She directed him to a hotel in a better part of town, near City Park. When he pulled to a stop at the entrance, neither of them moved or spoke for a measurable time. They turned to look at each other at the same instant.

Jimmy breathed in that perfume and said the first thing that came to mind. "That was some summer, twenty years ago. Every time I think about it, I have to smile. Nothing bad about goodbye, nothing to regret. The end was there in the beginning—you left for school in England and I...got on with life."

Emma nodded, and the corners of her mouth curved up. "It does seem strange to think that we didn't break up or get bored. So few relationships end painlessly." Regret claimed her face again.

"I figured you'd be married by now, with a couple of kids in boarding school."

"Boarding school is the last place I'd send my children. If I had any."

He reached out, stroked his knuckles down her cheek, touched by the note of sadness in her voice. The pad of his thumb lingered at the corner of her mouth, waiting to test texture and shape. A kiss was not a good idea. They hardly knew each other anymore.

But her soft lips tempted him, and he was losing the battle with good sense. If either of them even breathed...

Faster than he'd have believed possible, Emma had the door open and was standing on the sidewalk. "Good night. Be careful."

He fumbled to get out of the car. "I'll walk you to your door."

"No." She put up a hand for emphasis. "I can get to

my door by myself. Thanks for the ride, Jimmy. I'll look forward to dinner tomorrow.'' In a second or two she was on the other side of the glass door and lost in the lobby's shadows.

Jimmy dropped back into the driver's seat, then regretted it as his hip howled in protest. A vulgar word escaped his control. That fight tonight, even as little as he'd done, had aggravated his wrecked muscles.

He drove to his place slowly, thinking. The next week would be interesting. He'd never imagined seeing Emma again, especially once her letters had stopped coming. You could track down anybody on the Internet nowadays—that was how she'd found him. But he hadn't thought about looking for her. Their time together was in the past.

Or was it? There was still a current between them, part memory, part brand-new attraction. Jimmy hadn't followed an impulse in years, didn't believe in them anymore. He had his life set up the way he liked it. Why invite change?

Then he thought of Emma's blue eyes, her easy laugh, her lush curves. He remembered how she'd challenged him, taught him, loved him that summer. And the irrepressible question occurred to him.

Why not?

TIRED AS SHE WAS, Emma spent two restless hours trying to get to sleep before finally giving in and switching on the lamp again.

Her mind seemed to bounce from one problem to the next, without finding a solution and without settling down. She thought of those boys—Harlow was the Texan, she gathered, and Tomas the Indian—spending the night in detention. Horrible possibilities assailed her; American jails had a reputation for danger, even violence, from the people in charge. The officers had come close to assaulting the boys tonight. What would happen when there were no civilian witnesses?

Forcing herself to think of something else only brought her to Jimmy. Jimmy Falcon, whom she'd expected to know as easily, as intimately, as if they'd been together yesterday.

Even after twenty years, she remembered the beginning as clearly as she remembered yesterday. She'd been visiting her dad, at work on the Sioux reservation in South Dakota, before starting her studies at Oxford in October. Taking refuge from the fierce flatlands sun, she'd opened the door to a reservation trading post and been nearly knocked over by a young man—Jimmy—trying to sneak two bottles of beer without paying for them. The owner of the shop had grabbed him and threatened to call the police, but let him go when Emma laid down the cash.

Outside, Jimmy handed over one of the bottles. ''You paid for it,'' he said with that completely engaging grin. ''Let's go for a ride.'' He gestured at his beat-up truck.

They ran wild together that summer, while her dad spent meticulous hours recording stories and language. Jimmy took her to the mountains, to the rodeo, to the Badlands of South Dakota. More often than not, Emma paid for the truck's gas, the food, the tickets. If Jimmy showed up with money, she learned not to ask how he got it. Gambling was an answer she accepted, but stealing made her nervous. As long as she didn't know which route to wealth he'd taken, she could simply share and enjoy.

He'd made love to her for the first time in the mountains at midnight. She relived the moment now—cold air and the heat of his body against hers, the taste of whiskey on his mouth, the clean scent of his skin, the rasp of his tongue, the only sounds that of their heavy breathing, and of her own pounding heart.

Oh, God. Emma left the bed and opened the mini-fridge,

pulled out a can of ginger ale and pressed it against her cheeks, her forehead, her breastbone. This was the reason she'd kept the memory of Jimmy at the back of her mind all these years. It was almost too vivid to endure.

The man's magnetism had only intensified with time. He would have kissed her tonight. With the smallest movement, she could have joined her lips to his. A kiss for old times' sake—what would be the harm?

Turning off the lamp, she opened the curtains and stared into the city street—quieter here than outside The Indigo, nearly empty. No homeless boys to foolishly worry about.

Kissing Jimmy would be foolish, as well. They weren't so young now, so eager for experience, so confident of the future ahead of them. A relationship of any depth would complicate their lives, perhaps beyond possibility of resolution.

And Emma had too many complications already. Making a life without her dad's wry, loving support would be hard enough. The loss of one's employment ranked very high on the list of significant life changes, and within the last six months she'd lost not just a teaching position, but her entire career as a research historian. She'd lost a fiancé too, though she hardly regretted the fact—Eric Jeffries had simply used their relationship to further his own interests. Still, the knowledge that he hadn't really loved her hurt. As did her inner recording of things he'd said...

The bedside clock relentlessly counted the hours as she lay there, trying to sleep. She saw four-thirty, then five...and finally fell into an exhausted slumber just as the sun was coming up.

ON WEDNESDAY Jimmy stepped into the club and took off his sunglasses, relieved to be in the air-conditioned shadows after Denver's summertime heat.

"Tiffany? Tiff?"

His bartender came out of the kitchen. "Hey, Jimmy."

He gave her a grin. "Hey, beautiful. I hope you ordered me whatever you're having. It smells great, and I haven't seen food yet this morning."

"It's two o'clock, boss. That makes this the afternoon." She winked at him. "But listen. I've got good news and bad news."

"Hit me." He eased his sound hip onto a bar stool.

"The good news is that I ordered Chinese and there's enough for an army."

"And?"

"The bad news is I ordered in lunch because Hank quit." Hank Rawlins was the only cook he'd hired in the past year who'd stayed more than a couple of weeks.

Jimmy swore. "Why?"

"Something about a fight in the alley last night. He said he didn't get paid enough to risk his life."

"Great. Fantastic." Jimmy tossed his sunglasses onto the bar. "What a way to start the day." Thanks to Harlow and company, The Indigo was now missing a cook. And while the food wasn't the draw, people usually liked *something* to eat while they drank. "Did you call the agency, see if they had any temps?"

"I did. And they didn't. I also called to put an ad in the paper. But that'll take a few days to get results. Meanwhile…"

"Meanwhile, dammit, I do the honors." Eyes closed, he waited out the urge to throw something. He opened them again on a deep breath. "Those are the breaks, right?"

Tiffany shook her head, her smile sympathetic. "I can help you get ready."

Jimmy put a hand on her shoulder. "That's okay. You've got all you can handle out here. I think I can manage cutting up lettuce and tomatoes. I've got to make a call first, then I'll get started."

In the office, he pulled out the phone book and found the number for Emma's hotel. With his finger on the button, though, he stopped and put the handset down. Unlocking the desk drawer, he reached in, then sat looking at the walnut box resting on his palms.

Without lifting the lid, he could visualize the medallion inside. Most likely Navajo or Hopi or Zuni work, the Southwestern tribes were known for their expertise with metals and stone. The route the piece had traveled from Arizona to South Dakota might be interesting to follow. If you cared about things like that.

Jimmy didn't. He'd decided a long time ago that his Indian background created more trouble than it was worth. His ambition from the age of eight had been to get off the reservation and forget he'd ever been there. For the most part, he'd succeeded.

Until now. Emma had brought the reservation back into his life. Seeing her, getting at all close to her, would most likely involve him in the search for the background on the medallion.

But *not* seeing her again…he didn't like that option, either. She wasn't the girl he'd known that long-ago summer—redheaded, reckless and sassy, a strange combination of English manners and outright hell-raising. They'd caused some trouble and some talk when they were together, and why her dad hadn't horsewhipped him Jimmy never knew. Maybe Aubrey Garrett just never noticed what had gone on under his nose.

Now there were shadows in Emma's sweet blue eyes, pain in the set of her mouth. She'd just lost her dad, that was part of it. But there was something else, and he wanted to know what. He wanted to know about where she'd been these twenty years, and who'd been with her. There had been other women in his life, off and on. Had Emma loved other men? Had she been…was she married?

Jimmy swore and put the walnut box back in the drawer. It was a little late to be jealous. Or whatever the hell this gnawing in his gut was called.

The fact remained that he couldn't see her tonight for dinner. He tracked down the number for the hotel and dialed, then asked for her room and waited to be connected, wishing that Hank had quit just a week later. Or a week ago.

"Hullo?" She sounded barely awake.

"Hey, Emma. Still in bed?" Bad question, raising possibilities he shouldn't consider.

"Um…yes, actually." Jimmy could hear her waking up. "Jet lag, I suppose. How are you?"

"Okay. But I'm going to have to break our dinner date."

There was a pause. "Well, that's all right." Her tone had cooled down considerably.

"No, it's not. But my cook quit. I can't get hold of a temporary replacement this quick, and so I'm going to end up in the kitchen tonight."

"That's really too bad." Emma thought she heard exasperation in his voice, along with regret, which lightened her plummeting spirits considerably. "I was looking forward to a chance to talk."

"Me, too. I can't even promise tomorrow night, since I don't know when I'll be able to get somebody in the kitchen."

In the silence, she thought she heard drums. "Is that the band? Are they rehearsing?"

The sound stopped as he chuckled. "No, it's just me. I have a bad habit of beating on any flat surface nearby. Listen, how about lunch tomorrow, before I go to work?"

"That sounds good." A long time to wait, though. "I'll see you then."

"You bet."

After they'd hung up, Emma gazed around the hotel

room, wondering what she would do for the rest of the day. She did not want to play tourist—at least, not without Jimmy as the tour guide. For the first time in twenty years, she had no reading to do, no paper to write or examinations to grade. Just…time. Empty time.

Finally she connected her laptop computer to the Internet port provided by the hotel and signed on to check her e-mail—a couple of notes from friends, commiserating with her on the loss of her teaching fellowship, then the usual and irritating advertisements for sound equipment, airplane-fare discounts and instant riches. She replied to the notes and started to sign off, then reconsidered.

Her first search for Native American artifacts turned up thousands of sites. She went through them slowly, gathering scraps of information here and there. When she narrowed the search to metalwork, the Southwestern focus of that particular art became apparent. So Jimmy's medallion wouldn't have been made near the Sioux reservation. That argued for trade between tribes or, possibly, commerce between Southwestern tribes and whites, who then traded again with the groups on the Plains.

By dark she had quite a stack of note cards, her preferred method of keeping important information, and a few hints as to the meaning of the sun-over-mountains design. She also had a list of galleries and museums in Colorado, New Mexico and Arizona specializing in Native American metalwork. With a car, she could reach most of them in a day's drive.

Stretching out her stiff neck muscles, Emma acknowledged that she would much prefer a day's drive with Jimmy to one without him. If she didn't ask him to go back to South Dakota, but only to Santa Fe, or even across Denver, would he cooperate? Was it just the reservation, or was Jimmy avoiding a more fundamental issue?

And what right did she have to ask? Or to push him into

an enterprise he had already refused? After twenty years, she had no claim on Jimmy Falcon other than the fact that he had been her first lover and she, his. Not much of an obligation, especially since Jimmy had probably made love to any number of beautiful women since. His charm and magnetism guaranteed female attention.

But then again, her dad had asked them to trace the medallion. He felt "strongly," the note said, that Jimmy should have this particular piece. Aubrey Garrett had gotten a bit, well, mystic, as he grew older. He'd studied the Native American legends and myths with great intensity.

There would be a reason her dad wanted Jimmy to know the history of the disk. And a reason he'd insisted that she deliver the box herself. *Don't mail it or ship it,* he'd instructed. *Take it to him yourself.*

Perhaps he suspected Jimmy would resist the true message behind the medallion. And perhaps he counted on her to overcome that resistance. Her parents had enjoyed a long-standing joke comparing Emma's tendency to take charge of a situation with the heroine of Jane Austen's novel *Emma,* a young woman who considered herself an expert in the conduct of other people's business.

Thinking about the twinkle in her father's eye as he teased her, Emma smiled. Yes, Aubrey might well have been counting on her to see that Jimmy pursued this particular piece of business. She would hate to let him down.

An hour later, she once again stepped out of a cab across the street from The Indigo. She wouldn't press too hard tonight, when Jimmy was overworked and understaffed. But the music called to her. And if they happened to talk, and she happened to mention the medallion, what could it hurt?

BY 10:00 P.M., Jimmy wished he could close the club for the night. He was sick of lettuce, pickles, tomatoes and nacho cheese. Or maybe he should just close the kitchen down. People who really liked jazz didn't care about the food.

Darren came in with a tray full of paper plates and crumpled napkins. "She's back." He dumped the tray in the garbage can beside the back door.

Jimmy leaned back against the counter. His hip was on fire. "Who?"

"The lovely lady from last night. Tall, red hair…" A certain appreciative light in Darren's eyes said he was ready to elaborate on the description.

"Yeah, that's Emma. Did she ask to see me?"

The server shook his head. "She asked for a table and a drink—a Pimm's Cup, if you can believe it. She had to tell Tiffany how to make it—tall gin and lemonade, in case you're interested. Now she's just listening to the band."

"Great."

Knowing she was out front destroyed what was left of Jimmy's patience with food. He cleaned up fast, before Darren could bring in another order. Then he straightened his tie, pulled down his cuffs, locked the back door and went out to see Emma.

She looked up in surprise as he dropped into the chair at her table. "Jimmy! I didn't want to bother you while you were working."

"I just hung a Closed sign on the kitchen. You gave me the excuse I needed." Darren set a whiskey at his elbow and he nodded his thanks. "What brings you down tonight?"

"I was in the mood for jazz. Maybe not acid fusion," she said as the band went for a far-out chord progression, "but the silence in my room was deadly."

"TV?"

"All the police and attorney programs are reruns." She smiled at him, and his pulse jumped. "I thought live music would be more fun."

They listened for a couple of hours, talking during the quiet spots, trading glances at high points in the music... and low ones. During the last break, three different customers stopped to harass Jimmy about closing the kitchen.

"You'd think the food actually tasted good," he said after the last couple left. "The bread was fresh tonight, anyway. That might have impressed them."

"Fresh is always a good start." Emma's eyes laughed at him over the rim of her glass.

He enjoyed her good mood, maybe a little too much. "What do you know about cooking, Professor?"

"Quite a lot, actually. I've taken classes for years."

"No kidding? I'm glad you didn't take more than a bite of that sandwich last night, then. I didn't know I was feeding an expert."

Her smile was preoccupied. "You know, Jimmy..."

He recognized that look. Emma's troublemaking face hadn't changed in twenty years. "What?"

"I could cook for you."

"That'd be great some night." He deliberately misunderstood.

She didn't let him get away with it. "No, I mean here. At the club. I could be The Indigo's cook."

"But..." Jimmy shook his head, trying to get his bearings. "Emma, I can't hire you, especially not as a cook."

"Why not? I can do the work, I know I can."

"This isn't the kind of place you ought to be working at all. You could get a teaching job in any school in the state."

"But I'm not going to get a teaching position. I...I've taken some time off."

"A...what do they call it? A sabbatical?"

Her eyes avoided his face. "More or less."

"Then you really don't want to tie yourself down to a job like this. Anyway, I can't see me being your boss."

She folded her arms across her chest, which meant she was about to get stubborn. "I don't understand."

"We're friends." More than friends, for one summer. "That complicates the situation when you're working together."

"You aren't friends with your other employees?"

His face heated under her accusing stare. "Sure. Except when the club closes, they go their ways and I go mine."

Emma hesitated a few seconds, then cleared her throat. "We can do the same."

She watched as Jimmy's jaw dropped. "You mean—"

"I think that will work quite nicely, for us to see each other only at the club, as employee and employer." The whole idea was preposterous, insane…and yet felt exactly right. As if she'd been brought to Jimmy's club at this very moment for a purpose she wasn't sure she recognized.

All she had to do was convince Jimmy. "You do need a cook, don't you?"

"I thought so. Now I'm not sure."

"Good food would bring more customers in."

He shook his head. "The money's in the liquor."

"But food persuades them to stay longer and buy more drinks." She lifted her chin, daring him to contradict her. Silently praying he would allow her this chance.

Finally he shrugged and sent her one of his sexy grins. "We can give it a shot, I guess. I was planning to offer seven bucks an hour for six nights a week, five to two."

She fixed him with *that* look. "Fifteen."

Jimmy choked. "What's your experience working a restaurant?"

"What other choice do you have?"

"Jeez." He rolled his eyes. "Nine."

"Ten."

"Damn. Ten."

She smiled in relief. "That's good, then. You won't be sorry."

"I could never be sorry to see you again." Jimmy walked her to the front door and stood with her while she waited for a cab. "If you change your mind…"

"I won't." No uncertainty allowed. "I'll be back tomorrow morning to make some calls about provisions."

He put his hand on her arm. "What about lunch?"

Emma hated to give up the chance for a private encounter with this stunning man. But in the long term, resisting might prove a better plan. "I'll make lunch here—give you a sample of what I can do."

He tightened his grip, then stepped back quickly just as the cab drew up to the curb. Opening the door, he leaned in as she settled on the seat.

"This is crazy, you know. Not what I planned at all."

She took a risk and ran her fingertips lightly along the smooth line of his jaw. "Everything will work out, Jimmy. I'm sure of it."

With a smile, he shut the door. Emma turned to the window and saw him still standing on the pavement, watching the cab out of sight.

Back in her hotel room, combing out her hair, she acknowledged her own qualms. "Everything *will* work out," she assured herself. "I may have totally ruined the rest of my life. But surely I can manage to do this one thing right!"

CHAPTER THREE

HARLOW STAYED in the shadows at the street end of the alley, dragging on a cigarette as he watched Falcon put the English lady into a cab.

Ryan came up from behind, with Tommy following. "Hey, Harl—"

"Shut up." Harlow jerked a nod toward the street. "Falcon's still out there."

"Okay, okay." They froze in place until the door to the club opened and closed Falcon inside.

"Nice scenery," Ry commented. His voice sounded easy and light, the way it did after a rush. "I like my women on the big side."

"I like 'em big where it counts." Tomas cupped his hands in front of his chest. "Ya know?"

Ryan laughed. Harlow dropped his cigarette butt to the pavement and ground it out with the toe of his shoe. "Think with your brains for a change, Tommy. The lady could be useful."

"Women are built useful." This gesture was graphic and dirty.

"I was listening to what they said." Harlow ignored his friends' cackles. "She's cooking for the club."

"So?" Ryan yawned. "'Bout nap time, ain't it?"

"So…she's not likely to be a shithead like the last guy. Or like Falcon. Bet we can get some food off her."

"Hey, man, I'm all for free food." Tomas shook his head. "But food from this place is hard to swallow. My ma cooked better drunk.'' He scratched his head. '''Course, I don't think I ever knew Ma when she was sober.''

''Long as we keep out of Falcon's way, we could be in fat city.''

''Sounds good to me.'' Ry rubbed a hand over his chest. ''I get tired of puttin' holes in my belt. What's next? You gonna get us a house, too? We each get our own john, right?''

''You want a john?'' Tomas staggered back in fake surprise. ''You freaking 'selling' it now, dude?''

''Shut up.'' Harlow started up the sidewalk. That was one thing they'd managed to stay away from so far. They stole, sure, when they had to. They worked a little, when they could find a job. But they hadn't gotten into the sex business and they didn't deal drugs. He didn't have much pride left. But he did have some.

''If you can't say something nice,'' Ryan drawled beside him, ''don't say nothing at all.'' He yawned again. ''Man, I gotta crash. Think T-Bone is home? His squat's pretty empty most afternoons.''

''We'll check it out.'' Harlow could feel the need waking up in his belly, in his brain. He'd gotten Ry taken care of. If he could stash him somewhere safe, he'd be able to take care of himself.

A couple more blocks…a hundred more yards…just two flights of stairs. Funny, how the sickness got so much stronger, so much faster, these days.

He pounded on T-Bone's door as Ry all but fell asleep against the wall. The door swung back. ''What the…? Oh, it's you.'' The man with shoulders as straight as the bone of the steak he was named for ground the heels of his hands into his eyes. ''Whaddaya want?''

''Can Ry crash for a while? I'm going out.''

''Me, too.'' Tomas wiped his nose on his sleeve.

T-bone glanced over his shoulder into the bare room.

"Yeah, sure. Whatever." He turned, stumbled through an inner doorway and closed the panel behind him.

Harlow shoved Ryan and Tomas inside. "Get some sleep. And maybe tomorrow night we'll get a decent dinner." Before they could think of a word together between them, he shut himself out in the hall.

Claws raked at the inside of his head, and his stomach twisted as he stumbled down the steps. The closest supply wasn't the safest. But he didn't think he could make it farther. Sometimes, second best had to do.

I know a hell of a lot about second best, he thought as he tracked down the dealer, made the buy and ran for cover.

Big brother Mark had always been a tough act to follow. Captain of the Little League team, the Pop Warner team, the Y soccer team. Straight A's in every grade. Special awards in math and science. And that was all before high school.

Then the real stuff started happening. Scholarships and special sports camps and more math awards. Honor Society prez, top of the senior class. Headed for the Air Force Academy.

Until shithead little brother screws up. Big time. One minute, Mark's standing there yelling at him. The next, a car speeds by and big brother's flat on his back with blood everywhere.

Crouched behind a Dumpster at the back of a liquor store, Harlow tightened the band around his bicep, pumped his fist, took the syringe from between his teeth. Funny thing was, Mark had even more influence over his brother's life after he was dead. *We're number two, whether we try harder or not.*

But just a minute later, when he loosened the band on his arm and felt the power surge through his blood, being number two didn't matter anymore.

LUNCH in the club's kitchen, with Tiffany at the table and Emma cooking, was not Jimmy's number-one choice for their first date in twenty years.

But he couldn't deny that she knew her way around a kitchen. He watched as she sliced tomatoes, lettuce and onions, leaving them in neat stacks, instead of strewn across the table, which was the style he was used to. She skimmed the top off melted butter and then basted the rolls before piling on thin slices of ham and cheese, vegetables and a special sauce she threw together in about ten seconds flat.

The result was magic. "What'd you do to make ham and cheese taste like this?"

"Even the chips are different. Better," Tiffany added.

Emma smiled. "The right mustard, a few spices…oh, and bat's eyes. The bat's eyes are crucial."

Tiffany's face went white. She lifted a corner of the roll and stared suspiciously at the inside of her sandwich. "What are those little round brown things?"

Jimmy laughed—for what seemed like the first time in years. Emma put a hand on the bartender's shoulder. "Capers, Tiffany. The seeds of a pepper plant. I promise, no animal eyes of any kind."

"Oh." Tiffany sighed with relief, then gave Jimmy a dirty look because he was still chuckling. "How do I know what strange stuff foreigners put in their food? Far as I'm concerned, meat loaf with peppers in it is a gourmet dish." She got to her feet and walked stiffly to the door into the club. "Thanks for the lunch, Emma. I'd better get back to work."

Jimmy held up a hand. "Hey, Tiff, your limp beats mine today. What you'd do this time?"

She grinned. "In-line skating. There was this bump in the asphalt…"

He nodded. "I get the picture. Take it easy."

"Sure, boss."

Emma stacked the paper plates and took them to the trash. "She's very easy to like."

"Tiffany's almost as big a draw as the music. Half the customers come in just to flirt with the bartender."

As for himself, Jimmy enjoyed watching Emma move around the kitchen. The apron she'd tied on over her yellow dress did nothing to conceal her full breasts and shapely hips and legs. A breeze coming through the screen on the back door stirred the small curls at her temples and on the nape of her neck, made him think of how smooth her skin was in those places. And in others...

In just a minute or so, the kitchen looked spotless, which was as novel a concept for this room as decent food. Jimmy tamed his thoughts into innocuous words. "You really are good at this cooking stuff. I wouldn't have guessed that twenty years ago."

"I've learned a lot in twenty years." She folded the dish towel and sat in the chair across from him, her elbows on the table and her chin in her hands. Her fingers, he noticed, were bare.

"Who do you cook for?" Might as well make sure of his assumptions, not that he planned to take advantage of Emma any more than he already had by giving her a job.

"Friends, myself. Dad, when I could."

"No husband?"

She shook her head. "No husband. I was engaged, but we...broke it off." After a second her gaze met his. "No wife?"

Jimmy shook his head. "Not even an engagement. And no good explanation, either."

"You don't need to make one." She took a deep breath. "Listen, Jimmy, I wondered, have you thought any more about the medallion?"

The question hit from out of the blue, and he didn't have

a ready answer, except the truth. "It's a beautiful piece and I'm very honored that your dad wanted me to have it."

When she hesitated, he answered her next question before she asked. "But no, Emma, I don't want to trace the history. I told you—it doesn't matter."

"I've done some research on the Internet—we wouldn't necessarily need to visit the reservation. There are galleries and museums in the Southwest—"

"Which is where the metalwork probably came from. I know. I'm still not interested."

Her folded hands dropped to the table with a thump. "Why?"

He would have liked to avoid this confrontation, but couldn't. "Look. There was a man, an Indian, who made a big point of his heritage, his cultural pride. He knew the legends and the language of his tribe. He could trace his people back for a hundred years and more. He talked about forcing the whites to acknowledge Indian rights, to make reparations for the land they'd stolen. He wanted to bring the Indian race back to its rightful place of power, on the same level with whites."

Emma nodded without speaking. Her gaze encouraged him to finish.

"This man lived on land his family had claimed for generations. One day, a car pulls up in front of his house—a house hung with signs and symbols of Indian power. An Oklahoma oilman gets out, nice guy, good suit, and offers the Indian an indecent amount of money for that land."

"He took the money?"

"Of course not. It was Indian land. So the white men came back one night and caught him out at the barn, then beat him up until he agreed to sell."

"I know these evil things happened. But that doesn't explain—"

He held up a hand. "The man was my grandfather. My

mother was his youngest daughter. They moved to the reservation after that, where he drank himself to death. My dad did the same, a little while after he told me the story. I was eight years old.''

"Jimmy—''

"I figured out right then and there that being an Indian was an accident of birth. A correctable birth defect, even. I found the cure. I walked away from that history and I don't look back. For any reason.''

Emma stared at him from across the table with her twined fingers pressed tight against her lips. The hurt in her eyes said she'd taken the story into herself.

Shaking his head, Jimmy lurched to his feet. "Don't be so sad, Emma. All of this was a long time ago, and doesn't matter anymore. That's the point.''

He would have liked to comfort her. But that would mean controlling the contempt for his grandfather's weakness that roiled in his belly—not something he could handle in a minute or two. Without another word, he abandoned the kitchen, leaving Emma by herself.

ON HER THIRD AFTERNOON at work, Emma fortified herself with a deep breath, then left the kitchen and headed for Jimmy's office. She peeked in. "Do you have a moment?''

He looked up from his account book with that heart-stealing grin. "For you, always. What's up?''

They'd overcome their differences over the medallion by simply avoiding the subject entirely. Jimmy spoke with her, laughed with her—but not about anything that mattered. He didn't get to the club until midafternoon, when she was already deep into prep work. Once the club opened, Emma was too busy to do much more than breathe, and too exhausted afterward to argue when he paid for the cab to take her home. Their situation bore little resemblance to the easy enjoyable reunion she'd anticipated.

But then, nothing about Jimmy seemed to be as easy as it had been twenty years ago. He wore armor now, invisible but quite impenetrable. By unspoken consent they'd ignored the revelation he'd made of the tragedy in his past. A tragedy, as far as Emma was concerned, still active in his present.

But she knew better than to broach the subject again so soon. This was a different mission. "Have you ever considered a more…um…adventurous menu?"

His reaction was not the encouragement she expected. The engaging grin faded, and his straight eyebrows drew together. "I think I told you, the food isn't the draw."

"You also told me the guests are enjoying their meals now. Why not expand a little?"

"This isn't that kind of place."

"It could be." They both watched his long fingers rotate a pencil between point and eraser.

When he looked up, his gaze wasn't angry, just wary. "Why change what works?"

"Why do something halfway?"

He gave a choked laugh. "Did I hire you to argue with me?"

Emma shrugged. "You hired me with the understanding that I would do my best. I'm telling you I can do better than ham-and-cheese sandwiches and dill pickles. The music deserves more than that."

Jimmy shook his head. "Jazz is not polite music. It's down and dirty, gut-wrenching. It doesn't need polite food."

"Jazz is also elegant and sophisticated and profound. We could provide that kind of food."

"Your third day at work and you're already rocking the boat?" He pressed the heels of his hands against his eyes for a second. "What do you want to do?"

She sat in the chair across the desk. "A salad or two, I

thought. And a featured entrée—an actual dinner on an actual crockery plate.''

He rocked his chair back, putting more distance between them. "We don't have· plates. Or forks or spoons or knives."

"I can solve that problem with one telephone call."

He lifted a sardonic eyebrow. "You'll blow my profit, buying dishes. The margin's not all that great to begin with."

"Of course." She lifted her own eyebrow and regarded him skeptically. "What kind of car is it you drive? Some sort of animal… Pinto..? Bronco..?Cougar?"

"Might be worth a try, boss." Tiffany came in to stand at her shoulder. "Draw some folks in who stayed away because of the food."

After staring at them a few moments, his face unreadable, Jimmy shook his head. "Emma, I'm sorry. I just don't want to get into that kind of trade. Thanks for the effort, but no thanks."

She drew a deep breath. "Jimmy—"

He held up a hand. "I never argue with a beautiful woman. And especially not with two beautiful women. Take away the distractions so I can get back to my numbers here, okay?"

With a sigh of surrender, she made her escape, Tiffany following close behind.

"That went well." Emma sank into the chair at the kitchen table. "I'd say we left him at the point of conceding."

Tiffany gazed at her with a frown. After a moment, her face cleared. "Oh, I get it. You're joking again."

Emma propped her chin in her hand. "Yes. I'm joking." With the thumb of her free hand, she stroked the grain of the worn worktable. "Who'd have thought he would be so stubborn?"

"He's a man, isn't he? They're all like that. They want their own way."

"You sound as if you've had plenty of experience." Emma pushed her own losing encounters with the male drive for control to the back of her mind.

"Yeah, well, my Brad pretty much says what goes." The bartender put up a hand to massage her shoulder, wincing a little. "He's six-four and two-fifty, so most people don't argue."

"What's wrong with your shoulder?"

Tiffany dropped her hand. "Brad and me were fooling around last night—play fighting, you know. I hit a chair leg and got a bruise. That's all." She stepped through the doorway into the club. "See you later."

Could she really be that clumsy? Or... Emma followed her into the dark. This was meddling—again—but she had to ask. "Tiffany, does Brad hit you?"

Wiping down the bar, the other woman shrugged. "He gets mad sometimes. And he forgets how strong he is. Nothing major."

"How long have you two been together?"

"About three years."

"But you aren't married?"

Tiffany laughed. "I was already married once. To a real loser. I don't plan to be trapped like that again."

That should have been reassuring. Wanting to be convinced, Emma started back to the kitchen. At the doorway, she turned once more. "You probably have lots of friends and family already. But if you ever need help, please feel free to call me."

"Thanks." Intent on polishing a spotted glass, Tiffany didn't look over again.

Alone in the kitchen, Emma tried to put the matter out of her mind, without success. Tiffany probably didn't weigh much more than nine stone—one hundred twenty pounds or so—and she was half a foot shorter than Emma's five-ten. Why would such a big man even think about wrestling—"play fighting"—with someone so much smaller?

Sighing, she focused her attention on the food yet again—sweet, ripe tomatoes and crisp lettuce, fragrant onions. Block cheese didn't cost much more than fabricated cheese sauce for the nachos, especially when grated by hand, and tasted better. There was such peace in preparing food, a sort of rhythm…

Outside in the alley, glass hit concrete with an unmistakable shatter. Someone cursed, loudly and fluently.

Emma went to the screen door and peered out.

A boy stood just across the narrow lane, with a pile of rubbish at his feet, evidently fallen through the ripped bottom of the white plastic sack he held.

Harlow, the homeless boy she'd given money to her first night in Denver. The one Jimmy had rescued in the fight.

As Emma stepped outside, he looked over and grinned. "I guess I got greedy. Tried to carry too much."

Emma crossed her arms. "What in the world were you trying to do?"

"Just looking for some lunch." He started backing away. "Sorry if I bothered you."

"Lunch? In the rubbish bins?" She spared a glance for the mess at his feet. "You were going to eat that?"

His shoulders lifted in a shrug, and his face flushed. Emma watched him a moment, then ducked back into the kitchen for another sack and a dustpan. "Clean that up and put it back where you got it. Then come inside."

"That's nice 'n all, lady, but…"

"But?"

"Well, this part of town is where I hang out most of the time, and I've tangled with Mr. Falcon before. He's not big on handouts."

Jimmy had warned her about this boy and his friends. They were drug addicts, he'd said. Best left alone.

But Jimmy wouldn't expect her to ignore a hungry boy. "I'll pay for the sandwich, if that will make you—and Mr. Falcon—feel better. You've got five minutes."

Just as she set a full plate on the table, he tapped at the door. "Are you sure, lady? I wouldn't want to get you in trouble."

For an answer, Emma opened the screen and waved him inside. "Wash your hands and then sit down. And my name is Emma. Emma Garrett."

He grinned again, and she blinked against the shine of it. "Pleased to meet you, Emma Garrett. I really appreciate the lunch."

And he did—he ate every crumb in silent pleasure and asked for a refill on the glass of milk. Draining the last drop, he sat back with a sigh. "I won't be hungry again anytime soon. Thanks."

"You're welcome." She'd worked while he ate to give him privacy, but now she leaned back against the counter, watching him as she dried her hands. "Isn't there somewhere you call home where you can get a meal?"

"Not this side of Amarillo. I've been on my own for a couple of years now." He stood and picked up his paper plate and cup. "All right if I put these in the can over there?"

"Yes." She waited until he closed the lid. "You don't have a job?"

"Not steady work, no." He glanced at the table. "I got a drop of mustard on your table. Let me wipe it up."

Emma handed him the sponge. "Do you go to school?"

"Not since Amarillo." A sheaf of dark blond hair fell over his eyes as he bent to his task. He was too thin and not very clean. Except for his hands now. Beautiful hands.

With a glance at the door into the club, he placed the sponge in the sink and stepped back. "I'd better get lost.

Mr. Falcon's car is out front. He wouldn't like finding me in here.'' At the screen door he paused. ''Thanks again, Emma.''

''You're welcome, Harlow.'' She thought of urging him to come back. But he seemed convinced that Jimmy would disapprove. Until she had that situation figured out, she wouldn't press. ''Take care.''

With a quick nod, he slipped out the door. Emma looked outside an instant later to see which way he went. But the alley was empty. Harlow had disappeared into thin air.

WHEN EMMA CAME OUT of the kitchen at about six o'clock, Tiffany was in the storeroom, Jimmy had disappeared behind the closed door of his office, and Darren was sweeping the main room, with a book propped between his hands on the broom handle.

Smiling, Emma sat on a bar stool. ''I hope you're getting a lot of reading done, because you're missing quite a bit of the stuff under the tables.''

Jerked out of his concentration, he looked at the floor around him. ''I should know better.'' He sighed, slapping the book onto a tabletop. ''I guess I'll just pull another all-nighter after work.'' He ran a hand through his curly brown hair, then gripped the broom handle with grim determination.

The next question came automatically, after twenty years in academic life. ''What's the assignment?''

Darren bent to brush napkins and potato chips out from under a chair. ''I've got a paper to write for my history class. I have to get this primary-source reading done before I can even start thinking about what I want to say.''

''When is the paper due?''

''Tomorrow by three.''

''Darren! And you're just starting this afternoon?''

''Well, I had a music-theory final this morning. I've been studying for that all week.'' Darren's passion for music—

his dedication to the band he'd organized and played with—was the reason he worked at The Indigo. More than once he'd confided to Emma his dreams of performing and composing jazz.

"Are you a fast writer?"

"No. I hate it. But I have to take this history course to meet graduation requirements."

"How much do you have left to read?"

"Four stupid pages."

"Here." She crossed the room and held out her hand. "I'll sweep. You read."

"Nah, that's okay." He kept hold of the handle.

"Come on, Darren. I can sweep for you. I can't write your paper."

He grinned, an endearing, mischief-filled expression. "You sure? I hear you're an expert."

"Idiot."

Darren released the broom this time and Emma took over the job. Judging by the condition under some of the tables along the far wall, the server had been doing a good deal of double-duty work while sweeping up.

She was bending to whisk the last of the refuse into the dustpan when someone behind her cleared his throat. Upside down, Emma looked awkwardly around her jeans-clad legs and saw Jimmy's black shoes, the soft gray of his cuffed trousers.

Damn and blast.

She finished the task and straightened up. "Hello there."

Her face felt hot, wisps of hair stuck to her forehead and cheeks. She almost certainly had a swipe of dust over her nose, while Jimmy looked cool and controlled in a black shirt and silver tie. One of them had grown up quite nicely. The other had remained an adolescent mess.

His eyebrows were drawn together, but his eyes held amusement. "I could swear I hired somebody else to do that."

"A bit of sweeping is good for the soul now and again."

"Where's Darren?"

"Um...on break."

"On break." Jimmy thought that over. "He comes in at six. He needs a break before seven?"

"He needed a chance to finish up some reading for school. I'm ready for the evening—I thought I could help him out."

"Emma, you can't do everyone's work around here."

"Oh, I know. I haven't the faintest clue about mixing drinks." She offered him a cheeky grin. "Tiffany's job is safe."

He shook his head, chuckling. "I don't think I knew what I was getting into when I hired you to work here." With a smile, he headed back to his office.

Emma watched almost greedily. Even considering the limp that marred his once-athletic gait, he was a wondrously attractive man.

"Neither did I, Jimmy," she murmured. "Neither did I."

"NO SHIT, she gave you lunch?" Tommy pounded the heel of his palm against his forehead. "Why didn't I go?"

Stomach still full, Harlow grinned. "You're freakin' stupid, maybe?"

"Maybe." Tommy didn't mind knowing he was as dumb as a brick. He was big enough not to need brains. "Man! Ham and cheese."

"And milk."

"Chocolate milk?" Ryan stood beside Harlow, shivering in the summer heat.

"Not chocolate. Just cold. In a glass." Harlow hadn't had milk in a glass since he'd left home. Or a decent bed. Or a good pair of shoes.

But if he was gonna feel invisible, if people were gonna look at him like he'd just murdered somebody—which, to be truthful, he had—Harlow figured he might as well do it with strangers. Tommy and Ry and his other friends on the street didn't treat him like anything but what he was. A kid with nowhere to go.

"What I'm thinking," he said, distracting himself, "is that we can play Emma Garrett for a real good deal. She all but freakin' melted when I smiled at her. So I butter her up, put on some manners, she'll be giving me steak before too long. Then I'll bring in Ry, and he'll look real pitiful and she'll feed him. Then Tommy—you practice looking nice, okay? You scare the shit out of most people just standing there. Anyway, if we behave ourselves and keep out of Falcon's way, we'll be in fat city."

Tommy shook his head. "Falcon pulled some of that shit on us, remember? Gave us money, then tried to push rehab. I'm not going that route no more. I'm thinking it's too big a pain, just avoiding him."

"Then you're not hungry enough." Harlow looked at Ryan. "What do you think? You up for some decent meals?"

"Yeah, I think it's a good deal." He smiled, a sweet little boy's smile that reminded Harlow of his younger brother at home. "But what do I eat in the meantime?"

His eyes were big circles of brown with tiny black dots in the middle, his face white and dirty and sick-looking. He would need another hit in an hour or so. That would use up their last ten bucks.

Time for a couple hours of spanging. Hanging out near the financial district downtown, asking the suits for spare change, they always got enough for a burger or two each. Harlow put his arm around Ry's shoulders and gave Tommy a punch on the shoulder. "Like always, I got the answer to that, my man. You just stick with me."

CHAPTER FOUR

JIMMY HADN'T FAILED to notice that Emma was keeping to her promise, as far as their working together was concerned. She spoke and laughed with him if he came into the kitchen, said a friendly good-night when he walked her out to the cab he made sure was waiting when the club closed. Just as she'd predicted, they had developed a polite, uninvolved employer-employee relationship.

Too bad he had to work so damn hard to keep it that way.

Sunday night's crowd was thin and not very hungry. Jimmy leaned back against the bar a little after midnight, listening to the music, thinking about closing up early. Then Emma stepped up beside him.

"This band is quite good."

He nodded, trying not to take too deep a breath, needing to avoid getting caught by that scent she used. "There's a recording contract in the near future. Another year, and they'll be too busy to play here."

"You had something to do with that, I think."

"I made a phone call. The music did the rest."

She glanced at him, moved a step closer. "You must know some very influential people in the recording business."

Easing back, he shrugged. "I played drums for a year or so with a band that wasn't very good. After we broke up, one of the guys went back to the family business...which happens to be producing and recording. I let him know when something sounds good, he comes out from L.A. and we have a few drinks together while he listens. Not a big deal.''

The band moved into a slow number, showcasing the piano's heavy chords and the sax's sweet wail. Two couples at a nearby table got up to dance. Emma stirred, swayed slightly to the beat.

No. Jimmy threw himself a mental punch. *The last thing you want to do is dance. Get a drink, tell a joke. Just walk off.*

But he found himself looking at her when she turned his way. ''Want to dance, Emma?'' As soon as the words were out, he cursed himself for a fool.

She stared at him with caution in her eyes. Damned if he did or if he didn't at this point, Jimmy grinned. ''No strings. Just a friendly employer-employee conference...out on the floor.''

''Will it bother your hip?''

He took her hand and pulled her with him onto the small parquet square in front of the stage. ''No.'' Only a minor lie. He could handle anything from Emma Garrett except pity. ''Let's dance.''

Graceful they weren't. His stiff hip threw their rhythm off. After one brush with Emma's knees and thighs and breasts, Jimmy kept air between their bodies. His reaction to her softness was an echo of urges twenty years past.

And yet...completely in the present. Emma at eighteen had been a tall, thin, pale-skinned girl with unruly red hair, totally different from anyone he'd ever known. That uniqueness alone had been fascinating.

Emma at thirty-eight was a full-bodied temptress whose creamy skin and gold-red hair glowed, even under the harsh fluorescent lights in the kitchen. He'd met enough women in the past twenty years to make comparisons—she was still unique. And still fascinating.

Holding her away from him allowed them to talk. Jimmy went with the flow of his thoughts. "So what's happened to you in two decades, Emma? You got your degree. And then?"

"Another degree. And another. Academic life is addictive."

"If you say so." High school had been more than he could take, though he'd stayed in long enough to graduate. Because Emma had wanted him to. "What'd you study?"

"History—British colonial history, actually, with an emphasis on relations between the Crown and the indigenous peoples of America."

"Indians, you mean?" He grinned at her raised eyebrow. "I don't have to be politically correct. You said you taught college. In England?"

"At Cambridge, yes, then Edinburgh and Toronto. I spent two years at Harvard on a fellowship."

That hit him in the chest. "I've got a Harvard professor cooking in my kitchen?"

She looked away, toward the band. "An ex-professor." Her freckles darkened over a sweet rose blush. "I... um...was sacked about six months ago. Dismissed." The rose deepened to a splotched red.

His mind took a second to catch up. "You mean fired?" Emma nodded. "Why?"

With a soft glissando on the piano, the music ended. The bandleader said good-night, and the couples around them began to leave. Emma stepped back, needing to get away. Needing to avoid Jimmy's very reasonable, completely unanswerable question.

He kept hold of her arms, drawing her close again. "Why did you get fired, Emma? Too many parties? You couldn't get up in time for your eight-o'clock classes?"

Without looking at him, she pushed against his chest,

against the solid muscles under a deceptively soft black shirt. His hands retained their strong grip on her elbows.

"I wrote a paper," she said softly, desperately. "Had it accepted for publication in a major journal, was getting ready to be promoted to department head at an exclusive New England school. Just before I was to present the findings at a conference, the truth came out."

"Truth?"

"The central conclusions of my paper, the most important parts of the entire project, were based on a recently recovered set of letters, written from the colonies to England in the eighteenth century. I'd been reading for information about native cooperation with the English, but I discovered a remarkable peripheral thread."

"Yeah?"

"The letters revealed a traitor on the English military staff during the French and Indian war. The spy kept the opposing armies apprised of the movements of English troops. The fact that he was connected to some very highly placed figures in the governments of England and France widened the conspiracy. Or so I thought. The truly vital letters were found to be…to be…" She dragged in a breath. "Forged."

After a few moments of silence, Jimmy's hands softened. "Who did it?"

She threw her head back to stare at him. "The presumption is that I did, of course."

His grin was cynical, knowing. "Sure. But who really did the forging?"

Now she couldn't look at him at all. "That's the truly pitiful part. The forgery was discovered by Eric Jeffries, my…my colleague on th-the project. And…" Her voice did not want to work. "And my fiancé."

Jimmy muttered something under his breath.

When she pulled this time, he let her go. "It doesn't

really matter who forged the letters. As a historian, I should have been certain of the evidence and its provenance. I didn't check deeply enough, and for that mistake alone I deserved to lose my post.''

He followed her into the kitchen. ''Everybody makes a mistake once in a while. Some of us make more than one.''

Emma stood at the sink, staring down at the marred stainless steel. ''Better not to do it when there is…are people standing at your shoulder, ready to take your place. I doubt I'll ever be accepted as a serious historian again.''

''You think Jeffries planted the letters? So he could get the glory?''

''I…yes.''

Jimmy's warm hands closed on her shoulders and turned her around. Unwillingly she looked into his lean dark face, into eyes as black as the night sky over the desert.

''You might have lost one round, Emma.'' His thumbs stroked across her collarbones just above the neck of her shirt. ''But you're not a loser. Give yourself some time. You'll be back where you belong.''

The touch of his skin, light as it was, set her to trembling. Emma looked at his mouth, remembered his flavor as if they'd kissed only yesterday. Did he still taste the same?

His thumbs stilled. The pressure of his fingers on her shoulders increased, drawing her forward. Emma closed her eyes, waiting.

Not for long. Jimmy touched her mouth with his, softly, asking permission. She parted her lips, granting it. She expected to be swept away. She *wanted* to be swept away.

But the kiss stayed well within the boundaries of control. Touching, parting, touching again—a sweet torment that brought tears to her eyes and need into her chest. She had no defense against gentleness.

Jimmy drew back, leaned in again to press kisses on her eyelids, her forehead. ''You still taste like strawberries,'' he said softly. Then he let her go and stepped away. "I'll make sure the cab is waiting." Before she could gather her thoughts together, he had left the kitchen.

She managed a calm goodbye as he held the door of the cab for her. She kept herself together during the ride across town, the wait for the elevator and the ride up with two tired-looking men. Emma didn't react at all until she was safe behind the door to her private room.

There, she set free her self-disgust. "Haven't you learned anything?" She yanked the band out of her hair and jerked a brush through the tangles. "Throwing yourself at the man like…like a lovesick undergraduate. Surely you know better by now."

Even before the debacle that ended her research career, Emma's experience in academia had taught her more than historical facts. Over years of competition with male scholars and teachers, she had come to see herself in a realistic light. Her brain was formidable, her talents varied and useful.

But as a woman she lacked the spark to ignite men's hearts. Eric had as much told her so when he broke the engagement. "Thanks for the leg-up, Emma," he'd taunted. "I knew if I played you right, you'd believe me when I said those letters were authentic. What I do for my career…" He sighed. "Now, of course, there's no need for me to marry you. Amazons just aren't my type."

She wasn't anyone's type, apparently. That summer with Jimmy, they'd both been young, ready to learn the ways of love. Adolescent hormones and natural curiosity created a powerful chemistry. Only a fool would expect the reaction to last twenty years. Or to survive the twenty pounds she'd gained, the lines at the corners of her eyes, the awkwardness of being too tall, which she'd never managed to conquer.

Jimmy's charm, his charisma, were as natural to him as

breathing. But Emma knew better than to believe the fantasy. Cinderella she was not. When Jimmy was kind, when he was flattering, she would simply have to keep her head. He'd given her a job, given her a means to start over with her life.

How much more could she reasonably ask?

Turning off the bedside lamp, she burrowed under the sheet, arms folded tight against her chest, and acknowledged the answer to her own question.

Not nearly as much as I could want.

EVEN ON SUNDAY, the late-night streets weren't deserted. Long after Emma had left, Jimmy set the club's alarm, stepped out the front door and locked it, then turned to assess the situation. The cops patrolled fairly often until about midnight. After that, the pretense at control disappeared, and the street people reclaimed their territory. For a few hours, anyway.

Tonight's cast of characters included a couple of prostitutes stationed on a corner across from the club and their pimp in his gold Mercedes parked nearby, plus the usual assortment of addicts and dealers, the homeless and the helpless.

Jimmy shook his head. He'd once seen himself as someone who could help these people solve their problems. Now he just figured they all had a right to go to hell their own way.

As he approached the Jag in its usual spot, a trio of shadows separated from the nearby wall. Talking about lost causes...

"Hey there, Mr. Falcon. Great wheels." The Texas drawl identified Harlow.

"Thanks." Jimmy leaned back against the front fender. "After that mix-up the other night, I didn't expect to see you guys around here so soon. Doesn't look like the neighborhood's too safe, where you're concerned.''

"We go anywhere we want to." Tomas, part Mexican, part Indian, and all mouth, ran a hand over the roof of the Jag. "Nobody's telling us where we can and can't hang out."

"If you say so."

"Business doin' good, Mr. Falcon?" The smoke from Harlow's cigarette drifted on the late-night breeze.

"Same as usual."

"Been catching some great smells coming out that back door this week. You got a new cook?"

Every hair on his body stood on end. Jimmy forced himself not to move. "That's right." These three weren't the violent threat some folks pictured when they thought about heroin addicts—only boys who had nowhere else to go and nobody who cared. That was why he'd once thought he had a chance to get them off the streets, out of this lousy life.

But the drug had defeated him in the battle for their souls. He wasn't afraid of them, but he didn't want them hassling Emma. Just one more reason he never should have hired her.

Harlow wasn't going to let the subject drop. "You're gettin' real uptown for a dirty little hole in the wall. Next thing we know, you'll be paintin' the place."

"Don't worry—I don't expect to get an award from the Denver beautification committee anytime soon."

"Glad to hear it. Those types like to think our types live somewhere else, you know?" Harlow straightened away from the lamppost. He sounded almost…regretful.

But Jimmy had let that easy regret fake him out before. Harlow was a master con artist. "If you gentlemen will excuse me, it's been a long day." He wouldn't open the car door until they left. And all of them knew it.

"That it has." Ryan, the smallest of the bunch, was thin

to the point of disappearing. The hunger in his eyes was not for food. "Man with a car like this must carry some extra change. Whaddaya say, Mr. F.? How about a loan?"

"I could manage fifty cents for some gum."

Tomas barked a laugh. "Piss on that. As if gum wasn't eighty freakin' cents these days. Gimme a break, man."

Despite his size, he moved fast. Jimmy looked up into the swarthy, sweating face just inches from his own. If Harlow was the brains of the group, Tomas was the muscle. And he had a bad temper. "Get out of my way."

"I'm tellin' you, man—"

Harlow put a hand on Tomas's shoulder and jerked him backward, away from Jimmy. "Chill, Tommy. We're not gonna shake down Mr. Falcon. He's one of the good guys."

"Like hell he is."

"Harlow…" Ryan's voice had started to shake. In the few minutes of the conversation, his skin had paled and his eyes had clouded.

"Yeah, Ry. I'm coming." Harlow shrugged and gave Jimmy a conciliatory grin. "Sorry for the trouble, Mr. Falcon. We'll let you get home and get some sleep."

"Thanks." Jimmy didn't move until Harlow and friends started down the sidewalk toward the part of town where drugs were easier to score than ice-cream cones. Then, through the windshield, he watched until the three boys blended into the night. He reminded himself once again that he had tried with them. And failed.

Headed across town to his apartment, he turned on the seat warmer to ease the ache in his hip. He hadn't been keeping up with therapy the past few months, so a ten-minute dance had set up cramps in his shredded muscles. Small price to pay, though, for a chance to hold Emma in his arms.

But he shouldn't have kissed her. He'd known it ahead of time and ignored the knowledge. The very first time he'd ever dared, she'd just eaten a strawberry, brought back from Denver to the rez by her impractical, nearsighted, absent-minded father. Jimmy had never tasted strawberries—they didn't thrive in the arid canyonlands he'd grown up in. But that summer with Emma, he'd learned to crave the sweet, seedy fruit. Anytime since, when he'd allowed himself the indulgence of that special berry, he had thought of one special woman-child. And smiled.

He wasn't smiling now. He was trying to figure out how to keep control so that tonight's mistake didn't happen again. The easiest option was to fire Emma. Get her out of the club, out of his life.

Yeah, right. Kick her when she was already down. He couldn't do that to any woman.

Especially not to Emma.

He'd have to make himself scarce. Tiffany had worked for him long enough to know the liquor reps, the standing orders, the combination to the safe and where he kept the spare keys. She would handle the daily management duties as well as he could. Especially if he raised her pay.

That left only the nights—when the club was packed and Emma worked her magic in the kitchen. He'd stay out of her way, but he'd be sure to hang around. Harlow and his gang could not be allowed to hustle Emma. Unless something deep inside her had changed—and he could tell from her eyes that it hadn't—she'd have no problem throwing money into the bottomless well where these boys lived with their habit.

She would try to help them and, most likely, fail. Jimmy didn't want her hurt that way, didn't want to see the dis-illusionment in her eyes when she realized she'd only been a mark. Emma put her whole heart into everything she did. She'd done it the summer they spent together, and she was doing it now, just cooking up sandwiches in his club.

Somehow he was going to have to keep Emma from getting burned. By these boys...

And by his own fierce, out-of-line desire.

"JIMMY HASN'T BEEN HERE very often during this last week." Late Thursday morning, Emma sat down on a wobbly bar stool to watch Tiffany stack glassware.

"Nope. He said he was taking some days off."

"Did he say why?" Emma didn't really need to ask. Jimmy was avoiding *her,* embarrassed at being pressured into that kiss.

Tiffany shook her head. "He's done it before. I think he goes for weeks without sleeping more than a couple of hours a night, and then crashes and sleeps for about a month."

"That doesn't sound like much of a life." Why would an accomplished and charming man live such a sterile existence?"

"I guess that's the way he wants it."

Emma surrendered to her curiosity. "Has he always lived alone?"

"As long as I've known him."

Something loosened inside Emma's chest that she tried very hard to ignore.

"Of course, that doesn't mean he's a monk." Tiffany's smile was wicked. "There have been quite a few women in his life over the years."

"I'm sure." Her chest had tightened up again. She decided to change the subject. "How long have you known Jimmy?"

The bartender pondered. "I worked here for a couple of years before I got married. After the divorce I came back. So I guess that's maybe five or six years."

"Has Jimmy met your current...er...boyfriend?"

"Nope. No reason to. Brad's not into jazz." She grinned.

"But he likes the tips I get, so he doesn't mind me working."

"Does Brad work?"

"Off and on. He does demolition—taking down old buildings and stuff like that—but it's kind of an unsteady job market unless you run your own company. Which is okay with Brad, because he doesn't like life too predictable, anyway."

"Ah." If Tiffany didn't mind supporting a slacker, who was Emma to protest? She propped her chin in her hands. "Well, if Jimmy isn't here, he can't very well know what's going on, can he?"

Tiffany shot her a suspicious glance. "What's going on?"

The idea had occurred to her in the cab on the way home last night. "Suppose I changed the menu. He wouldn't realize until sometime during the evening. And by then, he'd see how much the customers enjoyed something new."

"Emma Garrett, you are nuts." The bartender shook her head. "Jimmy would kill you for something like that. He'd kill me, too, for letting you."

"But you know I'm right. Just think what this place could be with the right food, new furniture, paint—"

"Whoa! Furniture?" Tiffany backed into the counter opposite the bar, her hands held up as if to ward off danger. "Not another word. I want to be able to tell Jimmy I didn't know a thing about it!"

Before noon, Emma had ordered a minimum of dishware from a local shop and billed it to her credit card, along with knives, forks and spoons. If the idea failed, she wouldn't want Jimmy to bear the loss. Her savings could stand the damage. And though there would be more dirty dishes to deal with, the club's dishwashing machine functioned well enough to make the gamble worthwhile.

From their grocer, she requested the usual supplies for

sandwiches, but added mixed greens for salads, goat cheese and French bread. And chicken breasts—they were on special and would be easy to marinate and serve with sauce.

The woman on the other end of the line took the order without comment. After a moment's silence, she said, "Now where did you tell me this was for?"

"The Indigo."

"Jimmy's place?"

"That's right."

"Did Jimmy die?"

"Of course not. Why do you ask?"

The woman clucked her tongue. "He's the last guy in town I'd expect to serve fancy salads. I might have to show up tonight just to see that for myself!"

Emma prepped food for several hours, then went back to the hotel to change. When she returned at four, she noticed a young man leaning against the corner of the building, next to the alley. As she crossed the street, he turned. Harlow.

He threw away his cigarette and came toward her at an easy walk. "Hey, Emma. How are you this afternoon?"

"Well, thank you. I must say, you disappeared rather quickly last week."

His grin could melt sugar. "I make it a point to leave fast. Never can tell what you'll get blamed for if you hang around too long."

She pushed open the front door to The Indigo. "Would you like to come in?"

He glanced up and down the empty street. "Sure. For a minute, anyway."

As they stepped inside, Tiffany emerged from the back hallway. "Hey, Harlow. How's it going?"

"Good. What's Brad doing these days?"

Tiffany hesitated. "Uh…not much. He's between jobs."

Harlow laughed. "Me, too."

The front door opened again. Emma saw the boy freeze, then turn slowly to face the newcomer. She wondered what he expected Jimmy to do to him.

But a heavyset man stepped inside, not Jimmy. "I got a food delivery. Where do you want it?"

"In the alley, please. Tiffany, would you unlock the door?"

In fifteen minutes, with Harlow helping, the boxes of groceries sat on the kitchen table. Emma surveyed what she'd done with a sudden tremor of doubt. This was a lot of food. If it didn't sell...

Nonsense. "I should get those chicken breasts in the marinade."

Somehow Harlow became the unofficial kitchen boy, stowing the supplies where she directed. The new dishes were delivered, and he put those away, as well, after she washed them. He worked efficiently, always whistling a tune underneath his breath. Soon enough, the kitchen was back to normal, except for a large bowl of salad greens soaking in cold water.

The daylight in the alley had nearly disappeared. "I'd better be going," Harlow said. "Mr. Falcon'll show up soon."

Emma put her hand on the thin bones of his arm. "Let me make you something to eat first."

"That's okay. I'm good to go."

"But you've done a great deal of work this afternoon. Please, it's the least I can do."

He shook his head. "I'd like to, Emma. Your cooking is the best. But I don't want to be here when the boss comes in. That'll be bad for you and me. I can take it, but you shouldn't have to."

"Well, then, at least let me pay you. I won't feel right if I don't."

Again, that sweet grin. "I wouldn't want you feeling bad. Just a couple of bucks for a burger is plenty."

He'd worked for two hours. She gave him forty dollars—twice what she got paid, but her savings would make up the difference. In any event, she hadn't taken this job for the money. "Have a really good meal tonight. Vegetables, too."

"Yes, ma'am!" He saluted her from the door to the alley. His smile faded and his expression turned somber. "You're something special. Thanks."

Emma stared out the screen door for several minutes after he disappeared. Jimmy had warned her about Harlow, and his friend. But the boy she'd seen today seemed neither desperate nor dangerous. Just in need of help. Almost eager, in fact, to be helped. Perhaps he wanted to change his life and didn't know quite how to begin. Or how to ask.

"If we wait until we're asked to help," her mother had said more than once, "many good people with too much pride will be lost." Not long after Emma turned fifteen, Naomi Garrett had given her life for those good people—a victim of dengue fever, contracted while nursing the critically ill. Emma's dad had suffered recurrent malaria attacks for years, thanks to his work in Africa studying tribal dialects. Between them, they'd left her a very big example to live up to.

If anything positive were to come out of the end of her university career, Emma thought it might be the chance to provide the kind of help her parents had modeled for her. At least, she could try.

She smiled ruefully, thinking of her father's jokes about Emma-Knows-Best. Perhaps her penchant for meddling in other people's affairs could finally be turned to good use.

THE MUSIC WAS HOT and heavy by the time Jimmy showed up at the club. He made his way down the bar, greeting regulars with a handshake, checking out the room in general. An okay crowd for a Thursday night. Big enough to keep him occupied somewhere besides the kitchen.

Tiffany brought him a whiskey as he leaned against the end of the bar. Darren whizzed by, carrying a loaded tray on his shoulder. "Upper-body strength," he muttered. "I shoulda been lifting weights."

The comment didn't make sense until a break between sets, when Jimmy heard the clatter of dishes at a nearby table, the ping of knives and forks. The next time Darren came by, Jimmy stopped him.

"What's the deal with the food?"

The server shrugged. "Emma said to mention salads and lemon chicken when I took the orders. We got more people ordering that now than sandwiches." He shifted under the weight of the tray. "I gotta dump this, boss, or drop it."

Jimmy waved him away. When Tiffany worked her way down to him again, he called her over. "Emma changed the menu?"

The bartender avoided his eyes. "Yeah. The customers seem to like the variety."

"You didn't think I might want to know about this?"

She shrugged. "I didn't want to get between you and Emma."

Guilt grabbed him by the throat. He drummed a quick rhythm pattern on the bar. "You're right, Tiff. I'm a jerk for blaming you. There's only one person I should be talking to about this."

In the kitchen, Emma looked up from a plate of salad as he stepped through the door and let it swing shut behind him. "Hullo, Jimmy. How are you tonight?"

"Surprised. What are you doing, Emma?"

She met his gaze straight on. "I wanted to show you how successful a different menu could be. I think the customers are enjoying the wider selection of food."

Brains and beauty and guts. A powerful combination. The recognition expanded his irritation. "What's the profit margin on those salads?"

"The same as the sandwiches. I don't want you to lose money."

He leaned against the door frame to rest his hip. "Does that include the plates and silverware?"

Her face and throat flooded with red. "Um…no."

"Right." Hands in his pockets, he tried to figure out the real point here. A power struggle between them? Maybe. Emma was a woman used to running a classroom, a career. But he'd established his own life, ran his club to meet his own standards. He didn't like having decisions taken out of his hands, even by Emma Garrett.

"I meant this for the best, Jimmy."

"I'm sure you did." He sighed. Staying mad at Emma for any length of time had been impossible when they were kids, something between them that didn't seem to have changed. "The money doesn't really matter a damn."

"I know."

"But if I wanted this place to be something different, it would be."

"The question is, why wouldn't you want it?"

"Because…" He shook his head. "That doesn't matter, either. No more surprises, Emma, okay? At least talk to me first."

"I did talk to you."

"And then you ignored what I said."

"I was right—the customers like a more sophisticated menu."

"You were. You will be again." Jimmy straightened. "In fact, you might just be right about everything one hundred percent of the time. But this is my place and what I say goes. Clear?"

Emma lifted her chin. "Yes, sir. Perfectly clear."

"Thanks. You can keep the salads and the chicken. And the dishes. But that's as far as we go."

A minute later, behind the closed door of his office, Jimmy aimed a pencil and sent it flying, straight as an arrow, toward the opposite wall.

Emma was shaking up his world again. Only he wasn't seventeen anymore. He hadn't believed in happy-ever-afters since he was eight years old.

And he really hated being tempted to change his mind.

CHAPTER FIVE

DARREN'S FIVE-PIECE BAND played at The Indigo for the first time the following Sunday night. The crowd was small, but the music surprisingly good. Emma listened for most of two sets—she got only three orders, for nachos, all evening. When the last of the customers left about eleven-thirty, cleaning up the kitchen took her all of five minutes.

She stepped across the threshold into the darker club room and instinctively glanced to the right, toward Jimmy's office. He hadn't made any kind of appearance tonight. But a patch of light fell through his open doorway, signaling his presence. Now was as good a time as any, she supposed, to make her request.

He sat behind the desk with his chair turned sideways. At the sight of his strong profile, Emma caught her breath. Proud, intelligent, compelling, and obviously a man of Native American descent. A heritage he was determined to ignore.

Lost in thought, he didn't notice her for a moment. Then, though she hadn't moved, he turned his head. "Hey, Emma. I just called—the cab should be here in a few minutes."

"Good." She took a step into the room. "Before I go, I have a favor to ask."

"What's that?"

"I would like to borrow the medallion and its box."

His straight black brows drew together. "Any particular reason?"

A deep breath steadied her voice. "I've made a list of galleries in the area specializing in indigenous artifacts. I thought I would visit some of them tomorrow, since the club's closed on Mondays. The dealers will be able to give me more information if they can see the actual piece."

He shook his head. "Emma—"

She held up a hand. "I'm not asking you to participate. But I can't forget what my dad wanted, either. I'll pursue the research by myself, if you'll lend me the medallion."

Without a word he turned his chair to face the wall behind him. For the first time, she noticed a built-in safe there. The combination lock whirred, the door opened, then Jimmy turned back to set the box on the desk.

Emma picked it up and flipped the catch. Struck by the overhead lighting, the disk inside gleamed like an actual sunrise. "It's so unusual. I haven't found anything quite like it listed anywhere online." She traced a line of fine engraving with her fingertip. "I think it must be more than an ordinary concha," she said, referring to silver disks used as decorative elements in Indian jewelry. "Perhaps part of a necklace, for which the chain has been lost."

Jimmy cleared his throat. "There are rough places at two o'clock and ten o'clock that look like there might have been rings welded on at one point."

Holding the medallion close to her face, she squinted at the edges. "Ah. I see them. They've been polished smooth, but not quite erased." She glanced at the man across the desk. "You must have looked at this again."

"I've looked at it a lot. I really appreciate that your father thought of me." He let his head rest against the back of the chair. "Not that I know why—we didn't see each other even once after that summer. You went back to England to start college, he left for some other research site. And the Christmas cards stopped after a couple of years."

"Yes, they did." Emma sat down without being asked,

still cradling the disk in her palms. "Once you finished basic military training, you seemed to be awfully busy, and I couldn't tell if you wanted me to write or not."

"I liked hearing from you. But I didn't have all that much to say. Army life's pretty much the same every day."

"What you think about is always different."

Jimmy grinned slightly. "In the army, you're trained not to think."

"You didn't like the service?" After his curt behavior over the chicken and salads, she supposed she should be distant, reserved. But an opportunity to hear Jimmy talk about himself couldn't be wasted.

"More or less. I got to see places—not tourist spots, but the real world. I usually had a meal and a place to sleep, unless the operation went wrong. That didn't happen too often. Made a friend or two, learned to live with malaria—"

"My father contracted malaria in Africa."

Jimmy nodded. "Me, too. We were doing reconnaissance in Angola. I lost my pills in the mud somewhere and didn't get back to base before my immunity wore off. But at least there's treatment."

"Even a cure, these days."

"For a lot of people, yeah. Mine comes back occasionally, but the medicine knocks it down pretty fast." He tented his fingers and stared at them for a long moment. "Anyway, considering that about the most useful thing I did for Aubrey Garrett that summer was seduce his daughter, I'm pretty surprised he sent me such a gift. Unless—" leaning forward again, he propped his elbows on the desk "—unless it's cursed and brings torture and death to Indians who own it." His black eyes sparked with amusement, and a smile quirked his fine mouth. "That would make a lot of sense."

Emma had to smile, too. "I think you've solved that part

of the puzzle. Dad was a firm believer in enchantments and magic, especially Indian magic." The memory sobered her. "He wanted to come back to this country and have one of his friends perform a Healing Way ceremony for him. There wasn't time." Some internal demon drove her to add, "But I gather you don't concede the power of such Indian rituals."

Jimmy held up his hands to ward off the attack. "That's quite a change of mood. As a matter of fact, I think a person's beliefs are the power behind the ceremonies they use. If your dad really believed in the Healing Way, then having one might have made a difference to him."

Emma put the disk back in its box, then raised her gaze to his face. "The power of positive thinking?"

"Something like that." He took a second to line up his thoughts. "Look, I'm not anti-Indian. Other folks are welcome to whatever culture they want to claim, however they want to live, a history they can be proud of. I'm not running anybody else's life. Only mine. For me, being Indian just doesn't work. My grandfather gave the past away when he sold his land."

"You think he ought to have let them kill him—and perhaps his wife and children?"

"I think a true warrior would have done that, yeah. Indians have let themselves be pushed around, pushed out, for a couple of centuries now. That's not something to be proud of." He shrugged. "If Americans had done the same, the U.S. would still be part of the United Kingdom."

"The Indians chose to survive."

"Yeah, some standard of survival. My parents showed me what reservation life amounts to—alcoholism, disease, despair. I'm not buying."

They faced each other across the walnut box. Emma still didn't understand, he could see it in her eyes. Jimmy didn't know how else to explain.

He touched the medallion with two fingers. "This is a piece of artwork that I value because it came from your dad. Not because it connects me to the past."

"I see." She stood and picked up the box. Her eyes were shuttered. "Then you won't mind if I investigate for myself."

"No. No, I guess not." Instead of a peace treaty, this felt like a declaration of war. "Good luck."

"Thank you." As she turned to leave, Darren appeared at the door.

"Thanks, boss! It was a cool gig! We had a blast." His freckled face was flushed, his curly brown hair damp from three hours of beating drums.

"My pleasure. You did a good job."

"The music was exceptional, Darren." For the college kid, Emma had a wide smile. Jimmy beat down a wave of...jealousy? "You've really got something to build on."

"I'm totally psyched," he said, grinning. "Oh, and your cab's here."

"I'm on my way." She started to leave, hesitated in the hallway and turned halfway back. "Good night, Jimmy."

"'Night, Emma." When she and Darren had both left, Jimmy leaned back in his chair and closed his eyes. This wasn't the end of the issue between him and Emma. Only the beginning.

And he didn't have the slightest clue about what to expect next.

"OKAY, here's the plan." Harlow hunkered down next to Ryan on the floor of T-Bone's squat. "I've got her hooked. Helped her unload food and dishes and stuff, wouldn't let her feed me, then let her convince me to take forty bucks."

Tommy turned from the window. "Man! You got forty bucks? What are we doing wasting time in here?"

Harlow rolled his eyes. "It's called planning, Tommy."

Tommy gave him the finger.

"Yeah, right. Anyway, the next part is to get Ryan in there, make her feel sorry for him. I'll bring you with me next time, Ry. You might even get chocolate milk."

"Cool." He was nearly asleep. "You think she doesn't know what you're doing, Harlow? You really got her fooled?"

"Oh, yeah." He thought for a second about Emma Garrett's worried blue eyes, her warm smile. Too bad she was such a pigeon. "Yeah, Ry. I got the English lady completely snowed."

"Speaking of snow," Tommy said, crossing the room. "How about giving me my share of that forty bucks? There's this dealer I know…"

FRIDAY AFTERNOON, Emma looked up from the spices she was grinding with a mortar and pestle to see Harlow standing at the screen door. "Come in," she said without stopping. "You're just in time to try out a new recipe."

He opened the door, but stepped back to let someone else enter first. This boy seemed even more pitifully gaunt than Harlow, his brown hair dirty and long, his shirt hanging limply off his shoulders. His face was too white, his eyes too dark. She didn't need Jimmy to point out the face of a heroin addict.

"Emma, I've been telling Ryan here about your cooking."

Emma read the apology in Harlow's face. He hated to impose, but obviously his friend was in desperate need of decent food. "Word of mouth is excellent advertising," she said. "I just happen to have some fresh tomatoes to go with the chicken salad recipe I'm trying out. Let me make you both a sandwich."

Ryan ate two sandwiches, without saying anything beyond "Thank you, ma'am." Harlow filled the silence with descriptions of the fair they'd visited that morning in City Park.

"The guy on stilts was doing just great until he put one pole down in a puddle of melted ice cream. Next thing you know—bam!—he's on his butt in the street, with somebody's frozen drink spilled in his face and three dogs licking it off."

Emma laughed, and Ryan grinned absentmindedly, casting a glance toward the loaf of bread and bowl of chicken salad.

"Would you like another sandwich?" Emma went to the counter. "There's plenty."

"That would be…" he started in a rusty-sounding voice. And then stopped. When she looked around, he glanced at Harlow, then shook his head. "Thank you, ma'am. I'm just fine." But he downed his milk a little desperately.

Harlow got to his feet. "The salad's great. You've got another hit on your hands. We'd better get out of your way now, let you get ready for your late-night crowd. Come on, Ry."

Ryan pushed hard against the table to stand up. "This really has been great," he said, shuffling to the door. "I appreciate your help, ma'am." He yawned. "Have a good night."

With Ryan out the door, Harlow looked back. "I know I put you on the spot, Emma. Ry's…having some trouble. It'd been a coupla days since he ate much of anything at all, but I knew your cooking would tempt him. I've got some cash, if you'll just let me pay—"

"Don't be silly." She closed his hand around the bills. "We can certainly spare a few sandwiches. I'm glad I could help. Feel free to come again—anytime."

Harlow's sweet grin warmed her heart. He started to say something, then simply turned his hand in hers, squeezed her fingers and hurried down the alley. Catching Ryan by the waist as he passed, he pulled him around the corner, out of sight.

Moments later she heard the Jag's engine purr as Jimmy parked nearby. They hadn't talked much in the days since she'd borrowed the medallion. There wasn't really much to say about that—none of the gallery owners she'd consulted had ever seen a piece like this one. A curator at the Denver Museum of History suggested that the medallion might have come from Mexico, or even Peru. Online searches had showed her the fine metalwork of the Aztecs and Incas, and daunted her with the breadth of the research possibilities. Checking out all the available sources could take years. That explained why her father had put off the search.

Jimmy never asked what she'd discovered. He stayed as far away from her as possible while he was in the club, and left before she could finish her work and find him. There was always a prepaid cab at the front door to take her home.

But no personal escort from Jimmy Falcon. No conversation. He was polite, even cordial, when they chanced to meet. But he seemed to be making sure that didn't happen very often.

Emma set her jaw and went back to grinding spices. So be it. She was the one who'd set the rules to begin with. Employer-employee. No problem.

At least, that was what she'd like to believe.

As EMMA STEPPED into The Indigo on Saturday morning, a glass crashed against the floor. Tiffany's rude exclamation followed immediately.

"Are you all right?" Emma hurried over to the bar to peer at the scattered shards. "Did you cut yourself?"

Tiffany glanced back on her way to the storage room. "No cuts. I'm just lucky Jimmy doesn't take broken glasses out of my paycheck."

When she returned with the broom, Emma got her first

good look at the bartender. "What's wrong with your wrist?" An elastic bandage peeked out from either end of a lace-up brace.

"I was doing some in-line skating this morning. I fell and sprained it." She didn't meet Emma's gaze as she made the explanation.

Emma propped a hip on the nearest bar stool. "I don't believe you."

Tiffany flashed her an angry look and kept sweeping.

"Brad sprained your wrist for you, didn't he?"

No answer.

Emma drew a frustrated breath. "It won't get better, you know. He'll keep hurting you, and apologizing, until something dreadful happens. Or until you walk away."

Tiffany shook her head. "This wasn't his doing. I started falling and he caught my hand to keep me up and my wrist twisted the wrong way."

"Why won't you look at me when you explain?"

Another rude word blued the air. The bartender dumped broken glass into the garbage. Then she did meet Emma's stare straight on. "This isn't any of your business. Butt out."

"I thought we were friends, Tiffany. How can I sit by and watch him hurting you?"

"Nobody's asking you to watch anything. I'll say it again—butt out." She picked up a glass and held it under the water spigot with her good hand, wincing as she tried to work the lever with the injured arm. Switching the glass to her bandaged hand, she opened the spigot. The pressure of the spray pushed the vessel out of her grasp. Again the clatter of breaking glass.

This time, there was a whole string of curses. Emma waited until Tiffany had cleaned up the mess again. "You should call Jimmy—you can't work like this."

The bartender snorted a laugh. "Yeah, right. I don't

work, I don't get paid. You want to see some fireworks, watch me come home without a paycheck.''

"If you don't call him, I will.''

The bartender stared at Emma with active dislike. "Who died and left you in charge?''

Ignoring the question, Emma went down the hallway and picked up the pay phone, but only reached Jimmy's answering machine. Was he out…or just screening his calls, hoping to avoid her? The thought shook her, and she decided against leaving a message—she didn't want to try to explain Tiffany's situation to a tape recorder.

The crowd started out heavy that night, and hungry. Darren ran himself ragged until Jimmy appeared about nine o'clock. Emma knew the time because she stood in the kitchen doorway watching for him.

He caught sight of her across the room and paused for a second, then came close. "Hello. Things going okay?'' His face was grave and conveyed none of what he might be feeling. If indeed he felt anything at all.

Emma nodded toward the bar. "Tiffany's hurt her wrist and has trouble holding the glasses. Darren's helping out, but the customers are complaining about the longer wait.''

He cocked an eyebrow. "Somebody should have called me. I could have been here earlier.''

Darren stepped up beside them. "Well, you're here now, and we can use the help. I'm killing myself trying to get to everybody.''

Jimmy watched him make the rounds of the tables. "I guess I've got my assignment.'' When he looked back into Emma's face, the trouble there was easy to see. "What's wrong?''

"Can you come into the kitchen to talk about this? I really don't want—''

A large party poured through the front door. Moving tables together and scraping chairs across the floor, they settled noisily in the center of the room and started ordering drinks.

Jimmy shook his head. "I'd better get to work. We'll talk later, okay?"

"I...yes." Emma glanced at Tiffany, and the worry in her eyes doubled. "Later will be good."

Stepping behind the bar, Jimmy eased Tiffany out of the way and took over the mug of beer she'd been trying to draw. "What's got Emma so upset?"

His bartender shrugged a slender shoulder. "She's all bent out of shape because I sprained my wrist. No big deal."

Darren brought the drink order from the big table to the bar. "They want food, too. Emma's going to get a workout tonight."

Jimmy watched Darren go into the kitchen, then turned back to Tiffany. "You were skating again, weren't you? Seems like you get hurt every time you put those things on. Maybe you should consider a slower game." He grinned to take the sting out of the words.

Tiffany responded with a smile. "I'm thinking about taking up crocheting, as a matter of fact." She glanced at her bandaged wrist. "Guess I'll have to let this get better first, though."

The traffic picked up after that, keeping all of them occupied without a chance for any real communication or even a chance to think. Which was a good thing, because all Jimmy had done since yesterday was think, and it had gotten him nowhere.

He hadn't been sleeping well, anyway, and now the situation with Emma had wrecked the daylight hours, too. He'd always made it a rule not to get too involved with a woman, sexually or in any other way. Life ran much more smoothly when he kept the intensity of relationships to a minimum.

Now there was Emma. The antagonism between them wasn't too big a problem, although with Emma, *any* kind of conflict felt obscene. But it was the *other* emotions she stirred, which had nothing to do with anger...

Trying to avoid even thinking about those feelings, Jimmy focused his eyes in time to see a uniformed police officer making his way through the crowd. Then Zach Harmon, his former partner on the police force, slid onto the nearby bar stool.

"I was making my rounds and thought I'd step in and see what all the commotion was about. You've got a riot waiting to happen here tonight."

Jimmy shook his head, returning the cop's handshake. "Only if the booze runs dry."

Zach turned his head to follow Darren's progress with a loaded tray to the other side of the room. "The booze...or the food. Who's in the kitchen?"

"Emma Garrett." Tiffany set a Coke on the bar in front of Zach. "She's an old friend of Jimmy's, and a dynamite cook."

"Must be." When the bartender moved away, Zach glanced at Jimmy. "An old friend?"

"I knew her in high school."

"In other words, don't ask."

Jimmy shook his head. "Hell, you can ask anything you want. Emma's dad did language research on the reservation. Her mom was dead and so Emma came over during her school break. We hung out together until she went back to England in the fall to go to Oxford. I haven't seen her since."

"And now she's cooking for The Indigo? Quite a coincidence."

"Not at all. Her dad died a few months ago and he left me a...well, some kind of Indian artifact in his will. Emma brought it over and decided to stay a while. No big deal."

"I guess not." Zach turned on his seat to watch the crowd. "Do I get to meet her?"

"Sure. Some time when she's not so busy. Come by in the afternoon—she's usually here by one or two." Only when he stopped talking did Jimmy catch the whiff of fresh scent that heralded Emma's approach.

She set a covered dish on the counter behind the bar. "Tiffany's midnight snack," she said. She glanced at Zach, and smiled. "Hello, Officer."

After struggling for a second with his own envy for that smile, Jimmy did his duty. "Emma, this is Zach Harmon, a friend of mine. Zach—Emma Garrett."

Harmon's grin made his approval obvious. "Good to meet you, Emma. I'm hearing great things about the food at this place. You're giving The Indigo a touch of class."

Emma flushed. "That's kind of you. People do seem to appreciate the additions to the menu."

"I'll have to bring my wife in sometime soon. She's wanted Jimmy to upscale the meals here for a couple of years now." He rolled his eyes. "That's assuming I can get her to leave the baby, of course. We just had a little girl, Norah, six weeks ago. Shelley wouldn't leave our son—he's two years old—with a baby-sitter for almost six months."

Emma's eyes went soft. "They must be very sweet. What's your son's name?"

"Alex. And he's a wild one—I'm aging five years for every one of his." Soon enough, Zach had his wallet out and pictures displayed on the bar. Emma seemed to know a lot about children for someone without any. She laughed frequently and encouraged Zach to tell every story in his arsenal.

Jimmy didn't have a word to contribute, his total amount of experience with kids wouldn't fill a shot glass. He'd been his parents' only child. When they died, his aunt took him in, but her sons were older and didn't have time for a whiny little boy.

"I'd better get back to patrol," Zach said, pocketing his wallet. "Denver on Saturday night gets a little crazy."

Emma put out her hand. "It was so good to meet you. I hope I'll see you and your wife sometime soon."

"I'll do my best." He gave Jimmy a quick punch to the shoulder. "Take it easy, man. Call if you need anything."

"Thanks." Jimmy watched the patrolman work his way through the crowd and out the door, putting off the moment when he'd have to turn and face the woman beside him.

"Have you known him long?" Emma's question made the turn mandatory.

"We served together in the army a couple of years, and he was my partner on the police force before I got discharged. We still hang out together. Zach's laid-back enough that he doesn't care if he plays basketball with a gimp."

Her face flushed and her eyes turned fierce. "Jimmy—"

"Mr. Falcon?"

Jimmy turned away from Emma's protest. Darren handed in an order just as one of the latecomers approached the bar, an executive type in an expensive suit and shirt, his silk tie loosened and his top button free.

"I'm Jimmy. What can I get you?"

The man waved away the idea of a drink. "I'm good for now. But I wanted to ask if you ever host private parties here at The Indigo."

Jimmy shook his head as he poured the screwdriver Darren needed. "We're not that kind of place. Beer and jazz are our specialties."

"That's what I thought. But the wife and I come here a lot, and we've noticed the way your menu has picked up. We've got out-of-town clients coming in next week, and we were thinking they might enjoy just this kind of experience.''

"You're welcome to bring them in. Call ahead and we'll make sure there's a table waiting.''

"Of course.'' He hesitated, looking back at the band for a second. "But we need a less…hectic atmosphere. This will definitely be a business dinner.''

"There are some great restaurants in Denver. Any one of them—''

"What sort of menu did you have in mind?'' Emma stepped out of the shadows and joined them.

The man shrugged. "Something regional, interesting. Not too heavy. Can you do that?''

Jimmy said, "No, I'm sorry.''

At the same time Emma said, "As the cook, I'm certain we could accommodate your requirements.''

Jimmy felt his temper rise. "I've been explaining that this isn't a supper club. We don't have the facilities.''

She smiled at him and then at the businessman. "Did you have a particular day in mind?''

"My clients are arriving next Friday afternoon from Tokyo. They'll be here until Wednesday.''

Jimmy had to think fast to keep his jaw from dropping.

"So then you could bring them in on Monday night, when the club is closed?''

"I think that would work just fine, if you can get it together that quickly.''

Emma smiled again. "Oh, I think a week is plenty of notice. I'll work up three sample menus and you can choose the one you like. Jimmy will bring in a band—a fairly quiet group, so you'll be able to talk. Could I get your card, Mr….?''

"Owen. Ted Owen of Owen Pipe and Steel.''

Five minutes later Ted Owen sat down with his friends. Jimmy looked at Emma. "You're crazy.''

She shrugged. "We can handle a small dinner party with one hand tied behind our backs. I've been thinking about just this sort of event since I started work here. A few tablecloths, some napkins, flowers…and you make a name for yourself, not to mention a lot of money."

Swearing under his breath, Jimmy took hold of Emma's arm and herded her before him into the kitchen. "Who the hell do you think you are?" he demanded, not releasing her.

Her smile trembled. "That's the second variation I've heard on that question tonight."

"I'm not surprised. Did I miss the part where you get to run everybody's lives for them?"

"I am not—"

"I have no interest in making this place into some kind of diners' den. I don't want to work that hard. I don't want the hassle of dealing with people. I want to serve decent drinks and listen to good music and make a little money doing it. Got it?"

"I think—"

All his frustration from this last week around her seemed to condense into anger. "You've been meddling in my business since you first showed up here."

Emma jerked away, and her chin went up. "I did not intend to meddle."

"Well, that's what you're doing. And I'm asking you to stop. Right now. Before what we…" He dragged in a deep desperate breath. "Before what I remember about that summer becomes just one more thing I'm trying to forget."

CHAPTER SIX

EMMA WASN'T TALKING to him.

Jimmy didn't understand why she should be mad when she had caused the problem to begin with. She'd watched from the kitchen doorway on Saturday night as he explained to Ted Owen that there was a scheduling conflict and they wouldn't be able to host his event, after all. Owen was disappointed, but reasonably satisfied with Jimmy's offer to get him a spot at one of Denver's best restaurants. When Jimmy turned toward the kitchen after seeing the man to his seat, the temper and reproach in Emma's eyes set the seal on his own bad mood. He sent Tiffany home to rest her sprained wrist and spent the rest of the night furiously tending bar.

Sunday turned into the worst night Jimmy could remember at The Indigo in years. Maybe ever. The band was lousy, the crowd small but loud and rude. Darren dropped a tray of drinks into one woman's lap. Just as Jimmy finished apologizing and promising to pay the dry-cleaning bill, Tiffany tossed the contents of a beer mug into the face of a guy at the bar. Jimmy got the jerk outside without damage, but it wasn't pretty or quick.

So the last thing he expected on Monday morning was a call from Emma. "Hi, Jimmy."

He shouldn't be so glad to hear her voice. "Emma."

"I called to apologize. I was completely out of line Saturday night."

"Well…yeah. But I could have been more rational about the whole thing. I'm sorry I yelled at you."

"Don't worry about that."

"As long as you'll forget it."

"Of course." An awkward silence fell between them. Then Emma cleared her throat. "I…um…wondered if you could give me some advice."

"What's up?"

"Well…staying in a hotel is getting rather expensive. I've found some apartments in the newspaper, but I have no idea what part of Denver they're in. Could you…um…run over the list with me, so I'll have an idea of where to rent?"

That would be the simplest way out. Of course, a real friend would volunteer to drive her around and look at the apartments with her. But Jimmy knew what a day of Emma's company would do to him. She was so easy to like. So easy to want. He spent most of his time these days trying not to think about how much he wanted her.

Because acting on that desire would constitute a major mistake. She would be going back to England in October. Vulnerable, and at a significant crossroads in her life, she needed someone stable, someone permanent in her life. A short mind-blowing affair like the one they'd shared as teenagers wouldn't work this time around. Jimmy knew *he* couldn't take the risk. Hurting Emma was something he absolutely refused to do.

"Jimmy?" Her voice sounded nervous, unsure. Timid.

The rational, reasoned arguments fell apart. "Why don't I pick you up in half an hour or so? We can get some breakfast—I know a place that makes great omelettes— then I'll drive you around to look at these apartments. Sound okay?"

In her breathless hesitation, he could almost hear her going through the same arguments he'd just dismissed.

"That sounds great," she said strongly. "I'll be ready when you arrive."

FIFTEEN MINUTES LATER, Emma was still dithering over what to wear. "It's only breakfast, for God's sake," she muttered. "Not a presentation to the queen!" Finally deciding on a sleeveless green shirt and black jeans, she clipped her hair up high and put on a single coat of mascara. *Not too much,* she thought, evaluating the effect in the mirror. *It doesn't look as if I expect…anything. Just a couple of old friends having breakfast. That's all.*

But her palms were damp and her fingers trembling as she opened the door to Jimmy's knock. Coming face-to-face with the man himself did nothing to ease her nerves. In the clear morning light, she could see the gold flecks in his black eyes, the smoothness of the skin over his jaw. Her fingers curled with the urge to touch. In the pit of her stomach grew a sharp feeling of fear.

Or maybe just an unbearable excitement.

Emma drew breath against that feeling and stepped back. "So, where is this great omelette you mentioned?"

Jimmy's firm mouth tightened for a moment, and then relaxed. "Five minutes. Can you wait that long?"

She turned to get her purse, thinking of how long she'd waited already—twenty years. "Just barely."

"THAT'S THE REAL REASON we're here, isn't it?" Inhaling the aroma of dark, rich coffee, Emma sat down in the chair Jimmy had pulled out for her.

"Guilty as charged." He watched with a satisfied grin as the server filled a big white mug to the brim. "I need the high-octane stuff to get my brain in gear."

"Still addicted, hmm? I remember the smell of coffee in the mornings when we camped up on the mountain."

He nodded. "You always wanted to sleep in."

"And you were always up with the sun."

His grin faded. "Now I'm lucky if I get to bed before the sun comes up."

"It's not quite the life I pictured for you," she said after a moment. "I thought you might be running a ranch or a construction company. Something with a lot of work outdoors."

He stared into his cup. "I spent most of my time in the army outdoors. I decided then that I like central air-conditioning and heat."

"How long did you stay in?"

"Too long."

She wouldn't let him off that easily. "Jimmy?"

"Ten years. At that point I realized I would have to commit to becoming officer material or bail."

"You didn't want to stay in?"

Sipping coffee, he shook his head. "I couldn't see myself giving orders that could cost people their lives. Anyway, Zach was getting out and coming home—his dad was sick. I decided Denver looked as good as anyplace I'd seen to settle down in, so I came along."

The server set down their omelettes, and Emma occupied herself with the food for a few minutes. "You came to Denver and joined the police force?"

"More or less. There was a waiting list for the academy, so, like I told you, I bussed tables and played the drums for a blues band until I could get in."

"Did you like being on the force?"

He sidestepped her question. "I thought I could be useful. God knows the city needs all the good guys it can get."

She thought of Harlow. "I'm sure losing you hurt the department."

Jimmy shook his head. "Not that much. There were dozens of people waiting to take my place. Maybe they're having better luck putting the bad people away than I did."

Hands flat and spread wide, he stared at her across the table. "Anything else? My life's an open book." There was a hint of temper in his eyes. He didn't like her questions.

Emma refused to feel intrusive or intimidated. "I've got dozens of questions, as a matter of fact. But my omelette is getting cold."

They finished their meal in silence, then stepped out into the bright Monday-morning sunshine. Emma pretended to examine the windows of the shops they passed on the way to the Jag's parking place. In truth, she watched Jimmy's reflection in the glass. He was dressed more casually than she'd yet seen him, in snug jeans and a loose black T-shirt that somehow emphasized his physique rather than hiding it. Her heart beat faster just looking at him. And that was not a good sign.

"So let me see this list of yours," he said as they settled into the car. He pulled a pen out of the ashtray and scratched through one of the notices she'd gathered. "Nope." And another, and another. "Nope and nope and nope. You don't want to live in any of those places."

"And just where do I want to live?"

He gave her that wonderful grin. "Stick with me, babe. I'll show you the best this town has to offer."

Smiling with contentment, Emma relaxed against the seat. "Whatever you say, boss. Whatever you say."

EIGHT HOURS LATER they staggered into Emma's new apartment under the weight of a multitude of shopping bags. Jimmy didn't remember when he'd last spent quality time in a food store—his usual groceries were frozen dinners and beer. Emma bought fresh vegetables and meat, milk and cheese, and a few canned goods. She sat on the kitchen counter eating an apple while directing Jimmy's storage efforts.

"Big cans on the left side, smaller ones on the right."

"Yes, ma'am."

"Keep one kind of food together—black beans with black beans, tomatoes with tomatoes."

He sighed, rearranging containers. "That makes a difference? You can't read the labels?"

"Efficient storage means better cuisine, according to one of my cooking-school teachers. And it's easier to tell what you haven't got."

"Why cooking school?" If she could ask questions, so could he. Her interrogation from this morning still rankled. Or maybe it was the fact that he'd never done anything worthwhile in his life to report.

"After spending most days with papers and books, it was fun to mess about with food in the evenings."

"In between your dates, you mean?" He asked the question lightly and was surprised by his dread of the answer.

"Um…not all that many dates." When Jimmy turned from the cabinet, Emma wore that giveaway pink blush.

"There must've been a thousand guys ready to step out with a beautiful, intelligent woman professor."

Emma shrugged. "A big, freckled, managing female professor with a tendency to trip over her own feet wasn't quite so sought after."

"Managing?" Her voice and her accent were a pleasure to hear, but some of her English expressions required an interpreter.

"As you've…um…pointed out recently, I tend to take control of a situation, telling everyone else how to conduct their business better. Men, you included, don't like that."

Jimmy waved that issue away. "Big?" He'd never thought of her that way.

She jumped down off the counter and moved past him to throw her apple core away. He couldn't see her face, but he could see the deep rose flush at the nape of her neck. "Five foot ten and quite a few pounds over the definition of delicate.'' Her even voice couldn't disguise a quaver of hurt.

Stepping up behind her, Jimmy turned Emma to face him. Under his palms, her skin was warm and smooth, but her shoulders were stiff. "You look exactly like what you are—a generous, gracious, warmhearted woman. Any man who can't see that and recognize the benefits isn't worth your time."

She avoided his eyes. "That's a kind way of putting it."

"Emma…" He pulled her closer and stroked her back, running his palm along the curve of muscles from shoulder to waist. "I'm just being honest. You're an amazing, breathtaking female. Even more now than when you were eighteen."

Emma stirred, and he tensed against the surge of need that shot through him. Blood pounded in his ears like the roar of a waterfall. With everything he had inside, he wanted to tighten his hold, take the pleasure he knew he would find in Emma's arms.

Jimmy fought the impulse. This was not going to happen. She didn't need him hitting on her, now or ever.

But when she drew back far enough to look into his face, he used his thumb to trace her cheekbone and then ran the pad lightly over her damp, rosy lips. Her quick gasp undid him. With the next breath, Jimmy put his mouth where his thumb had been. Any sanity he might have held on to disappeared when Emma moved her lips against his and kissed him back.

She combed her fingers through his hair, ran her palms along his arms from shoulder to wrist. Their kisses were short as she broke for air again and again, each time coming back a little wilder, a little more desperate. He shifted, or she did, and his knee slipped between hers. She pulled his shirt from his jeans, sighing as her palms ran over the skin of his back.

Dragging kisses over Emma's cheek, along her jaw, down her throat, Jimmy was past caution now, or even thought. He knew only need and desire, and the way her every move, every sigh, every touch filled him. Her shirt was crisp under his chin, his cheek, across her soft breasts as he pressed his mouth against her. Emma moaned when he bit gently through the fabric. She jolted in his arms and he embraced the reaction. No other woman had ever felt so right. Only Emma.

In the end, though, the damn pain brought him down, as it always did. A flare of heat, then an actual aching in the bend of his hip told him he'd been standing in one position too long. Even as he tried to ignore the pain, his mind cooled, cleared. He didn't force himself to think. But he closed his hands on Emma's shoulders and took his mouth away from her sweet skin.

There was a sob in her breath as she pressed her forehead against his shoulder. "Emma. Emma, shh. It's okay." He changed his stance slightly and bit back a groan. So much for changing position. "Emma, I'm gonna have to let you go."

Her hands dropped to her sides as he backed clumsily away. She didn't look up as he leaned against the counter, taking most of the weight off his bad leg. The pain eased a little, only to be replaced by the frustration tearing at every other part of him.

After a few seconds, Emma put her fingers over her eyes and drew a shaking breath. She took her own stumbling step backward. Jimmy put out a hand to steady her, but she waved him off.

"I'm all right. Really." Her voice was rough, breathless. "I…I'll be back in a moment."

Shutting herself in the bathroom, Emma pressed a wet washcloth against her eyes, her temples, her wrists. When she raised her face to the mirror, she could see a faint redness on her neck where Jimmy's teeth had grazed her skin. Her knees trembled and she dropped to sit on the side of the tub, holding the cool cloth against her face.

Dear God, what had she done?

Nothing much, the rational part of her brain insisted. A spot of reminiscent lovemaking with the first lover she'd ever known. No harm done. Actually quite pleasant.

But her heart knew better. Her heart knew what kissing Jimmy Falcon revealed about the state of her emotions. Any hope she'd retained of coming out of this encounter intact had just vanished.

She heard the front door open and close as she sat there, and knew that Jimmy had left. That was okay. She didn't need him to stay and try to apologize or explain. What had happened between them was as clear as a mountain spring, as irresistible as the glaciers that had carved valleys into the mountains. At eighteen, she'd taken that power for granted, used it and then let it go.

At thirty-eight, she doubted she had the grace or the strength to act so unselfishly again.

AT WORK WEDNESDAY, Emma noticed the stiff way Tiffany held herself, the wince she gave if she had to bend over. When Jimmy went to the bank for change, Emma went out to the bar.

"What did you do this time?"

The bartender wrinkled her forehead. "What do you mean?"

"What did you do that made Brad so angry he had to hit you?"

"Nothing. I mean, he didn't."

"Are you lying to yourself, as well as me?"

"Drop it, Emma. Please." Her brown eyes were too bright, her face too pale. "Everything will be okay."

"You deserve better, Tiffany."

She didn't respond.

"Why do you stay with him? You're making the money. You're attractive and likable—you get asked out every night by the customers. You don't need to stay with a man who hurts you."

Tiffany propped her forearms on the edge of the bar and let her head hang down between her elbows. "I don't know."

Emma put a hand on one of Tiffany's. "You're welcome to move into my flat. There's plenty of room. You could get away."

The bartender shook her head. "If I disappeared out of Brad's life, this is the first place he'd look."

"That's what restraining orders are for."

"He wouldn't have to hurt me. He could hurt Jimmy or Darren. Or you. He'd go after my sisters in a heartbeat. How would that make anything better?"

"So is it your plan to stay with him until he kills you, and then the law will put him away and we'll all be safe? I'm sorry, but that doesn't sound very intelligent."

Cringing, the bartender straightened up. "An intelligent woman wouldn't have gotten involved with Brad in the first place. I pick losers. Every time."

"You can change the pattern. Choose to win."

Tiffany stared at Emma, her face weary beyond her age. "Sure. I'll work on it."

Emma couldn't push any further. Her friend already seemed to have her back to the wall.

Working through the evening, she tried to concentrate on food preparation, but her mind worried at the problems of those she cared about.

Jimmy, a strong man who had cut himself off from every aspect of his heritage and every possibility of change, of progress. How could he live in a limbo where there was no past and no future?

Tiffany, mired in a dangerous relationship, unable to reach the help she needed. Emma still hadn't spoken with Jimmy about that situation out of deference to Tiffany's wishes and a helpless hope that the bartender would tell him herself. Would the worst happen before anyone took steps to prevent it?

And Harlow, a boy on the street with his friends, but without reliable food or shelter or caring. She hadn't seen Harlow for almost a week. She wondered if something had happened to him or to Ryan. Cutting up onions, Emma mopped her tears with a dishcloth, knowing that only some of them were caused by the vegetables.

As if summoned by her thoughts, Harlow knocked on the screen door a short time after the band started its first set.

Emma nodded him in and got more than she'd bargained for. Ryan followed Harlow, and then Tomas—the burly, dark-skinned boy who'd held the gun on Jimmy that first night.

"Emma, you met Tomas before, right? We call him Tommy."

She smiled at Tomas and got a suggestive wink in return. "Why don't you sit down? Can I get you something to drink? To eat?"

Harlow gave his beautiful smile and pulled out a chair. "To tell the truth, I was hoping you'd ask. It's been kinda rough this week. We're all pretty hungry."

"You've come to the right place." She got the latest orders ready, then made sandwiches for the boys. Darren swung in with a tray full of dirty dishes just as Harlow had taken his first bite.

"Well, well." He raised an eyebrow. "Did we run out of seating in the front?" At the sink, he leaned close to Emma and lowered his voice. "Jimmy doesn't like these guys hanging around, you know."

"They're hungry! Jimmy would not expect me to let them starve."

The waiter shook his head. "I'm just telling you that if Jimmy walks in and sees you feeding strays, he won't be happy about it."

This attitude was another change she didn't understand. "I'm not hiding anything from Jimmy. And I'm not afraid of him."

"You're a better man than I am, then." Darren loaded his tray and went out again.

"He's right, Emma." Harlow finished his glass of milk. "I think we'd better stop coming by. I don't want to get you into trouble."

Ryan looked up in protest, but didn't say a word. Tomas made a rude sound and got a warning look from Harlow.

Emma shook her head. "If I get into trouble for helping you three out, then there's already a problem here which needs to be addressed. More sandwiches? Chips?"

The boys each ate three sandwiches, finished off a bag of chips and dealt quickly with bowls of ice cream. Harlow pushed back from the table. "I can't tell you how good it is to be full. We're gonna sleep sound tonight."

"*Where* are you going to sleep?"

Tomas shrugged. "We'll find a pad somewhere. We got friends."

"Do those friends have clean sheets? A shower?"

Ryan laughed, then was quiet.

Emma got her purse out of the broom closet. "At least go to a shelter." She extended her hand with the cash. "That way you'll get breakfast, too."

Harlow backed away. "No, ma'am. Put your money away. You fed us and that's enough."

"Jeez, Harl…" Tomas began.

He was stopped with a glance from those dark blue eyes. Then Harlow looked back at Emma. "I'm serious. We're not taking your money. And we're getting out of here right now." He pulled on the back of Ryan's shirt and the slight boy came to his feet.

Emma put the money in her pocket. "I can't argue with your pride. But if you ever do need help…"

"We know where to look. Thanks, Emma. You have a good night." Pushing Tomas and Ryan out the door ahead of him, Harlow gave her one last smile and vanished into the dark.

Later Darren staggered in under more used dishes. He looked around the room. "They're gone? That's good. How'd you get involved with those scavengers, Emma?"

"They are not scavengers. They're boys who need help."

"They're boys who need drugs."

Her cheeks heated. "I know."

"And they are playing you for all they're worth."

"Perhaps." She scraped the leavings on yet another plate into the rubbish. "But if I convince them to trust me, to believe that I care, then I can use some of that influence to get them help."

"That's your plan? Lure them in with food and money, then get them into rehab?"

"Something like that. Yes."

He whistled long and low. "Good luck. They look like heroin addicts to me, and that's a bitch of a habit to kick."

"It's not too late, though."

"Too late for what?" Stepping into the kitchen, Jimmy glanced from Darren to Emma. The conversation he'd interrupted looked intense.

Emma's cheeks flushed. "Getting the kitchen cleaned up for tomorrow. Darren's trying to convince me to leave the dishes undone."

"I've got an exam tomorrow I'd like to study for." The server picked up his empty tray and brushed by Jimmy.

''Would a few hours matter one way or the other?'' Before anyone could answer, the door swung closed behind him.

''Cleanup *was* easier with paper plates,'' Jimmy commented, handing Emma a plate for the dishwasher. Something felt…off.

''You can charge more for food on real dishware.'' Emma gave her usual answer, but her mind seemed to be somewhere else.

Watching her closely, he picked up another plate. ''You pay more, too.''

''You're impossible.'' She smiled at him as she said it, the smile that always went straight to his gut. Jimmy decided he was being paranoid—something to do with the headache he'd been fighting for two days now.

Darren staggered in under another full tray. ''This is the last of the dishes. Tiffany's stacking chairs on tables. What else?''

''That's it,'' Jimmy said.

''That's all,'' Emma said at the same time. Then she glanced at him. ''I'm sorry. You're the boss.''

Jimmy was beginning to doubt that. ''No problem. See you tomorrow night, Darren.''

''Right.''

Tiffany went home shortly after Darren, leaving Jimmy alone in the club with Emma. The quiet carried weight— and expectation. He'd scarcely had a waking thought in the past week that didn't recall those minutes in Emma's kitchen. His dreams were just as bad. She hadn't brought the subject up and neither had he, because he didn't know what to say. Should he apologize? He was anything but sorry. Having Emma's mouth against his was like stepping into spring sunshine after a long cold winter. Until that moment, he hadn't realized how much he needed the warmth.

Tonight…tonight he could coax her back to the office,

to the softness of his recliner and make love to her the way he'd been thinking about for the past week. Or he could take her home and ask to come in. She might say no. But her response in his arms last Monday night suggested she might say yes.

Then what?

Where could he and Emma go? Or, to be more accurate, where could Emma go with a second-rate club owner who had no great prospects and no interest in creating any? Her career might have taken a detour, but Jimmy knew she'd go back to work. Maybe it would take her a few years to recover her reputation. But Emma had energy and drive. He didn't doubt that she would get to the top again.

While he was going nowhere. Never had, never would. He wasn't complaining—he liked his life. But it wasn't enough for a woman like Emma.

The best answer to all of the questions in his head was simple. Forget the recliner. Forget taking her home and staying the night. Walk her to the cab, say goodbye. Go home, take a few aspirin. Get a good night's sleep, the first in more than a week.

"Well, that's that." Emma dried her hands and folded the towel, then took off her apron. "I do believe it's time for bed."

He just looked at her, grinning. Her face went scarlet. "I didn't mean... I wasn't thinking..."

Jimmy had to laugh. "I didn't take it as an invitation." He rubbed his temple with his knuckles. "I'd have to beg off, anyway. 'Not tonight, dear. I have a headache.'"

Concern replaced the embarrassment in Emma's face. "Why didn't you say something? You didn't have to stay so late washing up. I could have handled it. Do you need some medicine?" She went to the broom closet and pulled out her leather purse. "I've got pain pills in here some-where."

Through the pounding behind his eyes, he managed a grin. "That's okay, Emma. Aspirin is about as much as I need. Come on. The cab should be here by now."

Outside, the warm night air pressed even harder against his head. Jimmy took a deep breath and winced.

"Are you well enough to drive?" Emma put a cool hand on his cheek. "Why don't I take you home?"

Her palm felt like heaven against his skin. He was sorely tempted. "I'll be better off knowing that you got to your place with Landry, here." They'd found a driver who would take the job on a regular basis—Steve Landry, a good guy who kept pictures of his wife and four kids on the dash of his cab.

Jimmy opened the taxi door. "Get gone, gorgeous. I'll see you tomorrow afternoon sometime."

Emma slid onto the seat, still staring at him with worry in her eyes. Jimmy shut her inside, lifted a hand and watched her out of sight.

He wasn't sure exactly how he made it home, except that he and the car arrived in the parking garage together. Thankful for elevators, he rode up to his floor leaning back into the corner, eyes closed against the bright overhead light. A quick stumble to the right, a fumble with the key, and he was inside his dark apartment, breathing hard from pain and the effort to concentrate. He found the medicine cabinet by feel, swallowed three aspirin with a gulp of water and fell onto the bed. In a few minutes he'd feel like taking off his clothes. He just needed to rest first…

SOME NIGHTS MADE Harlow wish he'd never left home.

Eyes closed, he pressed his head hard against the wall behind him. The outside pain distracted him for a few seconds from the huge hurt inside.

On his left, Tommy stirred. "If you had taken the money, we wouldn't be sitting here with nothing—no food, no dope. How shithead stupid can you get?'' His thick voice slurred from word to word, taking the sting out of the insult.

But patience was not in Harlow's tool chest tonight. ''You're so smart, why don't you go back and finish the job, then? Beat her up a little—or a lot, hell, why not?—then walk out with her wallet. While you're at it, check the cash register. Maybe Falcon's got a safe in his office—take along a sledgehammer and you can clean that out, too. I don't see any problem with that game plan. Falcon'll only have every cop in the whole damn city looking for us.''

Ryan wandered back from the dark corners of the abandoned school building they'd holed up in. ''Man, I'm sick as shit.'' He dropped to the floor, curled up over his gut, shivering. ''I gotta have a hit, Harl. I can't do this.''

''You can do it, Ry. Just till the morning. I'll get Linda to pay me for cleaning off her parking lot before the breakfast crowd. She's cool—she'll give me twenty bucks, and that'll get us all a hit and some breakfast.''

Tommy doubled up, groaning. ''I'm not gonna make it to the morning.'' He staggered to his feet and stumbled into the dark, retching.

Harlow kept his eyes closed. Okay, he'd blown it. Emma had offered the money and he could have taken it, free and clear. But shit, he'd looked at her, her eyes so worried, so real…and he couldn't make himself finish the con. Taking advantage of Emma Garrett was getting harder every time he saw her.

What a time to develop a conscience.

His stomach drew itself into a tiny ball of incredible pain. He took a deep breath and waited out the cramp. They'd all gone without a fix before. They would survive a few miserable hours. Probably.

But he could remember when just breathing didn't hurt this much. When getting sick happened once a year, in the wintertime with the flu going around, not whenever the cash supply ran out. When being hungry meant waiting another fifteen minutes for a roast-beef dinner. When sleep didn't leave him open to some lunatic's attack.

No way to go home now. Did that mean no way out? Was there any other choice?

Did he really want to live like this anymore?

CHAPTER SEVEN

TIFFANY ANSWERED the phone Wednesday afternoon and hung up after a short conversation, with a worried frown wrinkling her forehead. "Jimmy's staying home tonight."

Emma's heart lurched against her breastbone. "What's wrong?"

"He said he's not feeling good and he didn't want to bring the flu in for everybody else."

"You don't look convinced."

The bartender shook her head. "It could be the flu. But it could be Jimmy trying to keep anybody from knowing he's having a malaria attack."

Emma wiped her shaking hands on her jeans. "He mentioned he has recurrences. Does he stay alone during these attacks?"

Tiffany smiled wryly. "I tried to play nurse once. He threatened to fire me if I stayed, and I believed him." She put her hand over Emma's on the bar. "He's an adult, Emma. He can take care of himself."

"Not if he's very sick." She slid off the bar stool. "Put a sign on the board by the door that the kitchen is temporarily closed. I'll let you know when I'm coming back in."

"But—"

"The drinks and the music, Tiffany. That's what matters, anyway." She scurried into the kitchen for her purse and found Harlow standing at the screen door.

"Oh...oh, hi." She pulled her purse out of the broom closet as he stepped inside.

"Not much cooking going on for a change." He smiled. "You didn't quit, did you?"

"No. I just closed the kitchen for the night. Did you want something to eat?" Guilt gnawed at her for hoping he would say no.

"Nah, I'm okay. Do you have time to talk a minute?"

Oh, God. "Of course. Sit down." Emma made herself take a chair and fold her hands together on the table. "What's going on?"

Harlow sat quietly for a moment, rubbing his fingertips across the grain of the wood. When he looked up, his eyes were completely serious. "It's about Ryan. He's sick."

"Do you mean physically ill?"

"Kinda." He took a deep breath. "You probably realized…he's totally hooked on some really bad stuff."

"Yes."

"It's killing him."

"What can I do?"

"That's just it—I'm not sure. But somebody's gotta do something before…" He shook his head.

Emma thought for a second. "There are treatment centers. If you take him to one of those…"

"Even if I could convince him, which I can't, he couldn't get in."

"Why not?"

"The city programs are all crowded, not taking anybody new. You need references to get into a private center or a doctor's referral to a hospital. *You* could arrange that kind of thing, though, couldn't you? You could get Ry into a rehab center and help him stay there, right?"

For the first time Emma felt daunted by the responsibility she'd assumed for these boys. "I don't know Ryan very well. Why would he trust me?"

"'Cause I'd tell him to."

''That won't make much difference when he's desperate, will it?''

Harlow sighed. ''Could you at least talk to him?''

''Now?''

''I can go get him—he's just a few blocks away.''

''No, don't do that.'' She sounded more desperate than she'd intended. ''I...I really have to leave—I have something else I must do.''

''Tomorrow afternoon?''

What shape would Jimmy be in tomorrow afternoon? ''I don't know if I'll be here.''

Harlow stood up, a closed look on his face. ''That's okay. I know it's asking too much.''

''No, Harlow.'' She stopped him with a hand on his arm as he turned away. ''It's not too much. Something else is going on, that's all. Look. I'll be here tomorrow at four. Can you come back then?''

He gave her a half smile. ''Sure. We'll be here right on the dot.'' His withdrawn trust was evident in his reserved tone. ''See you then.''

The screen door banged behind him as he left. Emma pressed her fingers against her temples. Would they come back? Or would Harlow allow his disappointment to keep Ryan away tomorrow?

Was Jimmy taking care of himself? That was the paramount question. She grabbed her purse and hurried out, determined to discover the answer for herself.

THE FIRST THING Jimmy knew was a cool palm on his forehead. He opened eyes that felt as if they'd been scrubbed with sand—and saw only darkness.

But he could hear, and it was Emma's whisper. ''Dear God, Jimmy.'' She went away, much to his disappointment. Maybe he was hallucinating. Sometimes the fever worked that way.

Then she came back, and her soft hands closed around his rigid one. "Your building manager let me in. I nursed my dad through a number of attacks," she said quietly. "Can you tell me if you've taken any medicine?"

He gave his head a shake that set off a rockslide inside his skull. Emma disappeared again—at least, she put down his hand. Jimmy floated for a while, thinking he should be mad that she'd come, that Tiffany had told her, and only able to feel a blessed sense of relief.

"Jimmy." Her fingers on his cheek opened his eyes. He focused a little better this time and saw the pale oval that must be Emma's face. "Jimmy, the next few minutes are going to be miserable. I want you out of those clothes and into bed. Can you help me a bit?"

His throat made a croak that might or might not have been "Sure."

"Let's get you sitting up."

The process was even worse than she'd predicted. Every muscle and bone ached, and moving was not a matter of will, but of luck. Sometimes his body cooperated, sometimes not. Emma seemed to understand. She hummed softly, unbuttoning his shirt, easing it off his shoulders with a gentleness that made him want to weep. Immediately she replaced it with something warm and soft and dry, before starting on his belt buckle.

Jimmy lifted a hand. "I can—"

"Don't bother. Just lie back." He gratefully followed orders. The slacks slid away, and cool air razed the skin on his belly, his hips, his thighs…

She would see the mess of scars on his hip.

He tried to pull down the fresh shirt, to hide the ugliness.

Still humming, Emma moved his hand out of the way without comment and covered the worst of the scars, then his legs and his feet with sweatpants and socks. It still hurt to move, but at least the sweat-damp clothes weren't fighting the fever with a chill that only made it worse.

"The last hurdle, love," Emma said. "It'll be easier to get comfortable if you stand up and let me pull back the covers." Kneeling on the bed, she helped him to sit up again. "Lean on me—I'm big enough to take it."

Jimmy put his hands on her shoulders, braced himself and somehow got to his feet. He swayed there for the seconds it took her to fold back the sheet and plump the pillows.

Her arm around his waist turned him to face the bed. "One more minute, Jimmy—take your medicine, and you can relax."

He swallowed the pill she gave him. And then somehow he was lying down again, still stiff and sore and aching, but with a cool pillow under his cheek and Emma's hand brushing back his hair. He felt like a child—cared for, wanted, loved. Squeezing his eyes shut against burning tears, he let go of the effort to think.

THE NEXT TIME Jimmy awoke, he recognized the absence of pain. He experimented by rolling onto his back, and sighed. "Aspirin is one of the world's greatest inventions."

Emma's soft, rich laugh came out of the room's shadows. "I'm glad you're feeling better." She sat down on the edge of the bed and touched his cheek. "Mmm. Still a fever, but not so high."

"What time is it?" He wanted to take hold of her hand and keep it—and he was feeling almost too sick to fight the urge.

"Just seven."

"Oh, good." Jimmy drew a deep breath. "I really appreciate you coming over, Emma. I might not have pulled it together to get the mefloquine started."

She smoothed the sheet over his chest. "You should have asked for help."

"But I'm doing okay now—I'll keep the aspirin up and the mefloquine and this will be over in a couple of days. You don't have to bother."

She looked at him skeptically. "You think I don't know what comes next?"

"Well—"

"First cold, then hot, then the sweats, right?"

He couldn't deny it.

"There isn't any reason I can't stay and help you out, Jimmy. Dry clothes, water, medicine—you can't possibly take care of yourself alone."

"I've managed."

"But this time you don't have to." As if they'd agreed, she stood up. "I noticed a food market just down the block. I'm going to get some ingredients for soup in case you feel like eating later."

"I usually don't."

"I wouldn't think so, if you have to face preparing it yourself." She gave him a sweet smile from the bedroom doorway and disappeared.

Jimmy tried to dredge up anger, irritation, even indignation at being treated like a little kid. But when the sweats started and Emma brought him towels and clean T-shirts, all he could feel was thankful. After the sweats eased up and she brought him a bowl of tomato soup, he realized he felt better for having something to eat.

And when he stumbled into the living room about midnight, wrung out from the day and dreading the inevitable repeat, he wondered how he was ever going to get through this again without Emma.

She set a glass of water for him on the nearby table, then sat at the other end of the sofa. "You look like death."

"That's approximately correct." He slumped down

against the cushions and closed his eyes. "Just another souvenir of army life."

"Does this happen often?"

"Last time was about four years ago. I'm a little surprised, actually. I thought maybe I'd finally worn it out."

"I hope you won't be angry—I talked with the doctor who prescribed the mefloquine. He seemed to think you would be fine as long as you got the doses you need."

Maybe he should have been mad—calling his doctor was above and beyond the call of duty, even for Emma. But he could only be glad she cared so much. "Sure. That's the way it always works."

"He also said there is a new drug that could prevent any more relapses. And he said he'd mentioned it to you in the past."

Jimmy shrugged. "Yeah, I just never got around to getting some. Like I said, I thought the last time was the end. I'll take care of it. And I'm doing great now, which is why you should go home."

Emma gazed at him for a minute. "Tomorrow," she said finally.

Jimmy tried to ignore the relief that hit him. But he really did think she should leave. "Emma…"

At the determination on her face, he gave up. She brought him the television remote and they found a soccer game to watch. Jimmy asked for more soup. When she brought the bowl back, she sat closer, close enough that when her head drooped, his shoulder was a convenient resting place. He let it happen, savoring the scent of her hair so close, the press of her knee into his thigh. The soccer game ended; he clicked off the TV and pressed a kiss to Emma's head. God knew, he could get used to this kind of ending to his days.

God also knew that was absolutely the wrong thing to do to the woman by his side.

THURSDAY MORNING, Emma decided to take a shower and change clothes while Jimmy slept on the sofa. She found a pair of his jeans that fit quite well, and a chambray shirt that felt as soft as flannel. She was making up his bed with clean sheets when she heard his step behind her.

"You look a hell of a lot better in my clothes than I do."

"I could use another couple of inches in the seat," she said, bending to get a pillow. "My hips are too wide."

When she turned, he was grinning. "Not from this perspective."

His face was less ravaged this morning, his eyes clearer, at least temporarily. "Would you like something to eat? Eggs and toast?"

"I'm not hungry, thanks. But I could use a cup of coffee."

"I'll make you some tea."

"I don't want tea."

"You don't need coffee."

"Tell that to my brain."

Emma walked close enough to knock lightly on his skull with her knuckles. "You don't need coffee." She couldn't resist slipping her fingertips lightly over his cheek. His skin was smooth, a little warm, and her heart started to stutter. "I'll make the tea sweet."

Jimmy took a deep breath. "Yeah. Okay."

He slept for most of the day, waking for an hour at noon to eat some soup and try to convince her to leave again. Emma held firm and, with a weary sigh, Jimmy gave in. He went back to bed without protest, and Emma curled up on the sofa.

She must have dozed, because the ringing of the telephone startled her awake.

"Emma? It's Tiffany. How's Jimmy?"

"Getting better. He'll be well in a few days."

"Glad to hear that. Listen. Harlow and Ryan are here."

"Oh my God. Is it four o'clock?"

"Just past."

"Is Ryan very sick?"

"He looks pretty good, actually. Probably just got a fix."
Damn, damn. "Can I talk to Harlow?"

"Sure."

The phone was handed over. She heard Harlow clear his throat. "Hello?"

"Harlow, I am sorry. Tiffany may have told you—Jimmy is sick. I came to his place to help out, and…and I fell asleep. I intended to be there. But with the traffic at this time of day, I probably couldn't get back for another hour at least."

"'Sokay. Ryan's not doing so bad this afternoon. Tommy lucked into some freelance work yesterday and came back with enough cash for dinner and…and a room. Don't worry about us."

"But I do! Tomorrow—could you come back with Ryan tomorrow?"

"I don't know…tomorrow might not be too good. But we'll stop by one day soon and catch you here. Then we'll talk, okay?"

"Harlow, please don't shut me out."

"Gotta go. Take care of Mr. Falcon." He hung up without putting Tiffany back on the line.

Emma dropped the phone back in its cradle. She'd let Harlow down, badly. The boys' problems were their own responsibility, of course. But she couldn't help feeling that her lapse had cost them all a precious chance.

"Emma?" When she turned, Jimmy stood in the bedroom doorway. "Everything okay?"

"Of course. How do you feel?"

"Not too bad. Well enough for more soup, if you've got some."

"Coming right up." She hurried into the kitchen, hoping to pull herself together while the soup heated.

But Jimmy followed her. "Did I hear the phone ring?"

"Tiffany called to ask about you. I told her you were malingering, as usual." Not exactly a lie. Just not the complete truth. When he'd recovered, Emma promised herself, they would get the whole situation with the boys straightened out.

"Did Tiffany know what that meant? I'm not sure I do."

"Loafing. Slacking off. Not doing the job."

"Ah. I imagine she wasn't surprised."

She smiled at him. "Not at all. Here's your soup."

AFTER A QUIET NIGHT, the chills rolled through him again about noon on Friday, making him shudder. Emma, who'd slept on the couch, got Jimmy to bed and then stood by helplessly as he shook, eyes closed, body stiff. There was nothing aspirin could do for this phase. Jimmy simply had to endure.

But she couldn't shut the door and sit down to read a book as if he wasn't suffering in the next room. Finally she gave in to her instincts and went to the far side of the bed. Jimmy lay on his side facing away from her, and she scooted over next to him, putting her arm over his waist, pressing her other hand against his quivering back. Now his tremors ran through her body, as well. He made a sound, as if to protest.

"Don't be upset," she said, hoping he could hear. "I don't mind. If this helps, I'm glad to stay. Just tell me if I make it worse."

He didn't say anything else. But somehow he got his hand over hers as it rested on his waist. His grip made going anywhere impossible. Smiling, Emma closed her eyes and held on.

A couple of hours later the chills subsided and his fever

started to climb. Aspirin kept things under control enough that he could sleep this time. As he relaxed, Emma got up and moved into a low chair in the corner of the bedroom and let her head rest against the cushion.

By tomorrow he would be much better, she knew, probably well enough to complain that she shouldn't have come over and certainly shouldn't have stayed.

But how could she have kept away? Why should he have to go through this ordeal without help? She didn't expect any recompense, other than the knowledge that she'd made Jimmy's life a little easier. He seemed so determined to go his way all alone. It couldn't hurt for him to depend on someone else just once.

Sitting in the darkened bedroom, Emma was honest enough to admit that ''just once'' was not what she wanted. She would be happy to give Jimmy everything she could for the rest of her life.

She allowed herself a moment to indulge that dream and then sighed. *If wishes were horses, beggars would ride.*

JIMMY WOKE UP when the fever broke Friday night and he started sweating. He knew he must look as grubby as he felt, so he decided to take a shower. Maybe the water would stay warm long enough to outlast this part of the process.

When he came out of the bathroom, Emma had changed the bed linens again. He had a very strong memory of her lying behind him this afternoon, her arm around his waist, anchoring him against the shakes. Even sick, he could feel her breasts against his back, the curve of her thighs into his. Of all the times to have Emma Garrett in his bed, he'd been too weak and exhausted to do anything meaningful about it.

In the main room, she had curled up in an armchair with an Elmore Leonard mystery. She looked up with a smile. ''Better?''

"Getting better all the time." He sat on the sofa and propped his elbows on his knees. "Well enough that you don't have to stay the night again, Emma. Tomorrow will be easy, compared to the last couple of days. By Sunday I'll be good as new."

"I'm glad." She nodded. "In other words, it's time for me to go home?"

As if he wanted her to leave. "I wouldn't put it that way. I really appreciate what you've done—this would have been a lot more miserable without you. But—"

"But you're on your feet again." She stood up and closed the book. "You don't need me any more."

"No, dammit, that's not what I mean." Jimmy crossed the room and took hold of her shoulders. "I'm trying to keep you from feeling obligated to stay, Emma. Having you here is the best thing that's happened to me in years." A dangerous confession, and completely true. "I just don't think it's the best thing for you."

"Why not?" Her hands came to rest on his chest. His heart thudded with a force that had nothing to do with fever.

"This is a dead-end street, Emma. Nowhere to go."

She pushed his hair back from his forehead. "I've done my share of traveling. I'd like to stay put for a while."

Against his will, his hands shaped her shoulder blades, the curve of her waist, drew her close enough to kiss. "You deserve more."

"I'll take what I'm offered."

Jimmy started to register a protest, but Emma stopped him with her mouth on his. Her lips were cool, his response anything but. He could have devoured her right there on the living-room floor.

Emma drew away instead. "As your nurse, I'm prescribing no strenuous exercise for another seventy-two hours. You need time to recover."

"I feel great." As long as Emma stayed around.

"You'll feel better after a good night's sleep. Go to bed."

"Come with me." He held out his hand.

She gazed at him for a minute, both doubt and longing in her eyes. Finally, she sighed, then joined her fingers with his.

"I suppose we can get a good night's sleep together." She resisted his pull. "But that's all. Just sleep."

"Sure. Whatever you say." He flicked off the light in the main room and brought her to stand between his knees as he sat on the bed. "Would you like a bundling board?"

Emma ran her fingers through his hair, and his breathing sped up again. "Do you have a bundling board?"

"I could improvise."

"I think I can protect your virtue without one." She bent to press a kiss against his forehead. "Go to sleep, Jimmy." After hesitating, she briefly kissed his mouth. "Get well soon."

The lamp on the table went out. Emma moved in the darkness to the other side of the bed. A zipper rasped, and Jimmy swallowed hard. Imagining Emma's bare legs so close was not a recipe for sleep.

When she climbed between the sheets, he turned to face her. She lay on her side, her back squarely to him. "G'night, Jimmy."

Chuckling, he rolled over again and punched the pillow into shape. "Good night, Emma. I'll get you for this."

She yawned. "I'm counting on that."

JIMMY FELT well enough on Saturday that Emma knew she must go back to her own apartment. She wasn't certain she could listen to him take another shower without joining him. She hadn't slept much Friday night. The desire…the need…to touch him nearly overpowered her a dozen times.

He seemed to want what she did, which made resistance all the harder.

That could be the result of being sick, of depending on her and appreciating her as his nurse. Jimmy still reeling from a bout of malaria was not the same man as Jimmy Falcon, in control of himself and sure of what he wanted from his world. After embarrassing herself, her department chair, her tutors, her university and her dad, Emma couldn't bear to put another foot wrong. Especially with Jimmy.

First, though, she made his breakfast and stayed to be sure he ate it. While she cleaned up the kitchen, he leaned against the door frame, finishing his coffee. Hands covered with bubbles, Emma had just picked up a juice glass when he cleared his throat.

"You still have the medallion, right?"

She turned to stare at him, and the glass slipped into the soapy water with a clank. "O-of course. I'm sorry I haven't brought it back, but I was thinking of going down to Santa Fe and showing it to some dealers there." Her cheeks heated as she felt around in the sink for the missing glass.

Jimmy hadn't moved. "Lots of Indian-art dealers in Santa Fe."

"Yes, and did you know that the earliest residents called that area 'The Dancing Ground of the Sun'?"

"No." He drew an audible breath. "No, I didn't."

Emma rinsed the glass and turned to face him. His eyes were tired, but the resistance she'd met in the past over this subject wasn't anywhere to be seen. "No one in Denver had an idea about what the medallion might mean, but a couple of people suggested Santa Fe, and when I started researching the city, I found a number of connections to the sun. It's an old city, a trading center for centuries. Surely there's a relationship between the sun on the medallion and the original inhabitants of Santa Fe."

"Could be." He set his mug where she could reach it to wash. "So you're flying down there?"

"I thought so. On a Monday, so I wouldn't be taking off more time from work."

"Yeah. That sounds good." She'd finished the kitchen cleanup completely before he spoke again. When she moved to leave the room, he stood in her way, considering her with a serious stare.

"Jimmy?"

"How about next Monday?"

"What are you asking?" Could he really have changed his mind so quickly?

"I can fly with you to Santa Fe on Monday, check out those names you got."

"Oh." Shock held her speechless for a moment. "That sounds…wonderful. I'd love to have you with me."

His appreciative grin made her heart beat faster. "Good. I haven't been there in years, but it's a great town. We'll have a good day."

As THEY DROVE into town from the Santa Fe airport, Jimmy smiled at Emma's pleasure in the mountains, the sunrise, the desert views. "For a person who was born and grew up in England, you sure do enjoy the heat and sun of the Southwest."

She relaxed into her seat, with the medallion box cradled in her lap. "England is lovely. Green and filled with flowers. But there is such energy here, in the sharp mountain peaks and the clear, bright air. I've always loved that sense of things evolving."

They drove without talking, and Jimmy found himself looking at the landscape through Emma's eyes. He'd never thought about the "energy" of the land, but now he could see what she meant. That had always been one of the pleasures of her company—she opened doors to new perspectives on just about everything she encountered.

Still, he'd never expected to go with her to check out the medallion's history. He couldn't believe he'd even suggested making the trip together. But standing in his kitchen that morning, he'd faced the knowledge that she was going back to her own place—a logical move, sure, and one he'd thought he wanted only the night before, but he'd felt as if something important was slipping away. The only plan he could think of to keep the connection strong was to use the medallion. To go with Emma to Santa Fe.

The air was crisp and the scent of piñon smoke rode a brisk breeze. They walked through the old town, with its stucco buildings, its winding streets, and ate lunch in The Pink House, Santa Fe's landmark restaurant. Galleries seemed to be tucked into every spare inch of space; there was always one around the next corner.

But none of the names on Emma's list could help with the medallion. Late in the afternoon, her shoulders had started to droop with more than just fatigue. She smiled and laughed, but Jimmy knew she was disappointed.

As they walked back to the rental car, they passed a small shop with blankets and baskets and pottery in the windows. The shopkeeper, an older Indian woman in a black shirt and jeans and boots, stepped outside to bring in the Welcome sign from the sidewalk. Jimmy gave the woman a smile and a glance…then stopped in his tracks.

"Did you see that?" He turned back to the shop door just as the shade went down.

"See what?" Emma stood behind him as he rapped on the glass.

"What she was wearing—a necklace with a big pendant. Inlaid with turquoise."

"Like ours?"

"I couldn't see the design, but…"

The woman lifted the shade and pointed to the Closed sign. "Tomorrow," she mouthed, starting to turn away.

"No, please, wait." Jimmy knocked again. The shopkeeper looked back, irritated. Then Emma held the medallion over his shoulder, so the woman could see.

She unlocked the door and peeked out. "What do you want? I have supper to fix for my son."

"I noticed your necklace," Jimmy said as gently as he could. "And we have a medallion we're trying to get information on. Can you help us?"

"Let me see." She held out a thin brown hand imperiously, and Emma handed over the medallion. When the woman turned back into the dark shop, Jimmy and Emma followed.

As the lights came up, he could see that the contents of the shop window had deceived him. The little store carried more than blankets and baskets and pottery. Filled with the glow of copper and silver and bronze, the soft shine of semiprecious stones on shelves staggered at different heights along the walls, this wood-paneled room felt like the inside of a treasure chest.

"I'm Irma White Buffalo," the shopkeeper said. She unfolded a square of velvet over the glass counter and set the medallion down. "Where did you get this?"

Emma touched a corner of the cloth. "My father got it as a gift from a friend."

Irma looked up sharply. "Here? In Santa Fe?"

"No. His friend lived on the Sioux reservation in South Dakota."

"Ah." The shopkeeper nodded. "That makes more sense."

Standing just behind Emma, Jimmy leaned an elbow on the counter. "You've seen pieces like this before?"

"A few. Mine is a small version." She held up the disk on her necklace. "Not so fancy or so expensive."

"What is it?" He could feel Emma's tension as a fine quiver through all her muscles. As for him, his throat felt locked, and he was having trouble getting a deep breath.

"It is a sacred piece," Irma said. "One of only a few." She looked at Emma, her dark eyes sharp and stern. "And it should never have been given to anyone but a full-blooded Sioux!"

CHAPTER EIGHT

THE LATE-NIGHT DRIVE to the Santa Fe airport, the wait to board the plane...Jimmy barely said a word, and Emma didn't push. The information Irma White Buffalo gave them hadn't been mentioned since they left the shop. Discovering the history of the medallion—or at least who made it and why—had placed a burden on Jimmy that he'd avoided all his adult life.

Emma waited until they were actually in the air before trying to start a conversation. The cabin was dim, the passengers quiet.

She turned sideways in her seat, the better to see him. "I'm fascinated by the idea that one tribe—the Navajo, in this case—would execute commissioned work for another tribe, like the Sioux, located so far away."

Jimmy had his head back, his eyes closed, his hand wrapped loosely around a glass of whiskey and soda. "Well, this *is* twentieth-century stuff. We're not talking about prehistory or anything. The telephone existed, and airplanes and trains crossed the country from all directions. Trade between tribes would be pretty reasonable." In the low lights of the plane, his profile seemed austere. Almost bleak.

"And I suppose the roots of cultural independence go back at least to 1890 and Wounded Knee."

His mouth quirked into a quick smile, as quickly gone. "Wounded Knee usually gets the credit, anyway."

"So—" Emma took a fortifying sip of wine "—what will you do now?"

He opened his eyes, took a long swallow of his own drink. Then he shrugged. "What's to do? You—we—got the information your dad wanted. Around 1927, Navajo smiths made ten medallions out of silver and gold and turquoise for a group of Sioux elders to wear during the Sun Dance. The medallions hung on chains of turquoise stones, with eagle feathers tied to each side of the disk, and the whole piece was blessed in a special ceremony. The one your dad got is missing the chain and feathers. But now we know what it was for."

She drew a deep breath. "You're avoiding the issue."

"No kidding." He sighed, sounding very weary. "You know about the Sun Dance, right?"

"Some."

"It was the most important Sioux ceremony of the year. A really big deal. Sometime in midsummer the people would get together and put up a huge tent, decorated with all sorts of symbolic buffalo and eagle parts, and the men would dance themselves into a trance."

"There was some ritualistic torture involved, too, wasn't there?"

"Oh, yeah. They threaded thorns through the skin of their chests, attached themselves to the tent pole with a rope, and danced until the thorns tore through flesh. It was supposed to stimulate visions and prophecy." He shook his head. "There's advanced thinking for you."

"Not so different from certain Eastern religious rites that are still practiced today."

"I guess you've got a point." With a last swallow, he drained his glass of all but ice.

Emma tightened her grip on her wine. "The ceremony—the medallion—there's a message in the observance."

He sighed again. "God, yes. The Sun, giver of life. The

Buffalo, sustainer of life. The Eagle, messenger between the Sun and the People. All moving in a circle of birth and death and rebirth that makes them one.''

''You know a lot about Sioux traditions for someone who's spent so many years ignoring them.''

Jimmy stirred in his seat. ''Yeah, well…I listened to the old men when I was little. Until I understood the truth.''

''The truth?''

''That it's all talk. All show. In the end, those elders gave away their traditions, their culture, just as surely as my grandfather gave away his land. Irma only knew of three medallions still in existence, including your dad's. The rest were probably melted down and sold to buy whiskey.'' He sat up straighter. ''Speaking of which…''

Emma grabbed his wrist before he could call the flight attendant. ''Don't, please.''

He looked at her, his dark eyes lightless. ''You think I drink too much, don't you?''

''I certainly think you could drink less without sacrificing anything at all.''

''You're probably right.'' Sitting back in his seat, he turned sideways until their knees touched. ''Are you always right?'' He took hold of her left hand in both of his and began to play with her fingers.

''Hardly.'' She caught her breath as his thumb massaged the hollow of her palm. ''Otherwise, I wouldn't have lost my research position.''

''Maybe sometimes, a mistake is…a gift in disguise.'' His dark gaze was anything but cool as he searched her face.

Tension, excitement—desire—flowed through her. ''Sometimes.'' Jimmy raked his teeth across his lower lip, and she barely found her voice. ''The worst mistake might be to ignore the gift.''

His white, sexy smile left her speechless. ''There you

go, Professor. Just one more example of you being absolutely right.''

They didn't say much else during the rest of the flight or on the drive into town from the Denver airport. At a traffic light, Jimmy looked over.

''Your apartment is five minutes away. Or—'' the pause both terrified and delighted her ''—or I can take you home with me.''

For an answer, Emma touched his lips with a fingertip. ''Home, James,'' she whispered, smiling.

They rode the elevator with their hands locked. Somebody's breathing was loud in the quietness. Emma wasn't sure if it was Jimmy's or hers. Entering his flat, she felt him behind her, but was afraid to look back, afraid of what she would—or would not—see in his face.

Then Jimmy closed the door. With no other option, Emma turned. He'd switched on a small lamp, and she could see in his eyes a reflection of the need screaming in her chest, need that caught her breath and made her shake. Mesmerized, speechless, she let him take her hand and lead her to the bedroom.

She'd imagined this often enough…and yet had no idea what would happen next. Her memories of sex with Jimmy were full of flash, passion mixed with uncertainty and laughter, a learning process for them both. No doubt he had learned a good deal more since then about lovemaking, about women.

She'd had only one lover in the twenty years apart. With her lack of experience, how could Jimmy be anything but disappointed in what they were about to do?

As they entered his bedroom, she released his hands and turned away, fumbling with the buttons that fastened the front of her dress. She got the second one loose as his arm came round her from behind, drawing her back against the warmth of his body.

"What is that flower?" He slipped the clip from her hair, murmured the question against her neck. "What do you smell like?"

The tension eased from her forehead as her hair fell down. "Gardenia." She felt as if she'd run up the stairs, instead of taking the elevator. "It's a hothouse flower in England, but I'm told it grows out of doors here in the States. In the South." Awkwardly she tried to finger-comb the untidy riot of curls he'd released.

"Ah." He drew her hands out of her hair, placed them at her waist. "I guess it does remind me of steamy Southern nights." Chin on her shoulder, he inhaled deeply from the hollow behind her ear. "I spent some time down there in the army." His fingers ran gently through her tangles, across her scalp. "Can I brush your hair?"

"What?" She heard her squeaky question with a blush. "I mean, give me a moment. I'll do it." Reaching into her purse, she fumbled for the brush.

"Not the point, Emma." Jimmy turned her toward him and took the brush from her hands. "Neatness doesn't count here." He pressed her to sit on the corner of the bed. Then, standing behind her, he gathered her long hank of hair in one hand and began to stroke through the strands.

Shivers of pleasure trailed down her spine and over her shoulders for long, exquisite minutes. She closed her eyes against the thrill, barely kept herself from moaning in sheer delight. When at last she got the courage to look into the mirror before them, the sight took her breath. Herself, a pale ghost in the dark, with the shadow that was Jimmy barely visible at her back. A glint of light from the lamp in the outer room struck his hair, and now and then showed her the absorption in his face. His silvered shirt gleamed as his hands moved. She'd never known hands so gentle. Her hair felt as if it had turned to silk.

But this wasn't lovemaking. She swiveled to face him. "Jimmy—"

"Shh." He reached over to set the brush on a chair. "I'm slow, but I get there in the end." His teeth flashed white as he grinned.

"I don't understand." She felt almost as stupid as she'd sometimes felt with Eric—not knowing what she was doing wrong or what she could do to make it right.

"You're beautiful," Jimmy said softly. "I want to enjoy that."

The concept struck her as absurd. She had freckles, for God's sake! She tried for a laugh, but it sounded as shaky as she felt. "Are you sure you know who I am?"

"Oh, yeah." Jimmy slowly slipped the dress buttons out of their holes. "Emma Mae Garrett, with fire-bright hair and sky-blue eyes, and freckles where the sun has never shone." He ran a fingertip along her breastbone to the valley inside her bra. "I'm looking forward to relearning the territory."

His finger retraced its path, moved along the arch of her throat and lifted her chin. He paused for a moment, holding her eyes with his. Then he bent close and claimed her mouth.

When his hands moved over her shoulders, across the bare skin of her back, Emma realized her dress was gone, tugged away at some point she hadn't noticed and didn't remember. She knelt before him now in her slip, barely covered. She thanked God for the darkness...until Jimmy leaned away to turn on the bedside lamp.

She protested, with an arm across her breasts. "No..." And cast a longing glance at the closet where his thick black robe hung.

But his smile was sweet and kind. "Strawberries and cream," he murmured, his fingers walking their way over her protective arm, from wrist to elbow to shoulder. "Loving you is the perfect dessert.'' His hand moved to her head again, pulling her close so that he could cover her lips with his. Any brains, any fear she might have once possessed, simply dissolved in that kiss.

Emma didn't protest when he slid the straps of her slip over her shoulders. She drew her arms free and circled them around his neck. In another second, her bra fell away. Then Jimmy took her breasts in his hands.

"Jimmy…oh, *Jimmy*."

The next time she opened her eyes, she was lying on her back, watching him pull off his tie and shirt. In the golden light his skin shone like polished sandstone, his blue-black hair like a raven's wing. As he came back to her, Emma ran her hands over his chest, his ribs, the flat of his belly. "You're so hard," she marveled.

"And you're so soft." His kisses traveled across the tops of her breasts, as his hands eased the rest of her clothes away. "What a fantastic combination."

Naked in Jimmy's arms, she found that words deserted her. With each touch, each kiss, Emma lost more awareness of herself, lost ever more comprehension of their differences. Jimmy was above her, beneath her, and then, with only the thinnest of barriers between them, inside her. She gave as much as she knew to give, opened her body and her soul for him…and it seemed to be enough.

JIMMY WASN'T SURPRISED when Emma fell immediately into a deep sleep in his arms. Even without the bedside clock, he knew dawn was close. She'd worked late Sunday night, spent most of the day on her feet…and taken him closer to heaven than he had any right to be.

He brushed her hair back from her face, shifted a little to ease his hip and closed his eyes. The relaxation in his muscles, the satisfaction in his brain, couldn't disguise how much he had just complicated the situation. Better to have left Emma to herself. Better...but impossible.

Now there were obligations involved, and expectations. He hadn't had nearly enough of her, and he couldn't imagine leaving her for long. Or letting her leave him.

At least he didn't have to deal with that employer-employee garbage anymore.

"NO WAY, man." Harlow ground his cigarette butt into the sidewalk with his toe. "No freakin' way."

"What's the problem? We need the cash." Tommy leaned back against the wall, a half-chewed toothpick in his mouth.

"We don't need that kind of money."

"Money's just money. It's all the same."

"Drug money's dirty."

Tommy laughed. "What is this? You take the stuff by the spoonful, you buy it for Ryan and me, but you don't want to make money selling it?"

"I'm not gonna deal."

"Then you ain't been hungry enough, man. Your kitchen angel keeps you from seeing the facts of life. You'll do anything it takes when your habit gets bad enough. Trust me."

Harlow was afraid Tommy was right. But he hadn't reached that point yet. "We're doing okay without dealing." Or they had been, until Emma Garrett let him down.

"But jeez, Harlow, dealing's a hell of a lot easier than carrying boxes. Loading furniture, picking up trash...we don't have to *do* that shit anymore. You should see Eddy's place. Black leather couches and glass tables and girls everywhere. Anything you want to eat, any time of the day or night. We could have that." He snapped his fingers. "This quick."

"We could end up dead. Or locked up. It's not worth it, Tommy."

Tomas shook his head and looked away. "You're blowing a good thing."

"All I'm blowing is a risk we don't have to take."

Ryan wandered up, smiling a little, looking like a walking skeleton. "Hey, guys. What's happenin'?"

Tommy didn't give up easily. "I was telling Harlow—"

Harlow gave his friend a look that stopped the words. "Tommy was telling me about a job moving boxes at a liquor store somewhere just off Colfax. Want to check it out?"

"Sure. What's for lunch?"

Harlow thought of the three bucks in his pocket. "I already ate, but we can get you a burger and fries on the way."

"Cool!" Ryan led the way. There was a little bounce in his walk that said his last hit had been a good one.

Tomas walked beside Harlow, shaking his head. "This is what's freakin' gonna get you killed—feeding him, buying for him, looking out for him like a damn baby. He oughta take care of himself or bail."

Harlow looked at Ryan, waiting at the corner ahead, and felt the weight of taking care of the little guy crash down on his head. Maybe Tommy was right. Maybe Ry should take care of himself. But when Harlow tried to picture letting go, he thought about his little brother. If Kyle was on the street somewhere, Harlow would sure as hell want somebody looking out for him. Even if the best that person could do was three bucks for lunch. Who the hell did he think he was, believing he could control the situation? Ryan, Tommy…himself, they would all go down hard, unless somebody, somewhere, gave them some help.

And if Emma Garrett could blow him off the way she

had, what hope was there anybody else in the entire friggin' world would do any different?

EMMA STARED OUT the window as she rode the bus to work on Tuesday afternoon, thinking that the world really should look different. The colors ought to be brighter, the faces happier. Surely something would reflect the miracle of last night.

She'd called a cab this morning at about ten to take her home. Jimmy slept deeply, despite the bright morning light, sleep he surely needed after a bout of malaria. Emma had ached for him to open his eyes, to give her that sexy, knowing grin, to say her name in his whiskey-rough voice.

But mornings-after had a bad reputation, one she didn't want to prove true. She wanted to keep the magic she'd awakened with—her head on Jimmy's pillow, his body warm and relaxed beside her, his hand on her hip. So she'd laid a finger gently on his lips, found her clothes and gone back to her own flat to relive her memories of the night.

Now the bus pulled away from the curb, leaving her on the sidewalk across from The Indigo. Jimmy hadn't yet arrived—the Jag was nowhere to be seen. That would make going in easier. She'd like to be on familiar ground—the kitchen—when she saw him again. Whatever Jimmy's reaction to what they'd done, at least she would know where she stood.

A car she hadn't seen before sat in front of the door to the club. Painted in a flashy purple, with dark windows and tires that seemed ridiculously small, the vehicle's body barely cleared the ground. Emma went around the rear end, stopping to read a bumper sticker on the fender. When the lewd meaning of the slogan finally reached her, her ears got hot. She hurried into the relative safety of the club.

The two people inside stared at her with wide, startled eyes.

Tiffany stood behind the bar, backed up against the shelves of bottles on the wall. "Um…hi, Emma."

"Hullo." She looked from the bartender to the big man leaning one elbow on the bar.

"This is Brad Renfroe. Brad, Emma Garrett, The Indigo's cook."

Brad nodded. "Hi, Emma. I hear your food is great." His smile was open and friendly, his faded jeans and white T-shirt fit tight over the kind of muscular development displayed in bodybuilding contests. He was tanned and gorgeous, with bright blond hair drawn back in a ponytail.

Emma couldn't find fault with the picture. "Thank you."

"So, babe." He turned back to the bar and Tiffany. "Want to sign those checks for me? I have to drive across town and I want to get there before the store closes."

"S-sure." Tiffany reached under the bar for her purse. "Two, you said?"

"Better make it four or five. They might not have all the supplies I need, and I'll have to go someplace else."

Emma heard the bartender sigh just as Brad turned his attention her way again. "Tiffany says you're from England. What part?"

"Oxford."

"I watch some soccer on TV—that's a really popular sport over there, isn't it?"

"Yes, it is." Emma caught herself in a shiver. Having all of Brad's attention made her nervous, though she couldn't have said exactly why.

"You go to the matches?"

"No, not often. I'm not much into sports."

"Probably just as well. Seems like people are always getting killed in the fan stampedes. Or the stadium collapses or something." He grinned, as if he'd told a joke.

"Here you go, Brad." Tiffany handed a checkbook across the bar. "That's five. Okay?"

"Sure, babe. Just great." He reached across and cupped his hand around the back of Tiffany's neck, bending her over the wide mahogany bar for a loud kiss. "You have a good night. I'll see you at home later." He crossed toward the door. Emma forced herself not to shrink away as he paused beside her. "Really good to meet you, Emma. I'll stop by soon and sample some of your cooking."

"We'll look forward to that."

He put a hand on her shoulder and squeezed briefly, then banged out into the sunlight and let the door slam behind him.

Tiffany had put her purse away and was wiping down the bar. Emma joined her. "He's very attractive."

"Yeah, he is." Tiffany didn't look up from her work.

"And personable. Seems to know just what to say."

"That's Brad." The other woman straightened up. "A real ladies' man." She glanced down at her cleaning cloth, then moved away, pulling down the rolled-up sleeves of her shirt as she went.

But Emma had already seen. She cornered Tiffany and caught at her wrist. "What's he done?"

Tiffany's hiss of pain answered the question, but Emma pushed the sleeves up, anyway. Both of the bartender's arms were mottled with bruises, red and deep purple. With a surge of nausea, Emma recognized fingerprints among the marks.

Frowning, she loosened her hold, and Tiffany drew her sleeves down again. "This can't go on. You shouldn't have to endure such abuse."

Tiffany laughed. "I can't leave him, Emma. He's got my checkbook."

"To hell with your checkbook. I'm worried about your life."

"Well…don't." Tiffany slipped past her to the open end of the space behind the bar. "I'll be okay."

Emma stayed where she was, near the bar phone. "That's unacceptable. I'm going to call Jimmy."

The other woman's hand clamped over hers with amazing strength as Emma started to pick up the handset. "You're not doing any such thing. You're not telling anybody."

"Yes, I am. Jimmy…or the police."

Tiffany stared at her a moment, then released Emma's hand. In the next instant, she grabbed the phone line, jerked it out of the wall and threw the receiver and handset into the shadows around the stage. "I'm warning you to leave me alone. If you don't, I'll…"

Emma crossed her arms over her chest. "You'll what?"

Desperation crossed Tiffany's pretty face, followed by a strangely dead calm. "If you breathe a word, I'll have some information of my own for the cops. About the three druggies who keep hanging around the kitchen. Casing the place, probably, for what they can steal. Usually high—they're easy marks for possession, if nothing else. You want Harlow and Ryan and Tommy arrested?"

"You wouldn't."

"Yeah, I would. You report Brad, I report the boys. The cops can clean up the neighborhood in one sweep."

If Harlow and his friends were arrested because of her, Emma was certain she would lose the last opportunity to help them. Any trust they might have placed in her—and after this week, who knew how much?—would be completely destroyed. She still had a chance with them, she thought. Should she risk that chance for Tiffany?

Emma dropped her hands to her sides. "You win. I'll keep quiet." She walked to the open end of the bar and slipped past Tiffany without a glance.

"It's for the best, Emma. Really."

"I hope you're right." In the kitchen, she dropped her

purse on the table, sank into a chair and put her head down on her arms.

Without a doubt, everything *had* changed since last night. For the worse.

CHAPTER NINE

ZACH HARMON CALLED just as Jimmy was getting ready to leave for the club. "I finally convinced Shelley to let Alex and Norah stay with my mother for a few hours. We thought we'd come down and check out Emma's cooking. Do you have a table free?"

"Uh...sure." Jimmy shook his head, trying to get his bearings. "Yeah, sure. I'll save you the best seats in the house."

"Great. Is everything okay?"

"Right as rain."

"You sound kinda stressed."

Yeah, well, the woman I made love to last night walked out this morning while I was still asleep. What does that mean? "I had a go-round with malaria last week. I might still be a little tired."

"Man, I bet. You sure you should be working?"

"I think I can stay on my feet till closing time. See you and Shelley later."

"Yeah, later."

First, though, he wanted to figure out what Emma was thinking. Preferably before he saw her again, he thought as he climbed into his car.

Was she sorry? Embarrassed? Ashamed? He swore as the possibilities occurred to him, and punched the Jag's steering wheel. Emma loved as generously as she did everything else. She gave back everything he offered, and more. She had to know how different last night was from anything they'd done together as kids...anything he'd ever done with another woman since.

Or did she think this was just the latest in a long string of one-night stands? Maybe she thought that it didn't matter to him, that *she* didn't matter to him more than any other woman.

That's crazy, Emma.

And he would tell her so as soon as he saw her. As soon as he looked into those bright blue eyes, he would know what she was thinking. He added weight to the gas pedal, trying to get there faster. He wasn't coping too well with the suspense.

But the club was a portrait of chaos. A liquor-supply truck that should have arrived yesterday was parked squarely in front of the door. As Jimmy approached, the fumes of good scotch reached him like an alcoholic fog. A handcart lay on the sidewalk, with four cases of Glenlivet shattered against the concrete.

Tiffany was going head to head with the delivery guy. "We are not paying for booze that didn't even get inside the door."

"I don't care where it broke. It's your merchandise and I'm marking it delivered. It ain't coming out of my paycheck."

"You're the one who can't handle a stupid piece of equipment designed for a four-year-old."

The deliveryman clenched his fists, and Jimmy stepped in. "Hey, Tiff. Albert. Looks like we've got a problem." He held up his hands to stop the spate of explanation from both sides. "No, no, that's okay. I get the general picture. Get me four more cases, Al, and add it to the bill. Yeah, in addition to the four that broke. Just clean up the glass and we'll call it even."

"Jimmy, we shouldn't have to pay!"

He put an arm around Tiffany's shoulders and walked

her into the club. "I'm guessing that Al can't afford to buy that much spilt whiskey. Four cases won't bankrupt us. You just see about getting the stuff put away."

She hesitated. "Um, can I wait for Darren? He'll be here in about an hour."

"Sure. Whatever." He looked at her closely, thought she was pale. "You okay?"

"Fine, boss. That wrist I sprained is still a little tender, that's all. I like to keep it rested for drawing beer."

"Good thinking." He grinned at her as Albert brought four new cases inside. "Put them down the hall near the storeroom, Al. We'll take it from there."

Jimmy stayed to referee, but the combatants kept their distance and peace resumed. Al swept up the glass and hosed scotch off the sidewalk.

Inside the club, Tiffany had disappeared. If she was with Emma, he'd have to put off any personal conversations until later. And he might very well go crazy waiting for the chance.

When he pushed open the kitchen door, Emma turned toward him, her eyes round in surprise, her jaw a little loose. Tiffany was nowhere to be seen.

But the rest of the company really grabbed his attention. Three pairs of eyes were trained on him in various stages of fear and defiance. Three pairs of hands held hefty sandwiches, packed with ham and cheese and thick slices of tomato. Three heroin addicts—young thugs who had threatened him not long ago—now confronted him from the kitchen table of his own club.

Jimmy looked at Emma again. "What the hell are *they* doing here?"

CAREFULLY, Harlow put down his sandwich and got to his feet. "We're going, Mr. Falcon. We're going." He jerked

Ryan up by the shoulder of his shirt and gave Tommy the sign to vamoose.

He hadn't counted on Emma Garrett. "None of you has finished your food," she said. "Sit down and eat."

Falcon's eyes narrowed and the air got even colder. Harlow shook his head. "We've had plenty, thanks. Come on, guys."

Before he could get Ryan to move, Emma stood in front of the outside door, arms crossed over her chest. "Sit. Down. And finish." She spoke to him, but she stared straight at Falcon. He was staring straight back at her.

Both exits were blocked. With a shrug, Harlow dropped back into his chair. He hadn't eaten in a couple of days. He wasn't going to argue with free food.

After a tight silence, Falcon repeated his question. "What are they doing here, Emma?"

"Eating, as you see. They're hungry most of the time. It doesn't hurt for me to feed them now and again."

Falcon leaned back against the door frame and put his hands in his pockets. "This isn't the first time they've been in here?"

He'd been defending himself on the streets for a long time, but Harlow would not have wanted to answer that question.

"No, it isn't." She lifted her chin. "Do you have a problem with that?"

"I have a major problem with that. But we'll talk about it when they're gone." The club owner glanced at Harlow. "Finish eating. Then hit the road."

"Yessir." Before he got the words out, Falcon slammed the kitchen door with the heel of his hand and let it swing closed behind him.

Emma stayed where she was for a few seconds, then seemed to lose all her stuffing. "That didn't go too badly, did it?" Her bright smile looked more than a little forced.

"I never meant to get you in trouble."

"You didn't, Harlow. I did that all by myself. I should have told him you'd been here before now."

He swallowed the last of his sandwich and got to his feet. "You can tell him we won't be back. I'm already on Mr. Falcon's sh-er, bad list."

"Please," she said, her eyes suddenly tired, "don't go away and never come back. We…we have some things to do." Her glance brushed over Ry. "This has been a bad week. But I'll get Mr. Falcon calmed down and I'm sure he'll be okay with having you here now and again. Please?"

Nobody had cared this much when he left home. It made doing the right thing too hard. "I'll be back. Come on, guys. Let's go." He poked his head back in the door after Tommy and Ry had left. "You take care, Emma."

She gave him that sweet smile. "I will. You, too."

"Sure." He let the door clatter behind him as he jogged to catch up with Ryan and Tommy. "That was close," he said as they crossed the street.

"I'm not sure he didn't go call the cops." Tommy spat out a toothpick. "We shoulda rolled him when we had the chance."

"Then he would have called the cops for sure, without letting us finish the food first."

"That woulda been a shame." Ryan stretched out his arms. "I'm feeling pretty damn good right this minute."

He looked worse than ever. If it hadn't been for Ry, Harlow might have cleared out of town altogether. But Emma was ready and willing to help him with Ryan. Somehow they had to get the little guy straightened out. Jimmy Falcon could help.

Or he could get out of the way.

ABOUT NINE, Darren brought an order into the kitchen. "Jimmy wants you to step out front."

Emma hesitated a moment, then looked up from the tab. "Would you tell him I'll be there as soon as I get these plates prepared?"

"Sure thing." But he stopped at the doorway. "He saw Harlow here, didn't he? What'd he say?"

"Nothing, really." Darren gave a disbelieving frown. "Yet. We haven't talked."

"Something for you to look forward to."

"Jimmy just doesn't understand. When I explain, he won't be angry anymore."

"Believing that will help you get through the night, won't it." Without waiting for an answer, the server went back into the club.

Emma made up the order he'd brought in, carefully thinking only about food, as she had all evening. When she couldn't delay any longer, she took off her apron and crossed the threshold into darkness and conversation and jazz.

Cigarette smoke burned her eyes as she searched the room. She found Jimmy seated at a table in the very center. The man to Jimmy's left had his back to her. On his right and facing her was an elegant, perfectly dressed, petite blonde. Emma recalled the illustrations in old-fashioned fairy-tale books. This woman could have modeled for the Faerie Queen.

Waiting for Jimmy to finish his conversation, listening to the music, Emma couldn't keep her mind blank any longer. How terrible that her first meeting with Jimmy after…last night had been so difficult. She felt as if she'd been riding horseback in the mountains these past twenty-four hours—cresting the peaks, rushing down into the valleys, veering close to the edge of terrifyingly sheer cliffs.

Where the journey would end was something she couldn't begin to predict.

The set ended and the band took a break. In the lull, Jimmy glanced over and saw Emma standing by the bar. He stood up and gestured for her to join them at the table.

Oh, dear. Their second encounter since last night would be in front of others, strangers to her, with no possibility for a personal word. Emma struggled for a smile that didn't betray her panic as she approached the trio.

Then the other man stood and turned, and her smile became more natural. Zach Harmon, unfamiliar out of his uniform, grinned at her as she reached him. "Wow, Emma, what a difference you've made in this place!" He took her hand and drew her close to kiss her cheek. "The Indigo is getting really upscale. Falcon's going to have to raise his prices." Without pausing a beat, he drew Emma to the free chair across from Jimmy, then introduced her to his wife.

Trying to ignore the sensation of towering over this small woman, Emma shook hands. "It's good to meet you, Shelley. Your husband showed me pictures of your children when we met last. They're beautiful."

Shelley's smile was sweeter than her flawless appearance had led Emma to expect. "We think so." She turned her smile on her husband, then back to Emma. "Your food is as wonderful as I'd been led to hope." Shelley put a hand on Jimmy's arm. "I've been trying for a couple of years to convince this man that he needed to update. How did you manage?"

When Emma hesitated, Jimmy said, "She shoots first and asks questions later, so to speak." He leaned back in his chair, looking relaxed and completely in control, not at all the man who had confronted her a short time ago in the kitchen, stiff with anger. "She tried out the food as sort of a surprise, and once the customers got a taste..." He shrugged. "I know a good thing when I see it."

Emma met his eyes across the table. There was humor in his face, but a sort of wariness, as well, as if he might feel dragged farther than he wanted to go. Was that in relation to Harlow and his friends? Or to last night and what she and Jimmy had done together?

"I always said you were smarter than you looked." Zach punched his friend lightly on the shoulder, then caught Darren as he eased by. "Emma needs a drink. What would you like?"

"Oh, no, I can't stay long. But thank you."

Darren shook his head. "We're in that midevening lull. You've got a few minutes. I'll bring you a Pym's." Before she could protest, he had taken off for the bar.

For the rest of the band's break, Jimmy listened with a lazy smile as Zach and Shelley kept up a lighthearted conversation ranging from sports to real estate—Zach's wife was a top Realtor—to the upcoming Policemen's Ball. Emma tried to participate, but she felt slow-witted in the couple's presence.

"How about buying a couple of tickets?" Zach brought out his wallet and a book of coupons. "There's usually a great live band and a pretty decent buffet dinner."

Jimmy sat up and propped his forearms on the table. "Have you convinced Shelley to leave the kids *again?*"

Blushing, Shelley rolled her eyes. "Is that what he tells you? *I* have to convince *him* to leave the house. We never go anywhere these days." The look she and her husband exchanged said more about the closeness of their relationship than any public display of affection could have.

Emma swallowed the lump in her throat and then realized Jimmy had asked her a question. "I'm sorry. What did you say?"

"Would you like to go?"

"Go?" Was she being stupid? What was he talking about?

"To the Policemen's Ball?"

"Oh." She sat staring at him, scarcely a coherent thought in her head. Was he asking for a date? Or a contribution?

Darren slipped up beside her. "Order up, Emma."

"I-I'll be right there." She looked at Zach and then at Shelley. "It's been lovely to meet you. I hope to see you again soon."

"At the ball, maybe," Shelley suggested.

Emma glanced at Jimmy and felt her ears begin to burn. "Perhaps."

The band had climbed back onstage. With the music beginning again and the voices around them getting louder in competition, the chance for any meaningful conversation vanished. Relieved, Emma made her escape.

At last she was back in her kitchen...Jimmy's kitchen, actually, but she thought of it as hers...in relative peace. The orders for food flowed in fairly quickly until after midnight, giving her a great deal of work to do and little time to think. Cleanup, interrupted by the occasional sandwich order, kept her working past two in the morning. The club grew gradually quieter, until she could hear the music undistorted by the noise of the crowd.

Not long after the band quit playing, she heard the distinctive pattern of Jimmy's footsteps approaching the kitchen door. He paused just outside.

"'Night, Tiffany. See you tomorrow." The door opened slightly, and Emma's heart pounded. But then Darren claimed his attention, something about a date for his band to play again at the club, and Jimmy let the door fall shut. Closing her eyes, Emma waited for her heartbeat to slow.

At last, he stepped into the room. She folded her towel carefully before turning around. In the kitchen's bright fluorescent light, he looked tired. He'd loosened his tie, and he carried the ever-present glass of whiskey.

"You shouldn't have come back to work so soon," she said without thinking. "Nothing would have been the worse if you'd stayed home until next week."

He lifted a skeptical eyebrow. "And then for a few more days you could have hidden the fact that you're letting those delinquents take you for whatever they can get."

"They are not delinquents. They are boys in trouble, boys who need help."

"How do they define delinquent in England, Emma? Over here, we consider them to be juveniles who are repeat offenders, who demonstrate no remorse over the cost or victims of their crimes, addicts who would do anything, including murder, for their next fix."

"That does not describe Harlow and Ryan and…and Tomas."

Jimmy nodded. "You have your doubts about Tommy. Smart thinking. He's the one with absolutely no conscience. But Harlow's no angel. His record is quite colorful, in fact. Burglary, theft, possession, vandalism—"

She crossed her arms over her breasts. "I know they're a challenge. But if someone doesn't help, the problem will only get worse."

He blew out an impatient breath. "Emma, the problem will get worse, anyway. You can't possibly baby-sit all the adolescent addicts in Denver."

"Change has to start somewhere. Why not here?"

"You want to turn The Indigo into a shelter for homeless boys?"

"Can you simply turn your back and pretend they don't exist? Do you really feel so little responsibility?"

His face darkened. "Look, I gave Harlow and company my best shot. I'm telling you from personal experience— they're a truly lost cause."

"You worked with them?" Had she made a fool of herself yet again? Or, worse yet, of Jimmy?

"I *tried.* I paid them for odd jobs around the club, found them a decent place to live. The only requirement was that they stay clean." He shook his head. "It was too much to ask then. And I'm sure it's too much to ask now."

Emma sank into a chair and propped her elbows on the table. "I can't just abandon them, Jimmy. Surely you see that."

"I see you believe you might actually make a difference." He downed the rest of his drink. "Look, I appreciate you want to help these kids. It's a free country, and you can try whatever you think will work."

"I believe—"

Jimmy held up his hand. "But having them here, inside the building, is asking for trouble. Your purse, the cash register, the storeroom—all accessible once they're inside. One bad fix could turn any one of those boys into a maniac. I can't—I won't—take that risk with you. Or Tiffany or Darren."

"What are you saying?"

"You want to give them money, fine—although you'd be better off just burning it. You want to feed them, okay—outside."

"That won't develop trust between us. If there's no trust, they won't let me help them." But she could feel the strength of Jimmy's resolve. She wouldn't budge him on this issue.

"The day they check themselves into rehab is the day I'll start thinking about trust."

Emma rubbed her aching eyes. "Very well. I'll see them outside the building."

"Thank you." After a moment, he straightened up from the wall. "You never did answer my question, you know."

"What question?" Though she knew perfectly well. And still didn't know what to say.

"Would you like to attend the Policemen's Ball? With me."

"I don't—"

"You already know I'm not a great dance partner." His smile mocked his own ability. "But I bought the tickets from Zach. And I think we'd have fun."

Emma gave him a genuine smile in return. "I would love to go."

The mockery disappeared, but not the grin. "Good. Are you ready to leave?"

A question loaded with possibilities. "Yes. All finished in here."

Jimmy locked the doors and set the alarm, then steered her out to the street. He put a hand at the small of her back. "I hope it's okay—I gave Landry the night off. I'll drive you home."

Did he mean *her* home or...

"Or," he murmured in her ear as they stood by the car, "I could take you back to my place for a surprise."

His lips moving against her cheek made thinking difficult. "Surprise?"

He nodded. "Just a small...celebration to say thanks for taking care of me last week. If you don't mind."

Emma felt breathless. "I don't mind. I'd be delighted."

When Jimmy unlocked his door twenty minutes later, only a square of light from outside brightened the darkness of the apartment. He squeezed Emma's shoulder. "Give me just a second."

In that second, he struck a match. Candles flared, one by one, dark red and blue and green, small, tall, fat, tapered. Filling nearly every available horizontal surface, they soon doused the room in a golden glow.

Jimmy set a covered plate in a small space between candles on the dining table, disappeared and returned with an insulated pitcher and mugs. "This establishment doesn't run to fine china.'' He poured them each a portion of coffee, adding milk and a lot of sugar to hers. ''I'm hoping the quality of the food compensates.'' He removed the cover of the plate.

Emma gasped in delight. ''Oh, Jimmy. Cheesecake.''

''I seem to remember that was your favorite dessert. Have you changed your mind over the years?''

''No. Of course not. This is just amazing.''

He smiled and cut her a generous piece, then one for himself. ''Sometimes I guess right. Why don't we sit on the couch to eat? It's more comfortable.''

And more intimate, she thought as he sat so close to her their thighs brushed.

When they'd both finished and set their empty plates on the coffee table, he looked at her a moment, then said, ''A penny for your thoughts.''

''That tasted incredibly good.''

He nodded. ''Why did you leave this morning?''

Taken by surprise, she struggled for an answer that would make sense. ''I thought…it would be easier.''

''Easier for whom? Didn't you enjoy last night?'' His fingers began playing over her hand, lightly touching, stroking over her palm and in the V's between her fingers.

''Oh, Jimmy, of course.'' She found herself close to tears. ''But I didn't want you to think I…I expect anything.''

''You don't?'' His palm stroked up the inside of her arm and down again. The backs of his fingers brushed her breast.

''I…um…'' She closed her eyes.

''Because I did.'' She stared at him and he leaned closer still. ''I expected the chance to make love to you in the morning light.'' His lips grazed hers. ''To brush your hair until it was smooth and soft, and then—'' he raked his teeth lightly on the angle of her jaw "—to completely mess it up all over again."

"Jimmy..." Emma took hold of his head with both hands and brought his mouth to hers.

Soft, desperate whispers. The slow slide of cloth across quivering skin. Sighs of satisfaction, sudden gasps of pleasure. Candlelight flickering over them, bronze and cream melded in the gentle shine.

A pause, limned with laughter, for Jimmy to retrieve a condom from the bedroom. "I thought I'd remembered everything. But then—" he leaned over her "—I thought I might feed you cheesecake and take you straight home."

Emma welcomed him back. "Surely you haven't forgotten—I'll do anything for cheesecake." She sighed as he joined his body with hers. "Oh, Jimmy..."

"Don't leave this time," Jimmy whispered later as Emma curled against him and drifted into sleep. She smiled and shook her head.

But he stayed awake for quite a while, wondering if his plea referred to the next morning...

Or to the rest of their lives.

CHAPTER TEN

LIFE ON THE STREETS wasn't so bad in the summertime, unless it rained. Denver didn't get all that much rain, but the occasional storm coming through could really screw up a decent day.

Harlow sat on the windowsill underneath a storefront awning, his clothes wet and his mood lousy. Tommy and Ryan had taken off this morning while he was still asleep. That was the trouble with going to a shelter—the cots were so comfortable that he sometimes had trouble waking up.

So now, behind his back, Tommy had pulled the little guy into who knew what kind of trouble—though Harlow had a pretty good idea. Word on the street was that Eddy Santos, one of the town's big drug suppliers, had openings for dealers. Tommy had talked more than once about getting in on the action. It would be like him to sneak off when Harlow wasn't watching and take Ryan to an addict's paradise—a clean, easy supply of all the dope he could handle, as long as he kept bringing in the profits from street sales.

Swearing to himself, Harlow threw his cigarette away; it hit the wet pavement with a hiss and a spiral of smoke. What was the point, anyway? How stupid was it to keep some outdated concept of honor in the middle of a life like his? The life he'd chosen to live. He hadn't ended up on the street by accident. Nobody had run him out of the house back in Amarillo. They just hadn't asked him to stay.

"Harlow?" He whipped his head around. Emma Garrett

stood three feet away, the edge of the awning dripping dirty water onto her bare head.

"What are you doing out in the rain?" he asked. "Come under here before you get soaked." He made room for her on the windowsill. "What're you doing in this part of town?"

She eyed his windowsill with distrust. "Why don't we go inside somewhere and have coffee? I passed a take-away restaurant just a block back."

The temptation to get warm and dry beat back his good intentions. "Okay."

They arrived at the hamburger joint breathless, stood in line with other dripping people, then sat down at a table that hadn't been cleared. Harlow did it himself, then came back to sit across from Emma. "I still want to know what you're doing here."

She patted a clean napkin over her spattered face. "Looking for you, of course."

"I'm flattered, but it's a bad idea. Why don't you find a phone and call a cab?"

"Not yet. You and Ryan and...and Tommy haven't come around in nearly two weeks. I worried that something had happened."

"No. Nothin'." He hoped. "Mr. Falcon was pretty clear about his orders, though. He wants us to stay away from the club and from you."

"Mr. Falcon doesn't choose my friends for me. Where is Ryan?"

"He and Tommy took off before I woke up. Haven't seen them yet today."

"How is Ryan holding up? Is he eating?"

Lying was against his nature. So who should he sacrifice? Ryan, or the nice lady who just wanted to help? "Off and on. I had a good three days of work last week at a construction site, picking up trash. So we've got some money.''

"Have you talked with him about getting off the street?''

"I try sometimes. But he's either high and asleep or strung-out and looking for his next hit. Makes talking about anything serious a little tough.''

"How does he come to be here to begin with? Where is his home? Where are his parents?''

Harlow shrugged. "He hitchhiked into town from somewhere up in the mountains. Said his mom had a new boyfriend and the house wasn't big enough for three. I think the guy liked to use Ryan as a punching bag. But he was already doing horse by the time I met him. I didn't get him hooked.'' It was important for her to believe that.

"I didn't think you had.'' Her fingers touched the back of his wrist for a second. "I just wondered—he seems so young.''

"Fourteen last month.''

"And how old are you?''

"Sixteen.'' Going on fifty.

"How did *you* get here?'' The question was so soft he could have pretended he didn't hear it.

But he owed her more than that. "Worked my way north from Amarillo. I was headed for California, but Denver's not a bad place for a layover. Then I met up with Ry and Tommy, and just never moved on.''

"Why did you leave home?''

Another quiet question he could refuse to answer. "I was tired of Texas.''

"Is that a polite way of telling me to mind my own business?''

He choked on his coffee, laughing. "Emma, you're too much.''

"I take that as a yes.''

Harlow wiped his mouth with the back of his hand. "It's

not a secret. My big brother got killed in a car accident. And after that it seemed like my folks weren't seeing me anymore. They sorta looked right through me, trying to see him. I figured I might as well hit the road, find a place to be real.''

When he looked up, Emma had tears in her eyes. ''I'm so sorry.''

''Don't cry for me, Miss Emma. It's not such a bad life.''

''It's dangerous and dirty, Harlow, and you know it.''

He took another swallow of coffee, instead of answering.

''Why don't you get off the street when Ryan does?''

Good question. ''Cause I'm not killing myself the way he is.''

''It's only a matter of time. You know that, too.''

He couldn't argue—the craving got stronger every day. ''I'm okay.''

Emma sat back in her seat. ''I won't argue with you. But I won't give up, either.''

She always made him smile. ''That's good to hear.''

When they stepped out on the sidewalk after finishing their coffee, the sun had slipped out from behind the clouds. The pavement was steaming, but a fresh wind was blowing. ''Thanks for the coffee. I'm warm from the inside out.'' And beginning to feel the need waking inside him. He had to get her out of here. Fast. ''That gas station across the street has a phone booth. I'm gonna call you a cab.'' She didn't object.

When he jogged back through the intersection, the effort started a headache. He was more winded than he wanted to admit. ''Cab'll be here in ten. I'll wait with you.'' All around them, the lowlifes were waking up after their late-night partying. Harlow saw several bad men eyeing Emma with interest. Hoping to God the cab came sooner than ten minutes, he squeezed his eyes shut against the pounding in his head.

"You may think you're doing better than Ryan," Emma said softly. He opened his eyes to the worry in hers. "But you look much worse today than you did a month ago when we met. You're losing weight, and your eyes are less alive. The drug has you, Harlow, and it's not going to let go without help."

"Yes, ma'am." He saw the cab approach and held up a hand. "You get back to the club." He shut the door hard on her goodbye and waved the driver on.

With his stomach cramping, he watched until the cab disappeared in traffic. Then he went looking for his dealer.

Later, when he could think again, Harlow recalled some of what he'd said. Emma had almost pulled the entire story out of him. He must be losing his nerve, because he wanted to tell her all of it, let her spend more of that amazing concern on him.

Except that the truth would drive her away. He couldn't afford to let her know everything, not until Ryan was off the street. Tommy had chosen his own path, and Harlow wasn't much inclined to change it. But the little guy deserved a chance to survive.

Harlow only wished he could say the same for himself.

AT THE CLICK of a key in the door lock, Jimmy looked up from his book. A second later, Emma closed the door to her apartment, turned and froze. "Jimmy!" Her reaction did not suggest that seeing him was a pleasant surprise.

He got to his feet with a smile. As he took in how wet she was, his smile faded. "Been for a walk in the rain?"

"Um, yes, as a matter of fact. I miss the English weather." She unbuttoned her raincoat, and he moved to lift it off her shoulders. Taking the damp coat from him without actually meeting his eyes, she hurried across the room to the hallway. "Just let me hang this in the lavatory."

Emma was always easy to read, and easiest when she was trying to hide something. Jimmy propped his hips against the back of the couch and waited for her to reappear. "What's going on?"

"Nothing." She still looked surprised. And distracted. "I mean, I just didn't expect to see you here."

Jimmy held out his hand. After an obvious hesitation, she took it and let him pull her close. He kissed her knuckles, her wrist, where her pulse pounded like a pile driver, her cheek and then her mouth. "Mmm. Coffee," he murmured against her lips. "Coffee and cream."

She relaxed finally and kissed him back the way she always did, with absolute surrender. He loved it…but it worried him, too. In two weeks Emma had never asked for anything personal, in bed or out of it. It was a nice change from the self-absorbed women he'd known in the past. But didn't she have some desires of her own?

He let the kiss end, let her step back, though he kept hold of her fingers. "I thought I'd drive you to work. But maybe I should have called first." They'd exchanged keys. This was the first time he'd used his, and now he knew why. He wasn't sure where the trouble lay, only that what had felt so right five hours ago now seemed awkward. Troubled. "Where'd you walk to?"

Emma closed her eyes and shook her head. "This is ridiculous. I should know better."

"What are you talking about?"

Still holding his hand, she pulled him around to sit on the couch with her. "I went to find Harlow."

Jimmy froze. "You did what?"

"I haven't seen him for two weeks. I wanted to know that he's all right."

"And is he?"

She gazed at him a second. "You're angry."

He stood up again. "Yeah, I guess I am. Where did you go looking for this drug addict, Emma?"

"Tiffany said—"

"Jeez…Tiffany told you where to look?"

Emma got to her feet. "Don't say that as if you intend to sack her."

"I'm not sure I can afford to keep a bartender that dumb." He pulled in a deep breath, drove his hands into the pockets of his slacks. "So you just went waltzing over to the worst part of town, asking anybody on the street for Harlow?"

"I took a cab. I asked a shop owner, who suggested a newspaper vendor, who had seen him. That's all. I was perfectly safe the entire time."

"Sure you were." Jimmy walked to the window and stared at the sliver of mountaintop visible over the next roof. "And what did you find out?"

"That Ryan's either asleep or strung-out. And that Harlow is losing ground to the heroin."

He shrugged, still without looking at her. "No surprise."

"No. But that doesn't mean we can't change the situation."

"I was afraid you would say that." He sighed. "What do you want to do?"

"I want to get Ryan into some sort of program that will allow him to withdraw from the heroin and start living again."

"Well, that's easy enough. I'll call Zach and we can have him arrested tonight. The city has a detox program attached to the jail system. He'll get good care."

"That's not the answer."

"Why not?" He turned around and faced the disappointment in her eyes.

"Because he doesn't need to be in jail at the mercy of criminals and…and who knows who else."

"Heroin possession and use is against the law. That makes him a criminal."

"He's a boy, Jimmy. Barely fourteen years old, abused by his mother's boyfriend, homeless and hungry."

"He doesn't have to be abused, homeless or hungry. There are shelters."

"Ryan needs care from people who are concerned about him as a person, not simply a case number."

"And the person to provide that care is you?"

"And you, and Tiffany, and Darren. I think we can all help."

Jimmy avoided the idea of Ryan as his personal crusade. "How do you propose to do that?"

"We have to talk with him. Convince him to enter a program."

"Which program?" He felt as if he were standing in quicksand up to his hips.

"We have to find the right one."

"And pay for it?" The mud had reached his shoulders.

"If that's what it takes, yes. He deserves a chance, Jimmy."

"Emma, this is just one kid. We can't be responsible for every addict in Denver."

She crossed her arms. "Why not?"

"Do you think you're Mother Teresa?"

Her cheeks turned pink. "I think I have the time and the money to make a difference."

"That's an illusion. All the time and money in the world won't change a single person who doesn't want to change himself."

"But we can give them the incentive. The support."

He shook his head wearily. "Why make an effort that's bound to fail?"

Her hands dropped to her hips. "Good God, Jimmy!

Why the hell *not* make the effort? What does it matter if it fails? At least we'll have tried!''

Emma's anger released his own. ''Look, I made the effort. For ten years in the army, I took extra duty, worked in every community outreach program my unit sponsored. Fed starving babies in Africa, cleaned up after monsoons in India, rounded up drug smugglers in Colombia. The world, in case you haven't noticed, is still a mess.''

''But you can't give up just because—''

He stopped her with a raised hand. ''No, that came later, when I took another shot at being a hero and joined the police force. Hopeless is arresting a dealer and seeing him out on the street five hours later, laughing in your face. Hopeless is getting kids into rehab programs and then catching them in an alley the next week, buying dope. Hopeless is watching a young girl die of gunshot wounds because her brother the gang leader pushed her out the door ahead of him.''

''Jimmy.''

''Hopeless is sponsoring a kids' baseball team, then hearing that one of your brightest hopes has OD'd on crack in his mother's basement.''

Emma stared at him, tears burning in her eyes. She'd lost the ability to say a word.

''I'm not bragging, but I think I've taken every chance I saw to make a difference. And at every chance, I got shot down, sometimes figuratively, sometimes—'' he hit his bad hip with the heel of his hand ''—not. So forgive me if I'm not into optimism.'' He drew a deep breath. ''I don't hope anymore. And I don't try. That way, I'm not disappointed.''

Emma could think of only one response. She crossed the room to lay her hands on his chest. ''I wish I could change the ways you've been hurt.''

He shook his head. ''Not me. I've gotten off pretty lightly, overall.''

"Your injuries are here." She pressed with her right hand, over his heart. "Much harder to heal."

"That's okay." He put a hand on the nape of her neck and drew her into his arms, then rubbed his cheek against her hair. "Having you back in my life for a little while makes a real difference."

Emma decided not to think about how long "a little while" would be. She tilted her face to his, asking for a kiss. When it ended, Jimmy was the one to step away.

"I'm just your boss, not your guardian. If you really think you've got a chance to help these guys, you're free to give it a shot."

There it was again, the emphasis on how small a part he expected to play in her life. Emma cleared her throat. "I know. I think I'd be even more successful if you helped. Those boys look up to you, whether they show it or not."

Jimmy laughed without humor. "Yeah, right. They know I've got connections with the cops."

She shook her head. "I won't bother you again about the boys. I can understand your reasons for staying out of this. I hope you understand why I can't."

This time he smiled in earnest. "Because of that famous, genuine, offered-free-to-all-comers Emma Garrett compassion. You look after everybody but yourself." The smile died away. "Just try to be careful, Emma. I will not stand back and let those boys hurt you."

"They won't," she promised. Jimmy might have given up on optimism. But she had enough for them both.

AT THE CLUB later that night, Jimmy shut the door to his office, sat behind the desk, opened the safe and removed the medallion box. With the same kind of apprehension running through him as he'd felt the first time, he flipped back the inlaid top to lift out the metal disk.

The Sun Dance. He remembered his eighth summer,

watching as the men erected the tall center pole, put a tent around it, and posted buffalo skulls and eagle feathers while the women cooked for the feast. There had been a sense of celebration and anticipation in the air—like before Christmas, but all-Indian.

His dad had stayed drunk for the whole week. His mother had been sick and in the hospital, her blood sugar out of control. Against a backdrop of drums and songs and the wails of men in pain, Jimmy had sat with his dad in the concrete block hovel they called home and learned his family history.

A few years later, he watched Indian activists fighting with the FBI. Later still, he'd met and loved Emma Garrett. And left the rez for good.

So what should he do with this relic of a history he didn't want to claim? If Emma had let well enough alone, he could have kept it as a remembrance of her dad…and of Emma herself, once she'd left, as she surely would. And should.

Now the disk carried more than just pleasant memories. To keep it—display it, even, in a frame on the wall or a case on a table—would be like implanting a thorn in his own chest. He would receive a vision, all right. A vision of failure, of loss, of regret. But to give it away meant giving up Aubrey Garrett's consideration, and Emma's good opinion. She would be furious, Jimmy figured, if he got rid of the disk. She took her father's transfer of the obligation seriously.

Frowning, Jimmy placed the medallion in its box and returned it to the safe, buried under envelopes containing stock certificates, investment papers and the like. Maybe if he didn't see the box, he wouldn't think about it, especially once Emma had gone. He'd lost sight of *her* twenty years ago, and she was eminently more memorable than a piece of jewelry.

Twenty years ago, of course, he'd had a life stretching

out in front of him. He'd said goodbye to Emma easily, because he'd thought he could afford the loss.

These days, he knew better. If he managed to hold on to his self respect and let her go without protest, there wouldn't be anything easy about it.

This time, he doubted he would ever recover from losing the only woman he'd ever really loved.

THE WEEK BEFORE the Policemen's Ball, Emma asked Tiffany to help her find a dress. "I haven't done any clothes shopping in Denver. I wouldn't have the first idea where to start."

Tiffany continued to polish the gleaming bar for a few moments. "When did you think about going?"

"Monday might be best, since we're off. But if you have something else to do…"

"No. I don't." Still, she hesitated. "Brad's used to me being home on Mondays, that's all." She considered, and then her face brightened. "He's going to a stock-car race down in Texas this weekend, though. He probably won't get back until late. Sure." Finally she gave Emma a sunny smile. "That'll be fun. I'll pick you up about one o'clock."

Emma started back to the kitchen, but paused at the end of the bar. "Tiffany? How are things going with Brad? Are you…all right?"

"I'm great." Another sunny smile. "We're doing just fine."

The shopping trip seemed to prove that Tiffany's life had smoothed out. She wore a sundress that left her arms and part of her back bare—there were no bruises to be seen, no bandaged wrists or sudden winces to ask about. Emma allowed her suspicions to relax. Maybe Tiffany had, in fact, endured a spate of accidents. Brad made her nervous, but he hadn't appeared to be blatantly violent.

Their hunt for a nice outfit took some time. Either the dress she liked was not available in her size, or the dresses in her size looked wrong. They showed far too much of her freckled arms and back, clung too closely to her hips, hung too short.

"I'm beginning to despair," she told Tiffany as they sifted through yet another rack of gowns. "American styles simply don't suit me. I'm the dowdy English type."

Tiffany punched her lightly on the arm. "No, no, don't give up. We're not finished, not by a long shot."

Emma sighed and continued the search. More than a few of the dresses she saw would have looked wonderful on Tiffany. She insisted that her friend try on one particularly lovely gown, a strapless sheath of shimmering burgundy that brought out the color of her eyes and the shine in her hair.

"Oh, Tiffany, that's fabulous. You look like royalty."

"That's stretching it," the bartender said. But she gazed at herself in the three-paneled mirror and smiled. "This would be fun to wear."

"With silver sandals and a silver purse." Emma enjoyed dressing her friend far more than she enjoyed dressing her own oversize frame. "And it's marked down, isn't it? I'm sure there are tickets left for the dance—you and Brad could come and you could show off your dress."

Tiffany seemed to hold her breath for a moment, then released it slowly. "That sounds like fun. But I'd better not." She turned her back to Emma. "Would you unzip me, please?"

When she returned from the dressing room, Emma tried once more. "Are you sure, Tiffany? That's such a special dress."

"I know." She gave the garment a long look, then hung it back on the rack. "But cash is a little tight at our house right now. I shouldn't be buying clothes I don't really need." She shook her head, and then smiled with a determination that blocked any further protest on Emma's part. "You're the one who needs a dress. And I think—" Tif-

fany's gaze was fixed on something across the aisle
"—we just found it." She wove her way quickly through
the racks.

Emma followed, though she couldn't tell where they
were headed. "Tiffany, what...? Oh."

Ten minutes later, Emma surveyed herself in that same
mirror and sighed in satisfaction. "This is right, isn't it?"

"Dynamite." Tiffany ran a finger along the satin lapel
of the creamy-white tailored jacket, then picked up the lay-
ers of matching chiffon in the skirt and let them float down.
"All you need is a pair of shoes, your hair fixed and your
toenails painted red. I can just imagine Jimmy's face when
he gets a look at you!"

Emma knew Jimmy would be appreciative, whatever she
wore and however she looked. He had an instinct for making women feel good about themselves. Something about
the way he focused his attention, about the way he really
listened to what she said, made her feel...treasured. He
didn't care only about the historical facts she could rattle
off or the theories she'd developed; he appeared to think
that *everything* she said mattered. Whether or not he
agreed—and he hadn't backed down one inch on the issue
of Harlow and Ryan—he gave her credit for having her
own opinion.

She spent all of Saturday getting ready for the ball.
Caught up in her career—because that was all she'd had,
really—Emma hadn't pampered herself so much in years.
Sleeping late, a long bath in scented water, a decadent
lunch of melon and prosciutto ham and provolone cheese,
followed by a nap...the day was nearly perfect. Especially
when she looked forward to spending the night with Jimmy.

She painted her toenails the red Tiffany had chosen and
pinned her hair into a smooth chignon on the back of her
head. Her hands remained their own practical selves—short
nails, no rings. At the last moment, she slipped her mother's

engagement ring onto her right hand. The diamond was small, but it added a touch of elegance.

Then, ready thirty minutes early, she perched on the edge of the sofa and waited for Jimmy to arrive.

SWEARING, Jimmy parked on the curb at The Indigo's front door. Two police cars were there ahead of him. His alarm system was screaming loud enough to wake the dead.

"Hey, Jimmy." Street cop Drew Rivers strolled around the corner from the alley. "Can't see any damage. No sign of forced entry. You think your alarm system's screwed up?"

"Hey, Drew. I don't know what's screwed up. Something sure is." He unbolted the door and then stepped back to let the cops go in first. They were carrying. He was just on his way to a dance. "The lights are to the left."

Weapons ready, Drew and his partner eased into the club under the glare of fluorescent lights. When they got to the center of the room without encountering any trouble, Jimmy stepped inside, too. "The alarm is down the back hall."

While Drew made a sweep of the kitchen and his partner checked out the storeroom, Jimmy turned off the alarm. Then he gathered with the cops back at the front door. "Doesn't look like anybody's been here," he admitted. "The safe was locked up same as usual, with nothing missing." He'd opened it up and made sure the medallion was still in the box. "Maybe the alarm got jumped by an electrical surge or something. Thanks for coming, guys."

"No problem." Drew clapped him on the shoulder. "As long as we gotta work on the night of the Policemen's Ball, we might as well have some excitement." He eyed Jimmy's suit. "You goin'?"

"Yeah. Zach made me buy tickets."

"That Harmon. He's out to win the door prize for most tickets sold."

"What's the door prize?"

Drew grinned. "*The Complete Elvis*—all his recordings and an official Elvis-in-Vegas doll."

Jimmy chuckled. "The look on his wife's face will be priceless if he wins." Shelley was completely in love with her husband. But she had ideas about decorating a house that did not include Elvis dolls. Jimmy wasn't sure Shelley had ever heard one of the King's songs all the way through.

"Take a picture for me." Drew waved and got back into his cruiser. The cruisers pulled away, and the street returned to normal.

Now almost twenty minutes late for his date with Emma, Jimmy double-checked the kitchen-door lock, set the alarm and bolted the front door. Throwing the Jag into gear, he swung across the empty street. Halfway into the intersection, his brain caught up with what his eyes had seen.

He pulled to a stop at the next curb and adjusted the rearview mirror to scan the street he'd just left.

Yeah, there they were. The Hardy Boys plus one—Harlow, Ryan and Tomas, hanging around the corner of the building across the street from the club. How much of a coincidence would it be that his alarm had sounded, and those three were in the vicinity?

Jimmy didn't indulge in optimism, and he didn't believe in coincidence. He considered calling the cops again, getting someone back to question the boys. He considered questioning them himself.

And then he glanced at the clock. Either way, he'd be tied up well into the evening. He'd been looking forward to a night out with Emma, away from the club. The opportunity to hold her in his arms while they danced was something he would hate to miss. Once she'd gone back to England, he wouldn't have the chance again.

So he mentally sent Harlow and his buddies to hell. He kept to the speed limit going across town—a traffic violation, even if he didn't get a ticket once the officer recognized him, would only make more delay. Emma had been waiting too long already.

The elevator in her building took forever to open its doors and another forever to go up. Jimmy clenched his teeth a little tighter every time the damn thing stopped.

On Emma's floor, he paused a second to straighten his tie and calm down. Then he took a deep breath and rang her doorbell.

She opened the door almost before the sound of the bell died away. Her face was pale, her eyes anxious. "Are you all right? I was beginning to worry."

That was a new experience, having someone worried about him. "I was leaving my place when the security company called—just some screwup in the club's alarm, but I had to check it out. I should have called on the way here, but I kept thinking that'd only take *more* time. I'm really sorry for leaving you hanging." He tilted his head, tried out a grin. "Forgive me?"

Her lips, painted a deeper red tonight, eased into a smile. "Of course."

"That's good. For a second there, I thought you might slam the door in my face. And I was looking forward to showing my date off to all the cops I worked with."

That made her laugh and her eyes lit up. "You're an idiot."

"No argument there. But…wow." He took the chance to look her up and down, appreciating every inch. "The alarm should have been here. Lady, you are hot tonight!"

Emma blushed. "I had to live up to my escort."

Taking her hand, he drew her out into the hallway and closed the door. "Well, then, let's go show these folks what real class is all about."

CHAPTER ELEVEN

THE POLICEMEN'S BALL could be heard long before it was seen. The hall at Denver's convention center fairly rumbled with voices and laughter.

Walking in on Jimmy's arm, Emma drew a deep breath. This was just for fun. She didn't have to impress anyone.

The reassurance did nothing to soothe her nerves.

A rich bass voice overwhelmed the crowd noise. "Well, Falcon. I heard Harmon talked you into coming."

Jimmy turned her toward a short, balding man who held a drink in each hand. "Yes, sir. Harmon's a hard man to refuse."

"Don't I know it. Every year he gets money out of me to buy those kids bats and balls and spikes." He looked expectantly at Emma.

Jimmy's hand at the small of her back brought her forward—which made her feel even taller, the man in front of her was so short. "Captain Langley, this is Emma Garrett. Emma, the captain was my supervisor when I was on the force."

She attempted a bright smile. "It's a pleasure to meet you, sir. Jimmy's told me how much he values his time spent with the police."

"He made himself useful now and again." Captain Langley gazed up at Emma. "How'd he get himself an English girlfriend?"

The heat started at her breastbone and rose like a tide across her face. "I...um..."

"Just lucky, sir." Jimmy's fingers moved gently along her spine, and Emma knew a sudden urge to straighten her back, to stand tall and be proud, because he was. "Emma and I knew each other in high school."

The captain nodded. "It happens like that sometimes. Me and my wife started dating in the tenth grade. Five kids and thirty years later, she's still telling me what to do. In fact—" he gestured with one of the drinks "—she'll probably give me hell for standing here talking, instead of bringing her drink back. You two have a good time." He made his way through the crowd to a woman no taller than he, who smiled and kissed his cheek when he handed her the drink.

"He talks tough," Jimmy said, "but he's a pushover for kids and his wife. When he had a heart attack last year, what worried him most was not whether he lived or died, but that Megan—his wife—would be taken care of."

"My dad worried about me, too. I'd just lost my position, and he fretted constantly about whether I would get along." Remembering that concern from a man whose life was slipping away brought her close to tears. "Even though I'd been on my own for more than half my life."

"Emma..." Jimmy began, then seemed to change his mind about what he was going to say. "Your dad was one of the good guys," he said. "Same as the captain. Would you like to dance?"

"I'd love to dance." She smiled as he led her onto the dance floor and drew her into his arms. But she couldn't help wondering what he'd thought twice about saying.

Soon enough, though, she gave herself up to the pleasure of the moment. Jimmy pulled her close, rested his cheek against her temple. The halt in his step had its own rhythm, and seemed to enhance the dance rather than spoil it. Emma closed her eyes and allowed the music to take over while she concentrated on Jimmy—the feel of his chest against her breasts, the scent of his cologne.

"May I cut in?"

She opened her eyes as Jimmy stopped dancing, and saw Zach and Shelley Harmon standing beside them. Shelley wore a simple black sheath that molded her excellent curves and showed off her smooth clear skin. Emma thought for a moment about her own height, her weight...and then dismissed the regret. Jimmy said she looked good tonight. If he thought so, nothing and no one else mattered.

He tightened his arm around her waist, then let her go. "I'd be happy to dance with one of the two most beautiful women in the room."

Zach nodded and the two men traded places. "We're definitely the luckiest guys here tonight." Smoothly he took Emma in his arms and danced her away.

Jimmy turned to Shelley with a grin. "Let's dance."

She put her hand on his arm. "Would you mind if we took a break, instead? I'd love something to drink."

Given the ache in his hip, he could only be grateful. "Sounds good. What will you have?"

Drinks in hand, they eased their way back to the edge of the dance floor just in time to take over a vacant table. Shelley sat down with a sigh. "I'm actually exhausted. Norah stayed up most of the night, and I had an appointment to show property this morning at ten, which kept me out until late this afternoon."

"Is the baby okay?" That seemed like the right question to ask.

"She's got a bit of a cold. Alex goes to a playgroup twice a week and brings back whatever the other children have caught from their older brothers and sisters. Then he gives it to Norah."

"Sounds complicated."

She laughed. "Children are definitely complicated. Thank goodness I've got Zach to keep things simple."

"Have you seen Allyson recently?" Shelley's oldest daughter, by a first marriage, lived with her father in Wyoming.

"She spent the early part of the summer with us. Now she's at an advanced horsemanship camp. Allyson loves the outdoors."

"I bet she loves her little brother and sister, too."

"Brothers—Dex and Claire have two sons now. We're a very large extended family." They were quiet, watching Emma with a new partner—Mick McGee, a recruit Jimmy hadn't worked with. He was tall enough that Emma had to look up to talk with him. Though he wasn't as good a dancer as Zach, Emma seemed to be having fun. Jimmy tried to be glad, while wishing he could get her back again without being rude to his friends.

"Emma's very sweet." Shelley had moved her chair close so they could talk over the noise. "The first time we met, she seemed very shy. But tonight she really shines."

"She knows she looks great." His face felt hot, his tie too tight.

Zach's wife nodded. "I find that being sure your man finds you desirable gives you a great deal of personal power."

"Shelley..." He shook his head at the assumptions she was making. "I don't intend to tie Emma down."

"What makes you think you have the final say?" She smiled, then turned to face Zach as he approached. "It's about time, Officer Harmon. I was beginning to get jealous."

Her husband put a hand at her elbow to help her stand. "I'm the one who has cause to be jealous. I was about to ask my friend here to step outside and explain what he was doing, sharing secrets with my wife."

She smiled up into his face, and Jimmy could see the love that connected them. "Let's dance, instead."

Zach grinned. "Whatever you say."

The band played two more tunes while Jimmy watched Emma. She'd traded partners again and now danced with Ben Tilden, a cop who'd come on the force just before Jimmy left. She moved smoothly to Tilden's rhythm, but some of her pleasure had faded. When the music stopped and Tilden walked her to the edge of the floor, Jimmy could see that the light had gone out of her face and her cheeks were flushed. He stood as they came close.

"Jimmy." She looked relieved to see him. "Do you know Ben Tilden?"

"Sure." They shook hands, then Jimmy pulled out a chair for her. "Want to join us?"

Tilden shook his head. "No, thanks. I think I'll get a beer—your lady here gave me quite a workout."

The words meant one thing, his tone implied something else. Something unpleasant. "Tilden—"

But the other man was on the move, already blending in with the crowd. "See you later, Emma. I'll catch you for that dance you promised."

Jimmy sat down and took Emma's left hand. "Are you okay?"

She nodded. "His compliments were rather...suggestive, that's all." Her fingers tightened around his. "I think I'd like to spend the rest of the evening dancing, or sitting, only with you."

"That can definitely be arranged." Satisfaction—possession?—warmed him like a winter fire.

THEY WERE SWAYING dreamily to a Cole Porter medley when Ben Tilden appeared again. "I'm here to claim that dance, Emma."

She stifled a gasp of dismay. She felt Jimmy stiffen. "We were just leaving, Tilden."

"You can wait a couple of minutes while I get my dance." His hand on her shoulder felt like an iron hook.

The chill of Jimmy's temper reached her. He let her go and stepped closer to Ben Tilden. "I don't think so."

Tilden drew himself up as if to argue.

Emma put her hand on Jimmy's arm. "It's all right, Jimmy. I'll be glad to give Ben one more dance." He looked at her, his eyes narrowed, questioning. "Truly." She smiled at him, covering her distaste.

He glanced at Tilden, then stepped back. "Okay. I'll wait for you at the table with the Harmons."

She didn't watch him walk away, but turned to Ben Tilden. The sooner this got started, the sooner it would end. "Shall we?"

He smelled of beer and he held her too tightly as he moved them toward the opposite side of the floor from Jimmy. She tried to push back, but he didn't budge. "You're sexy as hell," he breathed into her ear. "What're you doing with a gimp like Falcon?"

"That's a disgusting thing to say." Emma tried to draw back, but his hands dug into her shoulder and her hip. "Let me go."

She might as well not have spoken. "You need a man who's got all his parts working. A hot number like you shouldn't have to settle for leftovers."

The band changed the tune to something even slower, with a raunchy edge to it. Tilden dragged her up against him, and she could feel his erection pressing into her hip. If she could get through this one song without causing a scene...

Then he muttered in her ear, words so foul, so filthy, that she reacted without thought. She brought her knee up hard into his groin.

Tilden let go with a groan.

Aware of the couples around them stopping to stare, to comment, Emma stood panting, trying to quell her rage. She gazed around, saw the sign for the rest rooms. Suddenly the loo seemed the perfect refuge. She fought her way through the crowd.

In the ladies', she patted cold water on her forehead, cheeks and neck, let her hands and wrists hang under the cool stream. She was making too much of this, she knew. Most women would have handled Tilden with more aplomb. He was drunk, after all. Not completely responsible.

And perhaps she'd invited Tilden's lewdness. He had been pleasant at first, and she'd felt flattered. But then his comments had changed tone. She should have listened to Jimmy, should have refused the second dance.

Oh my God. Jimmy.

She rushed back to the ballroom and into bedlam. The center of attention became obvious as she pushed her way between bodies—Zach Harmon, holding Jimmy back from a bloody-faced Ben Tilden, on his knees in front of them, trying to rise.

Turning her back on Tilden, she raised her hands and cupped Jimmy's face. "Stop. Please stop."

His eyes were hard. "Are you okay?"

She nodded. "Yes, yes. He didn't hurt me. Please, let's just leave."

Zach released Jimmy's arms. "Good idea. Tilden's muttering about settling scores. He probably couldn't punch his way out of a doughnut sack, but why give him the chance?"

Jimmy seemed to come out of his trance. He blinked his eyes, shook his head. "Yeah, sure. We're out of here." He took Emma's hand and drew her after him, along a path cleared as the crowd backed away.

Only when they were in the Jag and his hands closed around the steering wheel did she notice his torn and bruised knuckles.

"Oh, Jimmy. Your hands."

He straightened his fingers. "Yeah, that's a mess. It'll probably hurt tomorrow."

"Let's go to my flat straight away. I have a first-aid kit. I'll clean you up."

His smile, tired, subdued, reassured her slightly. "Sounds good."

In her bathroom a short time later, she carefully blotted his hands with cleanser, then antiseptic.

"Don't worry, nothing's broken."

Emma clicked her tongue. "I'm not sure we can say the same for the other guy."

"I hope not."

She looked up, found the same hardness she'd seen earlier in his eyes. "You shouldn't have wrecked the party on my account. I wasn't really hurt."

"He wrecked the party by being an..." Jimmy cleared his throat, reconsidered the word he wanted to use. "...a jerk. I just let him know his behavior wasn't acceptable. Sort of negative reinforcement."

"I'll say." Emma wrapped bandages around the worst of the wounds, so gently he hardly felt her touch. "That will have to do, I suppose."

"It's great. Thank you." He followed her into the main room.

"You're welcome." She folded the towels she'd stained with his blood and put them into the closet that held the stacked washer and dryer. "Would you like something to eat? Some coffee?"

Jimmy shook his head. "You go ahead."

"I'm not hungry. Or thirsty, really." She glanced at him briefly, a question in her eyes.

That was all the invitation he needed. He closed the space between them, took her fingers in his. "You know the real problem with my hands right now?"

Emma looked puzzled. "What is it?"

"I'm not going to be very good with buttons."

Her cheeks flushed rose, and her smile widened in delight. "I'm sure we'll think of something." Then she led him to her room.

This time Emma switched on the lamp. Jimmy sat on the side of the bed and slipped off his shoes. She moved to stand between his knees and brushed his hair back from his face. "It was a truly special evening," she whispered, "despite the problems. I loved being there with you."

"Me, too." He ran his fingertip from the base of her throat, down her breastbone, into the deep V between the satin lapels of her jacket. "You look like heaven in this jacket."

Her laugh was a gasp.

"But now…" Smiling up at her, he let his hand fall away. "Now, I think you should take it off."

"Oh." She swallowed hard. Her shaking fingers came to the first of the three buttons, hesitated, then slipped it free.

Jimmy made himself breathe. "That's one."

After a fumbling second, the second button eased out.

"Two." Another breathless silence. "Three." The jacket fell open, revealing, yet still hiding. "Almost there."

Still holding his gaze, Emma shrugged her shoulders. The jacket's weight did the rest, dragging it down to her elbows and, when she straightened her arms, to the floor. She stood before him in the satin and lace of an elegant bra.

"Emma." His voice was more groan than whisper. "God, you're beautiful." He ran his fingertips across her ribs, along her collarbones, the lovely curve of her arms.

''You're so much more than I ever believed a woman could be.''

On a deep breath, she lifted her hands and unclipped the fastening between her breasts. ''Take whatever you want,'' she murmured.

After that, he lost track of…well, everything. Everything but Emma, her creamy skin, her soft voice, her trembling sighs and exciting hands. The night narrowed to just two people, giving and taking their pleasure in the soft lamplight…then falling asleep in each other's arms.

HE AWOKE when the phone rang, with a naked Emma sprawled half on top of him and no desire ever to move again. But the noise had woken her, as well. Making a sound between a groan and a sigh, she slid to the edge of the bed and stopped the raucous sound.

''Hullo.''

Jimmy rolled to his side and put his palm on her back, the skin marvelously smooth and scented. He felt the moment she stiffened and sat up straight.

''Of course. Here he is.'' She handed him the cordless receiver. ''It's Tiffany.'' Her eyes warned him of trouble ahead.

''Hey, Tiff. What's up?''

''Sorry, boss. The police called me because they couldn't find you. There's been a break-in at the club. I tried Emma's just in case…'' She cleared her throat.

''Yeah, sure. But is this really a break-in? There was a false alarm earlier tonight.'' He sat up on the side of the bed, looking for his slacks.

''Definitely. The door was broken in, the safe's been blown.''

He swore as he picked up his shirt. ''I'll be there in fifteen minutes.''

His knuckles wouldn't bend. Emma buttoned his shirt and tucked it in. "I'm going with you."

"No, you're not." He patted his pockets for wallet and keys. "Stay here and I'll call as soon as I can."

But when he reached the door, she was right behind him, dressed in jeans and a T-shirt, her hair pulled back with a clip. Jimmy stared into her eyes, read the determination there.

He sighed. "Okay. Let's go."

BY 5:00 A.M. even the hookers and pushers had called it a night, so nobody on the street noticed the commotion at the club. The flicker of red and blue and gold lights from the police cars sent shadows leaping along building walls in a bizarre, and somehow threatening, dance.

Jimmy parked the Jag across the street and looked at Emma. "I don't suppose you'd just sit here till I got back?"

She shook her head.

He smiled for a moment, cupped her cheek with his hand. Then he took a deep breath and pulled himself out of the car. The policeman standing at the entrance to The Indigo nodded at Jimmy, pushed open the blue door and let them inside.

The noise diminished, but that was the only good news. The room reeked of spirits—the bottles behind the bar had been smashed where they stood, presumably with the stool lying on its side on the bar. All the glasses above the bar and the mirror behind it were smashed, as well.

"Hey, Jimmy." The man coming toward them wore a wrinkled suit, carried a notepad and pen. "Sorry to wake you up."

"No problem. Bill, this is Emma Garrett. Emma, meet Detective Bill Spencer. I guess he's been assigned this case."

The detective nodded at Emma, then gave Jimmy his attention. "Let me show you what we found."

He took them to the kitchen first, where the solid door had been slammed back on its hinges, the lock ripped away. "Somebody really wanted to get in. Plastic explosives is not your usual burglary equipment."

"No, it's not."

"No damage in here otherwise. They came through the door, hit the bottles, I'm guessing, then made straight for the office and the safe."

In the office, the door to the safe had been opened with the same explosive. Spencer checked his notes. "Doesn't look like the safe was wired into the alarm system."

Jimmy's jaw tightened. "I couldn't afford that little detail when I put the safe in."

"In most cases, the external wiring would have been enough. Hard to figure out how he got this all done before the cops arrived. The response time was about eight minutes." Spencer flipped a page in his notebook. "But then, most burglars don't carry C4. We need you to tell us what was in the safe."

"About two thousand bucks, in tens and twenties and fives."

Staring into the hole in the wall, Jimmy started to jam his fists into his pockets, but winced and let them hang at his sides, instead. "Stock certificates, certificates of deposit, bonds. And…" His shoulders lifted on a deep breath as he turned to look at Emma. His eyes were bleak, his face shuttered. "And your dad's box, Emma. I'm sorry. They took the medallion."

She shook her head, wishing she could touch him, knowing that would only be a distraction, not a help. "Don't worry, Jimmy. It's not your fault." Later, she would mourn the loss of her dad's medallion. Right now, all that mattered was Jimmy.

"A medallion? I need a description."

Jimmy faced the detective and described first the box, then the disk itself. Spencer whistled when he heard the value Irma White Buffalo had given them.

"Jeez." He scribbled another note. "That thing shoulda been in a museum."

Seeing the guilt in Jimmy's expression, Emma pressed her lips together and went back into the front of the club.

"No noticeable prints," announced a man in a shirt that said Crime Scene Unit across the back, as he dusted the bar stool with a small fine brush. "I'd say he wore gloves."

"Footprints?" The detective came into the room, with Jimmy following.

"Not in the kitchen. Can't see much in the alley in the dark. But it's been dry for a week or so. I'm betting there's nothing to find."

"Great." Spencer sat on a stool at the end of the bar, flipped to a new page on his pad and looked at Jimmy. "Okay, now the question is—who do you think did it?"

Jimmy shrugged. "Good question. No answer."

"Try harder, Falcon. Could it be something personal? The whole job looks personal, as a matter of fact. Not just some random break-in, but a targeted attack. Who wants to hurt you?"

"Besides the dealers I put behind bars, if only for a couple of hours? The gang members I busted? Take your pick."

"Yeah, we can go through your case files, see who's still working the area. Anybody else?"

Staring at the ruined bottles behind the bar, Jimmy didn't say anything for a long time. The air seemed to chill as they waited for him to speak. Emma rubbed her hands over her bare arms, wishing she'd worn a sweater.

He shifted his stance as if his hip bothered him. Then he turned his head to look at Emma. She read anger in his face, despair, resignation. "Well, there's a drunk cop I punched out at the dance tonight. Ben Tilden."

"You beat up Tilden? What for?"

"He annoyed Emma."

Spencer glanced her way. "Oh." He wrote on the pad. "Anybody else?"

Again Jimmy hesitated. "There are three punks who've been giving me some trouble."

Emma pressed her fingers to her mouth, holding back a cry of protest. She prayed that she was wrong about what he would say next.

"Punks?"

"Addicts. Heroin, crack. They live on the streets most of the time. At least two of them have records."

Spencer nodded, still writing. "These punks have names?"

Emma shook her head. *No,* she pleaded silently. *They wouldn't do this. I* know *Harlow wouldn't let them do this to you. To me.*

But Jimmy didn't hear her. "Harlow," he said. "Harlow, Ryan and Tomas."

CHAPTER TWELVE

DAWN HAD ARRIVED by the time the police left the club. Emma sat at one of the tables with her chin propped on her hand, feeling totally useless, totally helpless. She'd tried cleaning up some of the broken bottles, the spilled liquor. Jimmy had glanced over and said, "Leave it."

Hearing the bitterness in his tone, she didn't try to argue.

His voice came to her now in a low murmur from his office as he talked with his insurance company. Presumably he would recoup the loss of the alcohol and the damage to the club. The break-in was a disaster, of course, but not a permanent setback. The Indigo would open again.

But what about Harlow and Ryan and Tommy?

Detective Spencer had taken their descriptions from Jimmy, painfully accurate in every detail. Neither man had asked her to corroborate, thank God. She didn't know what she would have said. Her first loyalty lay with Jimmy. But she knew he was wrong to blame Harlow for this crime.

She heard the silence just seconds before Jimmy's footsteps sounded on the hallway floor. He entered the main room and came directly to the table where she sat. His hand rested briefly on her shoulder, then he dropped into the chair across from her.

His face was gray with exhaustion. "I wish I could take you home. But I can't leave the place wide open..." He uttered a brief, mirthless laugh. "Not that there's anything else to steal. But I'd like to get the back door boarded up.

If you want to try to sleep, the recliner in my office is pretty comfortable.''

Emma shook her head. "I'm all right." She reached across the table to put her hand over his. "Are you sure I can't start cleaning up?"

"The insurance company wants to check things out first. They're sending somebody over this morning."

He didn't turn his palm up to grasp hers. She sat back and put her hands in her lap. "Harlow didn't do this, you know." The words were out before she even formed them in her head.

Jimmy drew a deep breath. "No, I don't."

"He wouldn't damage you this way. And Ryan and Tommy do what Harlow tells them to."

"Harlow and his pals don't give a damn about me, Emma. I told you before—the drug owns them and they'll do whatever it takes to stay high."

"I don't believe they would go this far."

"Yeah, I can see that." His sarcastic tone piqued her temper.

"Why are you so determined to make them guilty?"

"I was a cop. I look at the evidence and draw a conclusion."

"There is no evidence linking those boys to this break-in."

"Except that they've been running tame in here for weeks now. They have a great motive. And I saw them in the vicinity last night when I left to go to your place."

Emma caught her breath. She hadn't heard him give that information to the detective "They often spend time around here. That's not evidence."

"Just a really strange coincidence, I guess."

"Jimmy—"

He leaned heavily on the table as he got to his feet. "I know what you're going to say. So don't. It doesn't really matter whether your buddies did this or some psycho we never heard of. The point is, we deal with the damage and move on.''

That should have been an encouraging attitude—except for the deadness in Jimmy's eyes, the grim set to his mouth, the chill hanging in the air like winter fog. Before she could comment or try to help, he went back to his office and back to the phone, leaving Emma in serious doubt as to what ''moving on'' actually entailed.

She didn't take him up on his offer of his recliner but fell asleep sitting up, only to be woken by the teeth-grinding whir of an electric drill. The front room of the club was still dark, but the open door to the kitchen let in light and noise. With her head pounding and her eyes aching, Emma stumbled to the doorway to see what was happening to her kitchen.

A new door leaned against the counter in front of the sink while a man wearing overalls and a denim cap stood on a step stool to install a new hinge at the top of the empty doorjamb. The screen door had been taken away, and the new door looked solid, impregnable. Jimmy was going for real security this time.

Emma left the workman to his job and drifted aimlessly into the main room again. The smart thing to do would be to call a cab and go home. She could sleep all afternoon, and all night, if she chose. After weeks of being up until 3:00 or 4:00 a.m., the prospect tempted her.

But she hadn't brought her purse. And she couldn't see asking Jimmy for the fare. Remembering his face as she'd seen it earlier, remembering how certain he was that Harlow had been involved with the break-in, Emma wouldn't add insult to injury by asking for money.

If Harlow and Ryan and Tommy had done this, that made her responsible, as well. She'd let the boys in, encouraged them to come back. ''Running tame,'' Jimmy had called it. Had she never brought them into the kitchen, The Indigo might not have been burglarized.

Except that Harlow didn't do this. Emma refused to accept the possibility. She'd made mistakes in judgment before—she'd thought Eric Jeffries cared about her, believed they had a future together. If she'd been the least bit wary, perhaps she could have saved her career, if not the relationship.

She wasn't wrong this time, though. What she knew about Harlow went beyond the facts of his life, his problems, just as what she knew about Jimmy Falcon was far more than the image he wanted to project. She trusted both of them implicitly. They would not let her down.

The front door creaked open, letting in a slash of morning light before Tiffany shut it out again and crossed to Emma.

"What a mess." Her fist hit the bar in a series of sharp thuds, and all the time she swore. "What a hell of a mess."

Emma had moved beyond anger hours ago. She sighed. "Jimmy says to leave everything as is until the insurance company has investigated. I hope that's soon. I'm getting drunk off the fumes."

"Where is he?"

"His office. The phone rings every time he tries to put it down."

Tiffany nodded. "He's got friends in this town. He doesn't have to handle stuff like this by himself, if he'd only let them help."

"He doesn't seem to want to depend on anyone." Emma squeezed her eyes shut. *Even me.* "Tiffany, would you lend me money for a cab? I left my wallet at home."

"Sure." The bartender drew a thick fold of bills out of her slacks pocket. "A ten enough?"

"Plenty." Taking the money, she leaned over to give the bartender a kiss on the cheek. "Thanks. If Jimmy asks, will you tell him I've gone home? If he…anybody needs me, I'll be glad to come back. But right now…''

"I understand. You go. I'll call later and let you know what's going on."

"Thank you." Emma made a quick call to the cab company from the phone behind the bar. Then, without a word to Jimmy, she eased the front door open and stepped outside into the midmorning sunlight. The opposite side of the street was still in shadow, so she crossed the street to wait for the cab there. Leaning back against the building, she let her eyelids droop, hoping she wouldn't have to wait too long.

"You're out bright and early."

Emma opened her eyes. Harlow stood beside her, one shoulder propped against the bricks. She straightened and turned to face him. "It's been a long night."

The smile in his eyes dimmed. "What's wrong?"

She nodded at the club across the street, draped with yellow police tape from corner to corner.

His face gave nothing away—his surprise looked completely genuine. "Is everybody okay?"

"More or less. There was a break-in."

"Damn. What'd they take?"

Searching his eyes, she could find no trace of guilt. "Everything in the safe. And they broke all of the bottles and glasses at the bar, plus the mirror."

"Mr. Falcon must be pissed off."

"Do you know anything about this?"

His eyebrows rose and his eyes went round. "Me? Not a thing. Oh." He nodded. "We're on the list, huh? Me and Ry and Tommy are probably at the top."

"That's not unreasonable."

"Of course not." Jerking away from the wall, he paced a furious circle. "Shit, I'm surprised we're not already arrested. Cops must be sleeping late this morning.''

His frustration scourged her, but not as much as Jimmy's. "*Did* you do this?"

Harlow stopped his pacing. "Hell, Emma, you think I'm gonna admit to a crime?"

"You could tell me you didn't, don't know anything about it."

"Why should you believe me?"

"Would you be here this morning if you knew what happened?"

"Hell, us cons like to see the results of our work. You know—the torch watches the building go up in smoke, just to be proud of himself. Knocking over a safe's the same. I get a rush out of seeing what I've done."

The hurt behind his words gave her hope. "I don't believe you're responsible. And I don't think Ryan or...or Tommy would have done it, either."

He slumped back against the wall and pulled out his cigarettes, took several long drags before he looked at her again. "I didn't do this, Emma. I'm pretty sure Ryan didn't. I don't know about Tommy, but I'd bet on him, too."

The cab rounded the corner two blocks away, heading toward them. "Then that's what I'll believe, Harlow." She put her hand on his shoulder. "And I'll find some way to make Mr. Falcon believe it, too."

The boy shook his head. "That'll take a miracle."

With a squeal of brakes, the taxi pulled into the curb. Emma tightened her grip. "Where—how can I get in touch with you? We need to talk."

Harlow shook his head. "I'll find you." Stepping back, he waved her away. "Go home. We'll talk later."

She opened the car door. "Soon, Harlow."

Finally he gave her that sweet smile. "Soon."

Before she got the door shut again, her friend Harlow had disappeared.

WITH THE NEW BACK DOOR installed, Jimmy put out a sign, Closed Until Further Notice, and firmly locked the front door. Then he turned to the business of cleaning up his club.

Tiffany had already started in on the glass. "I'll do this, boss. Why don't you go home and get some sleep?"

The idea of sleep brought images of Emma, warm and soft in his arms. He shook his head. "I want to get this taken care of first." Because once he walked out, he might not be back for a long time. If ever.

"Did Emma go home?" He should know the answer to that question, but she'd slipped away while he dealt with all the paperwork on the stolen contents of the safe. His insurance company was not happy to hear about a museum-quality artifact going missing.

"Yeah. She was beat." Another dustpan of glass clattered into the garbage can. "So who do you think did this?"

"The Three Musketeers."

Tiffany stopped and stared at him. "You think Harlow and crew broke in?"

"Makes sense to me. Two grand buys a lot of dope."

She shook her head. "I don't know, boss. Harlow doesn't strike me as the type—"

Jimmy muttered a rude word. "And just what would 'the type' be?"

"Whoa." She took a step back, her hands held up for protection. "Sorry I said anything."

He thought about apologizing. He didn't mean to snap at Tiffany or anyone else. This wasn't her fault or Emma's. Hell, maybe it wasn't even Harlow's fault. Maybe some total stranger had trashed The Indigo after all, just for the hell of it.

But damn, he was fed up. Just when things had started

looking good, just when he'd begun to think there might be something—someone—in his future besides a string of empty days and nights, reality stepped in one more time to knock him flat. He thought back to the night Emma had arrived. Hell…maybe the disk *was* cursed.

"Go home, Tiff." He took her broom away. "This is my job. I'll give you a call when I know what's going on."

She looked back at him for a minute. "You don't have to do this alone, Jimmy. I want to help. So does Emma."

"I appreciate that. But for now, I need to do some thinking by myself. No offense meant."

"None taken." To his surprise, she put her arms around his shoulders and gave him a hug. "We'll get our feet back under us, boss. Just give things a day or two to settle."

"Sure." He patted her back, gave her a smile he didn't feel. "Enjoy the time off."

Her face changed, but the expression was gone so quickly he wasn't sure what he'd seen. "I'll do that. Take care of yourself."

"Yeah, sure." He unlocked the door for her, watched her walk to her car and lifted a hand as she drove past.

Then he locked the door again, leaned his broom against the bar and went to the storeroom for an unbroken bottle of whiskey.

HARLOW FOUND Ryan and Tommy at the same fast-food place he'd had coffee with Emma. Each of the guys had two burgers and fries and a milk shake. He sat down beside Ryan on the bench.

"Somebody win the lottery?"

"Hey, Harlow. Have some fries. Want a burger? I've already had two." Ryan pushed a sandwich his way.

"Yeah, thanks." Harlow took a bite and stared at Tommy while he chewed. "Where'd the cash come from?"

Tommy shrugged. "I did a job for Eddy Santos. He pays good."

"What kind of job?"

"What's with the questions?" He paddled the edge of the table with his fingers, like a drum. "What difference does it make? We got some cash for a change. I don't see you bringing in much except for Lady Emma's chicken salad."

"Hey, guys, chill. Don't spoil a good day." Ryan glanced from Harlow to Tommy and back again, his eyes bright, his face flushed. He looked almost healthy. "How about going to a movie this afternoon? Have we got enough for a movie, Tommy?"

"We got enough for a freakin' week's worth of movies."

Harlow put down the unfinished burger. "Falcon's club got broke into last night."

Tommy swallowed a gulp of milk shake. "Sucks for him."

"Did you do it?"

"Nope." Another gulp.

"Ry? You know something about this?"

Ryan was too far gone to be able to lie. He shrugged. "Not me, Harlow. Tommy and me hung out at Eddy's last night. Woke up about noon, came down here for breakfast."

Dead end. Harlow hadn't expected anything else. "If you guys hear something on the street about this job, let me know."

"You a cop now, man?" Tommy leaned back in his chair, arms crossed over his chest. "Is Falcon offering a reward?"

"Here's a question for you, Tommy. Who do you suppose is at the top of Falcon's shit list? Clue number one— it ain't Tiffany. Or Dumb Darren. Or Emma."

"They can't prove it, 'cause we didn't do it."

"With our records, they probably don't need proof. Falcon'll grab any excuse he can find to get us locked up."

"You worry too much." Tommy got to his feet. "Santos has got enough cops in his pocket to keep that from happening. At least for me and Ry." He lifted one eyebrow. "If you come to work for him, you can say the same."

Ryan pulled the used wrappers, boxes and cups onto a tray. "It's not so bad, Harlow. You can make a lot of money real quick."

"Yeah, Ry. I know. I've been paying Santos and his dealers for a while now, remember?" He got to his feet, feeling in his pockets for a cigarette, feeling his brain start to crumble inside his head. Convenient, one-stop shopping—he could buy a hit from his friends.

No way. "I'm outta here."

"Wait, Harlow!" Ryan caught up with him on the sidewalk. "Come to the movies with us. The new Stallone flick is out this week."

"Don't think so, Ry."

"But we never hang together anymore. You and Tommy are always fighting, and then you walk away pissed."

Harlow pulled his broken thoughts together. "Ryan, I don't like the direction Tommy's going in. And I don't like him taking you along. I'd be glad to have you on my side, but I'm not moving to his. Why don't you come with me this afternoon? We can find something to do."

Ryan looked over to where Tommy stood waiting. He took a step backward, then another. "I told Eddy I'd be back. He gets kinda mad when you don't do what you say you will, you know?"

"I know. Go on. I'll hunt you down later."

Tommy sent Harlow a salute before rounding the corner, with Ryan close behind.

Harlow took off in the opposite direction, hoping he

could find a supplier before the worms crawling under his skin found their way out.

AT THE END of a long, ugly day, Jimmy stepped into his apartment, which smelled like baking bread and roast beef. "Emma?"

She came out of the kitchen, close enough for him to touch. "My turn to surprise you. I thought you might need some food. Have you eaten anything today?"

"Not that I remember." He pulled her into his arms, rubbed his cheek against her soft hair. God, he was tired. Tired of working, even more tired of thinking. What he wouldn't give to simply shut down his brain.

"On a liquid diet, are you?" She drew back to stare into his face. "You smell like whiskey."

"I spent the day mopping it up."

Emma brushed her mouth across his. "You taste of whiskey, too."

"Don't you like whiskey?" He brought her face back to his, took them into the kind of kiss he'd dreamed about when Emma first came back, a kiss that rocked the foundations of the world. A kiss that blocked all thought.

"Jimmy." She pushed at his chest, pulled her head back. "You need a shower and some food."

His world-rocking kiss hadn't done much for her, he guessed. "Come with me." Two bare bodies under a nice warm spray...

She tugged against his hold. "No. I'm going to finish cooking. You get cleaned up. Now."

Jimmy could always tell when he'd lost the battle. "Yes, ma'am." Leaving his clothes on the bedroom floor a few minutes later, he stepped into a shower as cold as he could stand.

By the time he'd washed and dried off, he was awake again and more sober. He picked up his dirty clothes—he'd worn his dress shirt and slacks for most of the past twenty-four hours—and rolled them into a ball, then threw them in the bottom of the closet. He doubted he'd need them again.

His life was about to become very simple.

Wearing jeans and a T-shirt, he went back to the kitchen. Emma didn't hear his bare feet on the carpet, and he found her staring into space, stirring a pan of gravy.

"Penny for your thoughts."

She jumped. "Oh...they aren't worth even that." Her smile was sweet and more than a little nervous.

"I'm glad to hear it, because I don't know if *I'm* worth even a penny anymore." A pretty weak joke.

And Emma didn't get it. She frowned and shook her head. "Dinner is ready. Sit down and I'll bring you a plate."

He did as he was told and was rewarded with a mountain of food—meat and mashed potatoes and squash and rolls. "Trying to fatten me up?"

"You could use it." Emma sat down across from him, her own plate considerably less burdened.

"You're not eating much." Besides being something to talk about that didn't involve the club, it was true. Emma always seemed to be paring down what she ate.

"I don't need to fatten up. Exactly the opposite."

"Meaning?" His tone was harsher than he'd intended, but he couldn't call it back.

"I'd like to reduce a bit, is all. I've let myself take comfort in food too often this last year or so."

"Food *is* comfort." He took a bite of mashed potatoes. "So why not enjoy it?"

She stared at him, her forehead wrinkled. "Why are you arguing with me about this?"

He gave the question due consideration through another

sample of the potatoes. "Because you're dissatisfied with yourself. And there's no reason on earth you should be."

"I'm too heavy." She said it as if pronouncing a death sentence.

"For gymnastics, yeah. But do you want to be a gymnast?"

Emma gave a choke of laughter. "Be serious."

"I am. You're soft. You're smooth. You're comfortable and generous and warm. Those are gifts, not flaws."

"Oh, Jimmy." Her cheeks flushed. "You're such a good man."

"Just observant."

She shook her head. "No. Most men want women to conform to a particular image. And when they don't...well, things don't go very well."

"I take it you learned this from personal experience."

"Enough to realize I don't fit the mold."

"Why should you?" Before she could answer, he was pulling her out of her chair. "Why would any man want a woman who fits a plastic mold?" With a single motion, he lifted her T-shirt up and over her head. She wore nothing underneath. "How could any man want more—or less, dammit—than this?"

He sat on the sofa and pulled her into his lap, then reignited that seismic kiss. This time Emma was in it with him all the way. He filled his hands with her, filled his brain and body and soul with her, until there was no room left for thought, for despair, for regret. Only Emma.

When at last they broke apart, Emma needed a long time to recover her breath. Jimmy had taken her so far, whirled her through so much, she was not sure she would ever breathe normally again. Such passion. Such desire—for her, of all people! She might truly begin to believe she *was* beautiful.

But she was definitely too heavy to continue sitting on

his lap. Despite his protest, she moved to his side on the sofa, then turned so that she faced him, and they could hold each other close.

"You're wonderful," she whispered against his jaw, and felt him smile.

"Just trying to do my best, ma'am." After a moment, his smile faded. Little by little, she could feel the ease in his muscles give way to tension. She didn't need to be psychic to know where his thoughts had gone.

"You'll get over this, Jimmy. It's only a matter of time." He didn't reply, which surprised her. "A few days to air the place out—not that the customers would mind the smell of spirits—a new mirror and some new stock, and you can reopen. I'm sure you'll have a great crowd to celebrate."

He took a deep breath and put his head back against the cushion. "I don't know."

"Of course you do. Anyone in Denver who likes jazz has been to The Indigo. And they'll all want to be there for the reopening."

"If there is one."

Her heart stopped. "What do you mean?"

Jimmy got to his feet then, pulled on his jeans and T-shirt. Emma dressed, as well, her mind scampering after his words like a rabbit. "What do you mean, *if?*"

He sat at the table again, lifted a fork of potatoes, then set it down. Propping his head on one hand, he rotated the fork several times.

"Jimmy?" Emma clasped the back of her chair, barely keeping herself from screaming.

But he must have heard the frustration in her voice. "Sorry. I guess I don't want to say it out loud." He looked up at her with a slight smile and shrugged. "But I'm thinking about leaving The Indigo closed. For good."

CHAPTER THIRTEEN

EMMA SAT DOWN at the table and pushed her plate, now cold, away. "Why would you close the club permanently?"

Wishing he'd kept his mouth shut, Jimmy continued to play with his potatoes. "Seems like this might be the right time for moving on."

"To what?"

Good question. He shrugged. "Whatever's next."

"I could shake you until your teeth rattled."

His surprised gaze met her furious glare. "Why?"

"Because you're not talking. Not explaining. Not even excusing. Do you think you're some sort of Lone Ranger, above justifying your actions to the rest of us?"

"No." He got to his feet and carried his plate into the kitchen. "I do own the place, though. It's my decision."

She followed him and handed over her plate to be scraped and put in the dishwasher. "Your decisions affect other people. Shouldn't you consider their situations before you come to a conclusion?"

They worked together, putting away the leftovers, washing up the pots and pans, wiping the counter. When they left the kitchen, Jimmy turned off the light. He hadn't answered her question. Because she was right.

Emma sat down on the sofa. "Tiffany needs her job, Jimmy. She can't depend on Brad for a steady income. Darren can't stay in school without making money. What will they do if you close the club?"

"There are plenty of bartenders' jobs in Denver." Sitting

beside her would only distract him. Sitting in a different chair would deliver a message he wasn't ready for. So he walked to the window and stared at his reflection in the glass. "Darren can wait tables in any restaurant in town. I'm not essential to their survival."

"They're your friends. What are you going to do without them?"

He didn't have an answer for that, either. "I'll get by."

"Is that all you want to do? Get by?"

The phone rang, granting him a reprieve. "Jimmy, this is Spencer. We rounded up those three kids—Harlow, Ryan and Tomas. I thought you might want to be here when we question them."

"Thanks. I'll come right down."

Emma was waiting when he turned around. "The police have someone in custody?"

There was no way to avoid this. "Harlow and his crowd."

She stood up, her face suddenly pale, her eyes fierce. "They've been arrested?"

"No. Spencer has brought them in for questioning."

"And you want to be there."

He dug his hands into his pockets. "Yeah."

"Then let's go." She took her purse off the coatrack and started ahead of him to the front door.

"Emma…"

She stopped but didn't turn. "Yes?"

Jimmy closed the distance between them, put his hands on her shoulders and pulled her back against him. "You don't want to see this."

"No." For just a second, she melted into his hold. Then pulled away. "But I have to."

AT THE POLICE STATION, Emma watched a television screen that peered, via video camera, into a small, featureless room containing a table and straight chairs. Harlow sat at the narrow end of the table, an ankle propped on the opposite knee, his hands fidgeting with a coin. Tomas stood leaning back into the corner, arms crossed over his chest. Ryan had his head down on the table—Emma wondered if he'd fallen asleep.

The door at the end of the room opposite Harlow opened to admit Detective Spencer and Jimmy, followed by a thin, balding man in a suit. None of the boys moved.

"I thought Mr. Falcon here might be interested in what you three have to say." The detective pulled out the chair nearest Harlow and sat down, his notepad and pencil ready. "Since it is his club and all. This is Mr. Ashley from the Public Defender's office." He nodded toward the balding man. "He's here to guarantee you punks your rights."

Harlow looked Mr. Ashley over. "Impressive." Emma had never seen him sneer before, and she didn't like it.

Neither did Ashley. "Look, you—"

Tomas leaned over the attorney's shoulder. "You got something to say, freak?"

Hunching his shoulders, Ashley said nothing at all.

Jimmy sat down at the other end of the table, across from Harlow. "I saw you guys around the corner from The Indigo about seven-fifteen last night. Before the break-in."

Tomas shifted his weight. "And that makes us guilty?"

"It makes an alibi necessary," Spencer said. He looked at Ryan, who hadn't moved or made a sound, then at Harlow. "Is he okay?"

"He didn't get much sleep yesterday." The warmth Emma had always heard in Harlow's voice had completely vanished. "I guess he's catching up."

Jimmy folded his hands together on top of the table. "What was he doing, instead of sleeping?"

Harlow shrugged. "Don't ask me."

"What were you doing last night?"

"Hanging out."

"Where?"

"Different places. I got a lot of friends, you know?"

Detective Spencer looked at Tommy. "Where were you last night?"

"Can't remember, man. I got this knock on the head when I was little, so I have a hard time with dates and names."

The detective narrowed his eyes and glanced at Jimmy. Then he stood up and leaned across the table to shake Ryan's shoulder. "Wake up, kid. Come on, get your eyes open."

Emma gripped her hands together under her chin. Did he have to be so rough? Shouldn't the attorney say something?

Ryan stirred and looked up, bleary-eyed. "Wha'?" Ashley didn't make a move.

Spencer shook him again. "Where were you last night?"

The boy propped his head in his hands. "Dunno."

Tomas snickered. Jimmy stared at him until the grin dropped off his face.

Harlow sat up and shook Ryan's arm. "Get it together, Ry. We're being officially interrogated, y'know. We're supposed to cooperate."

"If you three can't prove where you were last night, we can detain you for a couple of days until we find out." Jimmy's voice was low, as cold as permafrost. "How many times a day do you need the dope, Harlow? What about your friend, here? How's he gonna feel, twenty-four hours into cold-turkey withdrawal?"

Emma closed her eyes against tears.

"I don't know what you're talking about, Mr. Falcon."

"We're not after you for possession and use," Detective Spencer added. "And we'll let you go just as soon as we're sure you didn't have anything to do with the break-in."

"What does it take for you to be sure?"

"Not much." Spencer leaned back in his chair. "Just somebody I trust who'll tell me you were with them when the lock on The Indigo's back door got blown off."

"That's all, huh?" Harlow scratched his head. "I'd be glad to oblige, but I'm pretty sure I don't know anybody you would trust."

"Okay. We'll play it your way." The detective stepped to the door and called in two uniformed officers. "Take these guys to detention. We'll talk to them tomorrow morning."

One of the policemen started waking Ryan again. The other grabbed Harlow's upper arm and lifted him out of the chair. With his free hand, the man shoved Tomas in the shoulder. "Let's go."

Tomas jerked away. "Leave me alone, pig."

Using a foul name, the officer shoved again. Tomas turned on him, and in an instant the policeman had his back to the wall as the boy pressed a beefy forearm over his throat. Mr. Ashley ran to the door and fled the room.

"Get off, Tommy." Harlow grabbed at his friend's arm and pulled, but made no impression. Tomas outweighed him by thirty pounds at least. Three other uniformed officers came into the room.

"Out of the way." Spencer pushed Harlow back and tackled Tomas himself. "Back off, punk. We can do this the hard way, but you'll be sorry."

Tomas snarled, then jerked himself away from the policeman. Spencer immediately pushed the boy face forward against the wall, drew his arms behind him and snapped on wrist restraints. "We'll see if these help you keep your temper."

Jimmy hadn't moved from his chair at the end of the table. He watched in silence as the three boys were marched out by a cadre of five big men. When the room was empty, he propped his elbows on the table and rubbed his eyes with the heels of his hands.

Emma turned away from the television screen, wiping her wet cheeks. She wondered if they would let her talk to Harlow for a few minutes. She didn't have to wonder what Jimmy would say if she asked.

The door to the observation room opened and Jimmy stepped in. He looked completely drained. "Would you like me to take you home now?"

"Is that the end? What will happen next?"

"Spencer's planning to talk to them individually later tonight."

"You'll be there, as well? And that very effective attorney?"

He nodded. The air vibrated with his resistance to her next question. Jimmy wanted her to go home. He did not want her here the next time they questioned Harlow.

"Could I talk to Harlow first?"

"Jeez, Emma, you don't ask much."

"They haven't been officially arrested, have they?"

Jimmy stared at her, his eyes bleak. "Whose side are you on here?"

"I want the truth. I'm assuming you do, too—and not simply a scapegoat."

His mouth thinned. "I think that answers my question. I'll see if I can get you in to see Harlow." He left the room, closing the door firmly behind him.

In about fifteen minutes, a policeman she didn't know looked in. "Miss Garrett? The detective said you wanted to talk with Harlow. We're bringing him in to the interrogation room right now."

She followed him and sat at the same table she'd seen through the video camera. The room looked even less appealing in reality than it had on television. And it smelled of sweat. Of fear.

The door behind her opened, and Harlow entered. He stopped just over the threshold, and the officer behind him pushed him forward. Wide-eyed, Harlow sat in the chair to her left.

"What the hell are you doing here? This is no place for you."

She put her hand over his on the table. "I was at Mr. Falcon's when they called him down. I...had to come."

He dropped his head back and closed his eyes. "You should have stayed away. There's nothing you can do."

"The detective and..." She began again. "The detective wants you to admit to the break-in."

Harlow gave her his angel's smile. "Sure he does. That'd make his job real easy."

"But you didn't do it."

His blue gaze fixed on her face. "I'm glad you think so. But you're not gonna convince him. You need to get out of here and let us take care of ourselves. We're used to that."

"Can't I help in some way?"

"Well..." He glanced at the policeman who had stayed in the room, then leaned closer. "Ry's gonna freak out pretty soon without a hit. Is there somebody you know who could get him transferred to a hospital? We might get him into rehab faster that way."

"Time's up." The guard stepped forward. "Come on."

"I'll try," Emma promised Harlow with a quick squeeze of his fingers. "As soon as possible."

He grinned. "Thanks. I—" The police officer jerked his arm. And Harlow disappeared again.

When she stepped out of the room, Jimmy waited, leaning against the opposite wall. "I can take you home. Or..." He hesitated, watching her with unreadable eyes. "Or I can call you a cab."

"Let me get a cab." His face hardened, his eyes shuttered. Emma shook her head. "Not because I don't want to be with you. But why should you drive me home and then drive back again? You're exhausted. Find somewhere to sit and have a cup of coffee." She smiled at him, tentatively. "And call me when you're finished?"

He shut his eyes for a moment, and his grin reappeared. "Sure." With an arm around her shoulders, he walked her to the lobby of the building and waited until a cab arrived. After dropping a kiss on her hair, he helped her into the back and shut the door.

But though she immediately twisted in her seat to wave out the rear windshield, Jimmy had already gone back inside.

RYAN TOOK one of the two cots in the cell and went to sleep again. Harlow sat down on the other and put his head in his hands.

Tommy sat next to him. "This sucks."

"Yeah." His head hurt, and the burritos they'd pigged out on for dinner had done a number on his stomach. "Did you hit Falcon's place, Tommy? Is that where the cash came from?"

"I told you—Eddy Santos pays me. He'll pay you, too. He figures people trust you to sell the good stuff."

"And I told you I'm not juggling for Santos or anybody else."

"So I'll sell the dope. You just bring me the buyers."

Harlow greeted that idea with a vulgar suggestion of his own.

The mattress bounced as Tommy dropped back to lie across the bed, with his head propped on the concrete wall. "You think it makes you some kind of hero, that you buy but don't sell?"

"Selling is bad news, Tommy. They can put you away for years."

"They gotta catch you first. And when they catch you, they gotta prove it. Santos don't let that shit happen to his runners."

"Santos will get caught one day."

Tommy just laughed.

Down the hallway, a door opened with a clang. Footsteps came nearer and the jingle of keys. A cop they hadn't seen before unlocked the cell.

"Wake the kid up," he said. "They want to talk to him."

DAWN HAD COME and gone by the time Jimmy left the station. His hip burned, his shoulders ached, his eyes barely focused.

Thanks to Ashley and the PD's office, Harlow, Tomas and Ryan had been back on the street for several hours.

He couldn't blame Spencer—there wasn't enough evidence to hold them, let alone charge them with a crime. There had been other people hanging around the club that evening, besides the boys. Any one of them could be as easily connected to the break-in. The problem with being a cop—ex-cop—was that you had to uphold all the laws, including the ones that put punks back on the street.

Even when you were convinced they were guilty.

He'd almost reached Emma's place before he realized where he'd gone. *Homing instinct,* he thought with a near smile.

But there were as many problems here as anywhere else. So far they'd managed to skirt the issue of Emma's involvement with Harlow, her belief in the boys' innocence, her certainty that they could be saved. In the same way she tried to rescue them, despite knowing their habits, Jimmy realized she accepted *him* while disagreeing with his fundamental principles. His beliefs.

He thought that over as he parked the Jag. He'd never

considered the possibility that he, too, was one of Emma's charity cases. That she might be trying to redeem him in some way. That she felt sorry for him for reasons other than his physical handicap.

His fingers found the key again to start the engine and drive away. He was nobody's charity case, least of all Emma's.

Exhaustion overwhelmed his indignation. The idea of shedding his clothes and crawling into Emma's bed for a few hours of sleep lured him out of the car and into the elevator, down the hall to her door.

She didn't answer his knock.

After an empty minute and another rap on the panel, he fished keys out of his pocket and let himself in. The front rooms were dim, shadowed, shut away from morning light. No aroma of coffee or tea greeted him, only that sweet gardenia scent she used. If Emma was here, she must still be asleep.

She lay on her side facing the door, one bare shoulder peeking out from beneath the covers that she'd barely disturbed. Her hair was wild on the pillow, the only spot of color in the darkened room. With a sigh, Jimmy pulled off his T-shirt and jeans, then sat as gently as he could on the far side of the bed. Easing in behind her, he smiled when Emma stirred and nestled back against him, one hand resting over his at her waist.

He'd never had much hope of heaven, but this would be close. Letting go of everything except how much he loved the woman in his arms, Jimmy shut his eyes and slept.

EMMA AWOKE with a sense of well-being, which she quickly attributed to the man who held her close. She remembered his kisses at the curve between her shoulder and neck, and then his complete surrender to sleep. His legs behind hers, the warmth of his chest at her back, whetted to a fine point the longing she now carried with her all the time. She never felt so whole as when she and Jimmy were one.

But whereas she'd slept for seven hours, he'd only been here for two. Love decreed that she let him rest. There would be time for lovemaking later.

Pulling on jeans and a T-shirt, she made a pot of coffee and some toast, spread generously with butter and raspberry jam. She hadn't eaten last night; she could afford the indulgence, she decided.

Now awake and fed, she allowed herself to think about Harlow and Ryan and Tomas. Had they spent the night in jail? Were they still there? Was there some way she could find out without waking Jimmy?

And how would she keep her promise to help Ryan find a rehabilitation program?

She was thumbing through the Denver telephone listings, taking note of the numerous facilities for the treatment of drug and alcohol abuse, when Jimmy appeared in the doorway.

"Good morning." His waking voice was husky, warm. He'd put his clothes on, including his boots.

Emma smiled. "Make that afternoon. Almost two o'clock, actually."

He rubbed his eyes with the fingers of one hand. "I could sleep for another twelve hours."

"Perhaps you should."

Shaking his head, he dropped his hand. "No. But what are the chances of getting some coffee?"

"It's waiting for you." She brought the cup to the dining table.

He picked it up and took a deep draft. She hadn't thought to close the telephone directory, and Jimmy pulled it close as he took a chair. He looked up, frowning. "Do you seriously believe you can get these guys into a program?"

"I think Harlow and I can persuade Ryan. He's at the

most risk. Since he's in police custody, it ought to be relatively simple…'' Jimmy was shaking his head. ''What?''

''Harlow and friends were released early this morning. There wasn't enough evidence to hold them.''

Emma quelled a surge of gladness. ''That was hard for Detective Spencer, and for you, I'm sure.''

He shrugged. ''The law's the law. Spencer will just have to work harder.''

''There must be ways to trace who bought the explosive. And we'll be searching for the medallion, won't we? We can't just let it disappear. Finding out who sold it would help, wouldn't it?''

''You watch too many cop shows.'' But he gave a faint grin. ''But, yeah, we'll definitely put out tracers on the medallion. And Spencer will look into the rest of it. Next time we'll have a solid cause for arrest.''

''Next time?'' His meaning gradually dawned on her. ''You mean, the next time you arrest those boys?''

Jimmy avoided her gaze. ''Or somebody. Tilden, maybe.''

''No, you meant Harlow and Ryan and Tomas.''

''Okay. Yeah, I meant Harlow and company.''

''Why can't you believe they didn't do this?''

''Why can't you believe they did? Are you so invested in the idea of saving them that you can't accept reality? You can't stand to fail?''

Emma got to her feet. ''My…my efforts to help them don't bear any relation to whether or not they are guilty of breaking into your club.''

Jimmy took another long swallow of coffee. ''I don't think you're seeing the situation clearly.''

''Perhaps neither of us sees the situation clearly.''

He looked up, held her gaze with dark and somehow distant eyes. ''I suppose we can work on that premise, till we know better, anyway.''

That hardly constituted a truce. But Emma chose to believe the best. She closed the telephone directory and returned it to the kitchen cabinet. "You know, I've been thinking." She poured herself more coffee then sat across the table from Jimmy.

"About what?"

"About The Indigo. This is another problem that could turn out to be a blessing in disguise."

Jimmy leaned back in his chair. "How so?"

"You'll be doing repairs as it is, correct?"

"Maybe."

She ignored the equivocation. "This would be the perfect moment to implement some exciting changes."

"Changes?"

"Oh, yes." Emma allowed her enthusiasm free rein. "From the very first time I walked in, I've been considering the sorts of renovation that could truly benefit you and the club and the customers."

"Such as?"

"New tables and seating, of course. New paint and artwork on the walls—posters, perhaps, framed in white—or primary colors, with an art deco feel to them. Or even authentic showbills for famous jazz artists. I'm sure there's a source for those sorts of things."

"Probably."

"We could get the bar refinished—it'd be beautiful, if only the scratches and stains were gone. I don't suppose carpet would be a reasonable investment, since people are always spilling drinks."

"Carpet changes the acoustics and the sound of the music."

"Well, the music does matter most." She smiled at him. "I haven't forgotten the most important point."

"Actually, Emma, I think you have." Jimmy stood up and took his mug into the kitchen. He saw disaster looming straight ahead, but couldn't figure out how to avoid it.

When he came back to the table, Emma's face was troubled. "What is it? What have I forgotten?"

"The Indigo Club is mine." He forced his voice to stay level. "And I've told you before, if I wanted to make changes, I would."

She rose from her chair, meeting him eye to eye. "I know that."

"So why bring this stuff up again?"

"Since you'll be having workmen in, anyway—"

"I also told you I was thinking of leaving the place closed."

"But you can't really mean that! You've made such a success out of The Indigo."

Like the crack of a whip, his restraint snapped. "How in hell do you know what I do or don't mean?"

"I...I thought we were friends." Her face flushed rose, then paled. "I thought we understood one another."

"I understand you." He stalked halfway across the room, then turned to look at her again. "I understand your enthusiasm and your energy and how easy you get carried away when an idea catches your interest."

She stiffened. "You make me sound like a child."

"You have a child's approach to life. For you, there's always another chance to ride the bike, to hit the ball, to make the grade."

"That's hardly true. I was quite...lost when I came to bring you the medallion. I had no idea where to turn."

Jimmy laughed, though the situation was far from funny. "Until you saw my club. That's been your official project ever since. My club...and me."

Emma's gaze hardened to steel blue. "I have never thought of you as a project."

Frustration welled up inside him, forced its way out. "You want to change the way I do business. You want me to acknowledge my Indian roots. You've involved me in a no-win situation over kids I failed with in the past, and you expect me to keep sticking my head out so they can kick me in the teeth.''

''That was not my intention.''

''Of course not, Emma. But facts count, not intentions. And the fact is, you set out from the very beginning to turn my life upside down. Hell—'' Jimmy shook his head ''—your dad can take some of the credit, too. He knew what would happen if he brought us together again.''

''You're ascribing motives to someone who can't defend himself.''

''What defense does he need? The problem is, he didn't predict how Harlow and friends would screw up the whole scheme. And he didn't understand something important about me.''

She crossed her arms over her breasts. ''What is that?''

''I gave up on happy-ever-after a long, long time ago. Then I figured out the sure way to avoid disappointment in this life.''

''Which is?''

Hands in his pockets, Jimmy said flatly, ''Don't hope, don't expect, don't plan.''

''That's hardly a real life.''

He ignored her comment. ''And I don't want anybody doing it for me. Not Tiffany, not Darren. Not Harmon. Not even you.''

Emma stared at the man across the room. Afternoon light through the window turned his skin to copper, struck sparks of silver in his hair. He was beautiful. But completely alone.

She lifted her chin, took a deep breath. ''The logical extension of that argument negates the possibility of relationships. Particularly if the other person has hope and believes in the value of change and making plans.''

''You're the professor—I don't know much about 'logical extensions.' But yeah, dealing with people on anything more than a surface level complicates life too much. I like to keep it simple.''

"That means everything between us...has been on the surface?"

He turned to the window again. "More or less."

"Look at me when you say that, Jimmy."

His gaze came back to hers. "Yes."

"This is just sex? A little slap and tickle between old acquaintances?"

There was a pause. And then he said, "Yes."

"And the things you've said to me, about my...my personality, my body, were a means to an end. A method of seduction, or manipulation. Not truth."

"Wait a minute, Emma. I—"

She stopped him with a raised hand, hoping he couldn't see how she trembled. "Too late. I have been betrayed and bereaved. I have seen the structure of my life dismantled by a man who pretended to care for me. I recognize defeat, and I accept it. But I don't have to embrace it as a way of life. I want you to leave."

He didn't move immediately.

Emma tightened every muscle in her body. "I will not be seduced or manipulated. I would much rather live with truth, no matter how bitter, and the possibility of change, than sweet, destructive lies. Get out, Jimmy. Do whatever the hell you please with your life and your club. I no longer work for you, and I no longer care one way or the other."

Still, he stayed motionless. The light had shifted past the window, leaving his face in shadow.

Choking on cold anguish, Emma strode to the door and jerked it open. "Go. Vamoose. Split. I don't have room in my life for a man who's going nowhere."

His boot heels beat an uneven tempo against the wooden floor as he approached. He stopped just in front of her. "Yeah," Jimmy said, "that's pretty much what I thought."

Then he took hold of the doorknob and shut himself out into the hall.

CHAPTER FOURTEEN

JIMMY STEPPED into the main room of the club, flipped on a light and then locked the door behind him. The place still reeked of alcohol. He surveyed the room—the beat-up chairs, the worn tables with cigarette burns and drink rings on the tops, the scratched and scuffed wood of the bar. Emma was right. The place was a wreck.

No surprise. It was, in fact, the point—what you see is what you get. He'd tried to tell her, to show her, that the theory applied to The Indigo and to him. She'd refused to believe.

He wished he could pretend that he'd staged tonight's fiasco for Emma's own good, that he was heroic enough to let her go because it was best for her. But he'd sworn off illusions years ago. His reaction to her plans had been pure defensive instinct. She wanted change. He couldn't face the prospect of trying—and failing—one more time. With The Indigo...or with Emma.

He hadn't seen the trap, though, until he'd stepped into it. He never meant to let her believe he'd lied about how he saw her, how he felt. Only when it was too late had he seen that in protecting himself, he was destroying what she'd just begun to build—her belief in her own worth.

Which was proof, if he needed any, that making changes only created pain. He and Tiffany and Darren would have gone on just as they were if Emma hadn't appeared out of nowhere. She wouldn't be hurting, and neither would anyone else.

Being right did not, Jimmy realized yet again, mean feeling good.

EMMA CALLED Tiffany the next morning. "I wanted to let you know that I…won't be back to work."

"Ever?"

"Yes. I quit."

"Look, Jimmy's probably being a real pain about this—he cares about the club a lot more than he likes to think or let people know. If you could cut him some slack…"

Emma's laugh came perilously close to a sob. "He has one or the other of us completely fooled. But he made it very clear that he doesn't want…me as part of his life. In any way."

"That's not like Jimmy. He's a pro when it comes to the easy letdown. All his women tend to stay friends, drop by occasionally for a drink, that kind of thing."

"Perhaps." There wasn't a word to describe this pain, Emma decided. She felt as if she would break in half. "He might have intended to end this the same way, but I pushed him too far."

"Or maybe," Tiffany said gently, "he cares so much more this time that he couldn't keep up the image."

Emma was having difficulty breathing. The air didn't seem to reach her lungs. "Be that as it may, I'll be staying around for a time to try to do something for Harlow and Ryan. If you need me, please phone."

"Sure, Emma." A door on the other end of the line slammed, and Brad's voice called for Tiffany. "I gotta go."

"Tiffany?"

"Yeah?" But only a portion of her attention remained with Emma.

"Try to look after Jimmy."

"I will. See you."

Before Emma could say goodbye, the line went dead.

She sat looking at the receiver in her hand. Jimmy was gone, which meant losing Tiffany and Darren, as well. What excuse did she have now to see them?

And the medallion was gone. She'd resolutely refused to think about that, putting off the moment when she acknowledged that a vital link to her father was lost. There were other reminders of him back in England—his favorite books, a worn sweater that smelled just like him, a few pieces of furniture that he and her mother had used together. Once back home, she could connect with them both.

The disk, however, had meant something more. Not just her dad, and not just Jimmy, but a sort of melding of the two with her memories of that summer, the happiest she'd ever known. Losing the medallion was like losing that part of her personal history.

Which was ridiculous, Emma told herself, putting down the phone and wiping her eyes. She was no worse off than she'd been before arriving in Denver. The medallion would have stayed with Jimmy anyway, when she went back to England.

If she'd gone back. After these last weeks, loving him, sharing his bed, she'd begun to think…to hope…

Shaking her head, she refused to revisit what she'd hoped. All of it was now in the past. Time to move forward with her life, to deal with problems she had some chance of solving.

Those, with luck, included Harlow and Ryan. She waited until the afternoon to contact Zach Harmon, in case he slept late the morning after his night shift.

"Emma, it's good to talk to you. What's going on?"

"I wanted to ask for your help, or at least advice."

"Shoot."

"How can I go about admitting someone to a rehabilitation program? And do you have any idea which of the many in this city would be suitable?"

"Suitable for who?"

"A homeless teenage boy addicted to heroin."

Zach whistled long and low. "Where are his parents?"

"I haven't any notion."

"Is this his idea?"

"No. A friend and I want to help him before...before he kills himself with the drug."

"That puts a lot of limitations on your options. No-cost programs are crowded, and not often residential. I don't know if he's a candidate for methadone treatment if he's a minor. Methadone isn't cheap. There's no easy fix for this one, Emma."

"I know. But I have to try."

"Okay. Let me check with some people around town, see what I can dig up. I'll get back to you in the next day or so."

"That would be wonderful. How are Shelley and the children?"

"Right now all three of them are taking a nap. Shelley's got Norah in one arm, Alex is curled under her other arm still holding a book, and Mom's as sound asleep as the kids. Cute picture, on which I've spent an entire roll of film in the last half hour."

"I'd love to see it sometime." Not that the possibility was at all likely. If she wasn't seeing Jimmy, wasn't working at The Indigo, she wasn't likely to run into Zach Harmon.

"I talked with our friend Falcon last night."

Emma held her breath, wondering if Jimmy had said something about her.

"He's taking the break-in harder than I would have expected. It's not like this hasn't happened before."

She swallowed her disappointment. "He's had other robberies?"

"A couple over the years. Not quite so much damage,

maybe, but crime is pretty much a given in that part of town.''

"I…I hope he'll recover eventually. It seems a shame that he would close down because of this.''

Zach was silent a moment. "Close down?''

"Didn't he mention that?'' She would have thought he would tell his best friend.

"No, he didn't, the jerk.'' A burst of anger came across the line. "I think I'll get back in touch with the man. In the very near future.''

That sounded promising. "Thank you, Zach. For being Jimmy's friend…and for looking into the rehabilitation prospects for me.''

"Emma, I apologize if I'm butting in, but…did something bad happen between you and Jimmy?''

There didn't seem to be an easy answer. "We aren't seeing each other anymore. Our…relationship didn't work out.''

"That doesn't make sense, either.'' He sighed. "I've never known anybody like Falcon for taking the wrong kind of risk. The guy— Uh-oh. We've got a baby 911 over here—a little girl who's thinking food and a clean diaper. I'd better respond. I'll call you, I promise.''

"Give Shelley my best.''

"Sure.''

Emma set down the telephone and curled onto her side on the bed as desolation swamped her. Despite her resolve of the morning, she felt empty inside. Her father and Jimmy, gone. Her career as a historian destroyed, her beloved cook's post lost.

She had nothing left.

HARLOW HAD SPENT two days trying to track Ryan down. He and Tommy had disappeared the morning after their night in jail. Harlow was beginning to wonder if they were dodging him. And why.

When he finally found Ry, it was after midnight. He'd gone into a video arcade and there was Ryan, huddled on a bench near the washroom, wearing a black shirt and jeans that blended in with the black walls of the arcade. Harlow would have missed him, except for the white sneakers. New white sneakers.

"Ry?" He sat down on the bench. "Hey, Ry, where you been? I was about to call Missing Persons, get your picture on a milk carton."

"I was waiting for you." His voice shook.

Harlow dragged the boy into the washroom. It was filthy, but there were lights. He got a look at Ryan's face and swore. "How long's it been, Ry?"

"A-a-a while." Gray skin, dull black eyes, a quiver in every muscle of his body. Ryan was on the edge of withdrawal.

And Harlow had used the last of his stash. "I've got some cash. Come on." He kept hold of his friend and started back out the door.

Ryan held back, with more strength than seemed possible. "No. No, Harlow. I can't."

"What does that mean?"

"E-Eddy's got a kit waiting for me at his place. I g-get it when I bring you w-w-ith me." He sagged against the wall. "I couldn't find you, and I got s-s-sicker while I was looking and just sort of g-gave up."

Harlow had to admire Santos's brains. He'd picked just the right tool for the job.

"Okay, Ry, you found me. Let's go."

Santos kept an office above the Rio Bravo Tex-Mex Restaurant in an upscale part of east Denver. The folks who ate there would be surprised, Harlow figured, to know who ran the place. And where the real money came from.

Ryan led him through the kitchen, empty now that midnight had come and gone, and up some steps to a black door with a big brass lock. The door opened in response to a knock, and a tall dude with three rings in his ear looked out at them. He must've recognized Ry, because he stepped back and let them go in.

Eddy Santos sat on a white couch across the room, surfing channels on a giant TV screen hanging on the wall. He glanced over as Ryan and Harlow approached. A grin split his face.

"Good job, little dude." He clicked off the television and sat up. "I'm glad to see you do what you're told."

Ryan didn't say anything. But he stood there shivering. Harlow felt the strength of his effort not to beg.

"Give him his reward, Ace." The guy with the earrings tossed Ry a plastic bag.

Ryan caught it, held it close to his chest. "Harlow, I... Do you need me to stay?"

He shook his head. "Nah. I'm cool."

Ryan managed a grin and disappeared through the black door.

Harlow looked at Santos. "Okay. I'm here. Now what?"

"Have a seat. Want a beer?"

"No. Just get to the point."

The drug dealer shook his head. "Man, you are so wound up. All I want to do is offer you a chance to make some money. Raise your standard of living, so to speak."

Harlow was tempted to tell Santos what he could do with his standard of living. But he wanted to get out of here alive. "You want me to sell for you."

"What could be easier?" Eddy gave an open-handed shrug. "You do for me, I do for you."

"Sounds good." Harlow pretended to consider. "But I got a problem."

"What problem?"

"Cops, man. They're crawling all over me. They think I did the job at Jimmy Falcon's club."

"You didn't?"

"Nah. Too much work, breaking all those bottles." He grinned, and Santos laughed.

"Yeah. So you got cops on your tail."

"Big time." Santos was eyeing him closely, and Harlow kept his face straight. "But when the heat dies down, I don't have a problem working for you. Just let me get clear first."

The dealer nodded. "I don't need any extra cops nosing around, for sure. How long you think it'll take them to drop you?"

"When they find somebody else. Or Falcon gives up. Who knows?"

Santos flopped back on the couch, picked up the remote. "Okay. I'll give you some time. Not too much time, though." He grinned again. "The 'hood belongs to me. You don't work for me, you don't stay."

Harlow nodded. "I got that." Ace opened the door for him. "See ya."

Santos nodded. "Sure, kid. Soon."

Harlow didn't breathe again until he was out on the street and several blocks away.

Now he had the cops on one side of him and Santos on the other. For a guy with no money, no house, no clothes and no family, his life had just become very complicated.

ZACH CALLED EMMA back late the next day, as he'd said he would, with a short list of programs that might accept Ryan. She thanked him, changed into jeans and a long-sleeved shirt and went out to find Harlow.

The new vendor who'd helped before hadn't seen him, and neither had the five merchants she asked. As she walked along the street, scanning the faces of people who passed, gazing into alleys, peeking into stores and bars she would never consider entering, the sun sank behind the Rockies. A short time later, the night turned dark.

But the lights came on, in bright greens and yellows and reds, neon blue and pink. Signs she had never noticed before suddenly appeared—women in fringed bikinis performing a stilted dance, a martini glass filling and emptying over and over again—lurid invitations for adult entertainment. The streets became busy, and her search for Harlow more difficult. In the dark, all faces looked the same. She might have to depend on Harlow's recognizing her.

She reached the last building with a neon sign and stood at the corner, waiting to cross the street. Footsteps scuffed across the pavement, out of her line of sight. Emma swallowed hard and did not turn around.

A man stepped up beside her. "What are you looking for, little lady? Maybe I can help."

"No, thank you." She kept her gaze fastened on the traffic light. *Change. Please, change.*

"I've been watching you for a while. You're a pretty thing. If you're looking for Mr. Right, I just might be your man."

When at last the light changed, Emma stepped into the street. The man followed at her side. A glance showed her that he was tall, with a mustache, a cowboy hat and a cigarette. His long strides easily matched her own. Jimmy's warnings about being on the street in this part of town suddenly took on new life.

Just as they reached the curb, a couple of drunks crossing in the opposite direction gave her a chance to draw away from the man. Walking fast, glancing over her shoulder every few seconds, Emma gave up the search for Harlow and concentrated on simply getting away unhurt. With a sob of relief, she saw an empty cab glide past, hailed it and scrambled inside.

Mr. Right reached the same spot a moment after she'd locked the door. As he cursed and complained, Emma told the cabdriver her address and, in the vernacular, got the hell out of Dodge.

Once behind her own door, she gave in to the shakes and the tears. Later, wrapped in her flannel robe, a cup of tea in hand, she huddled on the sofa.

"Oh, Jimmy." She sighed and sipped her tea. "Why do you always have to be right?"

WHEN THE PHONE RANG, Jimmy did one last curl, touched his elbows to his raised knees and unfolded back to the floor, breathing hard, while he listened to the call.

"Jimmy? It's Darren. I got your message, but are you sure? I mean, The Indigo has a rep on campus for giving new bands a chance. Some profs in the music department keep those calendars you hand out, and a couple give assignments that require showing up to listen. I can get another job, but there's no place like your place—" The answering machine cut him off.

Jimmy rolled onto his good side, braced a hand on the floor and started leg lifts. His hip hated it, and he clenched his teeth as he groaned out the count. "One, two, three, four..."

The damn phone rang again. He was popular today.

"Jimmy, it's Zach. I'm coming over about eight tonight, before my shift. Be there."

He sounded mad. Changing the flex of his ankle, Jimmy thought about where he could be at eight o'clock besides home.

Running away didn't solve much, though, so he answered the door when the bell rang that night. "Want a drink?"

Zach followed him into the living room, wearing the uniform Jimmy was honest enough to admit he still coveted. "No, thanks. What the hell do you think you're doing?"

They had never played word games with each other. "Have a seat. Somebody told you I'm closing the club?"

"Yeah. Why?"

"There doesn't seem to be much point in reopening."

"Income?"

Jimmy shrugged. "I've got investments. I can live for a year on what the Jag brings if I sell it."

"Exactly why are you deconstructing your life?"

"Big word." He grinned. Zach didn't. This was going to be one of *those* discussions. "Haven't you ever given up on anything?"

"Yeah. I gave up on professional basketball when I realized I was too short."

"Seriously."

"Seriously, no. If I want it, I do whatever's required to get it. Lucky for me, I'm not real high maintenance. I've got Shelley and the kids, a job I like, friends. What else do I need?"

"You figure that's what you deserve?"

Zach's blue eyes narrowed. "What the hell does deserving have to do with anything?"

He should have gone out to dinner at seven forty-five. "In general people get what they deserve."

Elbows braced on his knees, his friend stared silently at the floor for a long minute. Then he took a deep breath and said, "Leaving aside the issues of starving babies in Africa, young mothers with cancer, kids who get hit by drunk drivers and never walk again, you think you deserved to get those bullets in your hip?"

"Could be."

"Because…?"

"I gave up on them."

"The gangs?"

"The punks in general. Folks we were supposed to be trying to help."

Zach looked up and met his gaze. "You are not in control."

That felt like a stab between the ribs. "I could have done more, all along the line—in the army, on the force. I didn't make a difference."

"So this is about guilt. You'd have made a great priest."

Jimmy gave that joke the grin it deserved. "I ran into one or two on the rez when I was a kid. I learned fast."

"You blew Emma off because you're not good enough?"

He didn't remember ever wanting to slug Zach Harmon before. "That topic is off limits."

"Okay. You're dumping the club because you don't deserve to be...what? Solvent? Successful?"

"Because keeping the club requires me to care. And I don't." That was as honest as he could be.

Zach sat back in his chair. "Well, then, you won't mind lending The Indigo to the cops for a sting operation."

Because this was Zach, Jimmy ignored the immediate impulse to say no. "Who are you after?"

"Dealer named Santos. He works that side of town, has a whole string of runners and touts bringing him business. Crack, heroin, weed and some of the latest fads, like Ecstasy."

"Why do you need me?"

"We need a base in the area. We've got some undercover guys in place. The Indigo would be a contact point, and the site for us to set up a takedown. We picked you for the role of informant between Santos and us."

"Gee, thanks."

"You can say no." Zach didn't need to add, *That's what a man who doesn't care would do.*

Granted, Jimmy didn't believe the sting would make a

difference in the Denver drug scene. Remove Santos, there would be five guys waiting to take over his trade.

But the men on this project had been his comrades. Most were still his friends. And Zach was asking. Jimmy would not ignore his friends or leave them in danger if he could help it.

He got to his feet, went into the kitchen and brought back a cup of coffee for Zach and for himself. Then he sat down on the couch again.

"So what do you have in mind?"

"EMMA, IT'S JIMMY."

She hadn't heard his voice in five days. For a moment, she couldn't seem to breathe. Or think. Let alone speak into the phone.

"Emma, are you there?"

"Yes, yes, I'm here. How are you?"

After a second he gave a strange laugh. "Listen, I wanted to let you know that the cops have done some checking, trying to locate the medallion."

She could tell by his voice that the news wasn't good. "And?"

"None of the museems and upscale galleries have seen it."

"That's…too bad. I'm glad they tried."

"I wish I'd done something with it—brought it home, taken it to a bank." He drew a deep breath. "But the club is where I spend most of my time."

The admission told her a great deal. "Don't blame yourself. Anyway, we did what my father asked—we found out where the medallion came from and what it meant." *And we found each other again*…for a short time, at least. Tears burned in her eyes. "Thank you for calling." She needed to get off the phone before she completely broke apart.

But Jimmy didn't say goodbye. "One other thing, Emma. I…I want you to come back to work."

Pleasure lanced through her. "You're reopening The Indigo?"

"Tomorrow night. The crowd will want food."

That put her very quickly in focus. He wanted a cook. "I don't think so, Jimmy." He might be immune to agony, but she was not.

"I'll stay out of your way."

As if that was what she wanted. "Why did you change your mind?"

"Uh…it seems like a good idea. Maybe you were right, and I decided too fast. Tiffany's working, and Darren. I'll give you a raise."

"Don't bother." The very last thing she should do was return to the kitchen at The Indigo.

But the club was her link to Harlow. She could only wait for him to contact her—her narrow escape from Mr. Right had proved the futility, not to mention the stupidity, of trying to find him on his own ground. And she still felt responsible for Harlow, for Ryan. If she couldn't reach them, how could she take care of them?

"I'll be in tomorrow about four," she told Jimmy, then hung up before he could say anything else and spent the rest of the night sick with nerves, misery and dread.

But only Tiffany was present when she came in Saturday afternoon. "Hey, Emma. The place looks good as new, doesn't it?" Her face was bright, her voice loud.

"I'd say so." The mirror had been replaced, and the usual liquor bottles set out. New glasses hung from the racks above Tiffany's head. "Do you know why Jimmy changed his mind?"

"No idea." The bartender rubbed her polishing cloth furiously over the scarred mahogany. "But I'm glad he did. Money was getting a little tight."

"Brad's not working?"

"Off and on, as usual." Tiffany disappeared down the hallway and came back with a broom and dustpan. "Darren's gonna be here at seven. I told him I'd sweep up. Your food's in the kitchen—I put the cold stuff away."

"Thank you." She looked back as she paused at the kitchen door. Tiffany seemed more than nervous, almost hyperactive. Or uncomfortable. But why?

She fell into her usual kitchen routine quite easily, feeling more balanced, more stable, than she had in the past week. Twice she heard Jimmy's footsteps in the hallway; she tensed, but he always passed the kitchen door without the least hesitation. She might just be able to get through the night without seeing him at all.

As she finished setting the last of the chicken breasts in marinade, someone tapped on that solid, impenetrable back door. There was no indoor bolt; the door locked and unlocked only with a key. A key that, presumably, Jimmy carried.

Was she going to have to talk to him, after all?

She leaned close to the door panel. "Who is it?" A deliveryman could be directed around to the front door.

"Emma? It's Harlow."

Of course. The person she could not ignore, yet could not allow to enter. "I'll be there in just a moment."

Ignoring Tiffany's stare, still wearing her apron, Emma dashed across the main room and out onto the sidewalk. She met Harlow at the corner. "Where have you been? I've waited to hear from you, even went looking for you. Is Ryan all right? Are you?"

He wasn't smiling, and his eyes were tired. "The news isn't good, Emma. Ry's strung so high, he's gonna OD anytime now. He's in with a real bad crowd and I can't pry him loose. They give him the dope. Tommy's hooked on the money, as much as the drugs. I can't get through to him, and Ry won't leave if he doesn't.'' He leaned back against the wall, as if he couldn't stand without the support any longer.

Emma thought of Jimmy's predictions. And then she thought of Zach. ''Perhaps the police…''

''You can't trust the cops—some of them are on the payroll. Choosing the wrong one could get you wiped out permanently.''

''But Jimmy has friends—''

''A few, yeah.'' She hadn't heard him walk up behind her. Both she and Harlow turned to stare. ''What's going on?''

''Nothing at all, Mr. Falcon. Just stopped by to…uh…'' Harlow lifted his hands in a helpless gesture. ''Man, I can't do this. I'm outta here.''

''Not so fast.'' Jimmy grabbed the boy's arm and held on, even when Harlow tried to pull away. ''I want to talk to you. Inside.''

''Jimmy—'' Emma put out her hand.

''I told you before, man, I didn't do the break-in and I don't know anything about it.''

''Yeah, you told me before. So come inside and tell me again.'' Ignoring her protest, he drew Harlow through the club's front door.

Outraged, chagrined, frightened, she followed. ''Jimmy…Jimmy!'' He stopped at the end of the bar and looked back. His eyes flickered, then went to a dull black.

''What is it, Emma?''

''At least let me feed him first. He's nearly faint with hunger. He can wash up and get something to eat. And then—I promise—he'll come in to talk to you.''

He studied Harlow for a second. ''Okay. Go get something to eat. Then we'll talk.''

JIMMY WAITED for Harlow in his office. Emma's expression when she'd seen him tonight wouldn't leave his mind—a combination of sorrow and hurt and fear. God, he hated that he'd destroyed her faith in him.

The music hadn't started yet, and the squeak of sneakers in the hall announced Harlow's arrival. He halted in the doorway and waited, poised to run.

Jimmy nodded. "Come in and shut the door. Then have a seat."

The boy did as he was told. All the attitude, the self-confidence that was part of Harlow's act had disappeared. He looked very much like a boy tonight.

"You got enough to eat?"

Harlow's eyes widened. "Yessir."

"You say you don't know anything about the break-in and robbery here?"

"No sir. We were here that night, like you said. We were hoping…" He flushed and looked at the floor between his shoes.

"To get some food off of Emma. Right."

"Yessir. But when we saw that you weren't open, we split. Got some sandwiches. Tommy and Ry took off. I caught a movie, found a flophouse and went to sleep."

"So you don't really know what Tomas and Ryan did that night."

The thin shoulders lifted on a deep breath. "No." His hands fidgeted, tapping the cigarette box in his pocket, then moving away again.

"Go ahead and smoke. I'll survive."

Harlow grinned. "Thanks."

Jimmy understood how Emma could have been drawn in—that smile had a nearly hypnotic power. You wanted to do whatever you could to make it happen again.

But this was strictly police business, part of Harmon's overall plan. "Do you know a dealer named Santos? Eddy Santos?"

"I know about him, yeah." His deliberate evasion said that he knew a lot more.

"You buy from him?"

"Not if I can help it."

"You sell for him?"

"Why?" Jimmy stared until Harlow looked away to take a drag on his smoke. "He wants me to. I put him off, but he's holding Ry as a kind of hostage, trying to force me. Tommy went over a few weeks ago."

"What's stopping you?"

Harlow shrugged. "I don't sell drugs and I don't do sex for money. Even if I did, I wouldn't work for Santos. He's a bad man. Tommy's asking for deep trouble."

"You probably won't be surprised to hear that the cops want Santos out of business."

"Yeah, and I want a freakin' Harley from Santa Claus for Christmas."

Jimmy smiled. "Right. Would you consider helping?"

He sat up straight in the chair. "Me? Help the cops? Doing what?"

"Working for Santos. And for me."

HARLOW LEFT The Indigo without seeing Emma again. That was part of the deal Falcon had offered—stay away from the lady so she didn't get involved in their business. And in return for services rendered, Falcon would see to it that Ryan got into rehab—a place where he could live and stay off the streets until he was completely clean. Falcon even said he would pay.

Practically a fairy tale, Harlow thought, hanging out at his usual corner after a quick and easy fix. Complete with fairy godmother and godfather. Plus the wicked magician—that would be Santos. And Ry, the prince caught under a spell. Tommy would be the...what was that word?...the minion who lost out when the magician went down. He felt sorry for Tommy.

Laughing, because he hadn't thought about anything as silly as fairy tales for years, Harlow ignored the sound of somebody calling his name. But when it happened a second and third time, he looked around.

Before he knew what was going down, Tommy had him by the shoulders. "Come on, man. It's bad. You gotta get help."

Harlow went cold. "Ryan?"

Tommy nodded, panting, pulling him down the sidewalk. "He's passed out. Not just asleep. We crashed at T-bone's place for the night. Ry mainlined the dope Eddy gave him this afternoon and just keeled over. I can't wake him up."

They were running now, dodging people coming the other way. "Is he still breathing?"

"He was when I left."

Harlow reached the door of T-Bone's building and took two flights of stairs three steps at a time. T-Bone's door was wide open, and a crowd stood around, staring in. He shoved them out of the way to get through.

When he dropped to his knees beside the mattress on the floor, one look at Ryan's face convinced him he'd arrived too late.

CHAPTER FIFTEEN

ABOUT MIDNIGHT, the phone rang. Jimmy picked up in his office. "The Indigo."

"Mr. Falcon, it's Harlow. I gotta speak to Emma."

A current of panic underlay the boy's attempt to keep his voice calm.

"That's not part of the deal." Though all his instincts insisted that Harlow's desperation was real. "What's wrong?"

"God...please, let me talk to Emma."

Jimmy drew the line at torture. "Hold on." When he opened the kitchen door, Emma looked around from the dishwasher rack.

"Oh...Jimmy." He couldn't read whatever was in her face. He had to fight the need to touch her, just for... comfort.

Jeez. "Harlow wants you on the phone."

Her eyes widened in surprise. "Did he say what's happened?" She crossed to the door he held open.

"He wouldn't tell me." She reached for the phone on the bar. Jimmy put his hand over hers. "Take it in my office."

For a second they stood there, hand over hand, eyes locked. Everything inside him ached for Emma, and he saw the same need in her face.

But she pulled her hand away. "Thank you."

He wasn't above eavesdropping. He closed the office

door behind him and leaned back against it as Emma picked up the phone. "Harlow?"

Listening, she closed her eyes. "Where?" Her hand fisted just under her chin, as if holding something inside. "I'll be there as soon as possible."

She clicked off the phone, but held the receiver next to her ear in a sort of suspended animation. When her eyes opened, Jimmy saw the glisten of tears.

"Ryan has overdosed. He's at Denver General Hospital. I hate to leave while we're—while you're still open, but Harlow is there alone, waiting. You can dock my salary."

"Screw that." He straightened up and opened the door. "Get your stuff. I'll drive you to General."

Emma wanted to argue—he could see it in every line of her body. But after a second she just nodded. "Thank you."

Jimmy let himself touch her shoulder as she passed. "No problem."

He hoped.

AND NOW here they were, closed together within the confines of the car, and Emma could think of nothing to say. Jimmy wouldn't want to talk about Ryan or Harlow. Their failed personal relationship was hardly a topic she wanted to bring up. What did they have left except the weather?

Jimmy stopped the car at a traffic signal. Hands still wrapped firmly around the steering wheel, he looked at her. "Emma...I'm sorry."

Before she found her voice, the light changed and they moved forward. She gripped her hands together. "I'm not sure I understand."

He cleared his throat. "I made a mess of everything that night at your place. What you understood wasn't what I meant."

"How would you know what I understood?" She heard

the bitter echo of the question he'd thrown at her—*How the hell do you know what I do or don't mean?*

"Because I see it in your eyes. What you feel always shows."

"Oh." Emma drew a deep breath. "I don't like being so transparent. I'll have to...to work on dissembling." *As you do,* she could have added. But why be petty, even if she thought she might never recover from loving and losing Jimmy Falcon?

"I hope you won't. Your kind of honesty is rare and precious."

Her deep need for his approval, his...caring frightened her. She put a hand up to ward off the words. "Jimmy, don't do this. I can stand knowing that we...don't matter anymore." If they ever had. "But I can't bear being charmed, or soothed, or placated or whatever it is you're trying to do. Don't say nice things to me simply to salve your conscience."

His knuckles whitened on the steering wheel. "I was being honest."

"Very well. Apology accepted. You don't have to talk to me anymore."

He took her at her word and didn't speak again on the ride to the hospital. Emma had to be satisfied, because she'd gotten what she asked for. But being so close to him and so incredibly distant introduced her to an entirely new dimension of pain.

As they approached the hospital, she cleared her throat. "You can drop me at the emergency entrance. I do appreciate the ride over, and I know Harlow will be grateful. He shouldn't be here alone."

But Jimmy drove past the emergency room and into the nearest parking lot.

Emma stared at him as he cut the engine. "What are you doing?"

"I'm going in with you."

"That's not necessary."

"I didn't think it was."

Short of sounding like a pouting schoolgirl, there was no way to argue with him. "As you like." But she didn't give him time to get around the car to open her door.

The walk to the emergency entrance was quick and silent. Jimmy let her go through the automatic door first, and she saw Harlow immediately, sitting with his elbows propped on his knees and his head bowed.

"Harlow?" She put a hand on his shoulder as she took the seat beside him. "What's happened? What do you know?"

His eyes were red-rimmed, his cheeks splotched with dirt and tear marks. "Nothing. Nobody's come out since they took him in."

Jimmy sat on Harlow's other side. "Does anybody realize you're waiting?"

"I don't know. Everything happened so fast."

"Let me see what I can find out."

Emma gazed after him in surprise, then shook her head and returned her attention to Harlow. "Tell me about it."

He shrugged thin shoulders. "First thing I knew, Tommy was hollering for me. I thought—" he choked "—I thought for sure Ry was...dead. But the EMTs said not quite." The boy dropped his head into his hands. "Not quite."

"Where is Tomas?"

Harlow shook his head. "He split when the ambulance showed up. I haven't got a clue."

They waited without further conversation for Jimmy's return. Just when Emma thought she might have to go searching for him, he came down the hallway. In the cold light of the hospital, he seemed austere, unapproachable. There was no easy grin to assure her of welcome, no light in his eyes.

He sat beside Harlow again. "They didn't know you were waiting. As far as they can tell from what he's carrying in his pockets, Ryan mainlined some pretty powerful stuff—more than twice as pure as the usual street-caliber dope. They're doing what they can, and they promised you'd get some news as soon as they had any."

Harlow drew a deep breath. "Thanks, Mr. Falcon. I appreciate the help."

"No problem." Jimmy stood yet again. "I'm gonna see if I can find some food, coffee, drinks…" Without a glance at Emma, he left again.

The Denver General waiting area offered no privacy. Even thought was difficult above the noise of patients waiting with friends and family until they could be seen. Emma surveyed the room as discreetly as she could, trying to assimilate the sum of anguish around her—a teenage girl who gasped periodically and doubled up over her rounded, pregnant belly; an old man nearly asleep in his wheelchair, his spotted, twisted hand being patted by the younger woman—his daughter?—who'd brought him in; a tall, gangling youth in a sports jersey of some sort with his foot propped on a chair and covered with bags of ice; a young father holding his feverish and fussy little boy while his wife sat with a baby at her breast.

For the first time she saw everything clearly. Jimmy did have reality on his side. The world overflowed with problems that had no solution or only a weak solution at best. To have been exposed, day after day, for years, to the hopelessness of some people's lives would affect the strongest of men. Jimmy had obviously acquired his cynicism in a world that Emma had never truly experienced. But she was learning.

"Stale doughnuts, machine coffee or soft drinks. That's the best I could do." Standing before them, Jimmy held a box of assorted cans and cups and plastic-wrapped sweets.

Harlow didn't glance up. Emma stood and took a soda and doughnut out of the box. "Thank you, Jimmy. Anything will help. Harlow, you should eat a bit. It'll make the time go if nothing else."

He sighed deeply and took the food. "I'll try." One bite of doughnut later, he shook his head. "I think I'll stick with the drink."

"Good choice." Jimmy put his own doughnut back into the box. "They taste worse than they look." He picked up a cup of coffee and leaned back in his chair with his legs stretched out, as if he planned to spend what was left of the night in that place.

All three of them waited through the wee hours for news of Ryan. Jimmy glanced to his left about 3:00 a.m. and found Emma staring down at Harlow, who slept with his head against her shoulder. Her gaze was tender, almost like a mother might look at her child. Until that moment, he wasn't sure he'd fully realized the depth of her commitment to these kids.

He wasn't sure why he was here, either, except that he didn't want to leave her. Harlow had needed somebody and Emma had stepped in. But what if *she* needed someone? Jimmy wasn't sure Harlow was equal to the task.

Then again, he'd managed to wreck that aspect of their relationship pretty damn well, himself. Why should Emma depend on him for anything after that night? Why should anyone expect Jimmy Falcon to come through?

"Excuse me. Are you waiting for Ryan Cooper?" A young woman stood in front of them, exhaustion in her eyes. "I'm Dr. Ash."

Jimmy stood. "Yes. What can you tell us?"

"This was a very close call. A few minutes might have made the difference between Ryan living or dying." She smiled. "Fortunately time was on our side. He's stabilized for now." The smile died. "Of course, he'll wish he had died as he starts to withdraw from the heroin. And he's in terrible shape—malnourished and exhausted. Where are his parents?''

''They don't want him,'' Harlow said quietly. ''I try to take care of him.''

The doctor's eyes softened. ''You're not much older than Ryan, are you?'' He shook his head. ''He shouldn't be your responsibility. But the admitting department is asking about whom to bill.'' She looked at Emma, then Jimmy. ''And I think we should consider a methadone program that will get him off the heroin without such a horrible withdrawal.''

''That's what we've been working on,'' Emma said. ''The programs won't accept him without a doctor's prescription.''

Harlow sighed. ''And getting Ryan to the free clinic was like trying to teach a pig to sing. You don't get anywhere, and it annoys the hell out of the pig.''

Jimmy found himself chuckling. ''I'll work out the billing issues. Just take him where he needs to go and help him beat this habit.''

''Is he awake?'' Harlow got to his feet slowly, like an old man. ''Can I see him?''

Dr. Ash shook her head. ''Best to wait until later in the morning. Perhaps all of you should go home and get some sleep.''

Emma and Harlow stared at her, obviously at a loss. Jimmy made a decision. ''I'll leave my number with the nurses—you can call if you need to reach us.'' There would be time later to figure out his motive. Or if he'd gone crazy.

''Sounds good.'' The doctor smiled and put a hand on Harlow's shoulder. ''You've done the best you could for your friend. Now let the rest of us help.''

''You two sit down.'' As the doctor walked away, Jimmy faced Emma and Harlow, even put a hand on the boy's shoulder to push him into the chair. "I'll handle the paperwork. With luck, it won't take too long."

Still standing, Emma started to say something.

"Later," he told her with a glance at Harlow. "Let's just get this wrapped up."

Predictably, filling out forms and answering questions about a boy he barely knew took tons of patience and more than an hour. When he got back to the E.R. waiting room, both Harlow and Emma had fallen asleep.

The rush of…concern? tenderness? love?…that flowed through him was terrifying. And painful, like smashing his fist into a pane of glass.

Jimmy pushed the thoughts and the feelings away. "You two want to find a more comfortable place for a nap?" He shook Emma's shoulder, forced himself to let go and step back.

She opened heavy eyes and smiled straight at him. For a second, the last two weeks had never happened. "Sounds lovely."

Then she woke up completely, and the smile faded. "Harlow, wake up." She jogged his knee. "We're ready to leave."

The boy stood up, but he was scarcely awake. Only when they stepped outside into the cool night did he begin to revive. At the crosswalk leading to the parking lot, he stopped.

"I can make it from here," he said. "Thanks for coming, Emma. You made things better." He looked down at his feet and then at Jimmy. "Mr. Falcon, I know this is a lot of money, and for somebody who's done nothing but give you a hard time. I don't know how we'll pay it back, but we'll do our best."

"You can't walk all the way back from here in the middle of the night," Emma said, going into protective mode. "We can at least drive you over to your part of town. I mean—'' her glance at Jimmy was nervous, a little ashamed ''—if Mr. Falcon doesn't mind.''

Jimmy put a hand on Emma's shoulder, the other on Harlow's shoulder, and eased them across the street. ''I was thinking we would take Emma home. Then Harlow and I can go back to my place.''

Both Emma and Harlow stumbled and stopped. Both of them stared at him.

''Mr. Falcon—''

''Jimmy—''

He shook his head. ''Why don't we skip analyzing my reasons and just get some sleep?'' His reasons were a mystery to himself; he sure couldn't explain them to anybody else.

A short ride later, they left Harlow in the Jag while Jimmy walked Emma to her door.

They took the elevator to her floor without talking. Jimmy stood a little to the back so he could watch her without making her nervous. The jean skirt she wore fit loosely over her hips, as if she'd lost some weight. He tightened his jaw at the idea. Emma did not need to kill herself with some stupid diet. She was just right as she was.

But he couldn't say so to her. She wouldn't believe him. And he had only himself to blame.

After unlocking the door to her apartment, she hesitated, then turned to face him. ''Thank you for all you've done tonight.'' Her eyes didn't quite connect with his. ''For giving Harlow a place to stay—that's very generous. And for taking care of Ryan's bills. That's beyond generous, and a mere thank-you is totally inadequate.''

He shrugged. ''It's just money.''

Emma looked at him directly, her expression severe. ''It's a lot more than money, Jimmy.'' She leaned close, kissed his cheek. ''Good night.''

He'd intended to let her go. But somehow, without

thought, his hands came to cradle her face, to keep her close. He saw her eyes—surprised, hungry. And then he found her mouth with his.

Emma might have fought Jimmy's impulse. But she couldn't fight her own need to be close to him, to take what he gave and give back everything she had. Everything she was. His hands shaped her shoulders, her breasts, her ribs, then his arms closed around her, pulling her tight against him. She yielded, blending into him, answering his passion with her own. Her arms around his neck, she stroked his hair, the nape of his neck, absorbing every sensation to savor later, again and again. She thought about pulling him into her apartment, shutting the door, completing the union that seemed so necessary to her survival.

But Jimmy's arms loosened, his lips left hers. Breathing hard, he pressed a kiss to her forehead. "Sorry," he whispered. "I didn't mean—"

Emma shook her head. "No. Don't." She stepped back, out of his hold. Unable to resist, she touched two fingers to his mouth and felt his kiss one last time. "Good night."

"'Night, Emma."

Then she closed him out, knowing he would always stay in her heart.

HARLOW COULDN'T figure out this gig, even by the time they'd left Emma at her apartment and driven across town to Mr. Falcon's. He knew he liked the smell and the feel of an expensive car. He knew Ry was in good hands. The rest of the night made no sense at all.

Mr. Falcon unlocked the door and stepped inside. "Come in." Lights switched on, revealing a room like something out of a magazine—lots of empty space, black leather furniture, a few pictures on the walls.

Harlow whistled. "This is a great place." He saw a drum

set in the corner and a couple of guitar cases leaning against the wall. "You play?"

"Sometimes. Do you want something to eat?"

"Uh...no. Thanks." He was more tired than he was hungry. "I just need to crash." He'd taken a hit on the way to the hospital, so he was good to go for a while yet. "If you can spare a blanket..."

"How about a shower first?"

"A shower?"

"Yeah—water sprays down, you swipe soap everywhere, rinse it off." The laughter in Falcon's eyes took the insult out of the words.

"I think I remember the general idea. But—"

"Come on." Mr. Falcon led him through a bedroom to the cleanest bathroom Harlow had seen in years. "I'll find you something to wear. Take as long as you want."

Dangerous invitation, Harlow decided, standing under a pounding rain of hot water. He could have stayed there forever.

But his mother had taught him manners, so he made himself get out and dry off with the thickest towel he'd ever seen. There were fresh jeans and a T-shirt and—holy shit!—brand-new underwear lying just inside the door. He dressed slowly, enjoying the slide of clean cloth over his skin. The jeans were too big, but at least they didn't fall off.

Then he wiped up the bathroom, trying to make it look as if he'd never been there. Clothes and wet towel in hand, he walked back into the living room.

Mr. Falcon stood at the window, and he turned as Harlow came in. "That's a definite improvement. Still think you'd rather sleep than eat?"

"Uh...yeah."

He nodded toward the bedroom. "There's a closet in the

bathroom with a washer and dryer. Put your clothes in there. Then hit the sack.''

"You mean...the bed?"

"That's the best place to sleep."

"B-but what about you?"

"I sleep in the chairs out here sometimes, when lying flat bothers my hip. I'll be okay."

A huge yawn ambushed him. "You sure, Mr. Falcon?"

"I'm sure. And call me Jimmy. I'm tired of feeling old enough to be your dad."

Harlow gave up. "I appreciate this...Jimmy. I'll see you later."

"Sure."

The sheets were cool and soft, the pillows held him like a dream. Harlow stopped worrying about the whys and what-ifs, and dived deep into sleep.

WHEN EMMA STEPPED into the club the next afternoon, Tiffany and Darren were waiting at the bar.

"What happened?"

"Are they okay?"

Emma propped one hip on a bar stool. "Ryan overdosed, but he got to the hospital in time—that is, he's still alive. The antidote starts an immediate withdrawal process, so he's pretty miserable."

"When Jimmy didn't come back, I closed up the place without him." Tiffany wiped out a wineglass. "Where'd he go?"

"He took Harlow home with him." *After he kissed me.*

Darren and Tiffany let their jaws drop. "Be serious."

"I am. As far as I know, Harlow spent the night at Jimmy's flat. I called just before I left for work, but the machine answered. They might have gone to the hospital to see Ryan."

"Bizarre." Darren rubbed a hand over his hair. "I

thought Jimmy wanted to lock them up for the break-in. Not take them home for breakfast.''

''There's no proof they broke in anywhere.'' Without looking up, Tiffany started on another case of glasses. ''That's why the cops let them go.''

''But even before that—''

''Yeah, yeah, Jimmy thought Harlow and Ryan and Tommy were trouble.'' The bartender polished furiously. ''Doesn't mean he can't change his mind. Or just do a good deed when he feels like it.''

''No, it doesn't.'' Emma asked Darren to get the broom and start sweeping as far from the bar as possible. She wanted a private conversation with Tiffany. ''He's also paying Ryan's medical bills.''

''Jimmy's a good guy.''

''He seems to have some doubts about that.''

''I didn't say he was smart.'' The bartender grinned, then sobered after only a moment and picked up another glass to clean.

Emma leaned her elbows on the bar and propped her chin on her fists. ''Did Brad give you trouble when you thought you might be out of a job?''

''No, he didn't.'' Tiffany's vehemence made a lie out of her denial.

''That's good. But I imagine he's glad to have money coming in again.''

''Sure.'' Tiffany's shoulders relaxed slightly. ''Brad's always glad to have a steady supply of cash. He doesn't go through it as fast as he does when he gets one—''

''One…?''

She took a deep breath. ''One big payment. You know, finishes the whole job before he gets any of the money.''

''That would be difficult, unless you were very good at budgeting.''

Tiffany laughed. ''Brad? Budget? Ha.''

"Then you must be an expert."

"Nope. Numbers and me never did get along. I have a pretty good idea of what things cost, how much I get and how much I spend. But putting it all down on paper—no way."

"You're a better woman than I. If I don't write everything down, my life becomes total chaos." Emma slipped off the bar stool. "I suppose I'd better get cooking. The hospital said they would call here with any new information. I'll be glad to answer the telephone if it rings."

"You got it." Tiffany finished up the glassware and looked around nervously, straightening liquor bottles, wiping the bar yet again, as if she couldn't find enough to keep her busy. The relaxed, easy attitude she usually carried with her had vanished. She appeared anxious, even frightened. Almost hunted.

And Emma had a sickening feeling she knew the reason.

THE CALL JIMMY MADE to the hospital about 10:00 a.m. told him nothing new. But a couple of hours watching Harlow fidget on the couch, channel-surf and flip through books was more than enough.

"Why don't we go down and see what's going on with Ryan," he suggested after they ate pizza delivered from his favorite deli. "Stuff might be happening that the nurses at the desk don't know about."

"Yeah. Sounds good." Harlow had run his clothes through the washer and dryer—he looked fairly clean, though the shirt was ripped and jeans were worn to threads over the knees and butt. "I slept like a baby, Jimmy. And I ate like a pig. Thanks for everything."

Jimmy had a strong urge to ruffle the boy's blond hair. Or give him a one-armed hug, something you might do for a younger brother. He firmly stopped himself from doing either.

"I'm glad I could help. Let's go."

They found Ryan's room at the hospital without help. Nobody stopped them or asked where they were going, so Jimmy held the door for Harlow to slip through and then stepped in after him.

Ryan lay still on the bed, his face white against the blue of the pillowcase. The usual bags and tubes hung everywhere and connected to everything. Jimmy remembered the sense of suffocation those tubes had given him. He'd spent four weeks in a hospital room like this, fighting for every breath.

Harlow held Ryan's right hand, the one with the least tubes on and in it, between both of his. "Hey, Ry. Time to wake up. You're sleeping the freakin' day away, dude."

Ryan's eyes snapped open, conveying desperation and fear. His mouth moved, but no sound escaped past the tube down his throat.

"Don't try to talk, Ry. They got you hooked up to a machine to help you breathe. That was some major dope you scored last night. Musta cost you big. Did you buy from Eddy?"

Ryan tried to speak again and closed his eyes in frustration.

"Blink at me, Ry. Once for yes. Twice for no. Did you buy the stuff from Eddy?"

Two blinks.

"Somebody else?"

Two blinks.

Harlow stared blankly for a minute. "Oh...did he *give* you the stash, Ry?"

One blink.

"Free and clear?"

One blink.

"That doesn't sound like Santos."

Jimmy knew the comment was meant for him. "Unless he's fishing. Finding out what lever will work on you."

"He could've killed Ry." Harlow turned a defiant stare on Jimmy.

"I guess he knew that. It was worth the risk."

"Just to get me to sell for him?"

"You could bring in a lot of money, he thinks. Dealers are willing to do anything, use anybody, to net more cash."

The epithet Harlow used came out of the sewer. "He's not gonna get away with this."

"What are you going to do?"

The boy's face hardened, shaping planes and angles out of the soft cheeks, the round chin. Suddenly he looked like a man.

"I'm gonna take him down."

CHAPTER SIXTEEN

HARLOW SPENT the night after Ryan's overdose searching for Tommy. He finally caught up with him in an alley just as he took cash from a guy and handed over a plastic bag of white powder. From the size of the bag and the number of bills involved, Harlow judged that Tommy was selling crack, along with everything else. The idea set off explosives inside his head.

He waited until the guy had left, then came up behind and put a hand on Tommy's shoulder to pull him around. "Where the hell'd you go the other night?" Harlow let all his fury color the question. "I went to find you and you'd totally split."

One good look at Tommy and he felt his stomach heave. "What happened to you?"

His friend's face was a map of blue and red bruises, with one eye swollen almost closed. He shrugged, but didn't meet Harlow's eyes. "I ran into a door."

"Sure. Who beat you up, Tommy?"

"Punks."

"What did they take?"

"Uh…couple of nickel bags, all my cash."

"Why don't I believe you?"

"How should I know?" He shook off Harlow's hand and backed away. "I didn't stick around last night because I figured you had it covered. And I had three or four dime bags in my pockets—didn't want to get caught for possession or selling."

"Ryan was dying, Tommy. That didn't matter to you?"

"I couldn't do anything about it."

"Did you know the dope Santos gave him was almost seventy percent pure?"

"He buys it that way." Tommy shrugged. "I figured he cut it."

"But he didn't. Why do you think that was?"

"Not a clue."

"Maybe to show me what he could do to my friends if I don't work for him? Does that sound like Eddy Santos?"

"Could be."

"Yeah, right." Harlow paced down the alley and back. "And maybe he had you beat up a little for the same reason."

Tommy said nothing.

"Well, you can tell him it worked."

"You mean—"

"I can't let him hurt Ry…or you. I guess Santos wins this one. He can let me know what he wants me to do. But…"

"But?"

"But if anything happens to you or Ry or anybody else I know—" he couldn't mention Emma, in case the idea got back to Santos "—then I go to the cops. I don't give a shit where it gets me. If Santos doesn't leave my friends alone, I'll make sure he pays."

"You won't be sorry, Harlow. You can't believe how good it feels to eat three times every day." Tommy grinned, then winced. "And the girls… Ay yi yi."

"Right," Harlow said wearily. "I can hardly wait to see the girls."

JIMMY LEANED BACK in his chair. "So Santos took the bait?"

Across the desk, his mouth full of Emma's ham sandwich, Harlow nodded, swallowed. "He said he was glad I read the writing on the wall. The bastard."

"And he gave you dope to sell?"

"Crack and coke, some pills. Worth about a thousand on the street, I'm thinking."

At the newly installed safe, Jimmy disengaged the alarm and opened the door. "I got some money from the cops for you to take back to Santos. Let's make him really happy—let's give him twelve hundred." He counted out the bills, then came back to the desk.

Harlow was gulping down a glass of milk. The effects of the shower had worn off—he'd gone back to the homeless-grunge look. Jimmy felt the weight of the bills in his hand and considered what he was about to do. The money wasn't his, so he didn't care if it got lost. But if Harlow screwed up or decided to play the game his own way, there were people who could be seriously hurt.

When he looked at the boy again, he met a cool blue gaze. "Second thoughts, Jimmy?"

"Do you blame me? 'Solid citizen' is not the first description that comes to mind when I look at you."

"A solid citizen wouldn't be much good in this situation." Harlow grinned, and Jimmy blinked against the lightbulb brightness. "I'm playing this as straight as I can. He hurt my friends, almost killed one of them. There's not much I wouldn't do to see him flogged for that. Even if it means handing over every bit of that cash."

"Even if you're strung-out, ready for a fix?"

The boy squared his thin shoulders. "You're paying me to clean up the club. I've got the money to support myself."

"Okay, then. Take this to Santos. Leave the dope here." Harlow pocketed the money and put plastic bags of drugs on the desk. "Drop my name when you talk to him, mention that the action is getting dull at the club. Maybe I'm looking for extra cash." Jimmy took the bags and stowed them in the safe.

"Will do." Harlow got up from his chair, then stopped just before opening the door. "I can't even say thanks to Emma for the sandwich?"

"Leave her out of it. You know Emma—if she finds out what's going down, she's gonna end up involved. That absolutely cannot happen."

"Right." Harlow saluted. "See you tomorrow night."

Only a few minutes afterward, Emma knocked on the door frame. "He left rather quickly." She picked up the plate and glass.

Jimmy shrugged and pretended to examine his ledger. "He's got something to do, I guess."

When she didn't move or say anything, he looked up. "What can I do for you?" He kept his voice neutral, kept his face as blank as he could. If he allowed her to find the smallest chink, the whole wall would come down.

But damn, she looked good. Not glamorous or mysterious or knock-'em-dead sexy. Just Emma, with gold-red curls and smooth, creamy skin, and a shoulder to lend for anybody who needed it. Again he noted that her jeans were loose, even her T-shirt seemed to hang more. And again, he didn't have the right to comment.

Her eyes were a worried blue as she stared at him. "Why have you changed your mind about Harlow?"

"I haven't. He's still a junkie and a punk." He was sorely tempted to tell her about Harmon's operation, just to get her out of the room before he said all the wrong things. But that mistake could put Harlow *and* Emma at risk.

"You gave him a job, let him have the run of the club. Does that mean you don't think he did the break-in?"

"There wasn't enough evidence to pin on anybody. Tilden had an alibi—he was passed-out drunk on another cop's couch. With a broken nose." He grinned, but sobered quickly. "I'm chalking it up to experience and moving on. Sometimes that's all you can do."

She obviously wasn't convinced, but she gave up—on that issue, at least. "Well, then, do you know why he's avoiding me?"

He shook his head. "You'll have to ask him."

"If I can ever catch him."

"That shouldn't be too tough." If she didn't leave soon, he'd lose the strength to keep up this hard-ball act. He was doing it for her own good, but that didn't make it easy.

"I suppose not." Still, she hesitated. "Jimmy…"

"Yeah?" He showed reluctance when he finally glanced up from the books again.

"Never mind. Have a good night." She shut the door hard behind her.

And Jimmy fought every impulse he had to get up and follow.

RYAN WAS TRANSFERRED to an in-patient rehabilitation center five days after his overdose. Without Harlow to provide updates, Emma kept in touch with his condition through the nurses and staff. The doctors established Ryan on a methadone program, which mitigated the withdrawal symptoms. But he still needed a great deal of support.

Emma went to visit him as soon as she was allowed. He looked up eagerly when she stepped into the room. Some of his pleasure dimmed as he recognized her—he was probably waiting for Harlow. "Hi, Miss Emma."

"Hello, Ryan." She decided not to ask how he was or comment on his appearance—he looked and sounded as if death were only a breath away. "I brought you some things to read. Comic books," she explained when his face fell. "The woman at the shop assured me that these were some of the best."

She put them on his lap. His hand moved slowly to touch the colorful covers. He didn't look as if he could lift even one of them.

His smile was real and childlike. "Thanks, Miss Emma. I like these a bunch, 'specially Razor Man."

"Yes, I looked at that one. Quite a useful skill, being able to cut through doors and walls with one's hands."

"And ropes, when his buddies are tied up by the bad guy. Or his girlfriend, Lily."

"You sound as if you've followed Razor Man's career quite closely."

He shrugged, and the neck of the blue hospital gown showed a prominent collarbone. "I find 'em in the trash sometimes."

"Does Harlow read these comic books, too?"

"Nah. He likes real books. Sometimes one of the news-stand guys will give him brand-new paperbacks, just missing the covers. Harlow really gets into the stories set in olden times. He likes history."

Something she'd never known. She was tempted to pry further into Harlow's life, but resisted. Anything Harlow wanted her to know—his full name, for instance—he would tell her himself.

If he ever said more than "hello" and "goodbye" again.

They sat in a companionable silence for a few moments, while Emma gathered the courage to approach a difficult subject.

"Ryan, I wanted to talk with you about something."

"Yes, ma'am?"

"You're taking methadone now to replace the heroin."

"Yeah. It ain't as good, though. I feel okay. But I miss the rush."

"Have you thought about getting off drugs completely?"

He stared at her without expression. "No."

"Your life could be very different."

"Why would I want different?"

As with Jimmy, the question completely stonewalled her. If Ryan couldn't see the danger, the horror of living on the streets, how would he ever believe he had something to gain?

Behind her, the door opened. Ryan's face brightened. "Hey, Harlow!"

As Emma turned to look, Harlow stopped, as if surprised to see her. "Hey, Ry. Hey, Emma. How's it going?"

"Look what Emma brought, Harlow." Ryan's voice barely carried beyond the end of the bed. His friend came to the side opposite Emma and picked up the comic books.

"Cool, Ry. You got three Razor Man stories. That'll keep you busy for a while. They let you watch TV in here?"

"Yeah, but there aren't too many good shows. Kinda boring stuff. You got new threads?"

Emma noticed for the first time that Harlow did, indeed, have new clothes—not merely castoffs from a charity bin, but clothes that had obviously been purchased recently.

"Yeah. I've been doing some work for...for a guy. So I have some extra cash."

"Santos? You're working for Santos?" Ryan's tone was panicked. "You can't work for him, Harlow. He's a bad man."

Harlow put his hand on the boy's shoulder. "Hey, it's okay, Ry. I know what I'm doing."

"Get outta there, Harlow. He'll hurt you. I swear he will."

Emma looked at Harlow. "What does this Santos do?"

"He's a...businessman."

"He's a dealer," Ryan said. "He buys wholesale and gets people to sell for him."

"Drugs?" Cold filled her chest, and her heart seemed to stop.

Ryan nodded. "Yeah. He gave me the stuff I OD'd on. I think he meant that hit to go bad. He's always shoving Tommy around, making fun of him for being part Indian. An' he calls me a pissy little wimp."

Harlow hadn't yet met her eyes, though Emma hadn't looked away from his face. "You're selling drugs, Harlow?"

He shrugged one shoulder. "Sometimes."

A slap would have been kinder. "I see." Emma stood up on numb feet. She put a hand on top of Ryan's. "I'll come back in a few days to see how you liked the comics. Take care of yourself." She didn't look at Harlow. "Both of you be careful."

The room stayed quiet as she left. In fact, her ears seemed to be stuffed with cotton wool, because she couldn't hear anything around her. Just Harlow's affirmation that he was selling drugs.

She sat on a bench outside the hospital and closed her eyes. What chance did Ryan have now? With his closest friend selling the drug he craved, the boy had no reason to resist the habit. She'd never had much hope for Tomas, but she'd so wanted Ryan to escape.

And Harlow... She nearly moaned aloud. He would never get free with such simple access to heroin and an easy way to earn the money to buy it. He seemed so much thinner than when she'd first met him. The drug was claiming him, inch by inch. And now it appeared that the drug would win.

"Oh, Jimmy," she whispered. If she'd listened to him, if she'd given him credit for experience and for wisdom, she wouldn't have become involved with these boys, and she wouldn't now be suffering such terrible pain. *As if,* she thought with a sad smile, *Razor Man had used his hands on my heart.*

Even worse, had she listened, she might still be a part of Jimmy's life. They'd fought over the boys, but if she'd left them alone, there wouldn't have been such an issue between her and Jimmy. She might have dealt better with his weariness had she recognized the truth behind it. If she'd taken his word, heeded his warnings, his insistence on a surface life would have made much more sense. And she might have been able to settle for at least the surface of Jimmy Falcon. A cliché was a cliché because it was true...

Half a loaf was so much better than none.

JIMMY KNEW he had come on a fool's errand. There were enough pawnshops in the Denver metropolitan area to keep him busy for weeks, and no guarantee that the medallion had been sold to any of them. If the cops couldn't find it, what chance did *he* have? Still, he had to try.

He started with the dealer he knew best, in a neighborhood near the club. Quinn stayed legal, but he knew a lot about what kind of stolen merchandise was out there and who had fenced it.

Already involved with another customer when Jimmy stepped into the store, Quinn gave him a nod that promised he'd get free as soon as possible. Jimmy examined walls hung with guitars, violins and saxophones, cases of rings and bracelets and miles of gold necklaces. Quinn's customer, having decided which handgun he wanted to purchase, was drawing out his cash.

"I'll hold it for you," Quinn said, sliding a piece of paper across the counter. "You fill out this form and once the license board checks you out, the Glock's all yours."

"Give me a break. I'm not waiting for no license check."

"Yeah, I'm afraid you are." Quinn took the Glock off the counter. "Or you buy somewhere else."

"Look, buddy, don't give me that crap. I got good clean American cash to trade for that gun."

Jimmy stepped over to lean an elbow on the counter. "Take some advice from the police department—fill out the form nice and quiet, or we'll chase down the permits on every piece in your arsenal. Got that?"

Swearing under his breath, the customer filled out the simple form and left a deposit with Quinn. The bell on the door banged against the glass pane as the guy stormed out of the shop.

"Sunny personality," Jimmy commented.

"He has some trouble with authority figures." Quinn put the gun away and then turned back with a smile. "How's it going, Jimmy?"

"'Bout the same."

"Same as when I saw you—what? a year ago? I keep meaning to come down to The Indigo and listen, but I get a lot of late-night business, you know? Makes it hard to leave the shop."

"Well, you've still got a few chances. I'm closing the club in a couple of weeks."

"New ventures, I guess?"

"Something like that. Listen, I'm looking for a specific piece—an Indian medallion about four inches in diameter, inlaid with gold and silver and turquoise. Sound familiar?"

Quinn slowly shook his head. "Hasn't come in here. Where'd it get lost from?"

"The safe in my office."

"That stinks. So it's yours?"

"Yeah. And it's kinda special." Because it had brought Emma into his life again. "I'd like to get it back."

"Wish I could help. Do you know who stole it?"

"No." The more often he saw Harlow, the more convinced he was that Emma was right—the boy would not have trashed the club, even if he had stolen the cash. "Who in town do you think might see a piece like this?"

"I can give you a list of people who specialize in art and Indian stuff. And I'll ask some questions, see if I can hear anything useful."

"That'd be great, Quinn. I owe you."

"Nope. You straightened that last guy out. We're even." He walked Jimmy to the door. "You're looking a little tired, Jimmy. Maybe closing the club is a good idea. Give you a chance for a nice long vacation. Somewhere hot and sunny with lots of rum and lots of women to pour it."

Jimmy laughed. "Sure, Quinn. I'll let you know where I end up."

"Send me a postcard—with some of those women on the front!"

Quinn's was the first stop in a long, unproductive day. Describing the medallion, Jimmy found himself thinking about the day Emma brought it to him, the pleasure of seeing her again. He thought about Aubrey Garrett having cared enough to send a special gift. Aubrey might have been impractical, oblivious to realities, but he was the most patient man Jimmy had ever known. The memory inspired Jimmy to be patient, as well.

By late in the afternoon, his hip was starting to scream every time he got in and out of the car. The problem with exercise was that everything felt worse for about a month, until the muscles got toned again.

The good thing about exercise was that it tired him out enough to sleep. A few hours, anyway. Having Emma in his bed had been the only way to get a good solid sleep. Jimmy figured he had a lifetime of short nights ahead of him.

TWO DAYS LATER, Quinn's phone call caught him just as he walked into his office at the club. "I think I found what you're looking for."

"You're kidding."

"Nope. Guy in Aurora had an Indian piece come in about a week ago. He gave the guy two thousand bucks for it. Hasn't sold it, though, 'cause he knows it's worth about ten times that."

"Maybe more." Aurora was the part of Denver Tiffany lived in. Jimmy eased down into his desk chair. His heart was pounding as if he'd run a marathon. "Give me the address."

Quinn recited the location of the shop. "I told him I had a friend interested and not to ditch it until he'd talked to you."

"This is great, man. Thanks."

"Any time. Oh, and Jimmy?"

"Yeah?"

"The guy who wanted the Glock came up on the screen for illegal possession of weapons and a couple of assault charges in New Mexico."

"I thought he looked like trouble."

"Yeah. He hasn't been back."

"Surprise, surprise."

Jimmy drove out to Aurora the next morning. The business Quinn had described—a big, new building in which jewelry, weapons and household appliances were sold—was not the traditional pawnshop by any stretch of the imagination.

The owner was a big man with a big laugh. "I knew this wasn't your ordinary trinket." He took a velvet box out of a drawer. "Guy brought it in didn't have a clue. Just wanted cash for some race out in California last weekend."

Inside the box was more velvet. As the folds fell away, Jimmy sucked in his breath.

This was Aubrey's medallion. The gold and silver glinted in the overhead light, and the turquoise glowed like a sunrise sky.

"That's it." His voice sounded strained, even to his own ears. "That's what I'm looking for."

"Quinn said something about stolen property? I'm not a fence."

"I know. This was in a safe in my office until some creep blew the door open. A friend of mine brought it from England."

"How'd an Indian piece like this get to England?"

"Her dad was here, about twenty years ago, working on a reservation. One of his friends in the tribe gave him the medallion and he took it home. Now he's sent it back."

Along with Emma. Emma, who was out of a job, missing her dad, losing her faith in herself as a woman and a person. Aubrey had probably seen those things in his daughter. He'd sent Emma because he wanted Jimmy to help her out. Give her something new to do, restore her belief in her own worth.

Which he'd done pretty well, he thought. Until he let pride and fear and stupidity get in the way.

"So if this is stolen, I'm just out my two grand, right?" The big guy shook his head. "Man, I shoulda known. White guy comes in with an Indian piece, there's bound to be a catch."

Jimmy focused. "Tell me about this white guy."

"Tall, long blond hair in a ponytail. The studly type—muscle on muscle. Nice enough. But dumb."

"Yeah." The description could fit a thousand men in the Denver area, but not Harlow, Ryan or Tomas. "Listen, I'm not able to go the twenty grand you think it's worth. But I'll give you three."

After a second's consideration, the owner said, "Thirty-five hundred."

"Thirty-two-fifty."

"It's yours."

EMMA DELAYED the necessity as long as possible, but the time had come to get on with the rest of her life.

She thought about staying in Denver—she liked the dry heat, the gorgeous mountains. But the possibility that sometime, in this city of half a million people, she might run into Jimmy was simply too much of a threat. If she had to live without him, she couldn't risk seeing him. Even from a distance. These days of working near him at the club had completely convinced her—the wound simply went too deep.

Trying to work out a tentative schedule, she investigated the flights back to England on her Monday night off. Just before leaving, she'd taken a job in a small Yorkshire school whose headmaster cared little for her credentials, beyond a basic degree in history and the willingness to teach mischievous boys. Michaelmas term started in about a month. If she left for England by the first of October, she could give two weeks' notice to the landlord about vacating this flat and—

Someone knocked on her door. She didn't even consider Jimmy; this muffled beating was nothing like his crisp knock. With the chain still fastened, she peered through the eyehole. "Who is it?"

"Tiffany. Please, Emma, let me in quick."

As soon as the door swung free, Tiffany barreled in, then slammed it shut. Her fingers shook and fumbled as she latched the chain and threw the dead bolt. Only then did she turn around.

Emma gasped. "Oh my God."

Bruises covered the bartender's face and throat, as far as Emma could see into the V-neck shirt. Her jaw was swollen, her lip split. She carried her left arm cradled in her right hand.

"Damn him," Emma muttered, putting an arm around Tiffany's shoulders. "Oh, damn him."

She drew her friend into the bedroom and had her sit on the bed. Towels and cool water could do little for this kind of damage, but she tried. "Tiffany, I should take you to the hospital."

"Please, no. I…I can't face a doctor, asking questions, poking and peering. Please."

"But your shoulder…"

"He just… It was dislocated. But I pulled it back in its socket. He's done it a few times before." She tried a piteous smile. "So my tendons are pretty loose."

Emma blinked back tears. "But you look so awful."

"Gee, thanks." Another smile. "Just let me take a bath. A hot soak will do wonders."

In other words, there were more bruises Emma couldn't see.

She ran the tub full of water, added some mineral salts and left her friend alone. An hour later, the teakettle whistled as Tiffany came out of the bedroom. "Thanks for the gown and robe. Feeling clean again is great." Without makeup and with her hair hanging straight, she looked more like a young girl than a woman.

"I'm glad." Emma repressed her reaction to the bruises, the horror of what must have happened. "I've made some tea, and I put together a plate of cheese and fruit. I have some ham, though…"

Tiffany shook her head. "That sounds great. Especially the tea."

When Emma brought the tea to the coffee table, Tiffany took a sip of the hot drink. And then sighed. "What a mess I'm in now."

"Are your sisters safe? Your mother?"

She nodded. "I called them. They'll stay inside, keep the doors locked. Their boyfriends are coming over just in case. A cop lives in the building with my mom. She's gonna call him." Tiffany took a deep breath with a hitch in it. "I guess I'll have to call the cops, too. I can't…do this anymore."

Emma put a hand on her knee. "That's okay."

"Sure." She sniffed back tears. "I thought…he could be so sweet, and he always apologized. At the beginning, anyway. Lately…" She shook her head. "Lately, he doesn't care one way or the other."

"You can deal with all of this after you get a good night's sleep."

"Yeah. But I have to see Jimmy first."

"Jimmy?"

"That's how it started. I saw…I found out…" She drew another deep breath. "Brad was the one who broke into the club."

CHAPTER SEVENTEEN

GETTING A CALL from Emma was surprising enough. Being told that she and Tiffany were on their way over took surprise to an even higher level.

But nothing could have prepared Jimmy for the sight of Tiffany's face when he opened his door.

He stared for a second, his mind a total blank. "Come in," he said finally, and closed the door behind them.

Emma had taken his favorite place to stand, by the window. Jimmy turned to Tiffany. "Sit down. Tell me what… who…did this to you."

Tiffany perched on the couch. "Brad."

"Brad?" He couldn't latch on to the name at first. He sat down on the other end of the couch. "You mean Brad Renfroe? The guy you live with?" Tiffany nodded, and a burst of fury surged through him. He reached for the phone. "That sonofabitch will be locked up within thirty minutes. I promise."

Tiffany put her hand over his. "Wait a minute, boss. It's more complicated than that." While he watched, she took a deep breath. "Brad's the one who robbed the club."

"Excuse me?" He looked at Emma, who nodded, then back to Tiffany. "I don't get it."

"He needed extra cash to cover some bets he'd made, and decided that would be the easiest way." She rushed on. "He knew you kept cash in the safe—it wasn't a secret. And…and he got the alarm code and the door key from…from…'' She looked down at her hands. ''From me.''

''From you.''

She read his face. ''Not on purpose, Jimmy. You gotta believe I would never tell him stuff like that. But…but I wrote the code in my address book. You know how I am with numbers. I was afraid I'd forget it. He took the key out of my purse and put it back before I even knew it was gone.''

''When—how—did you find out?''

''Just tonight, for sure.'' She eased back on the cushion, supporting one arm with the other hand. ''I…I wondered, when he suddenly had all this cash to throw around. But tonight he was drinking with a couple of guys, watching a ball game at the house. I was cleaning up the bedroom, and…and I found that box, the one the medallion came in. It was empty, but there was only one way it could have gotten there. Then I heard Brad tell his friends how easy it was, knocking off a bar. Four grand for fifteen minutes' work, he said.''

The number fit. ''And why did he—'' Jimmy could barely look at her face without feeling sick ''—hit you?''

''He was bragging about how smart he'd been, how he'd gone in and turned off the alarm, blown the safe, then made it look like he set off the alarm when he blew the door open to get in. I was so furious I started yelling at him in front of his friends. They took off pretty quick. And then Brad started in on me.''

''God, Tiffany.'' Jimmy closed his eyes, wishing he could blank out the realization that this wasn't the first time or even the second that Tiffany had been Renfroe's punching bag. ''He's been…hurting you for a long time, hasn't he?''

Emma spoke for the first time. ''At least four episodes

since I've been here.'' Her lovely English tone shook with anger.

"Why didn't you say something, Tiff?" Jimmy demanded. "I would have taken care of the jerk."

"I don't like admitting I let him beat up on me. But when I tried to fight back, he only got worse."

"You should have left him. The first time he hit you, you should have walked away, come to me and let me take care of him. And you."

"Most women believe it won't happen again." Emma sat in the armchair. "Admitting you've made such an error in judgment takes a great deal of courage."

The echoes of their last night together—the things he'd said, the things she believed—hung in the air. Jimmy shook his head. "I just never thought…" He looked down at his hands, saw them clenched into fists, and deliberately relaxed. "So where is he now?"

"He left, probably to track down his friends—they said they were going to a bar."

"Does he know where to look for you?" His cop habits resurfaced without effort.

"He'll go to my sisters' place. Or my mom's. They're one reason I didn't say anything. He threatened them before."

Jimmy muttered a vicious curse. "I'm sure he did. Well, that'll be too bad for him." This time when he picked up the phone, she didn't stop him.

Since Tiffany lived in a different part of the city, he couldn't call on Harmon and friends to handle the situation. But he knew a few people in the Aurora department, and they remembered him well enough not to argue when he asked a favor.

"They're posting protection at your mom's and your sisters'. If Renfroe so much as bends a blade of grass, they'll pick him up." He took her good hand in his. "He won't get away with this, Tiff. And he won't ever hit you again."

She may have tried to smile, but whether from the pain of her face or the situation in general, all that happened was tears. Jimmy slid close enough to put his arms around her, holding her to his chest as she cried. It was the least he could do. He'd sure as hell failed her in every other way that counted.

After a few minutes, he realized that Tiffany had fallen asleep in his arms. He held her a little while, letting her get even deeper. Then he gently eased her down on the couch. When he looked up, Emma held out a blanket. He spread it lightly over Tiffany, dimmed the light above her head and stepped away.

The only other room in the apartment was the bedroom. "Do you want to talk?" he asked Emma with a nod toward that door.

"We can." Her shoulders lifted on a deep breath as she stepped over the threshold. Jimmy knew exactly what she was feeling because he felt the same way. Being with her in his bedroom and unable to take her in his arms hurt.

Emma turned on both bedside lamps, and the one on the chest of drawers. The bright light should have made the room less intimate. But she felt her desire increase, instead, because across the room from her stood Jimmy Falcon, looking worn and thin—and incredibly exciting. Being this close shortened her breath, quickened her heart. Her fingertips remembered the silkiness of his hair, the smoothness of his shoulders. Her body remembered being possessed by his.

He shut the door, and Emma swallowed hard.

"Did you know about...Renfroe?" His voice was different than it had been with Tiffany. Now his tone was harsh, flat.

She nodded. "I've been concerned all along. He would hurt her even when they were just playing games."

"Why the hell didn't you tell me?"

"I wanted to." Having his anger directed at her gave Emma an escape route from her desire. "She denied everything for weeks. Then she told me he would hurt her sisters. And she threatened to call the police about...about Harlow and Ryan."

Jimmy's eyes narrowed. "You chose those kids over Tiffany's safety?"

"I thought...hoped...that I could manage both. That Harlow and Ryan would be taken care of soon enough that Tiffany wouldn't have to suffer."

"You..." He put up a hand. "Never mind. The choice always rested with Tiffany. She had to be the one to break free. Nobody could do it for her."

"I did try, Jimmy. I talked to her again and again."

"If I had just known..." Abruptly, he laughed derisively. "Who the hell am I kidding? If you'd told me, I would have stuck my head in the sand, said it was her business and to stay out of it. I'm the world's best at ignoring the obvious. So what if one of my best friends gets pounded by her boyfriend on a regular basis? As long as she gets to work on time and doesn't complain about her pay or the hours, I only see the benefits—the profits—of the situation."

The raw bitterness in his voice burned her. "Tiffany camouflaged the problem, Jimmy. She didn't want you to know."

"You saw without being told."

"I'm a woman. More sensitive, maybe, to those kinds of undercurrents." Now it was Emma's turn to laugh. "Or maybe I'm just more inquisitive than you. You may have noticed, I rarely let well enough alone."

His teeth shone in the glimmer of a smile. "I've noticed." Then he sighed again. "Damn. She wouldn't be hurt tonight if I'd been a little less determined not to see the facts. Not to see anything that would make waves. If I'd just let in some light."

She couldn't think how to comfort him without touching him. And she couldn't touch him, because she couldn't guarantee she would ever stop. And she had no idea whether he would welcome or disdain the gesture.

So Emma left it unmade. She started across the room, wondering how to get through the door when he stood directly in her path. Stopping about halfway, she rested her hand on the dresser beside her. Her fingers fell on sleek wood…cool stone. She looked at what lay under her hand.

The medallion. Joy rushed through her. "How did you find it?" She picked up the disk and cradled it in both hands. "Surely Brad must have sold it."

"He did. I checked a couple of pawnshops, asked a few questions. The right people just happened to have the information I needed."

She stared at him. "Somehow I think there was much more to the process than that. But, oh, I'm glad you have it back. It brings Dad closer, don't you think, to have the medallion right here?"

"Definitely." The expression in Jimmy's eyes was one she didn't dare believe. She had trusted that desire once, only to have him throw it back in her face.

He stretched a hand toward her. "Emma, I—"

"Jimmy?" Tiffany called from the front room. "Jimmy? Emma? Where'd you go?"

"Right here, Tiff." Jimmy held Emma's eyes for a moment, then turned to open the door. "Are you ready to get this creep taken care of?"

AT THE AURORA police station, Jimmy shepherded Tiffany through the process of swearing out a complaint and put into motion the application for a restraining order.

The next step involved an argument.

"I don't need to go to a shelter, boss. I can go to my mom's."

"That's asking for trouble, Tiff. If Renfroe shows up and knows you're there, he could get crazy."

"You said there would be protection."

"Not forever."

Emma leaned forward from the back seat of the Jaguar and put a hand on Tiffany's shoulder. "You'd be welcome to stay with me. But Brad might come there, as well. An anonymous place, where he won't think to look, will be the safest."

Tiffany sighed. "What if he shows up at the club?"

"You won't be there."

Emma bit back a gasp. The bartender—ex-bartender?—drew a sharp breath. "Okay, so I'm fired. But that won't stop Brad if he's mad. He'll wreck the place all over again."

At the next stoplight, Jimmy took a hand off the steering wheel and gave Tiffany a light tap on the cheek. "You are not fired. As long as The Indigo stays open, you're tending bar."

"Boss—"

"But until Renfroe is locked up—and I do intend to see that happen—you don't need to be accessible. Just figure on getting a lot of reading done."

Emma blinked back tears. Tiffany sniffed, then sniffed again. They rode the rest of the way to the shelter Jimmy had located in a sweet, sad silence.

With Tiffany installed in the shelter, Jimmy drove Emma home. He wasn't sure what to say, so he didn't say anything. Emma stared out the window, which made approaching her even harder.

At the curb in front of her building, he let the car idle. He *was* sure she didn't want him to walk her to her door.

"Well." She finally turned to face him. "I hope the police will be able to work backward now and get proof that Brad robbed The Indigo."

"With a picture, they can probably find out where he bought the explosive. I've already got ID on him for selling the medallion. With any luck, he'll go away for a couple of years at least."

"That's good." Emma's gaze stayed locked with his, and the air started to vibrate deep and low. At last she said, "I've made a plane reservation. I'll be going back to England in three weeks."

Jimmy blinked, tried to reorient. This feeling was the same as being hit by a bullet. "You're leaving?" Brilliant deduction.

She nodded. "I've accepted a teaching post in Yorkshire for the fall. It won't be a university post, with research opportunities and prestige, but at least I'll be making a living."

"Yeah. Sure." Even though he'd known it would happen, he couldn't get past the main point. *Emma was going out of his life. Again.* "What about Harlow? Ryan?" *Me?*

She closed her eyes for a second. "I've come to the conclusion that you were right all along. Harlow is selling drugs now, which means that Ryan will no doubt be back on heroin as soon as he leaves the center. In my great conceit, I thought I could save them, and Tiffany, too. Perhaps this time I've learned my lesson."

"Emma, you don't..." He reconsidered. If he explained about Harlow, the whole operation might fall through. And the boy could end up in serious trouble.

When he didn't say anything, she nodded. "If you'd like, I'll stay until you find a new cook."

That gave him the excuse he needed, without having to

fire her or even to lie very much. "That's okay. I've got a line on a new guy already. I can bring him in and give it a shot."

"Oh. Well, then." Her face was pale, shocked, hurt. "That's good. I..." She stared at him and shook her head. Before he could close his hand around her arm, she was out of the car. "Thanks for helping Tiffany."

Jimmy sat without moving for a long time after Emma had disappeared. Her optimism had really taken a beating. He'd warned her, but he didn't like being proved right, not when that meant seeing Emma draw back from life. That was *his* approach, not hers.

Now it looked as if the more he got involved, the more Emma retreated. She planned to retreat all the way to England, take a lousy job in some damp school in the middle of nowhere. He remembered her saying that she missed the English mist. Maybe, but she was made for the sun, for brightness and laughter and joy.

Somehow, with everything else that was going on, he would simply have to make her realize that.

As a cook, Zach Harmon failed miserably.

"I can't follow Emma's recipes," he told Darren for the tenth time. "Tell them we've got ham sandwiches and chips, or roast-beef sandwiches and chips, or peanut butter and jelly. That's the menu."

Darren looked over at Jimmy. "This was the best you could do to replace Emma?"

"Just serve the drinks, Darren. Don't worry about anything else." The college student knew nothing about the plans being made. Jimmy intended to keep him in the dark.

"Yeah, right. It's not *your* tip they forget when the food's no good." Still muttering, Darren pushed the kitchen door open and let it slam behind him.

Zach shook his head. "You're going to have a mutiny

pretty soon. Between a missing bartender and a new cook, the natives are getting very restless.''

Jimmy shrugged. ''It won't matter much longer. Harlow brought me a message from Santos tonight. He'll be here Monday at nine to discuss selling drugs in the club. Him and me and Harlow and Tommy. I'm betting he brings at least one other goon along.''

''Yeah. But we have extra goons on our side, too. We'll set up the recording equipment in a van outside with a few extra cops standing by. I'll be in here with the door cracked open. And at least one of the undercover guys will get himself here somehow. All you have to do is wear the wire, tape what we need, and then we all come crashing in, guns ready, and ride out in a blaze of glory.''

''I think you're in the wrong movie. This is the one where both sides start shooting and everybody ends up dead except the guy under the table.''

Zach shook his head. ''Nah. We've got it covered. It'll be smooth as glass. Nothing's going wrong with this operation, I guarantee.''

Jimmy wished he felt that way in his gut. He lifted his whiskey glass in a toast to his friend. ''Here's hoping you're right about that.''

Harmon grinned. ''I'm always right.''

THE WEEK BEFORE her flight back to England, Emma decided she would visit Ryan to say goodbye. Though she hadn't seen Harlow since leaving her cook's post, she wouldn't try to find him again. What could she say? He'd made his choice. At least she wouldn't be in Denver to watch the inevitable end to his story.

No longer confined to bed, Ryan spent much of his time in the recreation room of the center, playing video games or a strange-looking contraption he called Foosball. Today she found him in the middle of a video war between galaxies, firing missiles at opponent planes and dodging their own.

"Hi, Miss Emma. Have a seat. Just let me finish…I'm about to beat the best score…" Ducking and pitching from side to side as if he occupied the pilot's chair in the plane, Ryan finished his battle successfully. "Two hundred forty-seven thousand points. All right!" When prompted, he typed in his initials—REC—at the top of a long list.

He relaxed with a sigh. "That was cool. I been trying all week to beat Wayne's top score. He'll be so pissed." Grinning, he finally turned his attention on her. "How are you?"

"I'm well, thanks. You look good."

"I'm okay. At least I get enough to eat here. But the group sessions are a real pain. I don't have anything to talk about and I have to just sit and listen. Boring."

"Or perhaps," Emma said gently, "you don't have anything you're ready to talk about right now."

Ryan's answer was a nonchalant shrug.

"I wanted to stop by to see you one last time. I'll be flying back to England next week, and I'd like to think you'll continue your progress after I leave."

His brown eyes went round. "Whaddaya mean, back to England?"

"That's my home. I'm going to teach at a school in the northern part of England. The term starts in October, so I'd best be heading back."

"B-but…you can't. You can't just walk off and leave us here."

"It won't be easy, Ryan. But you and Harlow can take care of yourselves. You'll be fine."

He muttered a rude word. "With Harlow and Tommy working for Santos, you think we'll be fine?"

Emma didn't have an answer because she knew he was right. As long as the boys were connected to a drug dealer, they would never be safe and well.

"I was counting on you to talk Harlow into quitting." Ryan wrung his hands. "He don't want the money. He's just doing it to take care of me—all these bills Mr. Falcon pays."

"I don't think I can talk Harlow into anything, Ryan. I can't say anything he would want to hear."

"You're giving up on him? On us?" Ryan lay back in his chair, eyes closed. "I never thought you would give up."

Her insides shriveled in shame. "I'm sorry, Ryan."

"Yeah, sure. Everybody's sorry." His lower lip stuck out in a pout.

She stood to leave, even took a step toward the door. Then she faced him again. "I...I could try one last time. To talk to Harlow, I mean. Do you know how I can find him?"

Ryan looked up at her, suspicion in his eyes. "You mean it?"

"Of course. I don't lie to you, do I?"

"I guess not." He still seemed unsure, and she waited. "Okay. Why don't you just talk to him at the club?"

"Mr. Falcon has a new cook. I'm not working there any longer. Besides, it's noisy and crowded, not the place for the kind of conversation I hope to have."

"So go over on Monday night. The club's closed, but Mr. Falcon usually wants Harlow over there to do some kind of cleanup work. It'll be quiet then."

She didn't want to see Jimmy again, didn't want to have to say goodbye once more. She'd barely held herself together the last time.

But she'd promised Ryan. "All right. I'll find Harlow at The Indigo tomorrow night." Taking a chance, she bent to put a kiss on his forehead. "Take care, Ryan."

He sighed. "You, too, Miss Emma."

THROUGH SUNDAY night and most of Monday she regretted having promised to try. A confrontation would only make both Harlow and herself uncomfortable. Maybe even angry. And if Jimmy was there...

On the other hand, if she didn't take this last chance, she would never know if she could have made a difference. This might be the one night she succeeded in setting Harlow and Ryan on a new path. If she abandoned them before she tried, she could never live with herself.

And so nine o'clock found her making one last trip to The Indigo. She watched the familiar cityscape roll past, trying to soak the image into her brain. It was nothing like England, but there was something vigorous and vital about Denver and its people. She felt comfortable here. Could have made it her home, if only...

When she stepped out of the cab, The Indigo displayed its usual run-down attitude, without the liveliness of a crowd and music to lend energy. Jimmy's Jaguar was parked down the street. That meant she would have to see him. She felt her heart crack at the prospect.

But she gathered her resolve, set her hand on the door, and stepped inside.

As she stood there, faces turned and stared, in various stages of shock. She saw Harlow and Tommy to her right, at the near end of the bar. Jimmy stood at the other end, elbows propped on the scarred mahogany surface, his face like stone. Close by, a man sat on a bar stool. As she closed the door, he swung his knees around and gazed at her. He was dark—Mexican, perhaps—and young. Slender but not thin; very good-looking, in fact, and well-dressed in a light-colored jacket and slacks with a dark blue shirt.

"Well, well," he said in a soft voice. "Who have we here?" He looked back at Jimmy. "I'm impressed, Falcon. I had no idea you were going to provide entertainment."

Jimmy straightened up from the bar. In the slow deliberation of his movements, Emma recognized the message that something was very, very wrong.

And she had just made it worse.

HARLOW HAD NEVER BEEN so scared. It was bad enough just knowing that Jimmy was wearing a wire and if Santos even suspected, they'd all be dead.

Now Emma was here, too.

At the other end of the bar, Jimmy straightened. "Hey, Emma. This isn't a real good time. Can you check back with me tomorrow afternoon?" His voice was even and low, but Harlow could hear the steel inside the words.

Eyes wide, Emma backed up a step. "Oh...um...of course. I'll just..."

Without a sound, Ace, the bodyguard with three earrings, appeared beside her. She glanced at him, at the door and then looked at Jimmy again.

"I don't think the lady needs to leave." Santos dropped off the bar stool and picked up his drink. "Give us some more light, Falcon. We can move to a table, be more comfortable. Talk."

Jimmy turned on every light in the place. The room went from shadows to midday. Then he walked to the table where Santos sat. "She doesn't matter. Let her leave."

"A pretty lady always matters." Santos looked over at Emma. "Come sit down, Emma. Have a drink."

"No, thank you. I'll just be—"

Ace took her arm and started toward the table. Emma tugged back without effect. In a second she was sitting across the table from one of the baddest men Harlow had ever known.

Eddy's guy backed up a couple of steps, but not so far that he couldn't get into the action in less than a second.

Jimmy pulled out a chair and sat on the other side of Emma. "Let's finish this up. I've got somebody else to see after you leave." His grin was sly. "And she's a lot nicer to look at."

"Than this lady?" Santos stroked the backs of his fingers down Emma's bare arm. "I don't see how that's possible."

Harlow saw Jimmy's jaw tighten, then relax. "So you and Emma can paint the town. Let's get our business done first."

Santos sighed. "You should relax more. All right. What do you want?"

"I'll let you put a paper boy in here with whatever stuff you want to sell. I think a fifty-fifty split on the money sounds reasonable."

"I think you're crazy."

Emma was looking from one man to the other, her expression puzzled. Harlow saw the minute understanding hit. And then her gaze went to his own face and stayed there, considering.

Jimmy was going through with the plan, even with Emma here. "I'm taking a hell of a risk. I've got cops dropping by all the time. This isn't going to be a picnic."

Santos rolled his eyes. "Eighty-twenty."

"Yeah, right. Maybe you'd like to just give the stuff away and we'll call it even."

"Settle down, Falcon. Let's make it seventy-thirty."

"Forty-sixty, Santos, or forget it."

"You want forty percent of the take just to let my guy sit in here on the chance that one of your lousy customers decides to snort a couple of lines? Remember, I got overhead—the carrier wants his cut."

"I've known a lot of my customers for years. And I know for a fact that some of them have very hefty habits. I'm offering you a chance to break into that market. Take it or leave it." Jimmy pushed away from the table and started to stand up.

"Okay, okay." Eddy waved him back into the chair. "So we'll split with sixty percent coming back to me, forty stays with you. Satisfied?"

"It'll do."

Santos looked at Emma. "He's a hard man to please. You find that to be true, pretty Emma?" His fingertip traced a line down her cheek. Emma sat like a rock. But her eyes were furious.

"So give me an idea of the inventory." Jimmy's voice was like wire stretched to the breaking point. "That way I can let customers know what'll be available. And for how much."

"You tell him, Tommy." Santos motioned Tommy forward.

"If I wanted to hear from Tommy, I would have asked him."

Santos swore. "You are way too freaked, man. Loosen up." He sighed. "We carry the usual—crack, coke, weed, horse. We got Ecstasy and meth. I can get LSD if somebody's interested. Or anything else. Got a shipment of Mexican tar coming up next week. Makes a great cocktail, huh, Harlow?"

Harlow groped for an answer. "The best."

"As for prices, fair market value's all I ever ask. No markups, like some guys out there."

"You're all heart." Jimmy stood again and held out his hand. "Sounds like a deal to me. You can put your boy here anytime I'm open. I'll just take my cut before he leaves for the night."

Santos stared up at him without taking Jimmy's hand. "Sure. Whatever. Now, how about a round of drinks for my lady and me? What'll you have, sweet Emma?"

Jimmy put a hand around Emma's arm and pulled her to her feet. "Lay off, Santos. Get your own."

Santos's smile turned ugly. "What I see is what I get, brother. Let the lady go. Or—"

"That's enough." Zach Harmon stepped out of the kitchen, gun aimed at Santos. "Eddy Santos, you're under arrest for possession of and conspiracy to sell illegal substances. Stand up and put your hands on your head."

Tommy turned to stare at Harlow. "You did this. You little sonofabitch."

"Interesting insight, Tommy." Santos had a gun out, too, pointed at Harlow's chest. And the goon behind Emma had his gun covering Zach. "The cop can leave, or else these two little junkies are going directly to the big rehab center in the sky." Harmon didn't move, and Eddy pulled back the hammer of the gun. "Don't push me. Falcon, get your buddy out of here or I'm taking your friends down with me."

Suddenly Emma started to scream.

CHAPTER EIGHTEEN

EMMA'S SCREAM distracted everybody for the two seconds Jimmy needed. He swung the chair in front of him up and around, onto Eddy Santos's shoulders.

The dealer dropped to his knees. As he started to get up, Jimmy lunged, taking Santos to the floor on his back. The gun went sliding across the floor, and Santos seemed to wilt. By the time Jimmy got two good punches in, the man underneath him had stopped fighting altogether.

"My hero," a voice said right above his head. "Get off and get up."

Tomas held the gun now, pointed straight at Jimmy's face. The struggle to stand gave Jimmy a few seconds to breathe. He also had a chance to see how the situation had changed. Harmon had Tomas covered. Good enough.

And Santos's bodyguard had Emma's arms drawn high behind her back. "Keep your mouth shut," the goon told her. He pushed a gun barrel into her temple.

Against every impulse, every desire in his body, Jimmy forced himself to look away, to face Tommy's gun. He held out his hand. "You're in deep enough already. Give me the weapon and let's call it a day." With luck, no more cops would come rushing in to the rescue. That was a guarantee that somebody would die.

Tommy snorted. "Yeah, right. You okay, Eddy?"

"Give me a hand here." Tommy pulled Santos to his feet. A nice shiner had started up over the dealer's left eye and his split lip was oozing blood. Jimmy had screwed up, though—he should have completely leveled the guy.

Emma would still have a gun to her head.

Santos looked that way. "I think we can keep the lady under control without bullets. Hand me your piece, Ace." Reaching across the table, without letting go of Emma, the goon laid his gun in Santos's hand. "I'm not into killing cops. Makes life too complicated. But pissant junkies are different." He swung around to face Harlow. "Nobody cheats me and nobody—nobody, you hear?—double crosses me. You're gonna eat it, boy. Big time."

"Wait a minute, Eddy." Tommy kept his gun and his eyes on Jimmy. "It's not Harlow's fault. Not really. He would have been cool with us, except for that bitch." A nod of his head indicated Emma. "I coulda talked him around, but she kept butting in, feeding him, making him think she cared about what happened to him. She got him involved with Falcon, and with the cops. If anybody's to blame for what happened tonight, it's her."

"That's bull, Tommy. And you know it." Harlow moved a couple of steps closer—closer to Jimmy and closer to Santos's gun. "The only reason I went to work for Santos was to take him down. He nearly killed Ry. He's got you totally brainwashed. Emma has nothing to do with any of that. It's me and you and him. That's all."

"We were friends, until her." Tommy steadied his gun with both hands. "After she came, Ry and I were out in the freakin' cold. We didn't have anywhere to go, until Eddy gave me a job."

Harlow came another step closer. "We're still friends, Tommy. All you have to do to prove it is choose the right side."

"How tender." Santos smiled. "Two boyhood friends, with divided loyalties, forced to choose between their relationship and making money. There's probably a film deal in the works already.'' His face hardened. "You're coming with us, rat. We'll deal with you on our own turf.'' He turned to Jimmy. "I suggest you relocate your joint to, say, California. You won't have five people willing to come in here by the time I'm finished with you."

Jimmy shook his head. "We've got you on tape, Santos.'' At his side, he felt Harlow tense. The kid was going to make a move—and end up dead. "Doesn't matter where you go. The cops'll have you by morning."

"I've got a real good lawyer, Falcon. One who knows how to yell 'entrapment' and wrap that red tape around your neck until your face turns blue. You're outta luck—"

Harlow sprang straight for Santos. A split second behind him, Jimmy shoved into the boy's hip with a shoulder, knocking him in Tommy's direction. Santos turned, intending to fire at Harlow, only to be tackled from behind by Ace the goon, also known as Dicky Sanders of the Denver P.D. Dicky had fifty pounds on Santos, and the dealer went down swearing.

Under Zach's cover, Jimmy pushed off the floor onto Santos's ribs, this time getting a grip on the hand with the pistol. Lying flat out, Jimmy slammed that hand into the floor, again and again and again, until the fingers finally loosened and the gun slipped free. Harmon picked it up, covering Santos with a weapon in each hand.

Jimmy slid to his knees on the floor, trying to find Emma, trying to figure out what had happened to Harlow.

Emma stood with a chair in her hands, legs forward, to ward off anyone who came near. She looked like an old-fashioned lion tamer. Jimmy would have grinned if Harlow hadn't still been in trouble. With one knee on the floor, he looked up at Tommy, who aimed the gun at his friend's face. When Tommy realized Jimmy was on his feet, he shifted targets—from Harlow to Jimmy and back again.

"You'll have to choose,'' Jimmy said quietly. "You

can't get both of us at the same time. As soon as you pull the trigger, whoever's left will be on top of you. Are you ready to go up for a murder rap? You know what happens to boys like you in the state pen? You can do better than that, Tommy. We can help.''

Tommy swallowed hard. ''What should I do, Eddy? Tell me what to do.''

But Santos was sprawled across the bar, having his hands cuffed and his rights read by Zach and Sanders.

''He's not the one to listen to,'' Harlow said. ''You can still get out of this, Tommy. Just put down the gun. That's all you have to do—put down the damn gun.''

Nobody breathed. Tommy sweated while he thought, his gun barrel twitching back and forth. Finally, still shaking, his arm started to lower. Jimmy felt sweat trickle between his shoulder blades as he kept his eyes on that gun. He prayed that nobody moved. Too many lives hung in the balance.

''Oh, man.'' Tommy's shoulders slumped, and he put his free hand over his eyes. Jimmy stepped close enough to take the gun from the boy's limp fingers. ''Oh, man.''

''It'll be okay.'' Harlow put his arms around his friend. ''Don't worry, Tommy. It'll be okay.''

AFTERWARD THERE WERE policemen everywhere, all talking at once. Sirens and flashing lights. Reporters and news-station vans. More commotion than Emma had ever seen in one small place. More commotion than she ever wanted to see again.

A post in a rural Yorkshire school should definitely limit her exposure to events such as this.

She gave her statement to an officer and then sat at a table, watching Jimmy. Surrounded by friends and colleagues, he was the man of the hour.

As soon as he'd given Tommy's gun to the bodyguard who had turned out to be a policeman, he'd come to her.

"Great scream. I'm glad you picked up my signal." He put his hands on her shoulders and appraised her from head to toe. "Are you okay?"

"My arms and shoulders are a bit sore," she confessed. "Otherwise, no problem. Is Tommy going to jail?"

Jimmy shrugged. "I don't know. We'll see what we can do." Someone near the bar called his name and beckoned him over. He looked back at Emma. "Don't go anywhere," he said urgently, intensely. "I want to talk to you when this zoo shuts down."

But what was there really to talk about? She understood a great deal now without needing to be told. Jimmy had reopened The Indigo specifically for the purpose of snaring Eddy Santos. Harlow had taken a job with the dealer for the same reason. Somehow the two of them had come to an understanding, had worked together on a project that took remarkable courage. Even Harlow's avoidance of her now became clear. If she'd had the least inkling of their plans, she would certainly have interfered, possibly derailed the entire operation. As it was, she'd caused a good deal of trouble and complicated the situation immeasurably.

Surely this time, at last, she had learned not to interfere.

Now Harlow would go back to his regular life. Or perhaps he could follow Ryan's example and withdraw from the drug before it killed him. Jimmy would close the club and drift wherever the wind blew. That seemed to be what he wanted. As little real life as possible.

They could say goodbye, she supposed. That hadn't been officially taken care of. But the last thing she wanted was to leave Jimmy Falcon. And saying goodbye would draw out the pain. Why not simply vanish?

Emma sighed. Because that was the coward's way. She didn't want to remember Jimmy as the man she ran away from. She would give him as much as she had until the very end.

And so she waited out the chaos in Jimmy's office, to avoid the reporters and the cameras and the gawkers. After hesitating, she sat in his chair, behind the desk, let its soft leather surround her as if Jimmy held her in his arms. This was the most peace she'd known in weeks.

"Hey there, Emma."

She opened sleep-heavy eyes to see Harlow standing in the doorway. "You're speaking to me now, are you?"

He ducked his head. "That was part of the deal with Jimmy. I had to stay away from you. We didn't want you involved."

"You must have been very pleased when I came waltzing into the middle of your plans."

"Things worked out okay. Santos is going away for a while. Ry's getting cleaned up. Tommy…well, I don't know about Tommy yet. Maybe he can cut a deal."

"And what about you?"

"Me?" He sat in the chair across the desk.

"What happens to you now? Where are you going?"

"Same place as always, I guess. Nowhere."

"You could change, as Ryan has." This was the conversation she'd promised she would undertake.

"I don't know, Emma. I'm not sure it's worth the effort."

"I think so." She brought even greater pressure to bear. "Jimmy thinks so, or he wouldn't have asked you to work with him."

"Yeah, well, no offense, but you two don't know everything."

"What do we need to know?"

He didn't say anything for a long time. "I told you my brother died."

"Yes. And your parents' grief overwhelmed them."

"I left out one big detail." Harlow stared down at his hands. "I was the one driving the car."

"I don't understand."

"I bugged him to let me drive that day. I didn't have a license, not even a learner's permit. But he let me get behind the wheel. The car had a manual transmission—you know what that means?"

She kept her smile to herself. "You have to shift the gears manually."

"Right. I had a hell of a time with the clutch. Never did get the hang of it. That day, I stalled the car in the middle of an intersection. We sat there for about ten minutes, people honking and swearing, me trying to get my foot from the clutch to the gas pedal without killing the engine. Finally Mark got out to come around and drive. I climbed over the stick to the passenger side." He drew in a deep breath. "Just as Mark cleared the front end of the car, one of the idiots behind us decided to pull out and speed past. He hit Mark, threw him about twenty feet."

Emma closed her eyes against the vision. "I'm so sorry."

"Me, too. Since it was my fault."

"You're smart enough to recognize that's not the case."

Harlow shrugged. "My folks thought so. My little brother asked me why I let Mark die." His voice faded to a whisper on the last word.

"Listen to me." She got down on her knees beside his chair. "Even if you caused the accident, which I don't accept, you still have a right to your life. You have a right to be safe, to have enough to eat. To go through your day without worrying where your next hit will come from. Everyone makes mistakes. You're letting yours destroy you. Make a different choice, Harlow. Decide to live."

In the hallway outside his office, Jimmy stepped back and returned quietly to the front room. Emma might have been talking to Harlow, but her words spoke to Jimmy, as well. He had his own choice to make. He could settle for existence. Or he could have a life. A life, if he was very lucky, with Emma.

When she came out with Harlow, both of them looked drained. Emma smiled wearily. "I'm sorry we kept you waiting."

"The last of the cops left just a few minutes ago. Are you two ready to leave?"

Emma nodded. Harlow headed for the door. "I'll catch y'all later, okay?"

Jimmy caught the boy's arm as he went by. "Where do you think you're going?"

"Uh…wherever."

"You can sleep at my place again. We'll figure out what to do with you in the morning."

Whatever had been holding Harlow together suddenly broke down. His shoulders slumped and he shook his head. "Thanks, Jimmy. I appreciate the help."

"Anytime." Jimmy looked over at Emma and caught her wiping her cheeks with her fingers. "You're about to drop where you stand. Let me take you home."

When they were parked at the curb outside her apartment, Emma turned and put a hand on Jimmy's knee. "He's fallen asleep back there. Don't worry about coming up with me." She gazed at him, and her eyes filled with tears. Before he realized what she was doing, she leaned forward and kissed him. Sweetly. Sadly.

And then drew back. "Goodbye, Jimmy. Take care of yourself."

She sounded very final. He knew what she was thinking, but now was not the time to change her mind.

So he said, "Good night, Emma. Sleep tight."

And then he let her walk away. For a little while.

IN THE END, Emma allowed Harlow to persuade her to postpone her flight to England until he was stabilized on a methadone program. There were repercussions, of course. The headmaster at the Yorkshire school was quite nasty about being left in the lurch. She had given notice on her flat and had to move back to a hotel. Her savings dwindled rapidly. But she couldn't abandon Harlow while he needed her.

If only Jimmy had needed her as much.

But Jimmy pretty effectively disappeared after that night at The Indigo. With Zach Harmon's help, Harlow found a halfway house where he could sleep and get decent meals, and an outpatient methadone clinic. He spent most of his time with Ryan at the inpatient center. Within days, the two of them began to look like regular teenage boys.

Emma stopped in to see them one October afternoon about three weeks after Harlow entered the program. She found Ryan immersed in the video game as usual. Harlow was stretched out on a sofa, holding a coverless paperback book in front of his face.

He looked up with a grin as she came into the room. "Hello there. You're particularly pretty today."

"Flattery will get you everywhere." She sat down in a chair nearby. "How are you?"

"Not bad. Kinda sleepy. But I've got a bed to snooze in now. That's a definite improvement."

One of many. "Have you thought any more about enrolling in school?" The counselors had talked with both boys about the wisdom of completing their education and preparing for a decent future. There were programs available for students who needed to make up missed years of study.

"I do think about it. Maybe in the new year. I'm taking things real easy for awhile."

Now they came to the hardest question of all. "And what about your family?"

His face was still, his eyes shuttered. "I called them, like you asked me to. My mom…cried."

"Are they coming to see you?"

"I didn't tell them where I was."

"Harlow—"

He held up his hands. "I will, I will. Eventually." Smiling ruefully, he met her gaze again. "One thing at a time, you know?"

She did know, and decided not to push further. "That sounds wise."

"Speaking of sounds…." Harlow got up off the sofa. "I've got something I want to show you. Come on."

Emma followed him into the hallway and upstairs. She noticed a sort of musical noise in the air, which grew louder as they climbed. Not a song, just disjointed notes and chords, accompanied by a completely arrhythmic drumbeat.

Harlow took her to a room at the front of the building and pushed open the unlatched door. Inside, a group of five or six boys sat in a circle. Two of the boys held guitars. One sat on the floor with bongo drums between his knees. Another perched on the stool behind a drum set.

Behind him stood Jimmy Falcon.

"Pa papa boom chink," he said. "Pa papa boom chink." The boy with the drumsticks attempted to mimic the pattern, with some success, though he missed the cymbal altogether once. "Good. Now just keep doing it. Pa papa boom chink. Pa papa boom chink."

Jimmy moved to a chair behind the boys with guitars. "Okay, guys. Show me your G-one chord. G four. Good. Now G five. Right. So your pattern is…" He led them through a series of chords, ones and fours and fives, in a rhythm similar to the one the drummer still played. "Now, if we all start at the same time, this should be music."

He went to stand behind the drummer again, with a glance toward the door. Emma couldn't manage a smile, she was so shocked to see him here. But Jimmy's eyes warmed and then that wonderful grin appeared, the one she never could resist.

Looking back at the boys, he started snapping his fingers. "Let's get this together now. One, two, one two three four. Pa papa boom chink. One…four…one…five…"

After several shaky repetitions, the boys found their mode. The chords got stronger, the beat more even. When the sound was solid, Jimmy started to sing.

"Twinkle, twinkle, little star." His mellow voice made the words important. Somehow, the drums and the guitars and the chords became a song. A slow song, true, but recognizable music.

"Cool!" The drummer stopped playing and threw his sticks in the air. "Let's start over." This time, he counted them off with taps on the rim of a drum.

Jimmy backed away, watching and listening, as the guitar players sang and played along. Eventually he came to stand beside Emma.

"Hey, boss." Harlow gave him a cheeky grin.

"Hey, yourself." He gave the boy a knock on the shoulder. "Hi, Emma. How are you?"

She found her voice. "I'm…well. What are you doing here?"

"Fooling around mostly." He avoided directly meeting her gaze.

Harlow rolled his eyes. "Give me a break. He's here three times a week giving some of the guys music lessons."

Emma looked back at Jimmy and saw his cheeks turn a dull red. "You're working with these boys? As a volunteer?"

He shrugged. "We jam a little, we talk some, that kinda thing. Nothing major."

"I see." Just under her breastbone, a smile was born. She felt it expand through her chest and throat until it reached her lips. "They seem to enjoy what they're doing."

"The music is pretty cool," Harlow volunteered. "In my group we're working on 'Hey, Jude' by the Beatles."

Jimmy nodded. "Next thing you know, you'll be singing at the club. Can a recording contract be far behind?"

"I wouldn't hold my breath, boss."

"I'm not. Why don't you go show those two some D chords and let me talk with Emma?"

"Sure." Harlow hunkered down beside the boys on the floor. Released from the rules, the drummer created a rhythm pattern of his own that involved loud cymbals and crashing bass drumbeats. Jimmy grinned and held the door open for Emma to step out into the hall.

"It gets kinda noisy sometimes."

She shook her head as they walked back toward the stairs. "I...I don't know what to say. I'm so glad you've decided there's hope for change."

"I couldn't ignore what was right in front of my eyes." She looked at him inquiringly. "Harlow and Ryan. I saw how confidence and caring really do make a difference."

Now Emma's cheeks were heating up. Jimmy's warm hand had taken hold of her elbow. When they reached the ground floor, he steered her toward the exit and, once outside, turned her toward the small parking lot. She could see the Jaguar parked under a leafless tree.

She resisted his progress. "Don't you need to get back to your class?"

"I should have left an hour ago. I was just waiting for you."

Her breath caught. "Me?"

"Harlow told me you were coming today. I thought we had some things to talk about. If you don't mind."

"Oh." Another of those smiles came into existence.

Since the last one still lingered, she was having trouble breathing around the happiness. "No. I don't mind."

She'd chosen a hotel within reasonable walking distance of the rehabilitation center, but Jimmy started the car and pulled into traffic without asking where she was staying. Content just to be with him again, Emma didn't question their destination, but watched his profile, his hands on the wheel, the set of his shoulders under a leather jacket. Once he glanced over and caught her staring. She started to blush, but Jimmy only grinned.

When the car stopped, she finally took notice of her surroundings. He'd brought her to The Indigo. Before she could open her door, Jimmy had come around to do it for her, to take her hand and help her out of the low-slung Jag. He locked the car, but didn't let her go, even to release the dead bolt on the club's faded blue door. The key turned with oiled ease. Then Jimmy led her across the threshold.

She expected darkness, but that was gone. Through the first-story windows high above, sunlight poured onto the floor of the main room. The ugly black ceiling, the pipes and ducts and the floorboards above it, had been completely removed.

"Jimmy?" Emma turned to stare at him. "What in the world has happened?" Behind the bar, all the bottles were gone. The mirror reflected Jimmy's back, herself and a huge empty space. All tables, chairs and bar stools had vanished and only the mahogany bar stayed behind. "Where is—" she gestured at the space "—everything?"

"Zach and a couple of guys helped me take out the ceiling. Of course, that took out the electricity and the lights, too. The windows definitely come in handy."

"But why?"

He came to her in the center of the space. "I decided that there never was enough room in here for a decent crowd. But the only direction I could really expand was up.''

"Up?"

One hand gestured toward the walls, as if painting a picture. "What I'm thinking about is a balcony around three sides, wide enough for tables and chairs and walking room. An open railing, so people up there can see the band." He brought his gaze from the emptiness above them to her face. "What do you think?"

"I—"

"The stairs are still sound, and I figure we can work it so they lead up to the balcony, but still have some space left to expand the stage. There should even be enough for a dressing room. Not too big, but these guys aren't stars quite yet."

Head spinning, Emma could only gaze at him. "You... you're renovating. That's wonderful."

She expected a quick funny answer. But Jimmy's eyes were steady and unsmiling, his mouth a straight serious line. "Do you want to be here to see it finished?"

Now she couldn't say anything at all.

He put his hands on her shoulders. "Emma, you have to know the things I said that night weren't true. What's between us has never been surface. You've filled a place deep inside me since I was seventeen."

Emma took hold of her courage. "You did the same for me."

Jimmy grinned. "Your dad knew it, too. That's the reason he sent you here with the medallion. He knew I needed you to bring me back to life."

"Perhaps almost as much as I needed you." She brushed his hair back from his forehead. "He knew I would be lost when he was gone. And he knew where I belonged."

Jimmy pressed a kiss to her forehead. "I didn't want to need anything. I'd given up, I guess, on ever winning. But you came, and I couldn't stop craving what you are—generous and bright and hopeful and curious and—"

"Please." She hid her face against his shoulder. "You're seeing so much more than there really is."

"Beautiful. Beautiful inside. And beautiful to look at." With a hand under her chin, he lifted her face. "I hated what you thought that night. I love to look at you just the way you are." He took the clip from her hair and put it in his pocket. "Clear blue eyes, rich red hair. Smooth white skin and incredible feminine curves." His palms traced those curves. "Doesn't matter where we are, what we're doing. One look at you and I'm wanting you. Always."

He brought her right hand to his mouth and kissed her knuckles. "I'm not a big success—just a guy who owns a jazz club. I don't know much about being a husband, and less about being a father. But I love you, Emma Mae Garrett. Forgive me for making you doubt yourself. And then marry me."

Before she could answer, Jimmy laid his hand along her jawline and brought their lips together. His arms wrapped around her waist, and Emma yielded, body and heart and soul. Light swirled inside her head like sparks from a bonfire. She could have this man for the rest of her life. She could look after Jimmy, and their children—oh, God, she'd believed she would never have children. At the thought, she started to cry.

The kiss got very wet, and she pulled away to bury her face in Jimmy's shoulder. He held her, stroking her back, her hair, as she sobbed away a lifetime of doubt.

"Does that mean no?" he asked quietly when she finally subsided to hiccups and sniffs.

"Of course not." She looked at him, knowing her eyes and nose were red, her hair mussed, her face splotched. Knowing, really knowing, that he saw only the beauty of the woman he loved. "How can I possibly say no to a dream come true?"

He shook his head. "I'm no dream. More like a nightmare."

"I'd say more like a knight errant, ready to come home after a lifetime of wandering."

Jimmy closed his eyes and sighed. "Home. With you. Oh, yeah."

They held each other for a long time, standing in the golden light pouring through the windows. At some point Jimmy started to hum, then to sing, an old Sinatra number. Emma caught snatches of words—about being lost and being found, just in time. She smiled into his shoulder and swayed with the tune until they were dancing, and the sparkling dust motes floated on the air around them like magic...or the graceful blessing of a father's contented love.

EPILOGUE

THE GRAND REOPENING party of The Indigo Club was a private affair. Champagne and punch were the only drinks available, served from big silver bowls reflected in the shining polish of the mahogany bar. White cloths and chrysanthemums graced the tops of the sleek stainless-steel tables in front of the stage and on the loft above, where festoons of ribbons and more mums draped the metallic sheen of the guardrails. Dancing had started even before the guests of honor arrived from the church, with music provided by a group of college musicians with fresh faces and a sophisticated sound.

Jimmy pulled the woman in his arms closer and spoke just above her ear. "You give a great party, Mrs. Falcon."

"Mmm." Emma's head rested on his shoulder for a second. "I'm enjoying it very much myself, now that I've taken off my shoes. Why is it a tradition that one wears excruciating footwear to one's wedding?"

"Probably for the same reason wedding dresses are hard to take off. You must have a thousand buttons on the back of this dress." He ran his fingertips along the line of her spine. "You know what I think of buttons."

"And I know what I think of what you think of buttons." She drew back and gave him a smile that held all the invitation he could ever need. "I'm looking forward to discussing the issue…later."

"Can I cut in?"

He looked around and found a personable young man

standing at his shoulder. "You clean up good, Nicholas Harlow. Sure, have a dance."

Harlow's smile—they'd decided to use the name they knew, even when he'd given them his first name—could light up Denver during a blackout, especially since he'd made contact with his family, his little brother in particular. The Harlows had come to Denver several times in the last year, and the youngest, Kyle, was a miniature of his big brother. A legal guardianship had given Jimmy and Emma the right to keep Harlow in Denver, where he wanted to be. The Harlows had signed reluctantly; Ryan's mother couldn't be found at all.

Both boys had kicked the heroin habit, and Harlow had come clean from methadone, as well. He'd filled out a lot in the last year, so his tux fit just right. There would be girl issues in the near future. Had Emma thought about that? The trouble with taking responsibility for kids was…well, you ought to know what you were doing. But what if you weren't so sure?

Jimmy sighed, just as a hand clapped his shoulder. "Congratulations, man. You have a beautiful wife," Zach Harmon said. "Almost as beautiful as mine."

"They're so different I think we can call it a draw." Nearby, Shelley supervised her son eating cake while her daughter pounded plastic keys on the table.

"Good idea. And when I find Ryan Cooper in this crowd, I'm gonna hand my kids over to him so I can dance with my beautiful lady. If you see him, send him our way."

"Sure," Jimmy said. Ryan was another one who'd changed, probably even more than Harlow. He still depended on methadone, but he succeeded pretty well in school and even held down a part-time job as a grocery clerk. After a couple of exposures to Alex and Norah Harmon, Ryan had demonstrated a real affinity for little kids. Zach and Shelley had used him as a distraction for the children several times, to give themselves a little break. Not bad for the strung-out kid on the street of a year ago.

Jimmy looked for Emma again and found her talking with Irma White Buffalo. Irma's contacts had helped Emma and Jimmy decide to donate the medallion to an Indian college in South Dakota. They had received photographs of the specially built exhibit case and the plaque dedicating the gift in Aubrey Garrett's name, but hadn't found time yet to see it for themselves. Once the club reopened, Jimmy had promised his wife a trip up north before the snows set in.

They would see the medallion exhibit…and they'd visit the rez. Jimmy wasn't looking forward to that part of the trip, but he knew he would go. He had to settle up with the past so the future would be free and clear. Though he wasn't sure how that would happen, he trusted Emma to be there and to help him through.

He frowned and looked at his watch. How long was this reception supposed to last, anyway? When could he have her to himself?

A hand slipped into the bend of his elbow. "No, boss, you can't leave yet. Emma hasn't thrown her bouquet."

"Details, details." He glanced at Tiffany and grinned. "Thanks for standing up with Emma. And for helping her out with this powwow. We wouldn't have had a wedding without you."

She shrugged, but smiled, too. "What're friends for?"

"So who's this guy you brought along?"

Tiffany caught the eye of a man across the room who gave her a smile and raised his glass in a toast. "He's a cop, actually. We met during all that business about Brad. I like him a lot."

Renfroe was spending this year plus several more behind bars. His sentence stipulated that when he did get out, he couldn't come within a mile of Tiffany. That was the best they could do. That and hope that some time spent in the joint would take the edge off Renfroe's temper.

Jimmy wasn't optimistic. Abusers tended to stay that way. But, hey, there was always a chance for change. Just look at his own life.

Still, he felt compelled to issue a warning. "Cops' wives have it hard, Tiff. Be careful."

"We're not anywhere near that far, boss. Don't worry about me." She moved off to dance with her man.

Watching the crowd, Jimmy was pleased—and a little surprised—to see how many people he counted as friends. A year ago, he would have been hard put to think of all their names. Amazing what having Emma in his life had done for his perspective.

The only person missing was Tomas. They had tried to find him, but after testifying against Eddy Santos, the boy had disappeared. Harlow kept checking, but no one on the street had seen him. It worried Emma, and more than once she'd mentioned trying to find him. Jimmy figured that if she put her mind to it—and his, too, no doubt—she would probably track the kid down.

"Deep thoughts?" Emma put a hand on his cheek. "You look awfully serious."

He turned his head to kiss her palm. "Just deciding whether to start at the bottom and work my way up, or start at the top and go down."

She stared at him in confusion. "What...?" Then she broke into that deep laugh of hers. "The buttons. I see. Hmm." She glanced around, then took his hand. "Come on."

They climbed the stairs and came out onto the balcony. The party looked even better from up here than it had on the floor, because the only person Jimmy needed to celebrate with had her arm around his waist.

"Tiffany!" She called out. "Tiffany!"

The bartender heard her name, and looked up. Emma waved the bouquet. Instantly a flock of women gathered just below them. Darren cut off the music and started a crescendoing drumroll.

Emma pulled her arm back and pitched. The bundle of white flowers sailed upward in a shallow arc, then down, down, down—to land in Harlow's grasp.

The women all protested, but Harlow refused to give up his prize. He looked up to the balcony, raised the bouquet in a gesture of triumph and grinned. Emma blew him a kiss.

Then she took Jimmy's hand again and led him to the stairway once more, where they climbed to the top story of the building and the space they had made their home. Desert colors on the walls were reflected by Indian rugs and blankets scattered all around. Like Emma herself, the apartment was a haven of light and comfort Jimmy had never realized he needed.

A bottle of chilled champagne waited. He poured them each a glass. "To you," he said, raising his glass. "The love of my life."

"To us," she corrected, "and a whole lifetime of love." They sipped the wine, smiling, her blue eyes never straying from Jimmy's. When both glasses were empty, Emma set them on the table and stepped into his arms.

"Now, Mr. Falcon," she murmured, easing the knot on his tie. "About those buttons…"

Jimmy grinned in anticipation and joy. "Consider it done, Mrs. Falcon. Consider it done."

*Harlequin truly does
make any time special. . . .
This year we are celebrating
weddings in style!*

A
Walk
Down
the Aisle
WEDDING CELEBRATION

To help us celebrate, we want you to tell us how wearing the Harlequin wedding gown will make your wedding day special. As the grand prize, Harlequin will offer one lucky bride the chance to **"Walk Down the Aisle"** in the Harlequin wedding gown!

There's more...

For her honeymoon, she and her groom will spend five nights at the **Hyatt Regency Maui.** As part of this five-night honeymoon at the hotel renowned for its romantic attractions, the couple will enjoy a candlelit dinner for two in Swan Court, a sunset sail on the hotel's catamaran, and duet spa treatments.

A HYATT RESORT AND SPA

Maui • Molokai • Lanai

To enter, please write, in, 250 words or less, how wearing the Harlequin wedding gown will make your wedding day special. The entry will be judged based on its emotionally compelling nature, its originality and creativity, and its sincerity. This contest is open to Canadian and U.S. residents only and to those who are 18 years of age and older. There is no purchase necessary to enter. Void where prohibited. See further contest rules attached. Please send your entry to:

Walk Down the Aisle Contest

In Canada	In U.S.A.
P.O. Box 637	P.O. Box 9076
Fort Erie, Ontario	3010 Walden Ave.
L2A 5X3	Buffalo, NY 14269-9076

You can also enter by visiting www.eHarlequin.com
Win the Harlequin wedding gown and the vacation of a lifetime!
The deadline for entries is October 1, 2001.

HARLEQUIN®
Makes any time special ®

PHWDACONT1

1. To enter, follow directions published in the offer to which you are responding. Contest begins April 2, 2001, and ends on October 1, 2001. Method of entry may vary. Mailed entries must be postmarked by October 1, 2001, and received by October 8, 2001.

2. Contest entry may be, at times, presented via the Internet, but will be restricted solely to residents of certain geographic areas that are disclosed on the Web site. To enter via the Internet, if permissible, access the Harlequin Web site (www.eHarlequin.com) and follow the directions displayed online. Online entries must be received by 11:59 p.m. E.S.T. on October 1, 2001.

   In lieu of submitting an entry online, enter by mail by hand-printing (or typing) on an 8½" x 11" plain piece of paper, your name, address (including zip code), Contest number/name and in 250 words or fewer, why winning a Harlequin wedding dress would make your wedding day special. Mail via first-class mail to: Harlequin Walk Down the Aisle Contest 1197, (in the U.S.) P.O. Box 9076, 3010 Walden Avenue, Buffalo, NY 14269-9076, (in Canada) P.O. Box 637, Fort Erie, Ontario L2A 5X3, Canada.

   Limit one entry per person, household address and e-mail address. Online and/or mailed entries received from persons residing in geographic areas in which Internet entry is not permissible will be disqualified.

3. Contests will be judged by a panel of members of the Harlequin editorial, marketing and public relations staff based on the following criteria:

   - Originality and Creativity—50%
   - Emotionally Compelling—25%
   - Sincerity—25%

   In the event of a tie, duplicate prizes will be awarded. Decisions of the judges are final.

4. All entries become the property of Torstar Corp. and will not be returned. No responsibility is assumed for lost, late, illegible, incomplete, inaccurate, nondelivered or misdirected mail or misdirected e-mail, for technical, hardware or software failures of any kind, lost or unavailable network connections, or failed, incomplete, garbled or delayed computer transmission or any human error which may occur in the receipt or processing of the entries in this Contest.

5. Contest open only to residents of the U.S. (except Puerto Rico) and Canada, who are 18 years of age or older, and is void wherever prohibited by law; all applicable laws and regulations apply. Any litigation within the Province of Quebec respecting the conduct or organization of a publicity contest may be submitted to the Régie des alcools, des courses et des jeux for a ruling. Any litigation respecting the awarding of a prize may be submitted to the Régie des alcools, des courses et des jeux only for the purpose of helping the parties reach a settlement. Employees and immediate family members of Torstar Corp. and D. L. Blair, Inc., their affiliates, subsidiaries and all other agencies, entities and persons connected with the use, marketing or conduct of this Contest are not eligible to enter. Taxes on prizes are the sole responsibility of winners. Acceptance of any prize offered constitutes permission to use winner's name, photograph or other likeness for the purposes of advertising, trade and promotion on behalf of Torstar Corp., its affiliates and subsidiaries without further compensation to the winner, unless prohibited by law.

6. Winners will be determined no later than November 15, 2001, and will be notified by mail. Winners will be required to sign and return an Affidavit of Eligibility form within 15 days after winner notification. Noncompliance within that time period may result in disqualification and an alternative winner may be selected. Winners of trip must execute a Release of Liability prior to ticketing and must possess required travel documents (e.g. passport, photo ID) where applicable. Trip must be completed by November 2002. No substitution of prize permitted by winner. Torstar Corp. and D. L. Blair, Inc., their parents, affiliates, and subsidiaries are not responsible for errors in printing or electronic presentation of Contest, entries and/or game pieces. In the event of printing or other errors which may result in unintended prize values or duplication of prizes, all affected game pieces or entries shall be null and void. If for any reason the Internet portion of the Contest is not capable of running as planned, including infection by computer virus, bugs, tampering, unauthorized intervention, fraud, technical failures, or any other causes beyond the control of Torstar Corp. which corrupt or affect the administration, secrecy, fairness, integrity or proper conduct of the Contest, Torstar Corp. reserves the right, at its sole discretion, to disqualify any individual who tampers with the entry process and to cancel, terminate, modify or suspend the Contest or the Internet portion thereof. In the event of a dispute regarding an online entry, the entry will be deemed submitted by the authorized holder of the e-mail account submitted at the time of entry. Authorized account holder is defined as the natural person who is assigned to an e-mail address by an Internet access provider, online service provider or other organization that is responsible for arranging e-mail address for the domain associated with the submitted e-mail address. **Purchase or acceptance of a product offer does not improve your chances of winning.**

7. Prizes: (1) Grand Prize—A Harlequin wedding dress (approximate retail value: $3,500) and a 5-night/6-day honeymoon trip to Maui, HI, including round-trip air transportation provided by Maui Visitors Bureau from Los Angeles International Airport (winner is responsible for transportation to and from Los Angeles International Airport) and a Harlequin Romance Package, including hotel accomodations (double occupancy) at the Hyatt Regency Maui Resort and Spa, dinner for (2) two at Swan Court, a sunset sail on Kiele V and a spa treatment for the winner (approximate retail value: $4,000); (5) Five runner-up prizes of a $1000 gift certificate to selected retail outlets to be determined by Sponsor (retail value $1000 ea.). Prizes consist of only those items listed as part of the prize. Limit one prize per person. All prizes are valued in U.S. currency.

8. For a list of winners (available after December 17, 2001) send a self-addressed, stamped envelope to: Harlequin Walk Down the Aisle Contest 1197 Winners, P.O. Box 4200 Blair, NE 68009-4200 or you may access the www.eHarlequin.com Web site through January 15, 2002.

Contest sponsored by Torstar Corp., P.O. Box 9042, Buffalo, NY 14269-9042, U.S.A.